I0823175

THE REVELATION SPACE COLLECTION: VOLUME 1

Also by Alastair Reynolds

NOVELS

Century Rain
Pushing Ice
House of Suns
Terminal World
The Medusa Chronicles (with Stephen Baxter)
Eversion
Halcyon Years

REVELATION SPACE

Revelation Space
Redemption Ark
Absolution Gap
Chasm City
Inhibitor Phase

THE PREFECT DREYFUS EMERGENCIES

(within the Revelation Space universe)
Aurora Rising (previously published as The Prefect)
Elysium Fire
Machine Vendetta

POSEIDON'S CHILDREN

Blue Remembered Earth
On the Steel Breeze
Poseidon's Wake

REVENGER

Revenger
Shadow Captain
Bone Silence

THE PREFECT DREYFUS EMERGENCIES

(within the Revelation Space universe)
Aurora Rising (previously published as The Prefect)
Elysium Fire
Machine Vendetta

SHORT STORY COLLECTIONS

Diamond Dogs, Turquoise Days
Galactic North
Zima Blue
Beyond the Aquila Rift
The Revelation Space Collection: Volume 1
The Revelation Space Collection: Volume 2

THE REVELATION SPACE COLLECTION: VOLUME 1

Alastair Reynolds

The collection first published in Great Britain in 2025 by Gollancz
an imprint of The Orion Publishing Group Ltd
Carmelite House, 50 Victoria Embankment
London EC4Y 0DZ

An Hachette UK Company

The authorised representative in the EEA is Hachette Ireland, 8 Castlecourt Centre, Castleknock Road, Castleknock, Dublin 15, D15 XTP3, Republic of Ireland (email: info@hbgi.ie)

1 3 5 7 9 10 8 6 4 2

A CIP catalogue record for this book is
available from the British Library.

ISBN (Hardback) 978 1 399 61191 6
ISBN (Export Trade Paperback) 978 1 399 61192 3
ISBN (eBook) 978 1 399 61194 7
ISBN (Audio) 978 1 399 61195 4

Typeset by Born Group
Printed in Great Britain by Clays Ltd, Elcograph S.p.A

www.gollancz.co.uk

Contents

DILATION SLEEP

Spacers tell people that the worst aspect of starflight is revival. They speak the truth, I think. They give us dreams while the machines warm us up and map our bodies for cell damage. We feel no anxiety or fear, detached from our physical selves and adrift in generated fantasies.

In my dream I was joined by the cybernetic imago of Katia, my wife. We found ourselves within a computer-constructed sensorium. An insect, I felt my six thin legs propelling me into a wide and busy chamber. Four worker ants were there, crouched in stiff mechanical postures. With compound vision I studied these new companions, observing the nearest of them deposit a pearly egg from its abdomen. A novel visceral sense told me that I, too, contained a ready egg.

'We're gods amongst them,' I told my wife's imago.

'We are *Myrmecia gulosa*,' she whispered into my brain. 'The bulldog ant. You see the queen, and her winged male?'

'Yes.'

'Those maggoty things in the corner of the cell are the queen's larvae. Her worker is about to feed them.'

'Feed them with what?'

'His egg, my darling.'

I rotated my sleek, mandibled head. 'And will I also?'

'Naturally! A worker's duty is always to serve his queen. Of course . . . you may exit this environ, if you choose. But you'll have to remain in reefersleep for another three hours.'

'Three hours . . . might as well be centuries,' I said. 'Then change it. Something a bit less alien.'

My imago dissolved the scenario, the universe. I floated in white limbo, awaiting fresh sensory stimulus. Soon I found myself brushing shimmering vermilion coral with eight suckered arms, an octopus.

Katia liked to play games.

Eventually the dreams ceased and I suddenly sensed my body, cold and stiff but definitely anchored to my mind.

I allowed myself a long primal scream, then opened my eyes. The eyes I opened were the eyes of Uri Andrei Sagdev, who was once a mainbrain technician at the Sylveste Institute but who now found himself in the odd role of Starship Heuristic Resource, a crewperson.

Under different circumstances, it is not a role I would otherwise have chosen. I was alone, the room cold and silent. My five companions remained in reefersleep around my own capsule; only I had been revived. I sensed, then, that something must be wrong. But I did not query Katia, preferring to remain in ignorance until she saw fit to enlighten me regarding our situation.

I hauled myself from the open reefer and took faltering steps out of the room.

It was several minutes before I felt confident to do anything more ambitious than that. I stumbled to the nearby health bay and exercised with galvanic activators, pushing my muscles beyond the false limits of apparent exhaustion. Then I showered and dressed, taking the expediency of wearing a thermal layer beneath my overalls. Breakfast consisted of fried ham and

Edam slices, followed by garlic croissants, washed down with chilled passion fruit and lemon tea.

Why was I not concerned to discover our difficulty? Simply because the mere fact of revival told me that it could not be compellingly urgent. Any undesirable situation upon a light-skimming starship that does not instantly destroy it – probably in a flash of exotic bosons – will act on such an extended timescale that the mainbrain-crew overmind will have days or weeks to engineer a solution.

I knew we were not home, and that therefore something was wrong. But for a moment it was good simply to lie back in the kitchen and allow the music of Roedelius to envelop me, and to revel in this condition called life. To simply suck air into my old lungs.

I who had been dead, or near death, for so long.

'Some more, Uri?' asked my wife's imago.

I was alone apart from a servitor. It was a dumb-bell shaped drone hovering on silently energised levitation fields above the metal floor. Extruding a manipulator from the matt-gold surface of its upper spheroid, it offered me the jug of pale juice.

With a well-practised subvocal command, I enabled my entoptic system. The implant supplied the visual and tactile stimuli necessary to fully realise the imago, the simulation of Katia, drawing it from the ship's mainbrain. Bright grids and circles interrupted my ocular field, then meshed and thickened to form my wife, frozen and lifeless but apparently solid. Copyright symbols denoting the implant company flashed, then faded. I locked her entoptic ghost over the dull form of the servitor, its compact size easily concealed within her body-space. Her blunt silver hair fell around a narrow pale face, black lips pursed like a doll's and eyes staring right through me. Her clasped hands emerged from a long hooded scarlet gown inlaid around the shoulder with the insignia of the Mixmaster geneticists, a pair of hands holding a cat's cradle of DNA. My wife was a geneticist to the marrow. On Yellowstone, where cybernetics was the primary creed, it made her a virtual pariah.

As the mainbrain-generated program took hold she grew vivacious and smiled, and her hand appeared now to grasp the jug.

'I was tiring of storage, my darling.'

'I'm not comfortable with this,' I admitted. 'Katia – my actual Katia – despised the whole idea of you. This illusion would have especially sickened her.'

'It doesn't sicken me,' Katia said.

'It ought to,' I said. 'Aren't your personalities supposed to be the same?'

She smiled, as if the point were settled. So infuriatingly like her original.

'I see that,' I said dubiously. The imago had been against my actual wife's wishes. When the Melding Plague hit us I saw my chance of escape via this craft. Katia was unable to become a crewperson, so I surreptitiously set about digitizing my wife's personality. The implant did all the hard work. It had assembled a behaviour map of Katia whenever we were together, studying her through the conduits of my own senses. The simulation grew slowly, limited by the memory capacity of the implant. But each day I downloaded more of her into an Institute mainbrain, performing this routine for weeks on end. I have no doubt that Katia suspected something, although she never made any mention of it.

Having completed my clandestine work, I then grafted the copy over the mind of the ship. It lacked her memories, of course, but I went to the expense and danger of having my own trawled and substituted instead, using software routines to perform the gender inversion. Katia's personality only assumed dominance when I was in rapport with the vessel. There was no doubt in my mind that the other crewpersons had also arranged for their own fictitious companions. They too would speak to their loved ones, or some idealised fantasy of a lover, when they addressed the ship.

But I preferred not to think about that.

A lie, then. But my entire life had been a lie, Katia's imago simply the most recent aspect of it. But why had she awoken me? Or rather: why had the ship chosen to awaken me, and not one of the others? Janos, Kaj, Hilda, Yul and Karlos still remained in reefersleep, displaying no signs of imminent thaw.

I upped from the table decisively. 'Thank you, Katia. I'll take a stroll, admire the view.'

'I must discuss something with you,' Katia said. 'But I suppose it can wait a few minutes.'

'Ah,' I said, grinning. 'You want to keep me in suspense.'

'Nothing of the sort, darling. Is the music fine?'

'Music's fine,' I answered, leaving the kitchen.

I entered a curving hexagonal corridor, bathed in dull ochre light. A node of Roedelius chased me, humming from piezo-acoustic panels in the walls. The gravity that held me to the floor arose from our one-gee thrust, and not from the centrifugal spin of the lifesystem, otherwise the vertical and horizontal axes would have been interchanged. This fact told me that we were not at home; not approaching the cluster of carousels and asteroids called Shiphaven, in the Trojan point that trailed Jupiter. We were still on stardrive, still climbing up or down from the slowtime of light-speed.

We might be anywhere between Epsilon Eridani and Solspace.

My stroll carried me away from the core of the vessel to her skin, where the hot neutron sleet wafted past us. The parts of the vessel through which I travelled grew darker and more machinelike, colder and less familiar. Irrationally, I began to imagine that I was being pursued and observed.

I have never enjoyed either solitude or the dark. I was a fool, then, to address this fear by turning around. Yet the hairs on my neck were bristling and my sweat had become chilled.

Most of the radial corridor was dark, apart from the miserly locus of light that had followed me like a halo. Nonetheless, it was still possible to make out a darker thing looming in the distance, almost lost in the convergence of the walls.

I was not alone.

It was a figure, a silhouette, regarding me. Not Katia's imago, for sure.

I felt a brief terror. 'Katia,' I croaked. 'Full lights, please.'

I jammed my eyes shut as the bright actinics snaped on. Red retinal ghosts slowly fading, I reopened them, not much more than a second later. But my watcher had gone.

I slowly emptied my lungs. I was wise enough not to leap to conclusions. This was not necessarily what it appeared. After all, I had only just emerged from reefersleep, after several years of being frozen. I was bound to be a little jittery, a little open to subconscious suggestion.

It seemed I was utterly alone. I vowed, shakily, to put the experience immediately out of mind.

Ten minutes later I had reached the outer hull, and was in naked space – or rather, seeing through the proxy eyes of a drone clamped on the outside with spidery grappling feet. The machine's camera head was peering through a porthole, into the room where I sat. I looked pale and strained, but I did not have company.

I looked away from the porthole, towards the bow of the ship. The vessel, the *Wild Pallas*, was a ramliner – a nearlight human-rated starship. Most of what I saw, therefore, was very dense neutron shielding. The vessel required protons for its bosonic drive process. Ahead, a graser beam swept space and stripped deuterium nuclei into protons and neutrons. Our gauss scoop sifted free the protons and focused them into the heart of the ship. The neutral baryons were channelled around the hull in a lethal radiative rain, diverted clear of the lifesystem and its fragile payload of sleepers. The drone sensed the flux and passed the data to me in terms of a swirling roseate aura, as if we were diving down the gullet of the universe.

To the rear, things were eclipsed by the glow of the exhaust. Gamma shields burned Cherenkov-blue. Within the ship, the proton harvest was extremely short-lived. Fields targeted the protons into a beam, lancing through a swarming cloud of heavy monopoles. The relativistic protons were decelerated and steered into the magnetic nodes. Inside each monopole was a shell of bosons which coaxed the protons to disintegrate. This was the power source of a ramliner.

I had studied all the tech before signing up for the overmind partnership, the human-cybernetic steering committee that commanded this vessel. When I say studied, I mean that I had downloaded certain eidetic documents furnished by the Macro that owned the ship. These eidetics entered my memory at an almost intuitive level, programmed of course to fade once my contract expired. They told me everything I needed to know and little else. We carried nine hundred reefersleep passengers and we crew comprised six humans, each of whom was an expert in one or more areas of starflight theory. My own specialties were scoop sub-systems – gauss collimators and particle-ablation shields – and shipboard/in-flight medicare. The computer that wore the masque of Katia was also equipped for these zones of expertise, but it was deficient – so the cybertechs said – in human heuristic thought modes. Crewpersons were therefore its Heuristic Resources – peripherals orbiting the hard glittering core of its machine consciousness.

Crewpersons thus rode at a more reduced level of reefer-sleep than our passengers: a little warmer, a little closer to the avalanche of cell death that is life. The computer could interrogate us without the bother of complete revival. Our dreams, therefore, would be dreams where matter and number flowed in technological tsunami.

I altered the drone's telemetry so that the neutron wind became invisible. Looking beyond, I saw no stars at all. Einsteinian distortion was squashing them up fore and aft, concealed by the flared ends of the ship. We were still accelerating towards light-speed.

'Well?' I asked, much later.

'As you know, we've yet to reach midpoint. In fact, we will not reach home for another three years of shiptime.'

'Is this a technical problem?'

'Not strictly. I'm afraid it's medical, which is why I was forced to bring you out of reefersleep between systems. Like the view, my darling?'

'Are you joking? An empty universe with no stars? It's the gloomiest thing I can remember.'

I was back in the coldroom where the six crew reefers were stored. Katia's data ghost stood at my side, and Mozart warmed our spirits. Mozart's joyous familiarity drowned out all the faint, distant sounds of the ship, and the frank necessity of this annoyed me greatly. I was not normally prone to nervousness.

'Janos is sick,' explained Katia. 'He must have contracted the Melding Plague on Yellowstone. Unless we act now he won't survive the rest of the journey. He needs emergency surgery.'

'He's sick?' I shrugged. 'Too bad. But SOP on this is clear, Katia. Freeze him down further, lock the condition in stasis.' I leaned over the smooth side of Janos's reefer, examining the biomed display cartouche under its coffin-lid rim. The reefer resembled a giant chrome chrysalis or silverfish, anchored by its head to a coiled nexus of umbilicals. Within this hexagonal fluted box lay Janos. His inert form was dimly visible under the frosted clear lid.

'Normally, that would be our wisest course of action,' Katia said. 'Earthside med skills will certainly outmode our own. But in this instance the rules must be contravened. Janos can't survive, even at emergency levels of reefersleep. You know about the Melding Plague.'

I did. We all knew about it only too well, for it had crippled Yellowstone. The Melding Plague was a biocybernetic virus, something new to our experience. Yellowstone's intensely cybernetic society had crumbled at the nanomolecular level, the level of our computers and implants. The Melding Plague had caused our nanomachinery to grow malign.

I permitted Katia to explain, walking to the kitchen and preparing salami rolls, stepping briskly through the dim corridors.

All crewpersons were fitted with such implants. Through these data windows we interfaced with the machinery of the reefers and the mainbrain of the ship as the ramliner cruised from star to star. Janos's virus had attacked the structure of his own implants, ripping them apart and reorganizing them into analogues of itself. From one implant node, a network of webbed strands was spreading further into his brain, in an apparent attempt to knit together all the infected locales.

'The experts on Yellowstone soon learned that cold does not retard the virus significantly – certainly not the kind of cold from which a human could ever be revived. We must therefore operate immediately, before the virus gains a stronghold. And I'm afraid that our routine surgical programs will fail. We can't use nanomachinery against the virus; it will simply subsume whatever we throw against it.'

I gobbled my rolls. 'I don't know neurosurgery; that wasn't on the skills eidetic.' I brushed crumbs from my stubbled chin. 'However, if Janos's life is in danger – '

'We must act. How are you feeling now?'

'A little stiff. Nothing serious.' I forced a very stiff grin. 'I'll admit, I was a little jumpy early on. I think those ants gave me the creeps.'

Katia was silent for a few seconds. 'That's normal,' she eventually said. 'Get plenty of rest. Then we'll examine the surgical tools.'

I went jogging. I mapped a sinuous, winding path through the lifesystem, feeling the megaton mass of the ship wheel about my centre of mass. I was ruthless with myself, deliberately selecting a route that took me through every dark and shadowy region of the lifesystem I could think of. I silenced Mozart and forbade myself the company of Katia, disabling my imago inducer.

My thoughts turned back to the figure I imagined I had seen. What kind of rationale had flashed through my mind in the few seconds when I permitted the figure to exist outside of my imagination? Perhaps one of the sleepers might have thawed by accident and was wandering the ship in dismay. That hypothetical wanderer would have been equally surprised by my own presence. Ergo the person was now hiding.

Of course, the figure was undoubtedly a hallucination. One need not be drooling at the mouth to hallucinate – indeed, one could easily retain enough facilities to recognise the experience as being totally internalised. After the uneventful hours of wakefulness that had subsequently passed, I was anxious to dismiss the whole incident.

I jogged on, my shoes slapping the deck. I was approaching the nadir of my journey, the part of the ship that until now I had studiously avoided. Sensing my nearing footfalls, cartwheel-shaped airlocks dilated open. I panted through an antechamber, into the vast room where nine hundred slept.

The chamber had the toroidal shape of a tokamak. Nine hundred deep-preservation reefers lined the inner and outer walls, crisscrossed by ladders and catwalks. I set about circumnavigating the chamber, to finally purge my mind of any stray ghosts. Hadn't that always been my strategy as a child: confront my fears head on? I suspected that the boy in me would have been richly amused by my motives here. Nonetheless I insisted on this one ridiculous circuit, convinced it would leave me eased.

Most of these sleepers would stay aboard when we arrived in the Earth system. They were refugees from the Melding Plague, seeking sanctuary in the future. At the nearlight speeds this vessel attained between suns, large levels of time dilation would be experienced. Our clocks would grind to an imperceptible crawl. After thirty or forty years of shiptime, a mere six or seven hops between systems, more than a century would have elapsed on Yellowstone, enough time for eco-engineers to exorcise the biome of the Melding Plague. The sleepers we carried had elected not to risk spending the time in the planet's community cryocrypts; in dilation sleep the effective time spent in reefers was less, and therefore their chances of completely safe revival were enormously increased.

I was jogging slowly enough to read the glowing name panels imprinted on each reefer. Men, women, children . . .

the rich of my world, able to pay for this exorbitant journey into a brighter future. I thought of the less wealthy, those who could not even afford spaces in the cryocrypts. I thought of the long queues of people waiting to see surgeons, people like Katia, anxious to lose their implants before the disease reached them. They would pay with whatever they could: organs or prosthetics or memories. Or if they chose not to pay they might consider becoming crew. My people made good crew-fodder. It called for a certain degree of yearning desperation to accept direct interfacing with the mainbrain. The hard price of our bargain was the simple fact that our reduced state of reefersleep meant we would continue to age as we slept away the years.

That was not a bargain Katia had felt she could make. And I had known that I could not stand to lose my implants. Thus the Melding Plague touched us.

I felt bitterness, and this was welcome to me. I was happy to find familiar anxieties polluting my thoughts. I cast a dismissive glance over my shoulder, back along the curving ranks of sleepers I had already passed.

I was being followed.

The shadow was pounding along the walkway, halfway around the great curve of the chamber. I could barely see it, just a man-shaped black aperture in the distance.

I quickened my pace. Only my feet thudded in the silence. Yet my chaser was also running faster. I felt sick with fright. I summoned Katia, but after alerting her was unable to grasp a sentence, a command, anything. The faceless silhouette seemed to be gaining on me.

Faceless was right. It had no features, no detail. Eventually I reached an exit. The airlock sequence amputated the chamber from me. I did not stop running, even when I realised that the doors behind me were remaining closed. The shadow-man remained with the sleepers.

But I had seen enough. It was not human. Just a man-shaped hole, a spectre.

I found the quickest route back to the command deck of the *Wild Pallas*. Immediately I ordered Katia to begin a rigorous search for intruders, though I knew of course that no intruder could have escaped her attention thus far. My Katia was omniscient. She would have known the exact location of every rat, every fly, aboard the craft; except that aboard the ship there were no flies, no rats.

I knew that the shadow was not a revived sleeper. None of the reefers had been opened or vacated. A stowaway was out of the question – what was there to eat or drink, apart from the supplies dispensed by the computer?

My mind veered towards the illogical. Could someone have entered the ship during its flight – someone dressed as a chameleon? That imagined intruder would have somehow had to achieve invisibility from Katia's eyes. Clearly impossible, even disregarding the unlikely manoeuvres required to match our velocity and position undetected.

I chewed on my lip, aware that each second of indecision counted against Janos. For my own defence, Katia would permit me access to a weapon, provided of course that the existence of the intruder was proven. Alternatively, I might best confront the situation by not confronting it. I could perform surgery on Janos without straying into those regions of the ship that the intruder had apparently claimed as its haunt. In a day or so, therefore, this ordeal might be over, and I could re-enter reefersleep. The most faceless, inhuman entities I would have to contend with upon my next revival would be Solspace Axis customs officials.

Let them worry about the unseen extra passenger. Hadn't the shadow permitted me safe slumber so far?

I chuckled, though to my ears it sounded more like a death-rattle. I was still frightened, but for once my hands had stopped playing arpeggios on the keys of an invisible piano.

I absorbed myself in technical eidetics outlining the medical systems Katia and I were about to employ. The gleaming semi-robotic tools were the culmination of Yellowstone's surgical sciences. Even so, they would undoubtedly appear crude by Earthside standards. This dichotomy galled me. Even if Janos would necessarily worsen by the time we arrived, how could we be certain that we were not reducing his chances with our outdated medical intervention? Perhaps Earth would have accelerated so far beyond our capabilities that the equation was no longer balanced in our favour.

Yet Katia would have weighed the issue minutely before selecting the appropriate course of action. Perhaps, then, it was best simply to silence one's qualms and do whatever was required.

Drones assisted me in carrying the medical machinery into the crew reefer room, where my five colleagues lay in frozen sleep. I wore a facemask and a gloved jumpsuit, inwoven with a heating circuit. Katia would lower the room's temperature before slightly increasing Janos's own.

'Ready, Uri?' she asked. 'Let's start.'

So we commenced, my eyes constantly flicking to the open reefer I hoped soon to re-enter. The room rapidly chilled, lights burning frigid blue from the overheads.

Janos's reefer cracked open with a gasp of released cold. I looked at Janos, still and white and somehow distant. Let that distance remain, I prayed. After all, we were about to open his head.

Katia, in fact, had already performed some preliminary surgery. The skull had been exposed, skin pulled back as if framing the white pistil of a flesh-leaved flower. Slender probes entered the scalp via drilled holes, trailing glowing coloured cables into a matrix of input points in the domed head of the reefer. The work was angstrom-precise, rendered with a robot's deadening perfection. I had been briefed: those cables were substituting for the cybernetic implants within his brain that had fallen victim to the Melding Plague.

'When you have the top of the skull free you should feed it back along the cables,' Katia told me. 'It's crucial that we don't lose cyber-interface with Janos.'

I prepped the mechanical bone-saw. 'Why? What use is he to us?'

'There are good reasons. If you're still interested we can discuss it after the operation.'

The saw hummed into life, the rotary tip glinting evilly. Katia vectored the blade down, smoothly gnawing into the pale bone. Little blood oozed free but the sound struck an unpleasant resonance with me. Katia made three expert circumferential passes, then retracted. I took a deep breath, then placed gloved fingers on the top of Janos's head. The scalp felt loose, like half of a chocolate egg. I eased the section of skull free with a wet, sucking slurp, exposing the damp pinkish mass of dura and gyrus, snuggling in the lower bowl of the skull. I took special care to maintain the integrity of the connections as I separated the bonework. For a while, humbled, I could only stand in awe of this fantastic organ, easily the most complex, alien thing my eyes had ever gazed on. And yet it managed to look so disappointingly vegetable.

'Husband, we must proceed,' warned Katia. 'I have warmed Janos to a dangerously high body temperature, while not greatly increasing his metabolic rate. We don't have time to waste.'

I felt sweat beading my forehead. I nodded. Inward, inward. Katia swung a new battery of blades and microlasers into play.

We operated to the music of Sibelius.

It was intriguing and repellent work.

I succeeded in detaching my mind to some extent, so that I was able to regard the parting brain tissue as dead but somehow sacred meat. The micro-implants came out one by one, too small for the naked eye to discern detail, barbed hunks of corroded metal. The corrosion, observable under a microscope, was the external evidence of the cybervirus. I studied it with rank feelings of abstract distaste. The virus behaved like its biological namesake, clamping onto the shell of the nanostructure and pulsing subversive instructions deep into its reproductive heart.

After three hours my back boiled with pain. I leaned away from the reefer, brushing a sleeve against my chilled forehead. I felt the room swimming, clotting with blobs of muggy darkness. For an instant I became disoriented, convinced that left was right and vice versa. I braced myself against the reefer as this dizziness washed over me.

'Not long now,' Katia said. 'How do you feel?'

'I'm fine. And you?'

'I'm . . . fine. The op's proceeding well.' Katia paused, then stiffened her voice with iron resolve, businesslike detachment. 'The next implant is the deepest. It lies between the occipital lobe and the cerebellum. We must take care to avoid lesion of the visual centre. This is the primary entoptic infeed node.'

'In we go, then.'

The machinery snicked obediently into place. Our ciliated microprobes slid into the tissue, like flexible syringes slipping into jelly. Despite the cold I found myself hot around the collar, iced sweat prickling my skin. Another hour passed, though time had ceased to have very much meaning.

And I froze, conscious of a presence behind me, in the same room.

Compelled, I turned. The watcher was with me.

I saw now that it could not be a man. Yet it did have a humanoid form, a humanoid of my build and posture.

A sculptor had selected ten thousand raven-black cubes, so dark that they were pure silhouettes, and arranged them as a blocky statue. That was the entirety of the watcher: a mass of black cubes.

As I turned, it swung towards me. None of the cubes from which it was formed actually moved; they simply blipped out and reappeared in an orchestrated wave, whole new strata of cubes forming in thin air. They popped in and out of reality to mould its altering posture. To my eyes, the motion had a beguiling, digital beauty. I thought of the coloured patterns that would sweep across a stadium of schoolchildren holding painted mosaic cards to image some great slogan or emblem.

I raised my left arm, and observed the shadow repeat the action from its point of view. We were not mirrors of one another. We were ghosts.

My terror had reached some peak and evaporated. I grasped that the watcher was essentially motiveless, that it had been drawn to me as inevitably as a shrinking noon shadow.

'Continue with the operation,' insisted Katia. I noticed hesitancy in her voice, true to her personality to the end. She liked games, my Katia, but she was never a convincing liar.

'Lesion of the visual centre, you say?'

'That is what we must be careful to avoid.'

I grimaced. I had to know for sure.

I scooped up one of the detached nanoprobes. In reality, the drones mimicked my intentions with their own manipulators, picking up the nanoprobe's platonic twin . . . Then I jammed it recklessly into Janos's head, into his occipital lobe.

This reality melted and shattered, as if a stone had fallen into and disturbed the reflections on a crystal-smooth lake.

I knew, then.

My vision slowly unpeeled itself, returning to normality in strips. Katia was doing this, attempting to cancel the damage in my visual centre by sending distorted signals along the optic infeeds. I realised that I no longer had control of the surgical tools.

'I am the patient,' I said. 'Not Janos. The surgeon is the one who needs surgery. How ironic.'

'It was best that you not know,' Katia said. And then, very rapidly, she herself flickered and warped, her voice momentarily growing cavernous and slurred. 'I'm failing . . . there isn't much time.'

'And the watcher?'

'A symptom,' she said ruefully. 'A symptom of my own illness. A false mapping of your own body image within the simulation.'

'You're a simulation!' I roared. 'I can understand your image being affected . . . but you – yourself – you don't exist in my head! You're a program running in the mainbrain!'

'Yes, darling. But the Melding Plague has also reached the mainbrain.' She paused, and then, without warning, her voice became robotically flat and autistic. 'Much of the computer is damaged. To keep this simulation intact has necessitated sacrifices in tertiary function levels. However, the primary goal is to guarantee that you do not die. The operation-in-progress must be completed. In order to maintain the integrity of the simulation, the tuple-ensemble coded KATIA must be removed from main memory. This operation has now been executed.'

She froze, her last moment locked within my implant, trapped in my eyes like a spot of sun-blindness. It was just me and the computer then, not forgetting the ever-present watcher.

What could I do but continue with the surgery? I had a reason now. I wanted to excise the frozen ghost of Katia from my mind. She was the real lesion.

So I survived.

Many years passed for us. Our ship's computer was so damaged by the Melding Plague that we could not decelerate in time to reach the Earth system. Our choice was to steer for 61 Cygni-A, around which lay the colony Sky's Edge. Our dilation sleepers consequently found themselves further from home both in time and space than they had expected. Secretly we cherished the justice in this, we who had sacrificed parts of our lives to crew their dream-voyage. Yet they had not lost so very much, and I suppose I would have been one of their number had I had their power. Concerning Katia . . .

The simulation was never properly reanimated.

The shipboard memory in which it lay fell prey to the Melding Plague, and much of its data was badly corrupted. When I did attempt to recreate her, I found only a crude caricature, all spontaneity sapped away, as lifeless and cruelly predictable as a Babbage engine. In a fit of remorse I destroyed the imago. It helped that I was blind, for even this facade had been programmed to exhibit fear, programmed to plead once it guessed my intentions.

That was years ago. I tell myself that she never lived. And that at least is what the cybertechs would have us believe.

The last information pulse from Yellowstone told me that the real Katia is still alive, of course much older than when I knew her. She has been married twice. To her the days of our union must seem as ancient and fragile as an heirloom. But she does not yet know that I survived. I transmitted to her, but the signal will not reach Epsilon Eridani for a decade. And then I will have to await her reply, more years still.

Perhaps she will reply in person. This is our only hope of meeting, because I . . .

I will not fly again. Nor will I sleep out the decades.

A SPY IN EUROPA

Marius Vargovic, agent of Gilgamesh Isis, savoured an instant of free fall before the flitter's engines kicked in, slamming it away from the *Deucalion.* His pilot gunned the craft towards the moon below, quickly outrunning the other shuttles that the Martian liner had disgorged. Europa enlarged perceptibly: a flattening arc the colour of nicotine-stained wallpaper.

'Boring, isn't it.'

Vargovic turned around in his seat, languidly. 'You'd rather they were shooting at us?'

'I'd rather they were doing *something*.'

'Then you're a fool,' Vargovic said, making a tent of his fingers. 'There's enough armament buried in that ice to give Jupiter a second red spot. What it would do to us doesn't bear thinking about.'

'Only trying to make conversation, friend.'

'Don't bother – it's an overrated activity at the best of times.'

'All right, Marius – I get the message. In fact I intercepted it, parsed it, filtered it, decrypted it with the appropriate one-time pad and wrote a fucking two-hundred-page report on it. Satisfied?'

'I'm never satisfied, Mishenka. It just isn't in my nature.'

But Mishenka was right: Europa was an encrypted document; complexity masked by a surface of fractured and refrozen ice. Its surface grooves were like the capillaries in a vitrified eyeball, faint as the structure in a raw surveillance image. But once within the airspace boundary of the Europan Demarchy, traffic-management co-opted the flitter, vectoring it into a touchdown corridor. In three days, Mishenka would return, but then he would disable the avionics, kissing the ice for less than ten minutes.

'Not too late to abort,' Mishenka said, a long time later.

'Are you out of your tiny mind?'

The younger man dispensed a frosty Covert Ops smile. 'We've all heard what the Demarchy does to spies, Marius.'

'Is this a personal grudge or are you just psychotic?'

'I'll leave being psychotic to you, Marius – you're so much better at it.'

Vargovic nodded. It was the first sensible thing Mishenka had said all day.

They landed an hour later. Vargovic adjusted his Martian businesswear, tuning his holographically inwoven frock coat to project red sandstorms; lifting the collar in what he had observed from the liner's passengers was a recent Martian fad. Then he grabbed his bag – nothing incriminating there, no gadgets or weapons – and exited the flitter, stepping through the gasket of locks. A slitherwalk propelled him forward, massaging the soles of his slippers. It was a single cultured ribbon of octopus skin, stimulated to ripple by the timed firing of buried squid axons.

To get to Europa you either had to be sickeningly rich or sickeningly poor. Vargovic's cover was the former: a lie excusing the single-passenger flitter. As the slitherwalk advanced he was joined by other arrivals: businesspeople like himself, and a sugaring of the merely wealthy. Most of them had dispensed with holographics, instead projecting entoptics beyond their personal space: machine-generated hallucinations decoded by the implant hugging Vargovic's optic nerve. Hummingbirds and seraphim were in sickly vogue. Others were attended by autonomous perfumes that subtly altered the moods of those around them. Slightly lower down the social scale, Vargovic observed a clique of noisy tourists – antlered brats from Circum-Jove. Then there was a discontinuous jump: to squalid-looking Maunder refugees who must have accepted indenture to the Demarchy. The refugees were quickly segregated from the more affluent immigrants, who found themselves within a huge geodesic dome resting above the ice on refrigerated stilts. The walls of the dome glittered with duty-free shops, boutiques and bars. The floor was bowl-shaped, slither walks and spiral stairways descending to the nadir where a quincunx of fluted marble cylinders waited. Vargovic observed that the newly arrived were queuing for elevators that terminated in the cylinders. He joined a line and waited.

'First time in Cadmus-Asterius?' asked the bearded man ahead of him, iridophores in his plum-coloured jacket projecting Boolean propositions from Sirikit's *Machine Ethics in the Transenlightenment.*

'First time on Europa, actually. First time Circum-Jove, you want the full story.'

'Down-system?'

'Mars.'

The man nodded gravely. 'Hear it's tough.'

'You're not kidding.' And he wasn't. Since the sun had dimmed – the second Maunder Minimum, repeating the behaviour the sun had exhibited in the seventeenth century – the entire balance of power in the First System had altered. The economies of the inner worlds had found it difficult to adjust; agriculture and power-generation handicapped, with concomitant social upheaval. But the outer planets had never had the luxury of solar energy in the first place. Now Circum-Jove was the benchmark of First System economic power, with Circum-Saturn trailing behind. Because of this, the two primary Circum-Jove superpowers – the Demarchy, which controlled Europa and Io, and Gilgamesh Isis, which controlled Ganymede and parts of Callisto – were vying for dominance.

The man smiled keenly. 'Here for anything special?'

'Surgery,' Vargovic said, hoping to curtail the conversation at the earliest juncture. 'Very extensive anatomical surgery.'

They hadn't told him much.

'Her name is Cholok,' Control had said, after Vargovic had skimmed the dossiers back in the caverns that housed the Covert Operations section of Gilgamesh Isis security, deep in Ganymede. 'We recruited her ten years ago, when she was on Phobos.'

'And now she's Demarchy?'

Control had nodded. 'She was swept up in the brain-drain, once Maunder Two began to bite. The smartest got out while they could. The Demarchy – and us, of course – snapped up the brightest.'

'And also one of our sleepers.' Vargovic glanced down at the portrait of the woman, striped by video lines. She looked mousy to him, with a permanent bone-deep severity of expression.

'Cheer up,' Control said. 'I'm asking you to contact her, not sleep with her.'

'Yeah, yeah. Just tell me her background.'

'Biotech.' Control nodded at the dossier. 'On Phobos she led one of the teams working in aquatic transform work – modifying the human form for submarine operations.'

Vargovic nodded diligently. 'Go on.'

'Phobos wanted to sell their know-how to the Martians, before their oceans froze. Of course, the Demarchy also appreciated her talents. Cholok took her team to Cadmus-Asterius, one of their hanging cities.'

'Mm.' Vargovic was getting the thread now. 'By which time we'd already recruited her.'

'Right,' Control said, 'except we had no obvious use for her.'

'Then why this conversation?'

Control smiled. Control always smiled when Vargovic pushed the envelope of subservience. 'We're having it because our sleeper won't lie down.' Then Control reached over and touched the image of Cholok, making her speak. What Vargovic was seeing was an intercept: something Gilgamesh had captured, riddled with edits and jump-cuts.

She appeared to be sending a verbal message to an old friend in Isis. She was talking rapidly from a white room, inert medical servitors behind her. Shelves displayed flasks of colour-coded medichines. A cruciform bed resembled an autopsy slab with ceramic drainage sluices.

'Cholok contacted us a month ago,' Control said. 'The room's part of her clinic.'

'She's using Phrase-Embedded Three,' Vargovic said, listening to her speech patterns, siphoning content from otherwise normal Canasian.

'Last code we taught her.'

'All right. What's her angle?'

Control chose his words – skating around the information excised from Cholok's message. 'She wants to give us something,' he said. 'Something valuable. She's acquired it accidentally. Someone good has to smuggle it out.'

'Flattery will get you everywhere, Control.'

*

The muzak rose to a carefully timed crescendo as the elevator plunged through the final layer of ice. The view around and below was literally dizzying, and Vargovic registered exactly as much awe as befitted his Martian guise. He knew the Demarchy's history, of course – how the hanging cities had begun as points of entry into the ocean; air-filled observation cupolas linked to the surface by narrow access shafts sunk through the kilometre-thick crystal ice. Scientists had studied the unusual smoothness of the crust, noting that its fracture patterns echoed those on Earth's ice shelves, implying the presence of a water ocean. Europa was further from the sun than Earth, but something other than solar energy maintained the ocean's liquidity. Instead, the moon's orbit around Jupiter created stresses that flexed the moon's silicate core, tectonic heat bleeding into the ocean via hydrothermal vents.

Descending into the city was a little like entering an amphitheatre – except that there was no stage; merely an endless succession of steeply tiered lower balconies. They converged towards a light-filled infinity, seven or eight kilometres below, where the city's conic shape constricted to a point. The opposite side was half a kilometre away, levels rising like geologic strata. A wide glass tower threaded the atrium from top to bottom, aglow with smoky-green ocean and a mass of kelp-like flora, cultured by gilly swimmers. Artificial sun lamps burned in the kelp like Christmas tree lights. Above, the tower branched, peristaltic feeds reaching out to the ocean proper. Offices, shops, restaurants and residential units were stacked atop each other, or teetered into the abyss on elegant balconies, spun from lustrous sheets of bulk-chitin polymer, the Demarchy's major construction material. Gossamer bridges arced across the atrium space, dodging banners, projections and vast translucent sculptures moulded from a silky variant of the same chitin polymer. Every visible surface was overlaid by neon, holographics and entoptics. People were everywhere, and in every face Vargovic detected a slight absence, as if their minds were not entirely focused on the here and now. No wonder: all citizens had an implant that constantly interrogated them, eliciting their opinions on every aspect of Demarchy life, both within Cadmus-Asterius and beyond. Eventually, it was said, the implant's nagging presence faded from consciousness, until the act of democratic participation became near-involuntary.

It revolted Vargovic as much as it intrigued him.

'Obviously,' Control said, with judicial deliberation, 'what Cholok has to offer isn't merely a nugget – or she'd have given it via PE3.'

Vargovic leaned forward. 'She hasn't told you what it is?'

'Only that it could endanger the hanging cities.'

'You trust her?'

Vargovic felt one of Control's momentary indiscretions coming on. 'She may have been sleeping, but she hasn't been completely valueless. She's assisted in defections . . . like the Maunciple job – remember that?'

'If you're calling that a success, perhaps it's time I defected.'

'Actually, it was Cholok's information that persuaded us to get Maunciple out via the ocean rather than the front door. If Demarchy security had taken Maunciple alive they'd have learned ten years of tradecraft.'

'Whereas instead, Maunciple got a harpoon in his back.'

'So the operation had its flaws.' Control shrugged. 'But if you're thinking all this points to Cholok having been compromised . . . Naturally, the thought entered our heads. But if

Mauncipле had acted otherwise it would have been worse.' Control folded his arms. 'And of course, he might have made it, in which case even you'd have to admit Cholok's safe.'

'Until proven otherwise.'

Control brightened. 'So you'll do it?'

'Like I have a choice.'

'There's always a choice, Vargovic.'

Yes, Vargovic thought. There was always a choice, between doing whatever Gilgamesh Isis asked of him and being deprogrammed, cyborgised and sent to work in the sulphur projects around the slopes of Ra Patera. It just wasn't a particularly good one.

'One other thing . . .'

'Yes?'

'When I've got whatever Cholok has—'

Control half-smiled, the two of them sharing a private joke that did not need illumination. 'I'm sure the usual will suffice.'

The elevator slowed into immigration.

Demarchy guards hefted big guns, but no one took any interest in him. His story about coming from Mars was accepted; he was subjected to only the usual spectrum of invasive procedures: neural and genetic patterns scanned for pathologies, body bathed in eight forms of exotic radiation. The final formality consisted of drinking a thimble of chocolate. The beverage consisted of billions of medichines which infiltrated his body, searching for concealed drugs, weapons and illegal biomodifications. He knew that they would find nothing, but was still relieved when they reached his bladder and requested to be urinated back into the Demarchy.

The entire procedure lasted six minutes. Outside, Vargovic followed a slitherwalk to the city zoo, and then barged through crowds of schoolchildren until he arrived at the aquarium where Cholok was meant to meet him. The exhibits were devoted to Europan biota, most of which depended on the ecological niches of the hydrothermal vents, carefully reproduced here. There was nothing very exciting to look at, since most Europan predators looked marginally less fierce than hat stands or lampshades. The commonest were called ventlings: large and structurally simple animals whose metabolisms hinged on symbiosis. They were pulpy, funnelled bags planted on a tripod of orange stilts, moving with such torpor that Vargovic almost nodded off before Cholok arrived at his side.

She wore an olive-green coat and tight emerald trousers, projecting a haze of medicinal entoptics. Her clenched jaw accentuated the dourness he had gleaned from the intercept.

They kissed.

'Good to see you Marius. It's been – what?'

'Nine years, thereabouts.'

'How's Phobos these days?'

'Still orbiting Mars.' He deployed a smile. 'Still a dive.'

'You haven't changed.'

'Nor you.'

At a loss for words, Vargovic found his gaze returning to the informational read-out accompanying the ventling exhibit. Only half-attentively, he read that the ventlings, motile in their juvenile phase, gradually became sessile in adulthood, stilts thickening with deposited sulphur until they were rooted to the ground like stalagmites. When they died, their soft bodies dispersed into the ocean, but the tripods remained; eerily regular clusters of orange spines concentrated around active vents.

'Nervous, Marius?'

'In your hands? Not likely.'

'That's the spirit.'

They bought two mugs of mocha from a nearby servitor, then returned to the ventling display, making what sounded like small talk. During indoctrination, Cholok had been taught Phrase-Embedded Three. The code allowed the insertion of secondary information into a primary conversation by means of careful deployment of word order, hesitation and sentence structure.

'What have you got?' Vargovic asked.

'A sample,' Cholok answered, one of the easy, pre-set words that did not need to be laboriously conveyed. But what followed took nearly five minutes to put over, freighted via a series of rambling reminiscences of the Phobos years. 'A small shard of hyperdiamond.'

Vargovic nodded. He knew what hyperdiamond was: a topologically complex interweave of tubular fullerene; structurally similar to cellulose or bulk-chitin but thousands of times stronger; its rigidity artificially maintained by some piezoelectric trick that Gilgamesh lacked.

'Interesting,' Vargovic said. 'But unfortunately not interesting enough.'

She ordered another mocha and downed it, replying, 'Use your imagination. Only the Demarchy knows how to synthesise it.'

'It's also useless as a weapon.'

'Depends. There's an application you should know about.'

'What?'

'Keeping this city afloat – and no, I'm not talking about economic solvency. Do you know about Buckminster Fuller? He lived about four hundred years ago; believed absolute democracy could be achieved through technological means.'

'The fool.'

'Maybe. But Fuller also invented the geodesic lattice that determines the structure of the buckyball: the closed allotrope of tubular fullerene. The city owes him on two counts.'

'Save the lecture. How does the hyperdiamond come into it?'

'Flotation bubbles,' she said. 'Around the outside of the city. Each one is a hundred-metre-wide sphere of hyperdiamond, holding vacuum. A hundred-metre-wide molecule, in fact, since each sphere is composed of one endless strand of tubular fullerene. Think of that, Marius: a molecule you could park a ship inside.'

While he absorbed that, another part of his mind continued to read the ventling caption: how their biochemistry had many similarities with the gutless tube worms that lived around Earth's ocean vents. The ventlings drank hydrogen sulphide through their funnels, circulating it via a modified form of haemoglobin, passing it through a bacteria-saturated organ in the lower part of their bags. The bacteria split and oxidised the hydrogen sulphide, manufacturing a molecule similar to glucose. The glucose-analogue nourished the ventling, enabling it to keep living and occasionally make slow perambulations to other parts of the vent, or even to swim between vents, until the adult phase rooted it to the ground. Vargovic read this, and then read it again, because he had just remembered something: a puzzling intercept passed to him from cryptanalysis several months earlier; something about Demarchy plans to incorporate ventling biochemistry into a larger animal. For a moment he was tempted to ask Cholok about it directly, but he decided to force the subject from his mind until a more suitable time.

'Any other propaganda to share with me?'

'There are two hundred of these spheres. They inflate and deflate like bladders, maintaining C-A's equilibrium. I'm not sure how the deflation happens, except that it's something to do with changing the piezoelectric current in the tubes.'

'I still don't see why Gilgamesh needs it.'

'Think. If you can get a sample of this to Ganymede, they might be able to find a way of attacking it. All you'd need would be a molecular agent capable of opening the gaps between the fullerene strands so that a molecule of water could squeeze through, or something that impedes the piezoelectric force.'

Absently Vargovic watched a squid-like predator nibble a chunk from the bag of a ventling. The squid's blood ran thick with two forms of haemoglobin, one oxygen-bearing, one tuned for hydrogen sulphide. They used glycoproteins to keep their blood flowing and switched metabolisms as they swam from oxygen-dominated to sulphide-dominated water.

He snapped his attention back to Cholok. 'I can't believe I came all this way for . . . what? Carbon?' He shook his head, slotting the gesture into the primary narrative of their conversation. 'How did you obtain this?'

'An accident, with a gilly.'

'Go on.'

'An explosion near one of the bubbles. I was the surgeon assigned to the gilly; had to remove a lot of hyperdiamond from him. It wasn't difficult to save a few splinters.'

'Forward-thinking of you.'

'Hard part was persuading Gilgamesh to send you. Especially after Maunciple – '

'Don't lose any sleep over him,' Vargovic said, consulting his coffee. 'He was a fat bastard who couldn't swim fast enough.'

The surgery took place the next day. Vargovic woke with his mouth furnace-dry.

He felt . . . odd. They had warned him of this. He had even interviewed subjects who had undergone similar procedures in Gilgamesh's experimental labs. They told him he would feel fragile, as if his head was no longer adequately coupled to his body. The periodic flushes of cold around his neck only served to increase that feeling.

'You can speak,' Cholok said, looming over him in surgeon's whites. 'But the cardiovascular modifications – and the amount of reworking we've done to your laryngeal area – will make your voice sound a little strange. Some of the gilled are really only comfortable talking to their own kind.'

He held a hand before his eyes, examining the translucent webbing that now spanned between his fingers. There was a dark patch in the pale tissue of his palm: Cholok's embedded sample. The other hand held another.

'It worked, didn't it?' His voice sounded squeaky. 'I can breathe water.'

'And air,' Cholok said. 'Though what you'll now find is that really strenuous exercise only feels natural when you're submerged.'

'Can I move?'

'Of course,' she said. 'Try standing up. You're stronger than you feel.'

He did as she suggested, using the moment to assess his surroundings. A neural monitor clamped his crown. He was naked, in a brightly lit revival room; one glass-walled side faced the exterior ocean. It was from here that Cholok had first contacted Gilgamesh.

'This place is secure, isn't it?'

'Secure?' she said, as if the word itself was obscene. 'Yes, I suppose so.'

'Then tell me about the Denizens.'

'What?'

'Demarchy codeword. Cryptanalysis intercepted it recently – supposedly something about an experiment in radical biomodification. I was reminded of it in the aquarium.' Vargovic fingered the gills in his neck. 'Something that would make this look like cosmetic surgery. We heard the Demarchy had tailored the sulphur-based metabolism of the ventlings for human use.'

She whistled. 'That would be quite a trick.'

'Useful, though – especially if you wanted a workforce who could tolerate the anoxic environments around the vents, where the Demarchy happens to have certain mineralogical interests.'

'Maybe.' Cholok paused. 'But the changes required would be beyond surgery. You'd have to script them in at the developmental level. And even then . . . I'm not sure that what you'd end up with would necessarily be human any more.' It was as if she shivered, though Vargovic was the one who felt cold, still standing naked beside the revival table. 'All I can say is, if it happened, no one told me.'

'I thought I'd ask, that's all.'

'Good.' She brandished a white medical scanner. 'Now can I run a few more tests? We have to follow procedure.'

Cholok was right: quite apart from the fact that Vargovic's operation was completely real – and therefore susceptible to complications that had to be looked for and monitored – any deviation from normal practice was undesirable.

After the first hour or so, the real strangeness of his transformation hit home. He had been blithely unaffected by it until then, but when he saw himself in a full-body mirror, in the corner of Cholok's revival room, he knew that there was no going back.

Not easily, anyway. The Gilgamesh surgeons had promised him they could undo the work – but he didn't believe them. After all, the Demarchy was ahead of Ganymede in the biosciences, and even Cholok had told him reversals were tricky. He'd accepted the mission in any case: the pay tantalising; the prospect of the sulphur projects rather less so.

Cholok spent most of the day with him, only breaking off to talk to other clients or confer with her team. Breathing exercises occupied most of that time: prolonged periods spent underwater, nulling the brain's drowning response. Unpleasant, but Vargovic had done worse things in training. They practised fully submerged swimming, using his lungs to regulate buoyancy, followed by instruction about keeping his gill-openings – what Cholok called his opercula – clean, which meant ensuring the health of the colonies of commensal bacteria that thrived in the openings and crawled over the fine secondary flaps of his lamellae. He'd read the brochure: what she'd done was to surgically sculpt his anatomy towards a state somewhere between human and air-breathing fish: incorporating biochemical lessons from lungfish and walking-catfish. Fish breathed water through their mouths and returned it to the sea via their gills, but it was the gills in Vargovic's neck that served the function of a mouth. His true gills were below his thoracic cavity: crescent-shaped gashes below his ribs.

'Compared to your body size,' she said, 'these gill-openings are never going to give you the respiratory efficiency you'd have if you went in for more dramatic changes – '

'Like a Denizen?'

'I told you, I don't know anything about that.'

'It doesn't matter.' He flattened the gill-flaps down, watching – only slightly nauseated – as they puckered with each exhalation. 'Are we finished?'

'Just some final bloodwork,' she said, 'to make sure everything's still functioning properly. Then you can go and swim with the fishes.'

While she was busy at one of her consoles, surrounded by false-colour entoptics of his gullet – he asked her, 'Do you have the weapon?'

Cholok nodded absently and opened a drawer, fishing out a hand-held medical laser. 'Not much,' she said. 'I disabled the yield-suppresser, but you'd have to aim it at someone's eyes to do much damage.'

Vargovic hefted the laser, scrutinising the controls in its contoured haft. Then he grabbed Cholok's head and twisted her around, dousing her face with the laser's actinic-blue beam. There were two consecutive popping sounds as her eyeballs evaporated.

'What, like that?'

Conventional scalpels did the rest.

He rinsed off the blood, dressed and left the medical centre alone, travelling kilometres down-city, to where Cadmus-Asterius narrowed to a point. Even though there were many gillies moving freely through the city – they were volunteers, by and large, with full Demarchy rights – he did not linger in public for long. Within a few minutes he was safe inside a warren of collagen-walled service tunnels, frequented only by technicians, servitors or other gill-workers. The late Cholok had been right: breathing air was more difficult now. It felt too thin.

'Demarchy security advisory,' said a bleak machine voice emanating from the wall. 'A murder has occurred in the medical sector. The suspect may be an armed gill-worker. Approach with extreme caution.'

They'd found Cholok. Risky, killing her. But Gilgamesh preferred to burn its bridges, removing the possibility of any sleeper turning traitor after they had fulfilled their usefulness. In the future, Vargovic mulled, they might be better using a toxin, rather than the immediate kill. He made a mental note to insert that in his report.

He entered the final tunnel, not far from the waterlock that was his destination. At the tunnel's far end a technician sat on a crate, listening with a stethoscope to something going on behind an access panel. For a moment Vargovic considered passing the man, hoping he was engrossed in his work. He began to approach him, padding on bare webbed feet, which made less noise than the shoes he had just removed. Then the man nodded to himself, uncoupled from the listening post and slammed the hatch. Grabbing his crate, he stood and made eye contact with Vargovic.

'You're not meant to be here,' he said. Then offered, almost plaintively, 'Can I help you? You've just had surgery, haven't you? I always recognise new ones like you: always a little red around the gills.'

Vargovic drew his collar higher, then relented because that made it harder to breathe. 'Stay where you are,' he said. 'Put down the crate and freeze.'

'Christ, that advisory – it was you, wasn't it?' the man said.

Vargovic raised the laser. Blinded, the man blundered into the wall, dropping the crate. He made a pitiful moan. Vargovic crept closer, the man stumbling into the scalpel. Not the cleanest of killings, but that hardly mattered.

Vargovic was sure the Demarchy would shortly seal off access to the ocean – especially when his latest murder came to light. For now, however, the locks were accessible. He moved into the air-filled chamber, his lungs now aflame for water. High-pressure jets filled the room, and he quickly transitioned to water-breathing, feeling his thoughts clarify. The secondary door clammed open, revealing ocean. He was kilometres below the ice, and the water here was both chillingly cold and under crushing pressure – but it felt normal; pressure and cold registered only as abstract qualities of the environment. His blood was inoculated with glycoproteins now, molecules which would lower its freezing point below that of water.

The late Cholok had done well.

Vargovic was about to leave the city when a second gill-worker appeared in the doorway, returning to the city after completing a shift. He killed her efficiently, and she bequeathed him a thermally inwoven wetsuit, for working in the coldest parts of the ocean. The wetsuit had octopus ancestry, and when it slithered onto him it left apertures for his gill-openings. She had been wearing goggles that had infrared and sonar capability, and carried a hand-held tug. The thing resembled the still-beating heart of a vivisected animal, its translucent components knobbed with dark veins and ganglia. But it was easy to use: Vargovic set its pump to maximum thrust and powered away from the lower levels of C-A. Even in the relatively uncontaminated water of the Europan ocean, visibility was low; he would not have been able to see anything were the city not abundantly illuminated on all its levels. Even so, he could see no more than half a kilometre upwards; the higher parts of C-A were lost in golden haze and then deepening darkness. Although its symmetry was upset by protrusions and accretions, the city's basic conic form was still evident, tapering at the narrowest point to an inlet mouth which ingested ocean. The cone was surrounded by a haze of flotation bubbles, black as caviar. He remembered the chips of hyperdiamond in his hands. If Cholok was right, Vargovic's people might find a way to make it water-permeable; opening the fullerene weave sufficiently so that the spheres' buoyant properties would be destroyed. The necessary agent could be introduced into the ocean by ice-penetrating missiles. Some time later – Vargovic was uninterested in the details – the Demarchy cities would begin to groan under their own weight. If the weapon worked sufficiently quickly, there might not even be time to act against it. The cities would fall from the ice, sinking down through the black kilometres of ocean below them.

He swam on.

Near C-A, the rocky interior of Europa climbed upwards to meet him. He had travelled three or four kilometres north, and was comparing the visible topography – lit by service lights installed by Demarchy gill-workers – with his own mental maps of the area. Eventually he found an outcropping of silicate rock. Beneath the overhang was a narrow ledge on which a dozen or so small boulders had fallen. One was redder than the others. Vargovic anchored himself to the ledge and hefted the red rock, the warmth of his fingertips activating its latent biocircuitry. A screen appeared in the rock, filling with Mishenka's face.

'I'm on time,' Vargovic said, his own voice sounding even less recognisable through the distorting medium of the water. 'I presume you're ready?'

'Problem,' Mishenka said. 'Big fucking problem.'

'What?'

'Extraction site's compromised.' Mishenka – or rather the simulation of Mishenka that was running in the rock – anticipated Vargovic's next question: 'A few hours ago the Demarchy sent a surface team out onto the ice, ostensibly to repair a transponder. But the spot they're covering is right where we planned to pull you out.' He paused. 'You did – uh – kill Cholok, didn't you? I mean, you didn't just grievously injure her?'

'You're talking to a professional.'

The rock did a creditable impression of Mishenka looking pained. 'Then the Demarchy got to her.'

Vargovic waved his hand in front of the rock. 'I got what I came for, didn't I?'

'You got something.'

'If it isn't what Cholok said it was, then she's accomplished nothing except get herself dead.'

'Even so . . .' Mishenka appeared to entertain a thought briefly, before discarding it. 'Listen, we always had a back-up extraction point, Vargovic. You'd better get your ass there.' He grinned. 'Hope you can swim faster than Maunciple.'

It was thirty kilometres south.

He passed a few gill-workers on the way, but they ignored him and once he was more than five kilometres from C-A there was increasingly less evidence of human presence. There was a head-up display in the goggles. Vargovic experimented with the read-out modes before calling up a map of the whole area. It showed his location, and also three dots following him from C-A.

He was being tailed by Demarchy security.

They were at least three kilometres behind him now, but they were perceptibly narrowing the distance. With a cold feeling gripping his gut, it occurred to Vargovic that there was no way he could make it to the extraction point before the Demarchy caught him.

Ahead, he noticed a thermal hot spot: heat bubbling up from the relatively shallow level of the rock floor. The security operatives were probably tracking him via the gill-worker's appropriated equipment. But once he was near the vent he could ditch it: the water was warmer there; he wouldn't need the suit, and the heat, light and associated turbulence would confuse any other tracking system. He could lie low behind a convenient rock, stalk them while they were preoccupied with the homing signal.

It struck Vargovic as a good plan. He covered the distance to the vent quickly, feeling the water grow warmer around him, noticing how the taste of it changed, turning brackish.

The vent was a fiery red fountain surrounded by bacteria-crusted rocks and the colourless Europan equivalent of coral. Ventlings were everywhere, their pulpy bags shifting as the currents altered. The smallest were motile, ambling on their stilts like animated bagpipes, navigating around the triadic stumps of their dead relatives.

Vargovic ensconced himself in a cave, after placing the gill-worker's equipment near another cave on the far side of the vent, hoping that the security operatives would look there first. While they did so, he would be able to kill at least one of them; maybe two. Once he had their weapons, taking care of the third would be a formality.

Something nudged him from behind.

What Vargovic saw when he turned around was something too repulsive even for a nightmare. It was so wrong that for a faltering moment he could not quite assimilate what he was looking at, as if the thing was a three-dimensional perception test; a shape that refused to stabilise in his head. The reason he could not hold it still was because part of him refused to believe that this thing had any connection with humanity. But the residual traces of human ancestry were too obvious to ignore.

Vargovic knew – beyond any reasonable doubt – that what he was seeing was a Denizen. Others loomed from the cave's depths – five more of them, all roughly similar, all aglow with faint bioluminescence, all regarding him with darkly intelligent eyes. Vargovic had seen pictures of mermaids in books when he was a child; what he was looking at now were macabre corruptions of those innocent illustrations. These things were the same fusions of human and fish as in those pictures – but every detail had been twisted towards ugliness, and the true horror of it was that the fusion was total; it was not simply that a human torso had been grafted to a fish's tail, but that the splice had been made – it was obvious – at the genetic level, so that in every aspect of the creature there was something simultaneously and grotesquely piscine. The faces were the worst, bisected by a lipless downcurved slit of a mouth, almost shark-like. There was no nose, not even a pair of nostrils; just an acreage of flat, sallow fish-flesh. The eyes were forward facing; all expression compacted into their dark depths.

The first creature had touched him with one of its arms, which terminated in an obscenely human hand. And then – to compound the horror – it spoke, its voice perfectly clear and calm despite the water.

'We've been expecting you, Vargovic.'

The others behind murmured, echoing the sentiment.

'What?'

'So glad you were able to complete your mission.'

Vargovic began to get a grip, shakily. He reached up and dislodged the Denizen's hand from his shoulder. 'You aren't why I'm here,' he said, forcing authority into his voice, drawing on every last drop of Gilgamesh training to suppress his nerves. 'I wanted to know about you . . . that was all – '

'No,' the lead Denizen said, opening its mouth to expose an alarming array of teeth. 'You misunderstand. Coming here was always your mission. You have brought us something we want very much. That was always your purpose.'

'Brought you something?' His mind was reeling now.

'Concealed within you.' The Denizen nodded: a human gesture that only served to magnify the horror of what it was. 'The means by which we will strike at the Demarchy; the means by which we will take the ocean.'

He thought of the chips in his hands. 'I think I understand,' he said slowly. 'It was always intended for you, is that what you mean?'

'Always.'

Then he'd been lied to by his superiors – or they had at least drastically simplified the matter. He filled in the gaps himself, making the necessary mental leaps: evidently Gilgamesh was already in contact with the Denizens – bizarre as it seemed – and the chips of hyperdiamond were meant for the Denizens, not his own people. Presumably – although he couldn't begin to guess at how this might be possible – the Denizens had the means to examine the shards and fabricate the agent that would unravel the hyperdiamond weave. They'd be acting for Gilgamesh, saving it the bother of actually dirtying its hands in the attack. He could see why this might appeal to Control. But if that was the case . . . why had Gilgamesh ever faked ignorance about the Denizens? It made no sense. But on the other hand, he could not concoct a better theory to replace it.

'I have what you want,' he said, after due consideration. 'Cholok said removing it would be simple.'

'Cholok can always be relied upon,' the Denizen said.

'You knew – know – her, then?'

'She made us what we are today.'

'You hate her, then?'

'No; we love her.' The Denizen flashed its shark-like smile again, and it seemed to Vargovic that as its emotional state changed, so did the coloration of its bioluminescence. It was scarlet now, no longer the blue-green hue it had displayed upon its first appearance. 'She took the abomination that we were and made us something better. We were in pain, once. Always in pain. But Cholok took it away, made us strong. For that they punished her, and then us.'

'If you hate the Demarchy,' Vargovic said, 'why have you waited until now before attacking it?'

'Because we can't leave this place,' one of the other Denizens said, the tone of its voice betraying femininity. 'The Demarchy hated what Cholok had done to us. She brought our humanity to the fore, made it impossible for them to treat us as animals. We thought they would kill us, rather than risk our existence becoming known to the rest of Circum-Jove. Instead, they banished us here.'

'They thought we might come in handy,' said another of the lurking creatures.

Just then, another Denizen entered the cave, having swum in from the sea.

'Demarchy agents have followed him,' it said, its coloration blood red, tinged with orange, pulsing lividly. 'They'll be here in a minute.'

'You'll have to protect me,' Vargovic said.

'Of course,' the lead Denizen said. 'You're our saviour.'

Vargovic nodded vigorously, no longer convinced that he could handle the three operatives on his own. Ever since he had arrived in the cave he had felt his energy dwindling, as if he was succumbing to slow poisoning. A thought tugged at the back of his mind, and for a moment he almost paid attention to it; almost considered seriously the possibility that he was being poisoned. But what was going on beyond the cave was too distracting. He watched the three Demarchy agents approach, pulled forward by the tugs they held in front of them. Each agent carried a slender harpoon gun, tipped with a vicious barb.

They didn't stand a chance.

The Denizens moved too quickly, lancing out from the shadows, cutting through the water. The creatures moved faster than the Demarchy agents, even though they only had their own muscles and anatomy to propel them. But it was more than enough. They had no weapons, either – not even harpoons. But sharpened rocks more than sufficed – that and their teeth.

Vargovic was impressed by their teeth.

Afterwards, the Denizens returned to the cave to join their cousins. They moved more sluggishly now, as if the fury of the fight had drained them. For a few moments they were silent, their bioluminescence curiously subdued.

Slowly, though, Vargovic watched their colour return.

'It was better that they not kill you,' the leader said.

'Damn right,' Vargovic said. 'They wouldn't just have killed me, you know.' He opened his fists, exposing his palms. 'They'd have made sure you never got this.'

The Denizens – all of them – looked momentarily towards his open hands, as if there ought to have been something there.

'I'm not sure you understand,' the leader said, eventually.

'Understand what?'

'The nature of your mission.'

Fighting his fatigue – it was a black slick lapping at his consciousness – Vargovic said, 'I understand perfectly well. I have the samples of hyperdiamond, in my hands – '

'That isn't what we want.'

He didn't like this, not at all. It was the way the Denizens were slowly creeping closer to him, sidling around him to obstruct his exit from the cave.

'What then?'

'You asked why we haven't attacked them before,' the leader said, with frightening charm. 'The answer's simple: we can't leave the vent.'

'You can't?'

'Our haemoglobin. It's not like yours.' Again that awful shark-like smile – and now he was well aware of what those teeth could do, given the right circumstances. 'It was tailored to allow us to work here.'

'Copied from the ventlings?'

'Adapted, yes. Later it became the means of imprisoning us. The DNA in our bone marrow was manipulated to limit the production of normal haemoglobin; a simple matter of suppressing a few beta-globin genes while retaining the variants that code for ventling haemoglobin. Hydrogen sulphide is poisonous to you, Vargovic. You probably already feel weak. But we can't survive without it. Oxygen kills us.'

'You leave the vent . . .'

'We die, within a few hours. There's more. The water's hot here, so hot that we don't need the glycoproteins. We have the genetic instructions to synthezise them, but they've also been turned off. But without the glycoproteins we can't swim into colder water. Our blood freezes.'

Now he was surrounded by them; looming aquatic devils, flushed a florid shade of crimson. And they were coming closer.

'But what do you expect me to do about it?'

'You don't have to do anything, Vargovic.' The leader opened its chasmic jaw wide, as if tasting the water. It was a miracle an organ like that was capable of speech in the first place . . .

'I don't?'

'No.' And with that the leader reached out and seized him, while at the same time he was pinned from behind by another of the creatures. 'It was Cholok's doing,' the leader continued. 'Her final gift to us. Maunciple was her first attempt at getting it to us – but Maunciple never made it.'

'He was too fat.'

'All the defectors failed – they just didn't have the stamina to make it this far from the city. That was why Cholok recruited you – an outsider.'

'Cholok recruited me?'

'She knew you'd kill her – you have, of course – but that didn't stop her. Her life mattered less than what she was about to give us. It was Cholok who tipped off the Demarchy about your primary extraction site, forcing you to come to us.'

He struggled, but it was pointless. All he could manage was a feeble, 'I don't understand – '

'No,' the Denizen said. 'Perhaps we never expected you to. If you had understood, you might have been less than willing to follow Cholok's plan.'

'Cholok was never working for us?'

'Once, maybe. But her last clients were us.'

'And now?'

'We take your blood, Vargovic.' Their grip on him tightened. He used his last draining reserves of strength to try to work loose, but it was futile.

'My blood?'

'Cholok put something in it. A retrovirus – a very hardy one, capable of surviving in your body. It reactivates the genes that were suppressed by the Demarchy. Suddenly, we'll be able to make oxygen-carrying haemoglobin. Our blood will fill up with glycoproteins. It's no great trick: all the cellular machinery for making those molecules is already present; it just needs to be unshackled.'

'Then you need . . . what? A sample of my blood?'

'No,' the Denizen said, with genuine regret. 'Rather more than a sample, I'm afraid. Rather a lot more.'

And then – with magisterial slowness – the creature bit into his arm, and as his blood spilt out, the Denizen drank. For a moment the others waited – but then they too came forward, and bit, and joined in the feeding frenzy.

All around Vargovic, the water was turning red.

GALACTIC NORTH

Luyten 726-8 Cometary Halo – AD 2303

The two of them crouched in a tunnel of filthy ice, bulky in spacesuits. Fifty metres down the tunnel, the servitor straddled the bore on skeletal legs, transmitting a thermal image onto their visors. Irravel jumped whenever the noise shifted into something human, cradling her gun nervously.

'Damn this thing,' she said. 'Hardly get my finger around the trigger.'

'It can't read your blood, Captain.' Markarian, next to her, managed not to sound as if he was stating the obvious. 'You have to set the override to female.'

Of course. Belatedly remembering the training session on Fand where they'd been shown how to use the weapons – months of subjective time ago; years of worldtime – Irravel told the gun to reshape itself. The memory-plastic casing squirmed in her gloves to something more manageable. It still felt wrong.

'How are we doing?' she asked.

'Last team's in position. That's all the tunnels covered. They'll have to fight their way in.'

'I think that might well be on the agenda.'

'Maybe so.' Markarian sighted along his weapon like a sniper. 'But they'll get a surprise when they reach the cargo.'

True: the ship had sealed the sleeper chambers the instant the pirates had arrived near the comet. Counter-intrusion weaponry would seriously inconvenience anyone trying to break in, unless they had the right authorisation. And there, Irravel knew, was the problem; the thing she would rather not have had to deal with.

'Markarian,' Irravel said, 'if we're taken prisoner, there's a chance they'll try to make us give up the codes.'

'Don't think that hasn't crossed my mind already.' Markarian rechecked some aspect of his gun. 'I won't let you down, Irravel.'

'It's not a question of letting me down,' she said, carefully. 'It's whether or not we betray the cargo.'

'I know.' For a moment they studied each other's faces through their visors, acknowledging what had once been more than professional friendship; the shared knowledge that they would kill each other rather than place the cargo in harm's way.

Their ship was the ramliner *Hirondelle*. She was damaged; lashed to the comet for repair. Improbably sleek for a creature of vacuum, her four-kilometre-long conic hull tapered to a needle-sharp prow and sprouted trumpet-shaped engines from two swept-back spars at the rear. It had been Irravel's first captaincy: a routine seventeen-year hop from Fand, in the Lacaille 9352 system, to Yellowstone, around Epsilon Eridani – with twenty thousand reefersleep colonists aboard. What had gone wrong should only have happened once in a thousand trips: a speck of interstellar dust had slipped through the ship's screen of anti-collision lasers and punched a cavernous hole in the ablative ice shield, vaporising a quarter of its mass. With a vastly reduced likelihood of surviving another collision, the ship had automatically steered towards the nearest system capable of supplying repair materials.

Luyten 726-8 had been no one's idea of a welcoming destination. No human colonies had flourished there. All that remained were droves of scavenging machines sent out by various superpowers. The ship had locked into a scavenger's homing signal, eventually coming within visual range of the inert comet the machine had made its home, and which ought to have been chequered with resupply materials. Irravel had been revived from reefersleep just in time to see that none of the goods were there – just acres of barren comet.

'Dear God,' she'd said. 'Do we deserve this?'

After a few days, despair became steely resolve. The ship couldn't safely travel anywhere else, so they would have to process the supplies themselves, doing the work of the malfunctioning surveyor. It would mean stripping the ship just to make the machines to mine and shape the cometary ice – years of work by any estimate. That hardly mattered. The detour had already added years to the mission.

Irravel ordered the rest of her crew – all ninety of them – to be warmed, and then delegated tasks, mostly programming. Servitors were not particularly intelligent outside of their designated functions. She considered activating the other machines she carried as cargo – the greenfly terraformers – but that cut against all her instincts. Greenfly machines were von Neumann breeders, unlike the sterile servitors. They were a hundred times cleverer. She would only consider using them if the cargo was placed in immediate danger.

'If you won't unleash the greenflies,' Markarian said, 'at least think about waking the Conjoiners. There may only be four of them, but we could use their expertise.'

'I don't trust them. I never liked the idea of carrying them in the first place. They unsettle me.'

'I don't like them either, but I'm willing to bury my prejudices if it means fixing the ship faster.'

'Well, that's where we differ. I'm not, so don't raise the subject again.'

'Yes,' Markarian said, and only when its omission was insolently clear added: 'Captain.'

Eventually the Conjoiners ceased to be an issue, when the work was clearly under way and proceeding normally. Most of the crew were able to return to reefersleep. Irravel and Markarian stayed awake a little longer, and even after they'd gone under, they woke every seven months to review the status of the works. It began to look as if they would succeed without assistance.

Until the day they were woken out of schedule, and a dark, grapple-shaped ship was almost upon the comet. Not an interstellar ship, it must have come from somewhere nearby – probably within the same halo of comets around Luyten 726-8. Its silence was not encouraging.

'I think they're pirates,' Irravel said. 'I've heard of one or two other ships going missing near here, but it was always put down to accident.'

'Why did they wait so long to attack us?'

'They had no choice. There are billions of comets out here, but they're never less than light-hours apart. That's a long way if you only have in-system engines. They must have a base somewhere else to keep watch, maybe light-weeks from here, like a spider with a very wide web.'

'What do we do now?'

Irravel gritted her teeth. 'Do what anything does when it's stuck in the middle of a web: fight back.'

But the *Hirondelle*'s minimal defences had only scratched the enemy ship.

Oblivious, it fired penetrators and winched closer. Dozens of crab-shaped machines swarmed out and dropped below the comet's horizon, impacting with seismic thuds. After a few minutes, sensors in the furthest tunnels registered intruders. Only a handful of crew had been woken. They broke guns out of the armoury – small arms designed for pacification in the unlikely event of a shipboard riot – and then established defensive positions in all the cometary tunnels.

Nervously now, Irravel and Markarian advanced around a bend in the tunnel, cleated shoes whispering through ice barely more substantial than smoke. They had to keep their suit exhausts from touching the walls if they didn't want to get blown back by superheated steam. Irravel jumped again at the pattern of photons on her visor and then forced calm, telling herself it was another mirage.

Except this time it stayed.

Markarian opened fire, squeezing rounds past the servitor. It lurched aside, a gaping hole in its carapace. Black crabs came around the bend, encrusted with sensors and guns. The first reached the ruined servitor and dismembered it with ease. If only there'd been time to activate and program the greenfly machines. They'd have ripped through the pirates like a host of furies, treating them as terraformable matter . . .

And maybe us, too, Irravel thought.

Something flashed through the clouds of steam: an electromagnetic pulse that turned Irravel's suit sluggish, as if every joint had corroded. The whine of the circulator died to silence, leaving only her frenzied breathing. Something pressed against her backpack. She turned slowly around, wary of falling against the walls. There were crabs everywhere. The chamber in which they'd been cornered was littered with the bodies of the other crew members, pink trails of blood reaching across the ice from other tunnels. They'd been killed and dragged here.

Two words jumped to mind: *kill yourself*. But first she had to kill Markarian, in case he lacked the nerve to do it himself. She couldn't see his face through his visor. That was good. Painfully, she pointed the gun towards him and squeezed the trigger. But instead of firing, the gun shivered in her hands, stowing itself into a quarter of its operational volume.

'Thank you for using this weapon system,' it said cheerfully.

Irravel let it drift to the ground.

A new voice rasped in her helmet. 'If you're thinking of surrendering, now might not be a bad time.'

'Bastard,' Irravel said, softly.

'Really the best you can manage?' The language was Canasian – what Irravel and Markarian had spoken on Fand – but heavily accented, as if the native tongue was Norte or Russish, or spoken with an impediment. "Bastard" is quite a compliment compared to some of the things my clients come up with.'

'Give me time; I'll work on it.'

'Positive attitude – that's good.' The lid of a crab hinged up, revealing the prone form of a man in a mesh of motion-sensors. He crawled from the mesh and stepped onto the ice, wearing a spacesuit formed from segmented metal plates. Totems had been welded to the armour, around holographic starscapes infested with serpentine monsters and scantily clad maidens.

'Who are you?' she asked.

'Captain Run Seven.' He stepped closer, examining her suit nameplate. 'But you can call me Seven, Irravel Veda.'

'I hope you burn in hell, Seven.'

Seven smiled – she could see the curve of his grin through his visor; the oddly upturned nostrils of his nose above it. 'I'm sensing some negativity here, Irravel. I think we need to put that behind us, don't you?'

Irravel looked at her murdered adjutants. 'Maybe if you tell me which one was the traitor.'

'Traitor?'

'You seemed to have no difficulty finding us.'

'Actually, you found us.' It was a woman's voice this time. 'We use lures – tampering with commercial beacons, like the scavengers'.' She emerged from one of the other attack machines wearing a suit similar to Seven's, except that it displayed the testosterone-saturated male analogues of his space-maidens: all rippling torsos and chromed codpieces.

'Wreckers,' Irravel breathed.

'Yeah. Ships home in on the beacons, then find they ain't going anywhere in a hurry. We move in from the halo.'

'Disclose all our confidential practices while you're at it, Mirsky,' Seven said.

She glared at him through her visor. 'Veda would have figured it out.'

'We'll never know now, will we?'

'What does it matter?' she said. 'Gonna kill them anyway, aren't you?'

Seven flashed an arc of teeth filed to points and waved a hand towards the female pirate. 'Allow me to introduce Mirsky, our loose-tongued but efficient information-retrieval specialist. She's going to take you on a little trip down memory lane, see if you can't remember those access codes.'

'What codes?'

'It'll come back to you,' Seven said.

They were taken through the tunnels, past half-assembled mining machines, onto the surface and then into the pirate ship. The ship was huge, most of it living space. Cramped corridors snaked through hydroponics galleries of spring wheat and dwarf papaya, strung with xenon lights. The ship hummed constantly with carbon dioxide scrubbers, the foetid air making Irravel sneeze. There were children everywhere, frowning at the captives. The pirates obviously had no reefersleep technology: they stayed warm the whole time, and some of the children Irravel saw had probably been born after the *Hirondelle* had arrived there.

They arrived at a pair of interrogation rooms where they were separated. Irravel's room held a couch converted from an old command seat, still carrying warning decals. A console stood in one corner. Painted torture scenes fought for wall space with racks of surgical equipment: drills, blades and ratcheted contraptions speckled with rust.

Irravel breathed deeply. Hyperventilation could have an anaesthetic effect. Her conditioning would in any case create a state of detachment: the pain would be no less intense, but she would feel it at one remove.

She hoped.

The pirates fiddled with her suit, confused by the modern design, until they stripped her down to her shipboard uniform. Mirsky leaned over her. She was small-boned and dark-skinned, dirty hair rising in a topknot, eyes mismatched shades of azure. Something clung to the side of her head above the left ear: a silver box with winking status lights. She fixed a crown to Irravel's head, then made adjustments on the console.

'Decided yet?' Captain Run Seven said, sauntering into the room. He was unlatching his helmet.

'What?'

'Which of our portfolio of interrogation packages you're going to opt for.'

She was looking at his face now. It wasn't really human. Seven had a man's bulk and a man's shape, but there was at least as much of the pig in his face. His nose was a snout, his ears two tapered flaps framing a hairless pink skull. His pale eyes evinced animal cunning.

'What the hell are you?'

'Excellent question,' Seven said, clicking a finger in her direction. His bare hand was dark-skinned and feminine. 'To be honest, I don't really know. A genetics experiment, perhaps? Was I the seventh failure, or the first success?'

'Do I get two guesses?'

He ignored her. 'All I know is that I've been here – in the halo around Luyten 726-8 – for as long as I can remember.'

'Someone sent you here?'

'In a tiny, automated spacecraft; perhaps an old lifepod. The ship's governing personality raised me as well as it could, attempted to make of me a well-rounded individual . . .' Seven trailed off momentarily. 'Eventually I was found by a passing ship. I staged what might be termed a hostile takeover bid. From then on I've built an organisation largely recruited from my client base.'

'You're insane. It might have worked once, but it won't work with us.'

'Why should you be any different?'

'Neural conditioning. I regard the cargo as my offspring – all twenty thousand of them. I can't betray them in any way.'

Seven smiled his piggy smile. 'Funny; the last client thought that, too.'

Sometime later, Irravel woke alone in a reefersleep casket. She remembered only dislocated episodes of interrogation. There was the memory of a kind of sacrifice, and, later, of the worst terror she could imagine – so intense that she could not bring its cause to mind. Underpinning everything was the certainty that she had not given up the codes.

So why was she still alive?

Everything was quiet and cold. Once she was able to move, she found a suit and wandered the *Hirondelle* until she reached a porthole. They were still lashed to the comet. The other craft was gone; presumably en route back to the base in the halo where the pirates must have had a larger ship.

She looked for Markarian, but there was no sign of him.

Then she checked the twenty crew sleeper chambers; the thousand-berth dormitories. The chamber doors were all open. Most of the sleepers were still there. They'd been butchered, carved open for implants, minds pulped by destructive memory-trawling devices. The horror was too great for any recognisable emotional response. The conditioning made each death feel like a stolen part of her.

Yet something kept her on the edge of sanity: the discovery that two hundred sleepers were missing. There was no sign that they'd been butchered like the others, which left the possibility that they'd been abducted by Captain Run Seven. It was madness – it would not begin to compensate for the loss of the others – but her psychology allowed no other line of thought.

She could find them again.

Her plan was disarmingly simple. It crystallised in her mind with the clarity of a divine vision. *It would be done.*

She would repair the ship. She would hunt down Seven. She would recover the sleepers from him. And enact whatever retribution she deemed fit.

*

She found the chamber where the four Conjoiners had slept, well away from the main dormitories, in a part of the ship through which the pirates were not likely to have wandered. She was hoping she could revive them and seek their assistance. There seemed no way they could make things worse for her now.

But hope faded when she saw the scorch marks of weapon blasts around the bulkhead; the door forced.

She stepped inside anyway.

They'd been a sect on Mars, originally; a clique of cyberneticists with a particular fondness for self-experimentation. In 2190, their final experiment had involved distributed processing – allowing their enhanced minds to merge into one massively parallel neural net. The resultant event – a permanent, irrevocable escalation to a new mode of consciousness – was known as the Transenlightenment.

There'd been a war, of course.

Demarchists had long seen both sides. They used neural augmentation themselves, policed it so that they never approached the Conjoiner threshold. They'd brokered the peace, defusing the suspicion surrounding the Conjoiners. Conjoiners had fuelled Demarchist expansion from Europa with their technologies, fused in the white heat of Transenlightenment. Four of them were along as observers because the *Hirondelle* used their ramscoop drives.

Irravel still didn't trust them.

And maybe it didn't matter. The reefersleep units – fluted caskets like streamlined coffins – were riddled with blast holes. Grimacing against the smell, Irravel examined the remains inside. They'd been cut open, but the pirates seemed to have abandoned the job halfway through, not finding the kinds of implants they were expecting. And maybe not even recognising that they were dealing with anything other than normal humans, Irravel thought – especially if the pirates who'd done this hadn't been amongst Seven's more experienced crew-members; just trigger-happy thugs.

She examined the final casket, the one furthest from the door. It was damaged, but not so badly as the others. The display cartouches were still alive, a patina of frost still adhering to the casket's lid. The Conjoiner inside looked intact: the pirates had never reached him. She read his nameplate: *Remontoire.*

'Yeah, he's a live one,' said a voice behind Irravel. 'Now back off real slow.'

Heart racing, Irravel did as she was told. Slowly, she turned around, facing the woman whose voice she recognised.

'Mirsky?' she said.

'Yeah, it's your lucky day.' Mirsky was wearing her suit, but without the helmet, making her head appear shrunken in the moat of her neck-ring. She had a gun on Irravel, but she pointed it half-heartedly, as if this was a stage in their relationship she wanted to get over as quickly as possible.

'What the hell are you doing here?'

'Same as you, Veda. Trying to figure out how much shit we're in; how difficult it'll be to get this ship moving again. Guess we had the same idea about the Conjoiners. Seven went berserk when he heard they'd been killed, but I figured it was worth checking how thorough the job had been.'

'Stop; slow down. Start at the beginning. Why aren't you with Seven?'

Mirsky pushed past her and consulted the reefersleep indicators. 'Seven and me had a falling out. Fill in the rest yourself.' With quick jabs of her free hand she called up different display modes, frowning at each. 'Shit; this *ain't* gonna be easy. If we wake the guy without his three friends, he's gonna be psychotic; no use to us at all.'

'What kind of falling out?'

'Seven reckoned I was holding back too much in the interrogation, not putting you through enough hell.' She scratched at the silver box on the side of her head. 'Maybe we can wake him, then fake the cybernetic presence of his friends – what do you think?'

'Why am I still alive, if Seven broke into the sleeper chambers? Why are *you* still alive?'

'Seven's a sadist. Abandonment's more his style than a quick and clean execution. As for you, the pig cut a deal with your second-in-command.'

The implication of that sunk in. 'Markarian gave him the codes?'

'It wasn't you, Veda.'

Strange relief flooded Irravel. She could never be absolved of the crime of losing the cargo, but at least her degree of complicity had lessened.

'But that was only half the deal,' Mirsky continued. 'The rest was Seven promising not to kill you if Markarian agreed to join the *Hideyoshi*, our main ship.' She told Irravel that there'd been a transmitter rigged to her reefersleep unit, so that Markarian would know she was still alive.

'Seven must have known he was taking a risk leaving both of us alive.'

'A pretty small one. The ship's in pieces and Seven will assume neither of us has the brains to patch it back together.' Mirsky slipped the gun into a holster. 'But Seven assumed the Conjoiners were dead. Big mistake. Once we figure out a way to wake Remontoire safely, he can help us fix the ship; make it faster, too.'

'You've got this all worked out, haven't you?'

'More or less. Something tells me you aren't absolutely ready to start trusting me, though.'

'Sorry, Mirsky, but you don't make the world's most convincing turncoat.'

Mirsky reached up and gripped the box attached to the side of her head. 'Know what this is? A loyalty shunt. Makes simian stem cells; pumps them into the internal carotid artery, just above the *cavernous sinus*. They jump the blood–brain barrier and build a whole bunch of transient structures tied to primate dominance hierarchies; alpha-male shit. That's how Seven kept us under his command – he was King Monkey. But I've turned it off now.'

'That's supposed to reassure me?'

'No, but maybe this will.'

Mirsky tugged at the box, ripping it away from the side of her head in curds of blood.

Luyten 726-8 Cometary Halo – AD 2309

Irravel felt the *Hirondelle* turn like a compass needle. The ramscoops gasped at interstellar gas, sucking lone atoms of cosmic hydrogen from cubic metres of vacuum. The engines spat twin beams of thrust, pressing Irravel into her seat with two gees of acceleration. Hardly moving now, still in the local frame of the cometary halo, but in only six months she would be nudging light-speed.

Her seat floated on a boom in the middle of the dodecahedral bridge. 'Map,' Irravel said, and was suddenly drowning in stars: an immense thirty-light-year-wide projection of human settled space, centred on the First System.

'There's the bastard,' Mirsky said, pointing from her own hovering seat, her voice only slightly strained under the gee-load. 'Map – give us projection of the *Hideyoshi*'s vector, and plot our intercept.'

The pirate ship's icon was still very close to Luyten 726-8; less than a tenth of a light-year out. They had not seen Seven until now. The thrust from his ship was so tightly focused that it had taken until this point for the widening beams of the exhaust to sweep over *Hirondelle*'s sensors. But now they knew where he was headed. A dashed line indicated the likely course, arrowing right through the map's heart and out towards the system Lalande 21185. Now came the intercept vector: a near-tangent that sliced Seven's course beyond Sol.

'When does it happen?' Irravel said.

'Depends on how much attention Seven's paying to what's coming up behind him, for a start, and what kind of evasive stunts he can pull.'

'Most of my simulations predict an intercept between 2325 and 2330,' Remontoire said.

Irravel savoured the dates. Even for someone trained to fly a starship between systems, they sounded uncomfortably like the future.

'Are you sure it's him – not just some other ship that happened to be waiting in the halo?'

'Trust me,' Mirsky said. 'I can smell the swine from here.'

'She's right,' Remontoire said. 'The destination makes perfect sense. Seven was prohibited from staying here much longer, once the number of missing ships became too large to be explained away as accidents. Now he must seek a well-settled system to profit from what he has stolen.'

The Conjoiner looked completely normal at first glance – a bald man wearing a ship's uniform, his expression placid – but then one noticed the unnatural bulge of his skull, covered only with a fuzz of baby hair. Most of his glial cells had been supplanted by machines, which served the same structural functions but also performed specialised cybernetic duties, like interfacing with other commune partners or external machinery. Even the organic neurons in his brain were now webbed together by artificial connections which allowed transmission speeds of kilometres per second; factors of ten faster than in normal brains. Only the problem of dispersing waste heat denied the Conjoiners even faster modes of thought.

It was six years since they'd woken him. Remontoire had not dealt well with the murder of his three compatriots, but Irravel and Mirsky had managed to keep him sane by feeding input into the glial machines, crudely simulating rapport with other commune members.

'It provides the kind of comfort to me that a ghost limb offers an amputee,' Remontoire had said. 'An illusion of wholeness – but no substitute for the real thing.'

'What more can we do?' Irravel had said.

'Return me to another commune with all speed.'

Irravel had agreed, provided Remontoire helped with the ship.

He hadn't let her down. Under his supervision, half the ship's mass had been sacrificed, permitting twice the acceleration. They had dug a vault in the comet, lined it with support systems and entombed what remained of the cargo. The sleepers were nominally dead – there was no real expectation of reviving them again, even if medicine improved in the future – but Irravel had nonetheless set servitors to tend the dead for however long it took, and programmed the beacon to lure another ship, this time to pick up the dead.

All that had taken years, of course – but it had also taken Seven as much time to cross the halo to his base; time again to show himself.

'Be so much easier if you didn't want the others back,' Mirsky said. 'Then we could just slam past Seven at relativistic speed and hit him with seven kinds of shit.' She was very proud of the weapons she'd built into the ship, copied from pirate designs with Remontoire's help.

'I want the sleepers back,' Irravel said.

'And Markarian?'

'He's mine,' she said, after due consideration. 'You get the pig.'

Near Lalande 21185 – AD 2328

Relativity squeezed stars until they bled colour. Half a kilometre ahead, the side of Seven's ship raced towards Irravel like a tsunami.

The *Hideyoshi* was the same shape as the *Hirondelle*; honed less by human whim than the edicts of physics. But the *Hideyoshi* was heavier, with a wider cross section, incapable of matching the *Hirondelle*'s acceleration or of pushing so close to C. It had taken years, but they'd caught up with Seven, and now the attack was in progress.

Irravel, Mirsky and Remontoire wore thruster-pack-equipped suits, of the type used for inspections outside the ship, with added armour and weapons. Painted for effect, they looked like mechanised samurai. Another forty-seven suits were slaved to theirs, acting as decoys. They'd crossed fifty thousand kilometres of space between the ships.

'You're sure Seven doesn't have any defences?' Irravel had asked, not long after waking from reefersleep.

'Only the in-system ship had any fire power,' Mirsky said. She looked older now; new lines engraved under her eyes. 'That's because no one's ever been insane enough to contemplate storming another ship in interstellar space.'

'Until now.'

But it wasn't so stupid, and Mirsky knew it. Matching velocities with another ship was only a question of being faster; squeezing fractionally closer to light-speed. It might take time, but sooner or later the distance would be closed. And it *had* taken time, none of which Mirsky had spent in reefersleep. Partly it was because she lacked the right implants – ripped out in infancy when she was captured by Seven. Partly it was a distaste for the very idea of being frozen, instilled by years of pirate upbringing. But also because she wanted time to refine her weapons. They had fired a salvo against the enemy before crossing space in the suits, softening up any weapons buried in his ice and opening holes into the *Hideyoshi*'s interior.

Now Irravel's vision blurred, her suit slowing itself before slamming into the ice.

Whiteness swallowed her.

For a moment she couldn't remember what she was doing here. Then awareness returned and she slithered back up the tunnel excavated by her impact, until she reached the surface of the *Hideyoshi*'s ice-shield.

'Veda – you intact?'

Her armour's shoulder-mounted comm laser found a line of sight to Mirsky. Mirsky was twenty or thirty metres away around the ship's lazy circumference, balancing on a ledge of ice. Walls of it stretched above and below like a rock face, lit by the glare from the engines. Decoys were arriving by the second.

'I'm alive,' Irravel said. 'Where's the entry point?'

'Couple of hundred metres upship.'

'Damn. I wanted to come in closer. Remontoire's out of line of sight. How much fuel do you have left?'

'Scarcely enough to take the chill off a penguin's dick.'

Mirsky raised her arms above her head and fired lines into the ice, rocketing out from her sleeves. Belly sliding against the shield, she retracted the lines and hauled herself upship.

Irravel followed. They'd burned all their fuel crossing between the two ships, but that was part of the plan. If they didn't have a chance to raid Seven's reserves, they'd just kick themselves into space and let the *Hirondelle* home in on them.

'You think Seven saw us cross over?'

'Definitely. And you can bet he's doing something about it, too.'

'Don't do anything that might endanger the cargo, Mirsky – no matter how tempting Seven makes it.'

'Would you sacrifice half the sleepers to get the other half back?'

'That's not remotely an option.'

Above their heads, crevasses opened like eyes. Pirate crabs erupted out, black as night against the ice. Irravel opened fire on the machines. This time, with better weapons and real armour, she began to inflict damage. Behind the crabs, pirates emerged, bulbous in customised armour. Lasers scuffed the ice, bright through gouts of steam. Irravel saw Remontoire now: he was unharmed, and doing his best to shoot the pirates into space.

Above, one of Irravel's shots dislodged a pirate.

The *Hideyoshi*'s acceleration dropped him towards her. When the impact came she hardly felt it, her suit's guy lines staying firm. The pirate folded around her like a broken toy, then bounced back against the ship, pinned there by her suit. He was too close to shoot unless Irravel wanted to blow herself into space. Distorted behind glass, his face shaped a word. She moved in closer until their visors were touching. Through the glass she saw the asymmetrical bulge of a loyalty shunt.

The face was Markarian's. At first it seemed like absurd coincidence. Then it occurred to her that Seven might have sent his newest recruit out to show his mettle. Maybe Seven wouldn't be far behind. Confronting adversaries was part of the alpha-male inheritance, after all.

'Irravel,' Markarian said, voice laced with static. 'I'm glad you're alive.'

'Don't flatter yourself you're the reason I'm here, Markarian. I came for the cargo. You're just next on the list.'

'What are you going to do – kill me?'

'Do you think you deserve any better than that?' Irravel adjusted her position. 'Or are you going to try to justify betraying the cargo?'

He pulled his aged features into a smile. 'We made a deal, Irravel; the same way you made a deal about the greenfly. But you don't remember that, do you?'

'Maybe I sold the greenfly machines to the pig,' she said. 'If I did that, it was a calculated move to buy the safety of the cargo. You, on the other hand, cut a deal with Seven to save your neck.'

The other pirates were holding fire, nervously marking them. 'I did it to save yours, actually. Does that make any sense?' There was wonder in his eyes now. 'Did you ever see Mirsky's hand? That was never her own. The pirates swap limbs as badges of rank. They're very good at connective surgery.'

'You're not making much sense, Markarian.'

Dislodged ice rained on them. Irravel looked around in time to see another pirate emerging from a crevasse. She recognised the suit artwork: it was Seven. He wore . . . things, strung around his utility belt in transparent bags like obscene fruit. She stared at them for a few seconds before their nature clicked into horrific focus: frozen human heads.

Irravel stifled an urge to vomit.

'Yes,' Run Seven said. 'Ten of your compatriots, recently unburdened of their bodies. But don't worry – they're not harmed in any fundamental sense. Their brains are intact – provided you don't warm them with an ill-aimed shot.'

'I've got a clear line of fire,' Mirsky said. 'Just say the word and the bastard's an instant anatomy lesson.'

'Wait,' Irravel said. 'Don't shoot.'

'Sound business sense, Captain Veda. I see you appreciate the value of these heads.'

'What's he talking about?' Mirsky said.

'Their neural patterns can be retrieved.' It was Remontoire speaking now. 'We Conjoiners have had the ability to copy minds onto machine substrates for some time now, though we haven't advertised it. But that doesn't matter – there have been experiments on Yellowstone that approach our early successes. And these heads aren't even thinking: only topologies need to be mapped, not electrochemical processes.'

The pig took one of the heads from his belt and held it at eye level, for inspection. 'The Conjoiner's right. They're not really dead. And they can be yours if you wish to do business.'

'What do you want for them?' Irravel asked.

'Markarian, for a start. All that Demarchy expertise makes for a very efficient second-in-command.'

Irravel glanced down at her prisoner. 'You can't buy loyalty with a box and a few neural connections.'

'No? In what way do our loyalty shunts differ from the psychosurgery your world inflicted on you, Irravel, yoking your motherhood instinct to twenty thousand sleepers you don't even know by name?'

'We have a deal or not?'

'Only if you throw in the Conjoiner as well.'

Irravel looked at Remontoire, some snake part of her mind weighing options with reptilian detachment.

'No!' he said. 'You promised!'

'Shut up,' Seven said. 'Or when you do get to rejoin your friends, it'll be in instalments.'

'I'm sorry,' Irravel said. 'I can't lose even ten of the cargo.'

Seven tossed the first head down to her. 'Now let Markarian go and we'll see about the rest.'

Irravel looked down at him. 'It's not over between you and me.'

Then she released him, and he scrambled back up the ice towards Seven.

'Excellent. Here's another head. Now the Conjoiner.'

Irravel issued a subvocal command; watched Remontoire stiffen. 'His suit's paralysed. Take him.'

Two pirates worked down to him, checked him over and nodded towards Seven. Between them they hauled him back up the ice, vanishing into a crevasse and back into the *Hideyoshi*.

'The other eight heads,' Irravel said.

'I'm going to throw them away from the ship. You'll be able to locate them easily enough. While I'm doing that, I'm going to retreat, and you're going to leave.'

'We could end this now,' Mirsky said.

'I need those heads.'

'They really fucked with your psychology big-time, didn't they?' Mirsky raised her weapon and began shooting at Seven and the other pirates. Irravel watched her carve up the remaining heads; splintering frozen bone into the vacuum.

'No!'

'Sorry,' Mirsky said. 'Had to do it, Veda.'

Seven clutched at his chest, fingers mashing the pulp of the heads still tethered to his belt. She'd punctured his suit. As he tried to stem the dam-burst, his face was carved with the intolerable knowledge that his reign had just ended.

But something had hit Irravel, too.

*

Sylveste Institute, Yellowstone Orbit, Epsilon Eridani – AD 2415

'Where am I?' Irravel asked. 'How am I thinking this?'

The woman's voice was the colour of mahogany. 'Somewhere safe. You died on the ice, but we got you back in time.'

'For what?'

Mirsky sighed, as if this was something she would rather not have had to explain this soon. 'To scan you, just like we did with the two frozen heads. Copy you into the ship.'

Maybe she should have felt horror, or indignation, or even relief that some part of her had been spared.

Instead, she just felt impatience.

'What now?'

'We're working on it,' Mirsky said.

Trans-Aldebaran Space – AD 2673

'We saved her body after she died,' Mirsky said, wheezing slightly. She found it difficult to move around under what to Irravel was the ship's normal two and a half gees of thrust. 'After the battle we brought her back aboard.'

Irravel thought of her mother dying on the other ship, the one they were chasing. For years they had deliberately not narrowed the distance, holding back but never allowing the *Hideyoshi* to slip from view.

Until now, it hadn't even occurred to Irravel to ask why.

She looked through the casket's window, trying to match her own features against what she saw in the woman's face, trying to project her own fifteen years into Mother Irravel's adulthood.

'Why did you keep her so cold?'

'We had to extract what we could from her brain,' Mirsky said, 'memories and neural patterns. We trawled them and stored them in the ship.'

'What good was that?'

'We knew they'd come in useful again.'

She'd been cloned from Mother Irravel. They were not identical – no Mixmaster expertise could duplicate the precise biochemical environment of Mother Irravel's womb, or the shaping experiences of her early infancy, and their personalities had been sculpted centuries apart, in totally different worlds. But they were still close copies. They even shared memories: scripted into Irravel's mind by medichines, so that she barely noticed each addition to her own experiences.

'Why did you do this?' she asked.

'Because Irravel began something,' Mirsky said. 'Something I promised I'd help her finish.'

Stormwatch Station, Aethra, Hyades Trade Envelope – AD 2931

'Why are you interested in our weapons?' the Nestbuilder asked. 'We are not aware of any wars within the *chordate* phylum at this epoch.'

'It's a personal matter,' Irravel said.

The Nestbuilder hovered a metre above the trade floor, suspended in a column of microgravity. They were oxygen-breathing arthropods that had once ascended to spacefaring capability. No longer intelligent, yet supported by their self-renewing machinery, they migrated from system to system, constructing elaborate, space-filling structures from solid diamond. Other Nestbuilder swarms would arrive and occasionally occupy the new nests. There seemed no purpose to this activity, but for tens of thousands of years they had been host to a smaller, cleverer species known as the Slugs. Small communities of Slugs – anything up to a dozen – lived in warm, damp niches in a Nestbuilder's intricately folded shell. They had long since learned how to control the host's behaviour and exploit its subservient technology.

Irravel studied a Slug now, crawling out from under a lip of shell material.

The thing was a multicellular invertebrate not much larger than her fist; a bag of soft blue protoplasm, sprouting appendages only when they were needed. A slightly bipolar shadow near one end might have been its central nervous system, but there hardly seemed enough of it to trap sentience. There were no obvious sense or communicational organs, but a pulsing filament of blue slime reached back into the Nestbuilder's fold. When the Slug spoke, it did so through the Nestbuilder: a rattle of chitin from the host's mouthparts which approximated human language. A hovering jewel connected to the station's lexical database did the rest, rendering the voice calmly feminine.

'A personal matter? A vendetta? Then it's true.' The mouthparts clicked together in what humans presumed was the symbiotic creature's laughter response. 'You *are* who we suspected.'

'She did tell you her name was Irravel, guy,' Mirsky said, sipping black coffee with delicate movements of the exoskeletal frame she always wore in high gravity.

'Amongst you *chordates*, the name is not so unusual now,' the Slug reminded them. 'But you do fit the description, Irravel.'

They were near one of the station's vast picture windows, overlooking Aethra's mighty, roiling cloud decks, fifty kilometres below. It was getting dark now and the stormplayers were preparing to start a show. Irravel saw two of their seeders descending into the clouds, robot craft tethered by a nearly invisible filament. The seeders would position the filament so that it bridged cloud layers with different static potentials; they'd then detach and return to Stormwatch, while the filament held itself in position by rippling along its length. For hundreds of kilometres around, other filaments would have been placed in carefully selected positions. They were electrically isolating now, but at the stormplayer's discretion, each filament would flick over into a conductive state: a massive, choreographed lightning flash.

'I never set out to become a legend,' Irravel said. 'Or a myth, for that matter.'

'Yes. There are so many stories about you, Veda, that it might be simpler to assume you never existed.'

'What makes you think otherwise?'

'The fact that a *chordate* who could have been Markarian also passed this way, only a year or so ago.' The Nestbuilder's shell pigmentation flickered, briefly revealing a picture of Markarian's ship.

'So you sold weapons to him?'

'That would be telling, wouldn't it?' The mouthparts clattered again. 'You would have to answer a question of ours first.'

Outside, the opening flashes of the night's performance gilded the horizon, like the first stirrings of a symphony. Aethra's rings echoed the flashes, pale ghosts momentarily cleaving the sky.

'What do you want to know?'

'We Slugs are amongst the few intelligent starfaring cultures in this part of the galaxy. During the war against intelligence, we avoided the Inhibitors by hiding ourselves amongst the mindless Nestbuilders.'

Irravel nodded. Slugs were one of the few alien species known to humanity that would even acknowledge the existence of the feared Inhibitors. Like humanity, they'd fought and beaten the revenants – at least for now.

'The weaponry you seek enabled us to triumph – but even then only at colossal cost to our phylum. Now we are watchful for new threats.'

'I don't see where this is leading.'

'We have heard rumours. Since you have come from the direction of those rumours – the local stellar neighbourhood around your phylum's birth star – we imagined you might have information of value.'

Irravel exchanged a sideways glance with Mirsky. The old woman's wizened, age-spotted skull looked as fragile as paper, but she remained an unrivalled tactician. They knew each other so well now that Mirsky could impart advice with the subtlest of movements, expression barely troubling the lined mask of her face.

'What kind of information are you seeking?'

'Information about something that frightens us.' The Nestbuilder's pigmentation flickered again, forming an image of . . . something. It was a splinter of grey-brown against speckled blackness – perhaps the Nestbuilder's attempt at visualising a planetoid. And then something erupted across the surface of the world, racing from end to end like a film of verdigris. Where it had passed, fissures opened up, deepening until they were black fractures, as if the world were a calving iceberg. And then it blew apart, shattering into a thousand green-tinged fragments.

'What was that?' Irravel said.

'We were rather hoping you could tell us.' The Nestbuilder's pigmentation refreshed again, and this time what they were seeing was clearly a star, veiled in a toroidal belt of golden dust.

'Machines have dismantled every rocky object in the system where these images were captured – Ross 128, which lies within eleven light-years of your birth star. They have engendered a swarm of trillions of rocks on independent orbits. Each rock is sheathed in a pressurised bubble membrane, within which an artificial plant-based ecosystem has been created. The same machines have fashioned other sources of raw material into mirrors, larger than worlds themselves, which trap sunlight above and below the ecliptic and focus it onto the swarm.'

'And why does this frighten you?'

The Nestbuilder leaned closer in its column of microgravity. 'Because we saw it being resisted. As if these machines had never been intended to wreak such transformations. As if your phylum had created something it could not control.'

'And – these attempts at resistance?'

'Failed.'

'But if one system was accidentally transformed, it doesn't mean . . .' Irravel trailed off. 'You're worried about them crossing interstellar space, to other systems. Even if that happened – couldn't you resist the spread? This can only be human technology – nothing that would pose any threat to yourselves.'

'Perhaps it was once human technology, with programmed limitations to prevent it from replicating uncontrollably. But those shackles have been broken. Worse, the machines have hybridised, gaining resilience and adaptability with each encounter with something external. First the Melding Plague, infection with which may have been a deliberate ploy to bypass the replication limits.'

Irravel nodded. The Melding Plague had swept human space four hundred years earlier, terminating the Demarchist *belle époque*. Like the Black Death of the previous millennium, it evoked terror generations after it had passed.

'Later,' the Nestbuilder continued, 'it may have encountered and assimilated Inhibitor technology, or worse. Now it will be very difficult to stop, even with the weapons at our disposal.'

An image of one of the machines flickered onto the Nestbuilder's shell, like a peculiar tattoo. Irravel shivered. The Slug was right: waves of hybridisation had transformed the initial architecture into something queasily alien. But enough of the original plan remained for there to be no doubt in her mind. She was looking at an evolved greenfly – one of the self-replicating breeders she had given Captain Run Seven. How it had broken loose was anyone's guess. She speculated that Seven's crew had sold the technology on to a third party, decades or centuries after gaining it from her. Perhaps that third party had reclusively experimented in the Ross 128 system, until the day when the greenfly tore out of their control . . .

'I don't know why you think I can help,' she said.

'Perhaps we were mistaken, then, to credit a five-hundred-year-old rumour that said you had been the original source of these machines.'

She had insulted it by daring to bluff. The Slugs were easily insulted. They read human beings far better than humans read Slugs.

'Like you say,' she answered, 'you can't believe everything you hear.'

The Slug made the Nestbuilder fold its armoured, spindly limbs across its mouthparts, a gesture of displeased huffiness.

'You *chordates*,' it said. 'You're all the same.'

Interstellar Space – AD 3354

Mirsky was dead. She had died of old age.

Irravel placed her body in an armoured coffin and ejected her into space when the *Hirondelle*'s speed was only a hair's breadth under light.

'Do it for me, Irravel,' Mirsky had asked her, towards the end. 'Keep my body aboard until we're almost touching light, and then fire me ahead of the ship.'

'Is that really what you want?'

'It's an old pirate tradition. Burial at C.' She forced a smile that must have sapped what little energy she had left. 'That's a joke, Irravel, but it only makes sense in a language neither of us have heard for a while.'

Irravel pretended that she understood. 'Mirsky? There's something I have to tell you. Do you remember the Nestbuilder?'

'That was centuries ago, Veda.'

'I know. I just keep worrying that maybe it was right.'

'About what?'

'Those machines. About how I started it all. They say it's spread now, to other systems. It doesn't look as if anyone knows how to stop it.'

'And you think all that was your fault?'

'It's crossed my mind.'

Mirsky convulsed, or shrugged – Irravel wasn't sure which. 'Even if it was your fault, Veda, you did it with the best of intentions. So you fucked up slightly. We all make mistakes.'

'Destroying whole solar systems is just a fuck-up?'

'Hey, accidents happen.'

'You always did have a sense of humour, Mirsky.'

'Yeah, guess I did.' She managed a smile. 'One of us needed one, Veda.'

Thinking of that, Irravel watched the coffin fall ahead of the *Hirondelle*, dwindling until it was only a tiny mote of steel-grey, and then nothing.

Subaru Commonwealth, Pleiades Cluster – AD 4161

The starbridge had long ago attained sentience.

Dense with machinery, it sang an endless hymn to its own immensity, throbbing like the lowest string on a guitar. Vacuum-breathing acolytes had voluntarily rewired their minds to view the bridge as an actual deity, translating the humming into their sensoria and passing decades in contemplative ecstasy.

Clasped in a cushioning field, an elevator ferried Irravel down the bridge from the orbital hub to the surface in a few minutes, accompanied by an entourage of children from the ship, many of whom bore in youth the hurting imprint of her dead friend Mirsky's genes. The bridge rose like the stem of a goblet from a ground terminal which was itself a scalloped shell of hyperdiamond, filled with tiered perfume gardens and cascading pools, anchored to the largest island in an equatorial archipelago. The senior children walked Irravel down to a beach of silver sand on the terminal's edge, where jewelled crabs moved like toys. She bid the children farewell, then waited, warm breezes fingering the hem of her sari.

Minutes later, the children's elevator flashed heavenward.

Irravel looked out at the ocean, thinking of the Pattern Jugglers. Here, as on dozens of other oceanic worlds, there was a colony of the alien intelligences. Transforming themselves to aquatic body-plans, the Subaruns had established close rapport with the aliens. In the morning, she would be taken out to meet the Jugglers, drowned, dissolved on the cellular level, every atom in her body swapped for one in the ocean, remade into something not quite human.

She was terrified.

Islanders came towards the shore, skimming the water on penanted trimarans, attended by oceanforms, sleek gloss-grey hybrids of porpoise and ray, whistlespeech downshifted into the human auditory spectrum. The Subaruns' epidermal scales shimmered like imbricated armour: biological photocells drinking scorching blue Pleiadean sunlight. Sentient veils hung in the sky, rippling gently like aurorae, shading the archipelago from the fiercest wavelengths. As the actinic eye of Taygeta sank towards the horizon, the veils moved with it like living clouds. Flocks of phantasmagorical birds migrated with the veils.

The purple-skinned elder's scales flashed green and opal as he approached Irravel along the coral jetty, a stick in one webbed hand, supported by two aides, a third shading his aged crown with a delicately watercoloured parasol. The aides were all descended from late-model Conjoiners; they had the translucent cranial crest through which bloodflow had once been channelled to cool their supercharged minds. Seeing them gave Irravel a dual-edged pang of nostalgia and guilt. She had not seen Conjoiners for nearly a thousand years, ever since they had fragmented into a dozen factions and vanished from human affairs. Neither had she entirely forgotten her betrayal of Remontoire.

But that had been so long ago . . .

A Communicant completed up the party, gowned in brocade, hazed by a blur of entopic projections. Communicants were small and elfin, with a phenomenal talent for natural languages augmented by Juggler transforms. Irravel sensed that this one was old and revered, despite the fact that Communicant genes did not express for great longevity.

The elder halted before her.

The head of his walking stick was a tiny lemur skull inside an egg-sized space helmet. He uttered something clearly ceremonial, but Irravel understood none of the sounds he made.

She groped for something to say, recalling the oldest language in her memory, and therefore the one most likely to be recognised in any far-flung human culture.

'Thank you for letting us stop here,' she said.

The Communicant hobbled forward, already shaping words experimentally with his wide, protruding lips. For a moment his sounds were like an infant's first attempts at vocalisation, but then they resolved into something Irravel understood.

'Am I – um – making the slightest sense to you?'

'Yes,' Irravel said. 'Yes, thank you.'

'Canasian,' the Communicant diagnosed. 'Twenty-third, twenty-fourth centuries, Lacaille 9352 dialect, Fand subdialect?'

Irravel nodded.

'Your kind are very rare now,' he said, studying her as if she was some kind of exotic butterfly, 'but not unwelcome.' His features cracked into a heart-warming smile.

'What about Markarian?' Irravel said. 'I know his ship passed through this system less than fifty years ago – I still have a fix on it as it moves out of the cluster.'

'Other ships do come, yes. Not many – one or two a century.'

'And what happened when the last one came through?'

'The usual tribute was given.'

'Tribute?'

'Something ceremonial.' The Communicant's smile was wider than ever. 'To the glory of Irravel. With many actors, beautiful words, love, death, laughter, tears.'

She understood, slowly, dumbfoundedly.

'You're putting on a play?'

The elder must have understood something of that. Nodding proudly, he extended a hand across the darkening bay, oceanforms cutting the water like scythes. A distant raft carried lanterns and the glimmerings of richly painted backdrops.

Boats converged from across the bay. A dirigible loomed over the archipelago's edge, pregnant with gondolas.

'We want you to play Irravel,' the Communicant said, beckoning her forward. 'This is our greatest honour.'

When they reached the raft, the Communicant taught Irravel her lines and the actions she would be required to make. It was all simple enough – even the fact that she had to deliver her parts in Subarun. By the end of evening she was fluent in their language. There was nothing she couldn't learn in an instant these days, by sheer force of will. But it was not enough. To catch Markarian, she would have to break out of the narrow labyrinth of human thought entirely. That was why she had come to Jugglers.

That night they performed the play, while boats congregated around them, top-heavy with lolling islanders. The sun sank and the sky glared with a thousand blue gems studding blue velvet. Night in the heart of the Pleiades was the most beautiful thing Irravel had dared imagine. But in the direction of Sol, when she amplified her vision, there was a green thumbprint on the sky. Every century, the green wave was larger, as neighbouring solar systems were infected and transformed by the rogue terraforming machines. Given time, it would even reach the Pleiades.

Irravel got drunk on islander wine and learned the tributes' history.

The plots varied immensely, but the protagonists always resembled Markarian and Irravel; mythic figures entwined by destiny, remembered across almost two thousand years. Sometimes, one or the other was the clear villain, but as often as not they were both heroic, misunderstanding each other's motives in true tragic fashion. Sometimes they ended with both parties dying. They rarely ended happily. But there was always some kind of redemption when the pursuit was done.

In the interlude, she felt she had to tell the Communicant the truth, so that he could tell the elder.

'Listen, there's something you need to know.' Irravel didn't wait for his answer. 'I'm really her – really the person I'm playing.'

For a long time he didn't seem to understand, before shaking his head slowly and sadly. 'No; I thought you'd be different. You seemed different. But many say that.'

She shrugged. There was little point arguing, and anything she said now could always be ascribed to wine. In the morning, the remark had been quietly forgotten. She was taken out to sea and drowned.

Galactic North, AD 9730

'Markarian? Answer me.'

She watched the *Hideyoshi*'s magnified image, looming just out of weapons range. Like the *Hirondelle*, it had changed almost beyond recognition. The hull glistened within a skein of armouring force. The engines, no longer physically coupled to the rest of the ship, flew alongside like dolphins. They were anchored in fields that only became visible when some tiny stress afflicted them.

For centuries of worldtime she had made no attempt to communicate with him. But now her mind had changed. The green wave had continued for millennia, an iridescent cataract spreading across the eye of the galaxy. It had assimilated the blue suns of the Subarun Commonwealth in mere centuries – although by then Irravel and Markarian were a thousand light-years closer to the core, beginning to turn away from the plane of the galaxy, and the death screams of those gentle islanders never reached them. Nothing stopped it, and once the green wave had swallowed them, systems fell silent. The Juggler transformation allowed Irravel to grasp the enormity of it; allowed her to stare unflinchingly into the horror of a million poisoned stars and apprehend each individually.

She knew more of what it was, now.

It was impossible for stars to shine green, any more than an ingot of metal could become green-hot if it was raised to a certain temperature. Instead, something was veiling them – staining their light, like coloured glass. Whatever it was stole energy from the stellar spectra at the frequencies of chlorophyll. Stars were shining through curtains of vegetation, like lanterns in a forest. The greenfly machines were turning the galaxy into a jungle.

It was time to talk. Time – as in the old plays of the dead islanders – to initiate the final act, before the two of them fell into the cold of intergalactic space. She searched her repertoire of communication systems until she found something as ancient as ceremony demanded.

She aimed the message laser at him, cutting through his armour. The beam was too ineffectual to be mistaken for anything other than an attempt to talk. No answer came, so she repeated the message in a variety of formats and languages. Days of shiptime passed – decades of worldtime.

Talk, you bastard.

Growing impatient, she examined her weapons options. Armaments from the Nestbuilders were amongst the most advanced: theoretically they could mole through the loam of spacetime and inflict precise harm anywhere in Markarian's ship. But to use them she had to convince herself that she knew the interior layout of the *Hideyoshi*. Her mass-sensor sweeps were too blurred to be much help. She might just as easily harm the sleepers as take out his field nodes. Until now, it had been too risky to contemplate.

But all games needed an end.

Willing her qualms from her mind, she enabled the Nestbuilder armaments, feeling them stress spacetime in the *Hirondelle*'s belly, ready to short-circuit it entirely. She selected attack loci in Markarian's ship; best guesses that would cripple him rather than blow him out of the sky.

Then something happened.

He replied, modulating his engine thrust in staccato stabs. The frequency was audio. Quickly, Irravel translated the modulation.

'I don't understand,' Markarian said, 'why you took so long to answer me, and why you ignored me for so long when I replied.'

'You never replied until now,' she said. 'I'd have known if you had.'

'Would you?'

There was something in his tone that convinced her he wasn't lying. Which left only one possibility: that he had tried speaking to her before, and that in some way her own ship had kept this knowledge from her.

'Mirsky must have done it,' Irravel said. 'She must have installed filters to block any communications from your ship.'

'Mirsky?'

'She would have done it as a favour to me; maybe under orders from my former self.' She didn't bother elaborating: Markarian was sure to know she had died and then been reborn as a clone of the original Irravel. 'My former self had the neural conditioning that kept her on the trail of the sleepers. This clone never had it, which meant that my instinct to pursue the sleepers had to be reinforced.'

'By lies?'

'Mirsky would have done it out of friendship,' Irravel said. And for a moment she believed herself, while wondering how friendship could seem so like betrayal.

Markarian's image smiled. They faced each other across an absurdly long banquet table, with the galaxy projected above it, flickering in the light of candelabra.

'Well?' he said, of the green stain spreading across the spiral. 'What do you think?'

Irravel had long ago stopped counting time and distance, but she knew it had been at least fifteen thousand years and that many light-years since they had turned from the plane. Part of her knew, of course: although the wave swallowed suns, it had no use for pulsars, and their metronomic ticking and slow decay allowed positional triangulation in space and time with chilling precision. But she elected to bury that knowledge beneath her conscious thought processes: one of the simpler Juggler tricks.

'What do I think? I think it terrifies me.'

'Our emotional responses haven't diverged as much as I'd feared.'

They didn't have to use language. They could have swapped pure mental concepts between ships: concatenated strings of qualia, some of which could only be grasped in minds rewired by Pattern Jugglers. But Irravel considered it sufficient that they could look each other in the eye without flinching.

The galaxy falling below had been frozen in time: light waves struggling to overtake Irravel and Markarian. The wave had appeared to slow, and then halt its advance. But then Markarian had turned, diving back towards the plane. The galaxy quickened to life, rushing to finish thirty thousand years of history before the two ships returned. The wave surged on. Above the banquet table, one arm of the star-clotted spiral was shot through with green, like a mote of ink spreading into blotting paper. The edge of the green wave was feathered, fractal, extending verdant tendrils.

'Do you have any observations?' Irravel asked.

'A few.' Markarian sipped from his chalice. 'I've studied the patterns of starlight amongst the suns already swallowed by the wave. They're not uniformly green – it's correlated with rotational angle. The green matter must be concentrated near the ecliptic, extending above and below it, but not encircling the stars completely.'

Irravel thought back to what the Nestbuilder had shown her.

'Meaning what?' she asked, testing Markarian.

'Swarms of absorbing bodies, on orbits resembling comets, or asteroids. I think the greenfly machines must have dismantled everything smaller than a Jovian, then enveloped the rubble in transparent membranes which they filled with air, water and greenery – self-sustaining biospheres. Then they were cast adrift. Trillions of tiny worlds, around each star. No rocky planets any more.'

Irravel retrieved a name from the deep past. 'Like Dyson spheres?'

'Dyson clouds, perhaps.'

'Do you think anyone survived? Are there niches in the wave where humans can live? That was the point of greenfly, after all: to create living space.'

'Maybe,' Markarian said, with no great conviction. 'Perhaps some survivors found ways inside, as their own worlds were smashed and reassembled into the cloud – '

'But you don't think it's very likely?'

'I've been listening, Irravel – scanning the assimilated regions for any hint of an extant technological culture. If anyone did survive, they're either keeping deliberately quiet or they don't even know how to make a radio signal by accident.'

'It was my fault, Markarian.'

His tone was rueful. 'Yes . . . I couldn't help but arrive at that conclusion.'

'I never intended this.'

'I think that goes without saying, don't you? No one could have guessed the consequences of that one action.'

'Did you?'

He shook his head. 'In all likelihood, I'd have done exactly what you did.'

'I did it out of love, Markarian. For the cargo.'

'I know.'

And she believed him.

'What happened back there, Markarian? Why did you give up the codes when I didn't?'

'Because of what they did to you, Irravel.'

He told her. How neither Markarian nor Irravel had shown any signs of revealing the codes under Mirsky's interrogation, until something new was tried.

'They were good at surgery,' Markarian said. 'Seven's crew swapped limbs and body parts as badges of status. They knew how to sever and splice nerves.' The image didn't allow her to interrupt. 'They cut your head off. Kept it alive in a state of borderline consciousness, and then showed it to me. That's when I gave them the codes.'

For a long while Irravel said nothing. Then it occurred to her to check her old body, still frozen in the same casket where Mirsky had once revealed it to her. She ordered some children to prepare the body for a detailed examination, then looked through their eyes. The microscopic evidence of reconnective surgery around the neck was too slight ever to have shown up unless one was looking for it. But now there was no mistaking it.

I did it to save your neck, Markarian had said, when she had held him pinned to the ice of Seven's ship.

'You appear to be telling the truth,' she said, when she had released the children. 'The nature of your betrayal was . . .' And then she paused, searching for the words, while Markarian watched her across the table. 'Different from what I assumed. Possibly less of a crime. But still a betrayal, Markarian.'

'One I've lived with for three hundred years of subjective time.'

'You could have returned the sleepers alive at any time. I wouldn't have attacked you.' But she didn't even sound convincing to herself.

'What now?' Markarian said. 'Do we keep this distance, arguing until one of us has the nerve to strike against the other? I've Nestbuilder weapons as well, Irravel. I think I could rip you apart before you could launch a reprisal.'

'You've had the opportunity to do so before. Perhaps you never had the nerve, though. What's changed now?'

Markarian's gaze flicked to the map. 'Everything. I think we should see what happens before making any rash decisions, don't you?'

Irravel agreed.

She willed herself into stasis, medichines arresting all biological activity in every cell in her body. The 'chines would only revive her when something – anything – happened, on a galactic timescale. Markarian would retreat into whatever mode of suspension he favoured, until woken by the same stimulus.

He was still sitting there when time resumed, as if only a moment had interrupted their conversation.

The wave had spread further now. It had eaten into the galaxy for ten thousand light-years around Sol – a third of the way to the core. There was no sign that it had encountered resistance – at least nothing that had done more than hinder it. There had never been many intelligent, starfaring cultures to begin with, the Nestbuilder's Slug had told her. Perhaps the few that existed were even now making plans to retard the wave. Or perhaps it had swallowed them, as it had swallowed humanity.

'Why did we wake?' Irravel said. 'Nothing's changed, except that it's grown larger.'

'Maybe not,' Markarian said. 'I had to be sure, but now I don't think there's any doubt. I've just detected a radio message from within the plane of the galaxy; from within the wave.'

'Yes?'

'Looks as though someone survived after all.'

The radio message was faint, but nothing else was transmitting on that or any adjacent frequency, except for the senseless mush of cosmic background sources. It was also in a language they recognised.

'It's Canasian,' Markarian said.

'Fand subdialect,' Irravel added, marvelling.

It was also beamed in their direction, from somewhere deep in the swathe of green, almost coincident with the position of a pulsar. The message was a simple one, frequency modulated around one and a half megahertz, repeated for a few minutes every day of galactic time. Whoever was sending it clearly didn't have the resources to transmit continuously. It was also coherent: amplified and beamed.

Someone wanted to speak to them.

The man's disembodied head appeared above the banquet table, chiselled from pixels. He was immeasurably old; a skull draped in parchment; something that should have been embalmed rather than talking.

Irravel recognised the face.

'It's him,' she said, in Markarian's direction. 'Remontoire. Somehow he made it across all this time.'

Markarian nodded slowly. 'He must have remembered us, and known where to look. Even across thousands of light-years, we can still be seen. There can't be many objects still moving relativistically.'

Remontoire told his story. His people had fled to the pulsar system twenty thousand years ago – more, now, since his message had taken thousands of years to climb out of the galaxy. They had seen the wave coming, as had thousands of other human factions, and like many they had observed that the wave shunned pulsars: burned-out stellar corpses rarely accompanied by planets. Some intelligence governing the wave must have recognised that pulsars were valueless; that even if a Dyson cloud could be created around them, there would be no sunlight to focus.

For thousands of years they had waited around the pulsar, growing ever more silent and cautious, seeing other cultures make errors that drew the wave upon them, for by now it interpreted any other intelligence as a threat to its progress, assimilating the weapons used against it.

Then – over many more thousands of years – Remontoire's people watched the wave learn, adapting like a vast neural net, becoming curious about those few pulsars that harboured planets. Soon their place of refuge would become nothing of the sort.

'Help us,' Remontoire said. 'Please.'

It took three thousand years to reach them.

For most of that time, Remontoire's people acted on faith, not knowing that help was on its way. During the first thousand years they abandoned their system, compressing their population down to a sustaining core of only a few hundred thousand. Together with the cultural data they'd preserved during the long centuries of their struggle against the wave, they packed their survivors into a single hollowed-out rock and flung themselves out of the ecliptic using a mass-driver that fuelled itself from the rock's own bulk. They called it Hope. A million decoys had to be launched, just to ensure that Hope got through the surrounding hordes of assimilating machines.

Inside, most of the Conjoiners slept out the next two thousand years of solitude before Irravel and Markarian reached them.

'Hope would make an excellent shield,' Markarian mused as they approached it, 'if one of us considered a pre-emptive strike against the other – '

'Don't think I wouldn't.'

They moved their ships to either side of the dark shard of rock, extended field grapples, then hauled in.

'Then why don't you?' Markarian said.

For a moment Irravel didn't have a good answer. When she found one, she wondered why it hadn't been more obvious before. 'Because they need us more than I need revenge.'

'A higher cause?'

'Redemption,' she said.

Hope, Galactic Plane – AD Circa 40,000

They didn't have long. Their approach, diving down from Galactic North, had drawn the attention of the wave's machines, directing them towards the one rock that mattered. A wall of annihilation was moving towards them at half the speed of light. When it reached Hope, it would turn it into the darkest of nebulae.

Conjoiners boarded the *Hirondelle* and invited Irravel into Hope. The hollowed-out chambers of the rock were Edenic to her children, after all the decades of subjective time they'd spent aboard ship since last planetfall. But it was a doomed paradise, the biomes grey with neglect, as if the Conjoiners had given up long before.

Remontoire welcomed Irravel next to a rock pool filmed with grey dust. Half the sun-panels set into the distant honeycombed ceiling were black.

'You came,' he said. He wore a simple smock and trousers. His anatomy was early-model Conjoiner: almost fully human.

'You're not him, are you?' Irravel asked. 'You look like him – sound like him – but the image you sent us was of someone much older.'

'I'm sorry. His name was chosen for its familiarity; my likeness shaped to his. We searched our collective memories and found the experiences of the one you knew as Remontoire . . . but that was a long time ago, and he was never known by that name to us.'

'What his name?'

'Even your Juggler cortex could not accommodate it, Irravel.'

She had to ask. 'Did he make it back to a commune?'

'Yes, of course,' the man said, as if her question was foolish. 'How else could we have absorbed his experiences back into the Transenlightenment?'

'And did he forgive me?'

'I forgive you now,' he said. 'It amounts to the same thing.'

She willed herself to think of him as Remontoire.

The Conjoiners hadn't allowed themselves to progress in all the thousands of years they waited around the pulsar, fearing that any social change – no matter how slight – would eventually bring the wave upon them. They had studied it, contemplated weapons they might use against it – but other than that, all they had done was wait.

They were very good at waiting.

'How many refugees did you bring?'

'One hundred thousand.' Before Irravel could answer, Remontoire shook his head. 'I know – too many. Perhaps half that number can be carried away on your ships. But half is better than nothing.'

She thought back to her own sleepers. 'I know. Still, we might be able to take more . . . I don't know about Markarian's ship, but – '

He cut her off, gently. 'I think you'd better come with me,' said Remontoire, and then led her aboard the *Hideyoshi*.

'How much of it did you explore?'

'Enough to know there's no one alive anywhere aboard this ship,' Remontoire said. 'If there are two hundred cryogenically frozen sleepers, we didn't find them.'

'No sleepers?'

'Just this one.'

They had arrived at a plinth supporting a reefersleep casket, encrusted with gold statuary: spacesuited figures with hands folded across their chests like resting saints. The glass lid of the casket was veined with fractures; the withered figure inside older than time. Markarian's skeletal frame was swaddled in layers of machines, all of archaic provenance. His skull had split open, a fused mass spilling out like lava.

'Is he dead?' Irravel asked.

'Depends what you mean by dead.' The Conjoiner's hand sketched across the neural mass. 'His organic mind must have been completely swamped by machines centuries ago. His linkage to the *Hideyoshi* would have been total. There would have been very little point discriminating between the two.'

'Why didn't he tell me what had become of him?'

'No guarantee he knew. Once he was in this state, with his personality running entirely on machine substrates, he could have edited his own memories and perceptual inputs – deceiving himself that he was still corporeal.'

Irravel looked away from the casket, forcing troubling questions from her mind. 'Is his personality still running the ship?'

'We detected only caretaker programs, capable of imitating him when the need arose, but lacking sentience.'

'Is that all there was?'

'No.' Remontoire reached through one of the casket's larger fractures, prizing something from Markarian's fingers. It was a sliver of computer memory. 'We examined this already, though not in great detail. It's partitioned into one hundred and ninety areas, each large enough to hold complete neural and genetic maps for one human being, encoded into superposed electron states on Rydberg atoms.'

She took the sliver from him. It didn't feel like much. 'He burned the sleepers onto this?'

'Three hundred years is much longer than any of them expected to sleep. By scanning them he lost nothing.'

'Can you retrieve them?'

'It would not be trivial,' the Conjoiner said, 'but given time, we could do it. Assuming any of them would welcome being born again, so far from home.'

She thought of the infected galaxy hanging below them, humming with the chill sentience of machines. 'Maybe the kindest thing would be to simulate the past,' she said. 'Recreate Yellowstone and revive them on it, as if nothing had ever gone wrong.'

'Is that what you're advocating?'

'No,' she said, after toying with the idea in all seriousness. 'We need all the genetic diversity we can get if we're going to establish a new branch of humanity outside the galaxy.'

She thought about it some more. Soon they would witness Hope's destruction, as the wave of machines tore through it with the mindlessness of stampeding animals. Some of them might try to follow the *Hirondelle*, but so far the machines moved too slowly to catch the ship, even if they forced it back towards Galactic North.

Where else could they go?

There were globular clusters high above the galaxy – tightly packed shoals of old stars the wave hadn't reached, but where fragments of humanity might already have sought refuge. If the clusters proved unwelcoming, there were high-latitude stars, flung from the galaxy a billion years ago, and some might have dragged their planetary systems with them. If those failed – and it would be tens of thousands of years before the possibilities were exhausted – the *Hirondelle* could always loop around towards Galactic South and search there, striking out for the Clouds of Magellan. Ultimately, of course – if any fragment of Irravel's children still clung to humanity, and remembered where they'd come from, and what had become of it, they would want to return to the galaxy, even if that meant confronting the wave.

But they would return.

'That's the plan then?' Remontoire said.

Irravel shrugged, turning away from the plinth where Markarian lay. 'Unless you've got a better one.'

GREAT WALL OF MARS

'You realise you might die down there,' said Warren.

Nevil Clavain looked into his brother's one good eye; the one the Conjoiners had left him with after the battle of Tharsis Bulge. 'Yes, I know,' he said. 'But if there's another war, we might all die. I'd rather take that risk, if there's a chance for peace.'

Warren shook his head, slowly and patiently. 'No matter how many times we've been over this, you just don't seem to get it, do you? There can't ever be any kind of peace while they're still down there. That's what you don't understand, Nevil. The only long-term solution here is . . .' he trailed off.

'Go on,' Clavain goaded. 'Say it. Genocide.'

Warren might have been about to answer when there was a bustle of activity down the docking tube, at the far end from the waiting spacecraft. Through the door Clavain saw a throng of media people, then someone gliding through them, fielding questions with only the curtest of answers. That was Sandra Voi, the Demarchist woman who would be coming with him to Mars.

'It's not genocide when they're just a faction, not an ethnically distinct race,' Warren said, before Voi was within earshot.

'What is it, then?'

'I don't know. Prudence?'

Voi approached. She bore herself stiffly, her face a mask of quiet resignation. Her ship had only just docked from Circum-Jove, after a three-week transit at maximum burn. During that time the prospects for a peaceful resolution of the current crisis had steadily deteriorated.

'Welcome to Deimos,' Warren said.

'Marshalls,' she said, addressing both of them. 'I wish the circumstances were better. Let's get straight to business. Warren; how long do you think we have to find a solution?'

'Not long. If Galiana maintains the pattern she's been following for the last six months, we're due another escape attempt in . . .' Warren glanced at a read-out buried in his cuff. 'About three days. If she does try and get another shuttle off Mars, we'll really have no option but to escalate.'

They all knew what would mean: a military strike against the Conjoiner nest.

'You've tolerated her attempts so far,' Voi said. 'And each time you've successfully destroyed her ship with all the people in it. The net risk of a successful breakout hasn't increased. So why retaliate now?'

'It's very simple. After each violation we issued Galiana with a stronger warning than the one before. Our last was absolute and final.'

'You'll be in violation of treaty if you attack.'

Warren's smile was one of quiet triumph. 'Not quite, Sandra. You may not be completely conversant with the treaty's fine print, but we've discovered that it allows us to storm Galiana's nest without breaking any terms. The technical phrase is a police action, I believe.'

Clavain saw that Voi was momentarily lost for words. That was hardly surprising. The treaty between the Coalition and the Conjoiners – which Voi's neutral Demarchists had helped draft – was the longest document in existence, apart from some obscure, computer-generated mathematical proofs. It was supposed to be watertight, though only machines had ever read it from beginning to end, and only machines had ever stood a chance of finding the kind of loophole which Warren was now brandishing.

'No . . .' she said. 'There's some mistake.'

'I'm afraid he's right,' Clavain said. 'I've seen the natural-language summaries, and there's no doubt about the legality of a police action. But it needn't come to that. I'm sure I can persuade Galiana not to make another escape attempt.'

'But if we should fail?' Voi looked at Warren now. 'Nevil and myself could still be on Mars in three days.'

'Don't be, is my advice.'

Disgusted, Voi turned and stepped into the green cool of the shuttle. Clavain was left alone with his brother for a moment. Warren fingered the leathery patch over his ruined eye with the chrome gauntlet of his prosthetic arm, as if to remind Clavain of what the war had cost him; how little love he had for the enemy, even now.

'We haven't got a chance of succeeding, have we?' Clavain said. 'We're only going down there so you can say you explored all avenues of negotiation before sending in the troops. You actually want another damned war.'

'Don't be so defeatist,' Warren said, shaking his head sadly, forever the older brother disappointed at his sibling's failings. 'It really doesn't become you.'

'It's not me who's defeatist,' Clavain said.

'No; of course not. Just do your best, little brother.'

Warren extended his hand for his brother to shake. Hesitating, Clavain looked again into his brother's good eye. What he saw there was an interrogator's eye: as pale, colourless and cold as a midwinter sun. There was hatred in it. Warren despised Clavain's pacifism; Clavain's belief that any kind of peace, even a peace which consisted only of stumbling episodes of mistrust between crises, was always better than war. That schism had fractured any lingering fraternal feelings they might have retained. Now, when Warren reminded Clavain that they were brothers, he never entirely concealed the disgust in his voice.

'You misjudge me,' Clavain whispered, before quietly shaking Warren's hand.

'No; I honestly don't think I do.'

Clavain stepped through the airlock just before it sphinctered shut. Voi had already buckled herself in; she had a glazed look now, as if staring into infinity. Clavain guessed she was uploading a copy of the treaty through her implants, scrolling it across her visual field, trying to find the loophole; probably running a global search for any references to police actions.

The ship recognised Clavain, its interior shivering to his preferences. The green was closer to turquoise now; the read-outs and controls minimalist in layout, displaying only the most mission-critical systems. Though the shuttle was the tiniest peacetime vessel Clavain had been in, it was a cathedral compared to the dropships he had flown during the war; so small that they were assembled around their occupants like medieval armour before a joust.

'Don't worry about the treaty,' Clavain said. 'I promise you Warren won't get his chance to apply that loophole.'

Voi snapped out of her trance irritatedly. 'You'd better be right, Nevil. Is it me, or is your brother hoping we fail?' She was speaking Quebecois French now; Clavain shifting mental gears to follow her. 'If my people discover that there's a hidden agenda here, there'll be hell to pay.'

'The Conjoiners gave Warren plenty of reasons to hate them after the battle of the Bulge,' Clavain said. 'And he's a tactician, not a field specialist. After the ceasefire my knowledge of worms was even more valuable than before, so I had a role. But Warren's skills were a lot less transferable.'

'So that gives him a right to edge us closer to another war?' The way Voi spoke, it was as if her own side had not been neutral in the last exchange. But Clavain knew she was right. If hostilities between the Conjoiners and the Coalition re-ignited, the Demarchy would not be able to stand aside as they had fifteen years ago. And it was anyone's guess how they would align themselves.

'There won't be war.'

'And if you can't reason with Galiana? Or are you going to play on your personal connection?'

'I was just her prisoner, that's all.' Clavain took the controls – Voi said piloting was a bore – and unlatched the shuttle from Deimos. They dropped away at a tangent to the rotation of the equatorial ring which girdled the moon, instantly in free-fall. Clavain sketched a porthole in the wall with his fingertip, outlining a rectangle which instantly became transparent.

For a moment he saw his reflection in the glass: older than he felt he had any right to look, the grey beard and hair making him look ancient rather than patriarchal; a man deeply wearied by recent circumstance. With some relief he darkened the cabin so that he could see Deimos, dwindling at surprising speed. The higher of the two Martian moons was a dark, bristling lump, infested with armaments, belted by the bright, window-studded band of the moving ring. For the last nine years, Deimos was all that he had known, but now he could encompass it within the arc of his fist.

'Not just her prisoner,' Voi said. 'No one else came back sane from the Conjoiners. She never even tried to infect you with her machines.'

'No, she didn't. But only because the timing was on my side.' Clavain was reciting an old argument now, as much for his own benefit as Voi's. 'I was the only prisoner she had. She was losing the war by then; one more recruit to her side wouldn't have made any real difference. The terms of ceasefire were being thrashed out and she knew she could buy herself favours by releasing me unharmed. There was something else, too. Conjoiners weren't supposed to be capable of anything so primitive as mercy. They were spiders, as far as we were concerned. Galiana's act threw a wrench into our thinking. It divided alliances within high command. If she hadn't released me, they might well have nuked her out of existence.'

'So there was absolutely nothing personal?'

'No,' Clavain said. 'There was nothing personal about it at all.'

Voi nodded, without in any way suggesting that she actually believed him. It was a skill some women had honed to perfection, Clavain thought.

Of course, he respected Voi completely. She had been one of the first human beings to enter Europa's ocean, decades back. Now they were planning fabulous cities under the ice; efforts which she had spearheaded. Demarchist society was supposedly flat in structure, non-hierarchical; but someone of Voi's brilliance ascended through echelons of her own making. She had been instrumental in brokering the peace between the Conjoiners and Clavain's own Coalition. That was why she was coming along now: Galiana had only agreed to Clavain's mission provided he was accompanied by a neutral observer, and Voi had been the obvious choice. Respect was easy. Trust, however, was harder: it required that Clavain ignore the fact that, with her head dotted with implants, the Demarchist woman's condition was not very far removed from that of the enemy.

The descent to Mars was hard and steep.

Once or twice they were queried by the automated tracking systems of the satellite interdiction network. Dark weapons hovering in Mars-synchronous orbit above the nest locked onto the ship for a few instants, magnetic railguns powering up, before the shuttle's diplomatic nature was established and it was allowed to proceed. The Interdiction was very efficient; as well it might be, given that Clavain had designed much of it himself. In fifteen years no ship had entered or left the Martian atmosphere, nor had any surface vehicle ever escaped from Galiana's nest.

'There she is,' Clavain said, as the Great Wall rose over the horizon.

'Why do you call "it" a "she"?' Voi asked. 'I never felt the urge to personalise it, and I designed it. Besides . . . even if it was alive once, it's dead now.'

She was right, but the Wall was still awesome to behold. Seen from orbit, it was a pale, circular ring on the surface of Mars, two thousand kilometres wide. Like a coral atoll, it entrapped its own weather system; a disk of bluer air, flecked with creamy white clouds which stopped abruptly at the boundary.

Once, hundreds of communities had sheltered inside that cell of warm, thick, oxygen-rich atmosphere. The Wall was the most audacious and visible of Voi's projects. The logic had been inescapable: a means to avoid the millennia-long timescales needed to terraform Mars via such conventional schemes as cometary bombardment or ice-cap thawing. Instead of modifying the whole atmosphere at once, the Wall allowed the initial effort to be concentrated in a relatively small region, at first only a thousand kilometres across. There were no craters deep enough, so the Wall had been completely artificial: a vast ring-shaped atmospheric dam designed to move slowly outward, encompassing ever more surface area at a rate of twenty kilometres per year. The Wall needed to be very tall because the low Martian gravity meant that the column of atmosphere was higher for a fixed surface pressure than on Earth. The ramparts were hundreds of metres thick, dark as glacial ice, sinking great taproots deep into the lithosphere to harvest the ores needed for the Wall's continual growth. Yet two hundred kilometres higher the wall was a diaphanously thin membrane only microns wide; completely invisible except when rare optical effects made it hang like a frozen aurora against the stars. Eco-engineers had invaded the Wall's liveable area with terran genestocks deftly altered in orbital labs. Flora and fauna had moved out in vivacious waves, lapping eagerly against the constraints of the Wall.

But the Wall was dead.

It had stopped growing during the war, hit by some sort of viral weapon which crippled its replicating subsystems, and now even the ecosystem within it was failing; the atmosphere cooling, oxygen bleeding into space, pressure declining inevitably towards the Martian norm of one seven-thousandth of an atmosphere.

He wondered how it must look to Voi, whether in any sense she saw it as her murdered child.

'I'm sorry that we had to kill it,' Clavain said. He was about to add that it been the kind of act which war normalised, but decided that the statement would have sounded hopelessly defensive.

'You needn't apologise,' Voi said. 'It was only machinery. I'm surprised it's lasted as long as it has, frankly. There must still be some residual damage-repair capability. We Demarchists build for posterity, you know.'

Yes, and it worried his own side. There was talk of challenging the Demarchist supremacy in the outer solar system; perhaps even an attempt to gain a Coalition foothold around Jupiter.

They skimmed the top of the Wall and punched through the thickening layers of atmosphere within it, the shuttle's hull morphing to an arrowhead shape. The ground had an arid, bleached look to it, dotted here and there by ruined shacks, broken domes, gutted vehicles or shot-down shuttles. There were patches of shallow-rooted, mainly dark-red tundra vegetation; cotton grass, saxifrage, arctic poppies and lichen. Clavain knew each species by its distinct infrared signature, but many of the plants were in recession now that the imported bird species had died. Ice lay in great silver swathes, and what few expanses of open water remained were warmed by buried thermopiles. Elsewhere there were whole zones which had reverted to almost sterile permafrost. It could have been a kind of paradise, Clavain thought, if the war had not ruined everything. Yet what had happened here could only be a foretaste of the devastation that would follow across the system, on Earth as well as Mars, if another war was allowed to happen.

'Do you see the nest yet?' Voi said.

'Wait a second,' Clavain said, requesting a head-up display which boxed the nest. 'That's it. A nice fat thermal signature too. Nothing else for miles around – nothing inhabited, anyway.'

'Yes. I see it now.'

The Conjoiner nest lay a third of the way from the Wall's edge, not far from the footslopes of Arsia Mons. The entire encampment was only a kilometre across, circled by a dyke which was piled high with regolith dust on one side. The area within the Great Wall was large enough to have an appreciable weather system: spanning enough Martian latitude for significant coriolis effects; enough longitude for diurnal warming and cooling to cause thermal currents.

He could see the nest much more clearly now, details leaping out of the haze.

Its external layout was crushingly familiar. Clavain's side had been studying the nest from the vantage point of Deimos ever since the ceasefire. Phobos with its lower orbit would have been even better, of course – but there was no helping that, and perhaps the Phobos problem might actually prove useful in his negotiations with Galiana. She was somewhere in the nest, he knew: somewhere beneath the twenty varyingly-sized domes emplaced within the rim, linked together by pressurised tunnels or merged at their boundaries like soap bubbles. The nest extended several tens of levels beneath the Martian surface; maybe deeper.

'How many people do you think are inside?' Voi said.

'Nine hundred or so,' said Clavain. 'That's an estimate based on my experiences as a prisoner, and the hundred or so who've died trying to escape since. The rest, I have to say, is pretty much guesswork.'

'Our estimates aren't dissimilar. A thousand or less here, and perhaps another three or four spread across the system in smaller nests. I know your side thinks we have better intelligence than that, but it happens not to be the case.'

'Actually, I believe you.' The shuttle's airframe was flexing around them, morphing to a low-altitude profile with wide, batlike wings.

'I was just hoping you might have some clue as to why Galiana keeps wasting valuable lives with escape attempts.'

Voi shrugged. 'Maybe to her the lives aren't anywhere near as valuable as you'd like to think.'

'Do you honestly think that?'

'I don't think we can begin to guess the thinking of a true hive-mind society, Clavain. Even from a Demarchist standpoint.'

There was a chirp from the console; Galiana signalling them. Clavain opened the channel allocated for Coalition–Conjoiner diplomacy.

'Nevil Clavain?' he heard.

'Yes.' He tried to sound as calm as possible. 'I'm with Sandra Voi. We're ready to land as soon as you show us where.'

'OK,' Galiana said. 'Vector your ship towards the westerly rim wall. And please, be careful.'

'Thank you. Any particular reason for the caution?'

'Just be quick about it, Nevil.'

They banked over the nest, shedding height until they were skimming only a few tens of metres above the weatherworn Martian surface. A wide rectangular door had opened in the concrete dyke, revealing a hangar bay aglow with yellow lights.

'That must be where Galiana launches her shuttles from,' Clavain whispered. 'We always thought there must be some kind of opening on the west side of the rim, but we never had a good view of it before.'

'Which still doesn't tell us why she does it,' Voi said.

The console chirped again – the link poor even though they were so close. 'Nose up,' Galiana said. 'You're too low and slow. Get some altitude or the worms will lock onto you.'

'You're telling me there are worms here?' Clavain said.

'I thought you were the worm expert, Nevil.'

He nosed the shuttle up, but fractionally too late. Ahead of them something coiled out of the ground with lightning speed, metallic jaws opening in its blunt, armoured head. He recognised the type immediately: Ouroboros class. Worms of this form still infested a hundred niches across the system. Not quite as smart as the type infesting Phobos, but still adequately dangerous.

'Shit,' Voi said, her veneer of Demarchist cool cracking for an instant.

'You said it,' Clavain answered.

The Ouroboros passed underneath and then there was a spine-jarring series of bumps as the jaws tore into the shuttle's belly. Clavain felt the shuttle lurch down sickeningly; no longer a flying thing but an exercise in ballistics. The cool, minimalist turquoise interior shifted liquidly into an emergency configuration; damage read-outs competing for attention with weapons status options. Their seats ballooned around them.

'Hold on,' he said. 'We're going down.'

Voi's calm returned. 'Do you think we can reach the rim in time?'

'Not a cat in hell's chance.' He wrestled with the controls all the same, but it was no good. The ground was coming up fast and hard. 'I wish Galiana had warned us a bit sooner . . .'

'I think she thought we already knew.'

They hit. It was harder than Clavain had been expecting, but the shuttle stayed in one piece and the seat cushioned him from the worst of the impact. They skidded for a few metres and then nosed up against a sandbank. Through the window Clavain saw the white worm racing towards them with undulating waves of its segmented robot body.

'I think we're finished,' Voi said.

'Not quite,' Clavain said. 'You're not going to like this, but . . .' Biting his tongue he brought the shuttle's hidden weapons online. An aiming scope plunged down from the ceiling; he brought his eyes to it and locked cross hairs onto the Ouroboros. Just like old times . . .

'Damn you,' Voi said. 'This was meant to be an unarmed mission!'

'You're welcome to lodge a formal complaint.'

Clavain fired, the hull shaking from the recoil. Through the side window they watched the white worm blow apart into stubby segments. The parts wriggled beneath the dust.

'Good shooting,' Voi said, almost grudgingly. 'Is it dead?'

'For now,' Clavain said. 'It'll take several hours for the segments to fuse back into a functional worm.'

'Good,' Voi said, pushing herself out of her seat. 'But there will be a formal complaint, take my word.'

'Maybe you'd rather the worm ate us?'

'I just hate duplicity, Clavain.'

He tried the radio again. 'Galiana? We're down – the ship's history – but we're both unharmed.'

'Thank God.' Old verbal mannerisms died hard, even among the Conjoined. 'But you can't stay where you are. There are more worms in the area. Do you think you can make it overland to the nest?'

'It's only two hundred metres,' Voi said. 'It shouldn't be a problem.'

Two hundred metres, yes – but two hundred metres across treacherous, potholed ground riddled with enough soft depressions to hide a dozen worms. And then they would have to climb up the rim's side to reach the entrance to the hangar bay; ten or fifteen metres above the soil.

'Let's hope it isn't,' Clavain said.

He unbuckled, feeling light-headed as he stood for the first time in Martian gravity. He had adapted entirely too well to the one-gee of the Deimos ring, constructed for the comfort of Earthside tacticians. He went to the emergency locker and found a mask which slithered eagerly across his face; another for Voi. They plugged in air-tanks and went to the shuttle's door. This time when it sphinctered open there was a glistening membrane stretched across the doorway, a recently licensed item of Demarchist technology. Clavain pushed through the membrane and the stuff enveloped him with a wet, sucking sound. By the time he hit the dirt the membrane had hardened itself around his soles and had begun to contour itself with ribs and accordioned joints, even though it stayed transparent.

Voi came behind him, gaining her own m-suit.

They loped away from the crashed shuttle, towards the dyke. The worms would be locking onto their seismic patterns already, if there were any nearby. They might be more interested in the shuttle for now, but that was nothing they could count on. Clavain knew the behaviour of worms intimately, knew the major routines which drove them; but that expertise did not guarantee his survival. It had almost failed him in Phobos.

The mask felt clammy against his face. The air at the base of the Great Wall was technically breathable even now, but there seemed no point in taking chances when speed was of the essence. His feet scuffed through the topsoil, and while he seemed to be crossing ground, the dyke obstinately refused to come any closer. It was larger than it looked from the crash; the distance further.

'Another worm,' Voi said.

White coils erupted through sand to the west. The Ouroboros was making undulating progress towards them, zig-zagging with predatorial calm, knowing that it could afford to take its time. In the tunnels of Phobos, they had never had the luxury of knowing when a worm was close. They struck from ambush, quick as pythons.

'Run,' Clavain said.

Dark figures appeared in the opening high in the rimwall. A rope-ladder unfurled down the side of the structure. Clavain, making for the base of it, made no effort to quieten his footfalls. He knew that the worm almost certainly had a lock on him by now.

He looked back.

The worm paused by the downed shuttle, then smashed its diamond-jawed head into the ship, impaling the hull on its body. The worm reared up, wearing the ship like a garland. Then it shivered and the ship flew apart like a rotten carcass. The worm returned its attention to Clavain and Voi. Like a sidewinder it pulled its thirty-metre-long body from the sand and rolled towards them on wheeling coils.

Clavain reached the base of the ladder.

Once, he could have ascended the ladder with his arms alone, in one-gee, but now the ladder felt alive beneath his feet. He began to climb, then realised that the ground was dropping away much faster than he was passing rungs. The Conjoiners were hauling him aloft.

He looked back in time to see Voi stumble.

'Sandra! No!'

She made to stand up, but it was too late by then. As the worm descended on her, Clavain could do nothing but turn his gaze away and pray for her death to be quick. If it had to be meaningless, he thought, at least let it be swift.

Then he started thinking about his own survival. 'Faster!' he shouted, but the mask reduced his voice to a panicked muffle. He had forgotten to assign the ship's radio frequency to the suit.

The worm thrashed against the base of the wall, then began to rear up, its maw opening beneath him; a diamond-ringed orifice like the drill of a tunnelling machine. Then something eye-hurtingly bright cut into the worm's hide. Craning his neck, Clavain saw a group of Conjoiners kneeling over the lip of the opening, aiming guns downward. The worm writhed in intense robotic irritation. Across the sand, he could see the coils of other worms coming closer. There must have been dozens ringing the nest. No wonder Galiana's people had made so few attempts to leave by land.

They had hauled him within ten metres of safety. The injured worm showed cybernetic workings where its hide had been flensed away by weapons impacts. Enraged, it flung itself against the rim wall, chipping off scabs of concrete the size of boulders. Clavain felt the vibration of each impact through the wall as he was dragged upwards.

The worm hit again and the wall shook more violently than before. To his horror, Clavain watched one of the Conjoiners lose his footing and tumble over the edge of the rim towards him. Time oozed to a crawl. The falling man was almost upon him. Without thinking, Clavain hugged closer to the wall, locking his limbs around the ladder. Suddenly, he had seized the man by the arm. Even in Martian gravity, even allowing for the Conjoiner's willowy build, the impact almost sent both of them towards the Ouroboros. Clavain felt his bones pop out of location, tearing at gristle, but he managed to keep his grip on both the Conjoiner and the ladder.

Conjoiners breathed the air at the base of the Wall without difficulty. The man wore only lightweight clothes, grey silk pyjamas belted at the waist. With his sunken cheeks and bald skull, the man's Martian physique lent him a cadaverous look. Yet somehow he had managed not to drop his gun, still holding it in his other hand.

'Let me go,' the man said.

Below, the worm inched higher despite the harm the Conjoiners had inflicted on it. 'No,' Clavain said, through clenched teeth and the distorting membrane of his mask. 'I'm not letting you go.'

'You've no option.' The man's voice was placid. 'They can't haul both of us up fast enough, Clavain.'

Clavain looked into the Conjoiner's face, trying to judge the man's age. Thirty, perhaps – maybe not even that, since the cadaverous look probably made him seem older than he really was. Clavain was easily twice his age; had surely lived a richer life; had comfortably cheated death on three or four previous occasions.

'I'm the one who should die, not you.'

'No,' the Conjoiner said. 'They'd find a way to blame your death on us. They'd make it a pretext for war.' Without any fuss the man pointed the gun at his own head and blew his brains out.

As much in shock as recognition that the man's life was no longer his to save, Clavain released his grip. The dead man tumbled down the rim wall, into the mouth of the worm which had just killed Sandra Voi.

Numb, Clavain allowed himself to be pulled to safety.

When the armoured door to the hangar was shut the Conjoiners attacked his m-suit with enzymic sprays. The sprays digested the fabric of the m-suit in seconds, leaving Clavain wheezing in a pool of slime. Then a pair of Conjoiners helped him unsteadily to his feet and waited patiently while he caught his breath from the mask. Through tears of exhaustion he saw that the hangar was racked full of half-assembled spacecraft; skeletal geodesic shark-shapes designed to punch out of an atmosphere, fast.

'Sandra Voi is dead,' he said, removing the mask to speak.

There was no way the Conjoiners could not have seen this for themselves, but it seemed inhuman not to acknowledge what had happened.

'I know,' Galiana said. 'But at least you survived.'

He thought of the man falling into the Ouroboros. 'I'm sorry about your . . .' But then trailed off, because for all his depth of knowledge concerning the Conjoiners, he had no idea what the appropriate term was.

'You placed your life in danger in trying to save him.'

'He didn't have to die.'

Galiana nodded sagely. 'No; in all likelihood he didn't. But the risk to yourself was too great. You heard what he said. Your death would be made to seem our fault; justification for a pre-emptive strike against our nest. Even the Demarchists would turn against us if we were seen to murder a diplomat.'

Taking another suck from the mask, he looked into her face. He had spoken to her over low-bandwidth video-links, but only in person was it obvious that Galiana had hardly aged in fifteen years. A decade and a half of habitual expression should have engraved existing lines deeper into her face – but Conjoiners were not known for their habits of expression. Galiana had seen little sunlight in the intervening time, cooped here in the nest, and Martian gravity was much kinder to bone structure than the one-gee of Deimos. She still had the cruel beauty he remembered from his time as a prisoner. The only real evidence of ageing lay in the filaments of grey threading her hair; raven-black when she had been his captor.

'Why didn't you warn us about the worms?'

'Warn you?' For the first time something like doubt crossed her face, but it was only fleeting. 'We assumed you were fully aware of the Ouroboros infestation. Those worms have been dormant – waiting – for years, but they've always been there. It was only when I saw how low your approach was that I realised . . .'

'That we might not have known?'

Worms were area-denial devices; autonomous prey-seeking mines. The war had left many pockets of the solar system still riddled with active worms. The machines were intelligent, in a one-dimensional way. Nobody ever admitted to deploying them and it was usually impossible to convince them that the war was over and that they should quietly deactivate.

'After what happened to you in Phobos,' Galiana said, 'I assumed there was nothing you needed to be taught about worms.'

He never liked thinking about Phobos: the pain was still too deeply engraved. But if it had not been for the injuries he had sustained there he would never have been sent to Deimos to recuperate; would never have been recruited into his brother's intelligence wing to study the Conjoiners. Out of that phase of deep immersion in everything concerning the enemy had come his peacetime role as negotiator – and now diplomat – on the eve of another war. Everything was circular, ultimately. And now Phobos was central to his thinking because he saw it as a way out of the impasse – maybe the last chance for peace. But it was too soon to put his idea to Galiana. He was not even sure the mission could still continue, after what had happened.

'We're safe now, I take it?'

'Yes; we can repair the damage to the dyke. Mostly, we can ignore their presence.'

'We should have been warned. Look, I need to talk to my brother.'

'Warren? Of course. It's easily arranged.'

They walked out of the hangar; away from the half-assembled ships. Somewhere deeper in the nest, Clavain knew, was a factory where the components for the ships were made, mined out of Mars or winnowed from the fabric of the nest. The Conjoiners managed to launch one every six weeks or so; had been doing so for six months. Not one of the ships had ever managed to escape the Martian atmosphere before being shot down . . . but sooner or later he would have to ask Galiana why she persisted with this provocative folly.

Now, though, was not the time – even if, by Warren's estimate, he only had three days before Galiana's next provocation.

The air elsewhere in the nest was thicker and warmer than in the hangar, which meant he could dispense with the mask. Galiana took him down a short, grey-walled, metallic corridor which ended in a circular room containing a console. He recognised the room from the times he had spoken to Galiana from Deimos. Galiana showed him how to use the system then left him in privacy while he established a connection with Deimos.

Warren's face soon appeared on a screen, thick with pixels like an impressionist portrait. Conjoiners were only allowed to send kilobytes a second to other parts of the system. Much of that bandwidth was now being sucked up by this one video link.

'You've heard, I take it,' Clavain said.

Warren nodded, his face ashen. 'We had a pretty good view from orbit, of course. Enough to see that Voi didn't make it. Poor woman. We were reasonably sure you survived, but it's good to have it confirmed.'

'Do you want me to abandon the mission?'

Warren's hesitation was more than just time-lag. 'No . . . I thought about it, of course, and high command agrees with me. Voi's death was tragic – no escaping that. But she was only along as a neutral observer. If Galiana consents for you to stay, I suggest you do so.'

'But you still say I only have three days?'

'That's up to Galiana, isn't it? Have you learnt much?'

'You must be kidding. I've seen shuttles ready for launch; that's all. I haven't raised the Phobos proposal, either. The timing wasn't exactly ideal, after what happened to Voi.'

'Yes. If only we'd known about that Ouroboros infestation.'

Clavain leaned closer to the screen. 'Yes. Why the hell didn't we? Galiana assumed that we would, and I don't blame her for that. We've had the nest under constant surveillance for fifteen years. Surely in all that time we'd have seen evidence of the worms?'

'You'd have thought so, wouldn't you?'

'Meaning what?'

'Meaning, maybe the worms weren't always there.'

Conscious that there could be nothing private about this conversation – but unwilling to drop the thread – Clavain said: 'You think the Conjoiners put them there to ambush us?'

'I'm saying we shouldn't disregard any possibility, no matter how unpalatable.'

'Galiana would never do something like that.'

'No, I wouldn't.' She had just stepped back into the room. 'And I'm disappointed that you'd even debate the possibility.'

Clavain terminated the link with Deimos. 'Eavesdropping's not a very nice habit, you know.'

'What did you expect me to do?'

'Show some trust? Or is that too much of a stretch?'

'I never had to trust you when you were my prisoner,' Galiana said. 'That made our relationship infinitely simpler. Our roles were completely defined.'

'And now? If you distrust me so completely, why did you ever agree to my visit? Plenty of other specialists could have come in my place. You could even have refused any dialogue.'

'Voi's people pressured us to allow your visit,' Galiana said. 'Just as they pressured your side into delaying hostilities a little longer.'

'Is that all?'

She hesitated slightly now. 'I . . . knew you.'

'Knew me? Is that how you sum up a year of imprisonment? What about the thousands of conversations we had; the times when we put aside our differences to talk about something other than the damned war? You kept me sane, Galiana. I've never forgotten that. It's why I've risked my life to come here and talk you out of another provocation.'

'It's completely different now.'

'Of course!' He forced himself not to shout. 'Of course it's different. But not fundamentally. We can still build on that bond of trust and find a way out of this crisis.'

'But does your side really want a way out of it?'

He did not answer her immediately; wary of what the truth might mean. 'I'm not sure. But I'm also not sure you do, or else you wouldn't keep pushing your luck.' Something snapped inside him and he asked the question he had meant to ask in a million better ways. 'Why do you keep doing it, Galiana? Why do you keep launching those ships when you know they'll be shot down as soon as they leave the nest?'

Her eyes locked onto his own, unflinchingly. 'Because we can. Because sooner or later one will succeed.'

Clavain nodded. It was exactly the sort of thing he had feared she would say.

She led him through more grey-walled corridors, descending several levels deeper into the nest. Light poured from snaking strips embedded into the walls like arteries. It was possible that the snaking design was decorative, but Clavain thought it much more likely that the strips had simply grown that way, expressing biological algorithms. There was no evidence that the Conjoiners had attempted to enliven their surroundings; to render them in any sense human.

'It's a terrible risk you're running,' Clavain said.

'And the status quo is intolerable. I've every desire to avoid another war, but if it came to one, we'd at least have the chance to break these shackles.'

'If you didn't get exterminated first . . .'

'We'd avoid that. In any case, fear plays no part in our thinking. You saw the man accept his fate on the dyke, when he understood that your death would harm us more than his own. He altered his state of mind to one of total acceptance.'

'Fine. That makes it alright, then.'

She halted. They were alone in one of the snakingly-lit corridors; he had seen no other Conjoiners since the hangar. 'It's not that we regard individual lives as worthless, any more than you would willingly sacrifice a limb. But now that we're part of something larger . . .'

'Transenlightenment, you mean?'

It was the Conjoiners' term for the state of neural communion they shared, mediated by the machines swarming in their skulls. Whereas Demarchists used implants to facilitate real-time democracy, Conjoiners used them to share sensory data, memories – even conscious thought itself. That was what had precipitated the war. Back in 2190 half of humanity had been hooked into the system-wide data nets via neural implants. Then the Conjoiner experiments had exceeded some threshold, unleashing a transforming virus into the nets. Implants had begun to change, infecting millions of minds with the templates of Conjoiner thought. Instantly the infected had become the enemy. Earth and the other inner planets had always been more conservative, preferring to access the nets via traditional media.

Once they saw communities on Mars and in the asteroid belts fall prey to the Conjoiner phenomenon, the Coalition powers hurriedly pooled their resources to prevent the spread reaching their own states. The Demarchists, out around the gas giants, had managed to get firewalls up before many of their habitats were lost. They had chosen neutrality while the Coalition tried to contain – some said sterilise – zones of Conjoiner takeover. Within three years – after some of the bloodiest battles in human experience – the Conjoiners had been pushed back to a clutch of hideaways dotted around the system. Yet all along they professed a kind of puzzled bemusement that their spread was being resisted. After all, no one who had been assimilated seemed to regret it. Quite the contrary. The few prisoners whom the Conjoiners had reluctantly returned to their pre-infection state had sought every means to return to the fold. Some had even chosen suicide rather than be denied Transenlightenment. Like acolytes given a vision of heaven, they devoted their entire waking existence to the search for another glimpse.

'Transenlightenment blurs our sense of self,' Galiana said. 'When the man elected to die, the sacrifice was not absolute for him. He understood that much of what he was had already achieved preservation among the rest of us.'

'But he was just one man. What about the hundred lives you've thrown away with your escape attempts? We know – we've counted the bodies.'

'Replacements can always be cloned.'

Clavain hoped that he hid his disgust satisfactorily. Among his people the very notion of cloning was an unspeakable atrocity, redolent with horror. To Galiana it would be just another technique in her arsenal. 'But you don't clone, do you? And you're losing people. We thought there would be nine hundred of you in this nest, but that was a gross overestimate, wasn't it?'

'You haven't seen much yet,' Galiana said.

'No, but this place smells deserted. You can't hide absence, Galiana. I bet there aren't more than a hundred of you left here.'

'You're wrong,' Galiana said. 'We have cloning technology, but we've hardly ever used it. What would be the point? We don't aspire to genetic unity, no matter what your propagandists think. The pursuit of optima leads only to local minima. We honour our errors. We actively seek persistent disequilibrium.'

'Right.' The last thing he needed now was a dose of Conjoiner rhetoric. 'So where the hell is everyone?'

In a while he had part of the answer, if not the whole of it. At the end of the maze of corridors – far under Mars now – Galiana brought him to a nursery.

It was shockingly unlike his expectations. Not only did it not match what he had imagined from the vantage point of Deimos, but it jarred against his predictions based on what he had seen so far of the nest. In Deimos, he had assumed a Conjoiner nursery would be a place of grim medical efficiency; all gleaming machines with babies plugged in like peripherals, like a monstrously productive doll factory. Within the nest, he had revised his model to allow for the depleted numbers of Conjoiners. If there was a nursery, it was obviously not very productive. Fewer babies, then – but still a vision of hulking grey machines, bathed in snaking light.

The nursery was nothing like that.

The huge room Galiana showed him was almost painfully bright and cheerful; a child's fantasy of friendly shapes and primary colours. The walls and ceiling projected a holographic sky: infinite blue and billowing clouds of heavenly white. The floor was an undulating mat of synthetic grass forming hillocks and meadows. There were banks of flowers and forests of bonsai trees. There were robot animals: fabulous birds and rabbits just slightly too anthropomorphic to fool Clavain. They were like the animals in children's books: big-eyed and happy-looking. Toys were scattered on the grass.

And there were children. They numbered between forty and fifty; spanning by his estimate ages from a few months to six or seven standard years. Some were crawling among the rabbits; other, older children were gathered around tree stumps whose sheered-off surfaces flickered rapidly with images, underlighting their faces. They were talking amongst themselves, giggling or singing. He counted perhaps half a dozen adult Conjoiners kneeling among the children. The children's clothes were a headache of bright, clashing colours and patterns. The Conjoiners crouched among them like ravens. Yet the children seemed at ease with them, listening attentively when the adults had something to say.

'This isn't what you thought it would be like, is it.'

'No . . . not at all.' There seemed no point lying to her. 'We thought you'd raise your young in a simplified version of the machine-generated environment you experience.'

'In the early days that's more or less what we did.' Subtly, Galiana's tone of voice had changed. 'Do you know why chimpanzees are less intelligent than humans?'

He blinked at the change of tack. 'I don't know – are their brains smaller?'

'Yes – but a dolphin's brain is larger, and they're scarcely more intelligent than dogs.' Galiana stooped next to a vacant tree stump. Without seeming to do anything, she made a diagram of mammal brain anatomies appear on the trunk's upper surface, then sketched her finger across the relevant parts. 'It's not overall brain volume that counts so much as the developmental history. The difference in brain volume between a neonatal chimp and an adult is only about twenty percent. By the time the chimp receives any data from beyond the womb, there's almost no plasticity left to use. Similarly, dolphins are born with almost their complete repertoire of adult behaviour already hardwired. A human brain, on the other hand, keeps growing through years of learning. We inverted that thinking. If data received during post natal growth was so crucial to intelligence, perhaps we could boost our intelligence even further by intervening during the earliest phases of brain development.'

'In the womb?'

'Yes.' Now she made the tree trunk show a human embryo running through cycles of cell-division, until the faint fold of a rudimentary spinal nerve began to form, nubbed with the tiniest of emergent minds. Droves of subcellular machines swarmed in, invading the nascent nervous system. Then the embryo's development slammed forward, until Clavain was looking at an unborn human baby.

'What happened?'

'It was a grave error,' Galiana said. 'Instead of enhancing normal neural development, we impaired it terribly. All we ended up with were various manifestations of savant syndrome.'

Clavain looked around him. 'Then you let these kids develop normally?'

'More or less. There's no family structure, of course, but then again there are plenty of human and primate societies where the family is less important in child development than the cohort group. So far we haven't seen any pathologies.'

Clavain watched as one of the older children was escorted out of the grassy room, through a door in the sky. When the Conjoiner reached the door the child hesitated, tugging against the man's gentle insistence. The child looked back for a moment, then followed the man through the gap.

'Where's that child going?'

'To the next stage of its development.'

Clavain wondered what were the chances of him seeing the nursery just as one of the children was being promoted. Small, he judged – unless there was a crash program to rush as many of them through as quickly as possible. As he thought about this, Galiana took him into another part of the nursery. While this room was smaller and dourer it was still more colourful than any other part of the nest he had seen before the grassy room. The walls were a mosaic of crowded, intermingling displays, teeming with moving images and rapidly scrolling text. He saw a herd of zebra stampeding through the core of a neutron star. Elsewhere an octopus squirted ink at the face of a twentieth-century despot. Other display facets rose from the floor like Japanese paper screens, flooded with data. Children – up to early teenagers – sat on soft black toadstools next to the screens in little groups, debating.

A few musical instruments lay around unused: holoclaviers and air-guitars. Some of the children had grey bands around their eyes and were poking their fingers through the interstices of abstract structures, exploring the dragon-infested waters of mathematical space. Clavain could see what they were manipulating on the flat screens: shapes that made his head hurt even in two dimensions.

'They're nearly there,' Clavain said. 'The machines are outside their heads, but not for long. When does it happen?'

'Soon; very soon.'

'You're rushing them, aren't you. Trying to get as many children Conjoined as you can. What are you planning?'

'Something . . . has arisen, that's all. The timing of your arrival is either very bad or very fortunate, depending on your point of view.' Before he could query her, Galiana added: 'Clavain; I want you to meet someone.'

'Who?'

'Someone very precious to us.'

She took him through a series of child proof doors until they reached a small circular room. The walls and ceiling were veined grey; tranquil after what he had seen in the last place. A child sat cross-legged on the floor in the middle of the room. Clavain estimated the girl's age as ten standard years – perhaps fractionally older. But she did not respond to Clavain's presence in any way an adult, or even a normal child, would have. She just kept on doing the thing she had been doing when they stepped inside, as if they were not really present at all. It was not at all clear what she was doing. Her hands moved before her in slow, precise gestures. It was as if she were playing a holoclavier or working a phantom puppet show. Now and then she would pivot round until she was facing another direction and carry on doing the hand movements.

'Her name's Felka,' Galiana said.

'Hello, Felka . . .' He waited for a response, but none came. 'I can see there's something wrong with her.'

'She was one of the savants. Felka developed with machines in her head. She was the last to be born before we realised our failure.'

Something about Felka disturbed him. Perhaps it was the way she carried on regardless, engrossed in an activity to which she seemed to attribute the utmost significance, yet which had to be without any sane purpose.

'She doesn't seem aware of us.'

'Her deficits are severe,' Galiana said. 'She has no interest in other human beings. She has prosopagnosia; the inability to distinguish faces. We all seem alike to her. Can you imagine something more strange than that?'

He tried, and failed. Life from Felka's viewpoint must have been a nightmarish thing, surrounded by identical clones whose inner lives she could not begin to grasp. No wonder she seemed so engrossed in her game.

'Why is she so precious to you?' Clavain asked, not really wanting to know the answer.

'She's keeping us alive,' Galiana said.

Of course, he asked Galiana what she meant by that. Galiana's only response was to tell him that he was not yet ready to be shown the answer.

'And what exactly would it take for me to reach that stage?'

'A simple procedure.'

Oh yes, he understood that part well enough. Just a few machines in the right parts of his brain and the truth could be his. Politely, doing his best to mask his distaste, Clavain declined. Fortunately, Galiana did not press the point, for the time had arrived for the meeting he had been promised before his arrival on Mars.

He watched a subset of the nest file in to the conference room. Galiana was their leader only inasmuch as she had founded the lab here from which the original experiment had sprung and was accorded some respect deriving from seniority. She was also the most obvious spokesperson among them. They all had areas of expertise which could not be easily shared among other Conjoined; very distinct from the hive-mind of identical clones which still figured in the Coalition's propaganda. If the nest was in any way like an ant colony, then it was an ant colony in which every ant fulfilled a distinct role from all the others. Naturally, no individual could be solely entrusted with a particular skill essential to the nest – that would have been dangerous over-specialisation – but neither had individuality been completely subsumed into the group mind.

The conference room must have dated back to the days when the nest was a research outpost, or even earlier, when it was some kind of mining base in the early 2100s. It was much too big for the dour handful of Conjoiners who stood round the main table. Tactical read-outs around the table showed the build-up of strike forces above the Martian exclusion zone; probable drop trajectories for ground-force deployment.

'Nevil Clavain,' Galiana said, introducing him to the others. Everyone sat down. 'I'm just sorry that Sandra Voi can't be with us now. We all feel the tragedy of her death. But perhaps out of this terrible event we can find some common ground. Nevil, before you came here you told us you had a proposal for a peaceful resolution to the crisis.'

'I'd really like to hear it,' one of the others murmured audibly.

Clavain's throat was dry. Diplomatically, this was quicksand. 'My proposal concerns Phobos . . .'

'Go on.'

'I was injured there,' he said. 'Very badly. Our attempt to clean out the worm infestation failed and I lost some good friends. That makes it personal between me and the worms. But I'd accept anyone's help to finish them off.'

Galiana glanced quickly at her compatriots before answering. 'A joint assault operation?'

'It could work.'

'Yes . . .' Galiana seemed lost momentarily. 'I suppose it could be a way out of the impasse. Our own attempt failed too – and the interdiction's stopped us from trying again.' Again, she seemed to fall into reverie. 'But who would really benefit from the flushing out of Phobos? We'd still be quarantined here.'

Clavain leaned forward. 'A co-operative gesture might be exactly the thing to lead to a relaxation in the terms of the interdiction. But don't think of it in those terms. Think instead of reducing the current threat from the worms.'

'Threat?'

Clavain nodded. 'It's possible that you haven't noticed.' He leaned forward, elbows on the table. 'We're concerned about the Phobos worms. They've begun altering the moon's orbit. The shift is tiny at the moment, but too large to be anything other than deliberate.'

Galiana looked away from him for an instant, as if weighing her options. Then said: 'We were aware of this, but you weren't to know that.'

Gratitude?

He had assumed the worms' activity could not have escaped Galiana. 'We've seen odd behaviour from other worm infestations across the system; things that begin to look like emergent intelligence. But never anything this purposeful. This infestation must have come from a batch with some subroutines we never even guessed about. Do you have any ideas about what they might be up to?'

Again, there was the briefest of hesitations, as if she was communing with her compatriots for the right response. Then she nodded towards a male Conjoiner sitting opposite her, Clavain guessing that the gesture was entirely for his benefit. His hair was black and curly; his face as smooth and untroubled by expression as Galiana's, with something of the same beautifully symmetrical bone structure.

'This is Remontoire,' said Galiana. 'He's our specialist on the Phobos situation.'

Remontoire nodded politely. 'In answer to your question, we currently have no viable theories as to what they're doing, but we do know one thing. They're raising the apocentre of the moon's orbit.' Apocentre, Clavain knew, was the Martian equivalent of apogee for an object orbiting Earth: the point of highest altitude in an elliptical orbit. Remontoire continued, his voice as preternaturally calm as a parent reading slowly to a child. 'The natural orbit of Phobos is actually inside the Roche limit for a gravitationally-bound moon; Phobos is raising a tidal bulge on Mars but, because of friction, the bulge can't quite keep up with Phobos. It's causing Phobos to spiral slowly closer to Mars, by about two metres a century. In a few tens of millions of years, what's left of the moon will crash into Mars.'

'You think the worms are elevating the orbit to avoid a cataclysm so far in the future?'

'I don't know,' Remontoire said. 'I suppose the orbital alterations could also be a by-product of some less meaningful worm activity.'

'I agree,' Clavain said. 'But the danger remains. If the worms can elevate the moon's apocentre – even accidentally – we can assume they also have the means to lower its pericentre. They could drop Phobos on top of your nest. Does that scare you sufficiently that you'd consider co-operation with the Coalition?'

Galiana steepled her fingers before her face; a human gesture of deep concentration which her time as a Conjoiner had not quite eroded. Clavain could almost feel the web of thought looming the room; ghostly strands of cognition reaching between each Conjoiner at the table, and beyond into the nest proper.

'A winning team, is that your idea?'

'It's got to be better than war,' Clavain said. 'Hasn't it?'

Galiana might have been about to answer him when her face grew troubled. Clavain saw the wave of discomposure sweep over the others almost simultaneously. Something told him that it was nothing to do with his proposal.

Around the table, half the display facets switched automatically over to another channel. The face that Clavain was looking at was much like his own, except that the face on the screen was missing an eye. It was his brother. Warren was overlaid with the official insignia of the Coalition and a dozen system-wide media cartels.

He was in the middle of a speech. '. . . express my shock,' Warren said. 'Or, for that matter, my outrage. It's not just that they've murdered a valued colleague and deeply experienced member of my team. They've murdered my brother.'

Clavain felt the deepest of chills. 'What is this?'

'A live transmission from Deimos,' Galiana breathed. 'It's going out to all the nets; right out to the trans-Pluto habitats.'

'What they did was an act of unspeakable treachery,' Warren said. 'Nothing less than the pre meditated, cold-blooded murder of a peace envoy.' And then a video clip sprang up to replace Warren. The image must have been snapped from Deimos or one of the interdiction satellites. It showed Clavain's shuttle, lying in the dust close to the dyke. He watched the Ouroboros destroy the shuttle, then saw the image zoom in on himself and Voi, running for sanctuary. The Ouroboros took Voi. But this time there was no ladder lowered down for him. Instead, he saw weapon-beams scythe out from the nest towards him, knocking him to the ground. Horribly wounded, he tried to get up, to crawl a few inches nearer to his tormentors, but the worm was already upon him.

He watched himself get eaten.

Warren was back again. 'The worms around the nest were a Conjoiner trap. My brother's death must have been planned days – maybe even weeks – in advance.' His face glistened with a wave of military composure. 'There can only be one outcome from such an action – something the Conjoiners must have well understood. For months they've been goading us towards hostile action.' He paused, then nodded at an unseen audience. 'Well now they're going to get it. In fact, our response has already commenced.'

'Dear God, no,' Clavain said, but the evidence was all there now; all around the table he could see the updating orbital spread of the Coalition's dropships, knifing down towards Mars.

'I think it's war,' Galiana said.

Conjoiners stormed onto the roof of the nest, taking up defensive positions around the domes and the dyke's edge. Most of them carried the same guns which they had used against the Ouroboros. Smaller numbers were setting up automatic cannon on tripods. One or two were manhandling large anti-assault weapons into position. Most of it was war-surplus. Fifteen years ago the Conjoiners had avoided extinction by deploying weapons of awesome ferocity – but those ship-to-ship armaments were simply too destructive to use against a nearby foe. Now it would be more visceral; closer to the primal templates of combat, and none of what the Conjoiners were marshalling would be much use against the kind of assault Warren had prepared, Clavain knew. They could slow an attack, but not much more than that.

Galiana had given him another breather mask, made him don lightweight chameleoflage armour, and then forced him to carry one of the smaller guns. The gun felt alien in his hands; something he had never expected to carry again. The only possible justification for carrying it was to use it against his brother's forces – against his own side.

Could he do that?

It was clear that Warren had betrayed him; he had surely been aware of the worms around the nest. So his brother was capable not just of contempt, but of treacherous murder. For the first time, Clavain felt genuine hatred for Warren. He must have hoped that the worms would destroy the shuttle completely and kill Clavain and Voi in the process. It must have pained him to see Clavain make it to the dyke . . . pained him even more when Clavain called to talk about the tragedy. But Warren's larger plan had not been affected. The diplomatic link between the nest and Deimos was secure – even the Demarchists had no immediate access to it. So Clavain's call from the surface could be quietly ignored; spysat imagery doctored to make it seem that he had never reached the dyke . . . had in fact been repelled by Conjoiner treachery. Inevitably the Demarchists would unravel the deception given time . . . but if Warren's plan succeeded, they would all be embroiled in war long before then. That, thought Clavain, was all that Warren had ever wanted.

Two brothers, Clavain thought. In many ways so alike. Both had embraced war once, but like a fickle lover Clavain had wearied of its glories. He had not even been injured as severely as Warren . . . but perhaps that was the point, too. Warren needed another war to avenge what one had stolen from him.

Clavain despised and pitied him in equal measure.

He searched for the safety clip on the gun. The rifle, now that he studied it more closely, was not all that different from those he had used during the war. The read-out said the ammo-cell was fully charged.

He looked into the sky.

The attack wave broke orbit hard and steep above the Wall; five hundred fireballs screeching towards the nest. The insertion scorched inches of ablative armour from most of the ships; fried a few others which came in just fractionally too hard. Clavain knew that was how it was happening: he had studied possible attack scenarios for years, the range of outcomes burned indelibly into his memory.

The anti-assault guns were already working – locking onto the plasma trails as they flowered overhead, swinging down to find the tiny spark of heat at the head, computing refraction paths for laser pulses, spitting death into the sky. The unlucky ships flared a white that hurt the back of the eye and rained down in a billion dulling sparks. A dozen – then a dozen more. Maybe fifty in total before the guns could no longer acquire targets. It was nowhere near enough. Clavain's memory of the simulations told him that at least four hundred units of the attack wave would survive both re-entry and the Conjoiner's heavy defences.

Nothing that Galiana could do would make any difference.

And that had always been the paradox. Galiana was capable of running the same simulations. She must always have known that her provocations would bring down something she could never hope to defeat.

Something that was always going to destroy her.

The surviving members of the wave were levelling out now, commencing long, ground-hugging runs from all directions. Cocooned in their dropships, the soldiers would be suffering punishing gee-loads . . . but it was nothing they were not engineered to withstand; half their cardiovascular systems were augmented by the only kinds of implant the Coalition tolerated.

The first of the wave came arcing in at supersonic speeds. All around, worms struggled to snatch them out of the sky, but mostly they were too slow to catch the dropships. Galiana's people manned their cannon positions and did their best to fend off what they could. Clavain clutched his gun, not firing yet. Best to save his ammo-cell power for a target he stood a chance of injuring.

Above, the first dropships made hairpin turns, nosing suicidally down towards the nest. Then they fractured cleanly apart, revealing falling pilots clad in bulbous armour. Just before the moment of impact each pilot exploded into a mass of black shock-absorbing balloons, looking something like a blackberry, bouncing across the nest before the balloons deflated just as swiftly and the pilot was left standing on the ground. By then the pilot – now properly a soldier – would have a comprehensive computer-generated map of the nest's nooks and crannies; enemy positions graphed in realtime from the down-looking spysats.

Clavain fell behind the curve of a dome before the nearest soldier got a lock onto him. The firefight was beginning now. He had to hand it to Galiana's people – they were fighting like devils. And they were at least as well co-ordinated as the attackers. But their weapons and armour were simply inadequate. Chameleoflage was only truly effective against a solitary enemy, or a massed enemy moving in from a common direction. With Coalition forces surrounding him, Clavain's suit was going crazy trying to match itself against every background, like a chameleon in a house of mirrors.

The sky overhead looked strange now – darkening purple. And the purple was spreading in a mist across the nest. Galiana had deployed some kind of chemical smoke screen: infrared and optically opaque, he guessed. It would occlude the spysats and might be primed to adhere only to enemy chameleoflage. That had never been in Warren's simulations. Galiana had just given herself the slightest of edges.

A soldier stepped out of the mist, the obscene darkness of a gun muzzle trained on Clavain. His chameleoflage armour was dappled with vivid purple patches, ruining its stealthiness. The man fired, but his discharge wasted itself against Clavain's armour. Clavain returned the compliment, dropping his compatriot. What he had done, he thought, was not technically treason. Not yet. All he had done was act in self-preservation.

The man was wounded, but not yet dead. Clavain stepped through the purple haze and knelt down beside the soldier. He tried not to look at the man's wound.

'Can you hear me?' he said. There was no answer from the man, but beneath his visor, Clavain thought he saw the man's lips shape a sound. The man was just a kid – hardly old enough to remember much of the last war. 'There's something you have to know,' Clavain continued. 'Do you realise who I am?' He wondered how recognisable he was, under the breather mask. Then something made him relent. He could tell the man he was Nevil Clavain – but what would that achieve? The soldier would be dead in minutes; maybe sooner than that. Nothing would be served by the soldier knowing that the basis for his attack was a lie; that he would not in fact be laying down his life for a just cause. The universe could be spared a single callous act.

'Forget it,' Clavain said, turning away from his victim.

And then moved deeper into the nest, to see who else he could kill before the odds took him.

But the odds never did.

'You always were lucky,' Galiana said, leaning over him. They were somewhere underground again – deep in the nest. A medical area, by the look of things. He was on a bed, fully clothed apart from the outer layer of chameleoflage armour. The room was grey and kettle-shaped, ringed by a circular balcony.

'What happened?'

'You took a head wound, but you'll survive.'

He groped for the right question. 'What about Warren's attack?'

'We endured three waves. We took casualties, of course.'

Around the circumference of the balcony were thirty or so grey couches, slightly recessed into archways studded with grey medical equipment. They were all occupied. There were more

Conjoiners in this room than he had seen so far in one place. Some of them looked very close to death.

Clavain reached up and examined his head, gingerly. There was some dried blood on the scalp, matted with his hair; some numbness, but it could have been a lot worse. He felt normal – no memory drop-outs or aphasia. When he made to stand from the bed, his body obeyed his will with only a tinge of dizziness.

'Warren won't stop at just three waves, Galiana.'

'I know.' She paused. 'We know there'll be more.'

He walked to the railing on the inner side of the balcony and looked over the edge. He had expected to see something – some chunk of incomprehensible surgical equipment, perhaps – but the middle of the room was only an empty, smooth-walled, grey pit. He shivered. The air was colder than any part of the nest he had visited so far, with a medicinal tang which reminded him of the convalescence ward on Deimos. What made him shiver even more was the realisation that some of the injured – some of the dead – were barely older than the children he had visited only hours ago. Perhaps some of them were those children, conscripted from the nursery since his visit, uploaded with fighting reflexes through their new implants.

'What are you going to do? You know you can't win. Warren lost only a tiny fraction of his available force in those waves. You look like you've lost half your nest.'

'It's much worse than that,' Galiana said.

'What do you mean?'

'You're not quite ready yet. But I can show you in a moment.'

He felt colder than ever now. 'What do you mean, not quite ready?'

Galiana looked deep into his eyes now. 'You took a serious head wound, Clavain. The entry wound was small, but the internal bleeding . . . it would have killed you, had we not intervened.' Before he could ask the inevitable question she answered it for him. 'We injected a small cluster of medichines into your head. They undid the damage very easily. But it seemed provident to allow them to grow.'

'You've put replicators in my head?'

'You needn't sound so horrified. They're already growing – spreading out and interfacing with your existing neural circuitry – but the total volume of glial mass that they will consume is tiny: only a few cubic millimetres in total, across your entire brain.'

He wondered if she was calling his bluff. 'I don't feel anything.'

'You won't – not for a minute or so.' Now she pointed into the empty pit in the middle of the room. 'Stand here and look into the air.'

'There's nothing there.'

But as soon as he had spoken, he knew he was wrong. There was something in the pit. He blinked and directed his attention somewhere else, but when he returned his gaze to the pit, the thing he imagined he had seen – milky, spectral – was still there, and becoming sharper and brighter by the second. It was a three-dimensional structure, as complex as an exercise in protein-folding. A tangle of loops and connecting branches and nodes and tunnels, embedded in a ghostly red matrix.

Suddenly he saw it for what it was: a map of the nest, dug into Mars. Just as the Coalition had suspected, the base was deeper than the original structure; far more extensive, reaching deeper down but much further out than anyone had imagined. Clavain made a mental effort to retain some of what he was seeing in his mind, the intelligence-gathering reflex stronger than the conscious knowledge that he would never see Deimos again.

'The medichines in your brain have interfaced with your visual cortex,' Galiana said. 'That's the first step on the road to Transenlightenment. Now you're privy to the machine-generated imagery encoded by the fields through which we move – most of it, anyway.'

'Tell me this wasn't planned, Galiana. Tell me you weren't intending to put machines in me at the first opportunity.'

'No; I wasn't planning it. But nor was I going to let your phobias stop me from saving your life.'

The image grew in complexity. Glowing nodes of light appeared in the tunnels, some moving slowly through the network.

'What are they?'

'You're seeing the locations of the Conjoiners,' Galiana said. 'Are there as many as you imagined?'

Clavain judged that there were no more than seventy lights in the whole complex now. He searched for a cluster which would identify the room where he stood. There: twenty-odd bright lights, accompanied by one much fainter. Himself, of course. There were few people near the top of the nest – the attack must have collapsed half the tunnels, or maybe Galiana had deliberately sealed entrances herself.

'Where is everyone? Where are the children?'

'Most of the children are gone now.' She paused. 'You were right to guess that we were rushing them to Transenlightenment, Clavain.'

'Why?'

'Because it's the only way out of here.'

The image changed again. Now each of the bright lights was connected to another by a shimmering filament. The topology of the network was constantly shifting, like a pattern seen in a kaleidoscope. Occasionally, too swiftly for Clavain to be sure, it shifted towards a mandala of elusive symmetry, only to dissolve into the flickering chaos of the ever-changing network. He studied Galiana's node and saw that – even as she was speaking to him – her mind was in constant rapport with the rest of the nest.

Now something very bright appeared in the middle of the image, like a tiny star, against which the shimmering network paled almost to invisibility. 'The network is abstracted now,' Galiana said. 'The bright light represents its totality: the unity of Transenlightenment. Watch.'

He watched. The bright light – beautiful and alluring as anything Clavain had ever imagined – was extending a ray towards the isolated node which represented himself. The ray was extending itself through the map, coming closer by the second.

'The new structures in your mind are nearing maturity,' Galiana said. 'When the ray touches you, you will experience partial integration with the rest of us. Prepare yourself, Nevil.'

Her words were unnecessary. His fingers were already clenched sweating on the railing as the light inched closer and engulfed his node.

'I should hate you for this,' Clavain said.

'Why don't you? Hate's always the easier option.'

'Because . . .' Because it made no difference now. His old life was over. He reached out for Galiana, needing some anchor against what was about to hit him. Galiana squeezed his hand and an instant later he knew something of Transenlightenment. The experience was shocking; not because it was painful or fearful, but because it was profoundly and totally new. He was literally thinking in ways that had not been possible microseconds earlier.

Afterwards, when Clavain tried to imagine how he might describe it, he found that words were never going to be adequate for the task. And that was no surprise: evolution had shaped language to convey many concepts, but going from a single to a networked topology of self was not among them. But if he could not convey the core of the experience, he could at least skirt its essence with metaphor. It was like standing on the shore of an ocean, being engulfed by a wave taller than himself. For a moment he sought the surface; tried to keep the water from his lungs. But there happened not to be a surface. What had consumed him extended infinitely in all directions. He could only submit to it. Yet as the moments slipped by it turned from something terrifying in its unfamiliarity to something he could begin to adapt to; something that even began in the tiniest way to seem comforting. Even then he glimpsed that it was only a shadow of what Galiana was experiencing every instant of her life.

'Alright,' Galiana said. 'That's enough for now.'

The fullness of Transenlightenment retreated, like a fading vision of Godhead. What he was left with was purely sensory; no longer any direct rapport with the others. His state of mind came crashing back to normality.

'Are you alright, Nevil?'

'Yes . . .' His mouth was dry. 'Yes; I think so.'

'Look around you.'

He did.

The room had changed completely. So had everyone in it.

His head reeling, Clavain walked in light. The formerly grey walls oozed beguiling patterns; as if a dark forest had suddenly become enchanted. Information hung in veils in the air; icons and diagrams and numbers clustering around the beds of the injured, thinning out into the general space like fantastically delicate neon sculptures. As he walked towards the icons they darted out of his way, mocking him like schools of brilliant fish. Sometimes they seemed to sing, or tickle the back of his nose with half-familiar smells.

'You can perceive things now,' Galiana said. 'But none of it will mean much to you. You'd need years of education, or deeper neural machinery for that – building cognitive layers. We read all this almost subliminally.'

Galiana was dressed differently now. He could still see the vague shape of her grey outfit, but layered around it were billowing skeins of light, unravelling at their edges into chains of Boolean logic. Icons danced in her hair like angels. He could see, faintly, the web of thought linking her with the other Conjoiners.

She was inhumanly beautiful.

'You said things were much worse,' Clavain said. 'Are you ready to show me now?'

She took him to see Felka again, passing on the way through deserted nursery rooms, populated now only by bewildered mechanical animals. Felka was the only child left in the nursery.

Clavain had been deeply disturbed by Felka when he had seen her before, but not for any reason he could easily express. Something about the purposefulness of what she did; performed with ferocious concentration, as if the fate of creation hung on the outcome of her game. Felka and her surroundings had not changed at all since his visit. The room was still austere to the point of oppressiveness. Felka looked the same. In every respect it was as if only an instant had passed since their meeting; as if the onset of war and the assaults against the nest – the battle of which this was only an interlude – were only figments from someone else's troubling dream; nothing that need concern Felka in her devotion to the task at hand.

And what the task was awed Clavain.

Before he had watched her make strange gestures in front of her. Now the machines in his head revealed the purpose that those gestures served. Around Felka – cordoning her like a barricade – was a ghostly representation of the Great Wall. She was doing something to it.

It was not a scale representation, Clavain knew. The Wall looked much higher here in relation to its diametre. And the surface was not the nearly-invisible membrane of the real thing, but something like etched glass. The etchwork was a filigree of lines and junctions, descending down to smaller and smaller scales in fractal steps, until the blur of detail was too fine for his eyes to discriminate. It was shifting and altering colour, and Felka was responding to these alterations with what he now saw was frightening efficiency. It was as if the colour changes warned of some malignancy in part of the Wall, and by touching it – expressing some tactile code – Felka was able to restructure the etchwork to block and neutralise the malignancy before it spread.

'I don't understand,' Clavain said. 'I thought we destroyed the Wall; completely killed its systems.'

'No,' Galiana said. 'You only ever injured it. Stopped it from growing, and from managing its own repair-processes correctly . . . but you never truly killed it.'

Sandra Voi had guessed, Clavain realised. She had wondered how the Wall had survived this long.

Galiana told him the rest – how they had managed to establish control pathways to the Wall from the nest, fifteen years earlier – optical cables sunk deep below the worm zone. 'We stabilised the Wall's degradation with software running on dumb machines,' she said. 'But when Felka was born we found that she managed the task just as efficiently as the computers; in some ways better than they ever did. In fact, she seemed to thrive on it. It was as if in the Wall she found . . .' Galiana trailed off. 'I was going to say a friend.'

'Why don't you?'

'Because the Wall's just a machine. Which means if Felka recognised kinship . . . what would that make her?'

'Someone lonely, that's all.' Clavain watched the girl's motions. 'She seems faster than before. Is that possible?'

'I told you things were worse than before. She's having to work harder to hold the Wall together.'

'Warren must have attacked it.' Clavain said. 'The possibility of knocking down the Wall always figured in our contingency plans for another war. I just never thought it would happen so soon.' Then he looked at Felka. Maybe it was imagination but she seemed to be working even faster than when he had entered the room; not just since his last visit. 'How long do you think she can keep it together?'

'Not much longer,' Galiana said. 'As a matter of fact I think she's already failing.'

It was true. Now that he looked closely at the ghost Wall he saw that the upper edge was not the mathematically smooth ring it should have been; that there were scores of tiny ragged bites eating down from the top. Felka's activities were increasingly directed to these opening cracks in the structure; instructing the crippled structure to divert energy and raw materials to these critical failure points. Clavain knew that the distant processes Felka directed were awesome. Within the Wall lay a lymphatic system whose peristaltic feed-pipes ranged in size from metres across to the submicroscopic, flowing with myriad tiny repair machines. Felka chose where to send those machines; her hand gestures establishing pathways between damage points and the factories sunk into the Wall's ramparts which made the required types of machines. For more than a decade, Galiana said, Felka had kept the Wall from crumbling – but for most of that time her adversary had been only natural decay and accidental damage. It was a different game now that the Wall had been attacked again. It was not one she could ever win.

Felka's movements were swifter; less fluid. Her face remained impassive, but in the quickening way that her eyes darted from point to point it was possible to read the first hints of panic. No surprise, either: the deepest cracks in the structure now reached a quarter of the way to the surface, and they were too wide to be repaired. The Wall was unzipping along those flaws. Cubic kilometres of atmosphere would be howling out through the openings. The loss of pressure would be immeasurably slow at first, for near the top the trapped cylinder of atmosphere was only fractionally thicker than the rest of the Martian atmosphere. But only at first . . .

'We have to get deeper,' Clavain said. 'Once the Wall goes, we won't have a chance in hell if we're anywhere near the surface. It'll be like the worst tornado in history.'

'What will your brother do? Will he nuke us?'

'No; I don't think so. He'll want to get hold of any technologies you've hidden away. He'll wait until the dust storms have died down, then he'll raid the nest with a hundred times as many troops as you've seen so far. You won't be able to resist, Galiana. If you're lucky you may just survive long enough to be taken prisoner.'

'There won't be any prisoners,' Galiana said.

'You're planning to die fighting?'

'No. And mass suicide doesn't figure in our plans either. Neither will be necessary. By the time your brother reaches here, there won't be anyone left in the nest.'

Clavain thought of the worms encircling the area; how small were the chances of reaching any kind of safety if it involved getting past them. 'Secret tunnels under the worm zone, is that it? I hope you're serious.'

'I'm deadly serious,' Galiana said. 'And yes, there is a secret tunnel. The other children have already gone through it now. But it doesn't lead under the worm zone.'

'Where, then?'

'Somewhere a lot further away.'

When they passed through the medical centre again it was empty, save for a few swan-necked robots patiently waiting for further casualties. They had left Felka behind tending the Wall, her hands a manic blur as she tried to slow the rate of collapse. Clavain had tried to make her come with them, but Galiana had told him he was wasting his time: that she would sooner die than be parted from the Wall.

'You don't understand,' Galiana said. 'You're placing too much humanity behind her eyes. Keeping the Wall alive is the single most important fact of her universe – more important than love, pain, death – anything you or I would consider definitively human.'

'Then what happens to her when the Wall dies?'

'Her life ends,' Galiana said.

Reluctantly he had left without her, the taste of shame in his mouth. Rationally it made sense: without Felka's help the Wall would collapse much sooner and there was a good chance all their lives would end, not just that of the haunted girl. How deep would they have to go before they were safe from the suction of the escaping atmosphere? Would any part of the nest be safe?

The regions through which they were descending now were as cold and grey as any Clavain had seen. There were no entoptic generators buried in these walls to supply visual information to the implants Galiana had put in his head, and even her own aura of light was gone. They only met a few other Conjoiners, and they seemed to be moving in the same general direction: down to the nest's basement levels. This was unknown territory to Clavain.

Where was Galiana taking him?

'If you had an escape route all along, why did you wait so long before sending the children through it?'

'I told you, we couldn't bring them to Transenlightenment too soon. The older they were, the better,' Galiana said. 'Now though . . .'

'There was no waiting any longer, was there?'

Eventually they reached a chamber with the same echoing acoustics as the topside hangar. The chamber was dark except for a few pools of light, but in the shadows Clavain made out discarded excavation equipment and freight pallets; cranes and deactivated robots. The air smelled of ozone. Something was still going on here.

'Is this the factory where you make the shuttles?' Clavain said.

'We manufactured parts of them here, yes,' Galiana said. 'But that was a side-industry.'

'Of what?'

'The tunnel, of course.' Galiana made more lights come on. At the far end of the chamber – they were walking towards it – waited a series of cylindrical things with pointed ends, like huge bullets. They rested on rails, one after the other. The tip of the very first bullet was next to a dark hole in the wall. Clavain was about to say something when there was a sudden loud buzz and the first bullet slammed into the hole. The other bullets – there were three of them now – eased slowly forward and halted. Conjoiners were waiting to get aboard them.

He remembered what Galiana had said about no one being left behind.

'What am I seeing here?'

'A way out of the nest,' Galiana said. 'And a way off Mars, though I suppose you figured that part for yourself.'

'There is no way off Mars,' Clavain said. 'The interdiction guarantees that. Haven't you learned that with your shuttles?'

'The shuttles were only ever a diversionary tactic,' Galiana said. 'They made your side think we were still striving to escape, whereas our true escape route was already fully operational.'

'A pretty desperate diversion.'

'Not really. I lied to you when I said we didn't clone. We did – but only to produce brain-dead corpses. The shuttles were full of corpses before we ever launched them.'

For the first time since leaving Deimos Clavain smiled, amused at the sheer obliquity of Galiana's thinking.

'Of course, there was another function,' she said. 'The shuttles provoked your side into a direct attack against the nest.'

'So this was deliberate all along?'

'Yes. We needed to draw your side's attention; to concentrate your military presence in low-orbit, near the nest. Of course we were hoping the offensive would come later than it did . . . but we reckoned without Warren's conspiracy.'

'Then you are planning something.'

'Yes.' The next bullet slammed into the wall, ozone crackling from its linear induction rails. Now only two remained. 'We can talk later. There isn't much time now.' She projected an image into his visual field: the Wall, now veined by titanic fractures down half its length. 'It's collapsing.'

'And Felka?'

'She's still trying to save it.'

He looked at the Conjoiners boarding the leading bullet; tried to imagine where they were going. Was it to any kind of sanctuary he might recognise – or to something so beyond his experience that it might as well be death? Did he have the nerve to find out? Perhaps. He had nothing to lose now, after all: he could certainly not return home. But if he was going to follow Galiana's exodus, it could not be with the sense of shame he now felt in abandoning Felka.

The answer, when it came, was simple. 'I'm going back for her. If you can't wait for me, don't. But don't try and stop me doing this.'

Galiana looked at him, shaking her head slowly. 'She won't thank you for saving her life, Clavain.'

'Maybe not now,' he said.

He had the feeling he was running back into a burning building. Given what Galiana had said about the girl's deficiencies – that by any reasonable definition she was hardly more than an automaton – what he was doing was very likely pointless, if not suicidal. But if he turned his back on her, he would become something even less than human himself. He had misread Galiana badly when she said the girl was precious to them. He had assumed some bond of affection . . . whereas what Galiana meant was that the girl was precious in the sense of a vital component. Now – with the nest being abandoned – the component had no further use. Did that make Galiana as cold as a machine herself – or was she just being unfailingly realistic? He found the nursery after only one or two false turns, and then Felka's room. The implants Galiana had given him were again throwing phantom images into the air. Felka sat within the crumbling circle of the Wall. Great fissures now reached to the surface of Mars. Shards of the Wall, as big as icebergs, had fractured away and now lay like vast sheets of broken glass across the regolith.

She was losing, and now she knew it. This was not just some more difficult phase of the game. This was something she could never win, and her realisation was now plainly evident in her face. She was still moving her arms frantically, but her face was red now, locked into a petulant scowl of anger and fear.

For the first time, she seemed to notice him.

Something had broken through her shell, Clavain thought. For the first time in years, something was happening that was beyond her control; something that threatened to destroy the neat, geometric universe she had made for herself. She might not have distinguished his face from all the other people who came to see her, but she surely recognised something . . . that now the adult world was bigger than she was, and it was only from the adult world that any kind of salvation could come.

Then she did something that shocked him beyond words. She looked deep into his eyes and reached out a hand.

But there was nothing he could do to help her.

Later – it seemed hours, but in fact could only have been tens of minutes – Clavain found that he was able to breathe normally again. They had escaped Mars now; Galiana, Felka and himself, riding the last bullet.

And they were still alive.

The bullet's vacuum-filled tunnel cut deep into Mars; a shallow arc bending under the crust before rising again, thousands of kilometres away, well beyond the Wall, where the atmosphere was as thin as ever. For the Conjoiners, boring the tunnel had not been especially difficult. Such engineering would have been impossible on a planet that had plate tectonics, but beneath its lithosphere Mars was geologically quiet. They had not even had to worry about tailings. What they excavated, they compressed and fused and used to line the tunnel, maintaining rigidity against awesome pressure with some trick of piezo-electricity. In the tunnel, the bullet accelerated continuously at three gees for ten minutes. Their seats had tilted back and wrapped around them, applying pressure to the legs to maintain bloodflow to the head. Even so, it was hard to think, let alone move, but Clavain knew that it was no worse than what the earliest space explorers had endured climbing away from Earth. And he had undergone similar tortures during the war, in combat insertions.

They were moving at ten kilometres a second when they reached the surface again, exiting via a camouflaged trapdoor. For a moment the atmosphere snatched at them . . . but almost as soon as Clavain had registered the deceleration, it was over. The surface of Mars was dropping below them very quickly indeed.

In half a minute, they were in true space.

'The Interdiction's sensor web can't track us,' Galiana said. 'You placed your best spy-sats directly over the nest. That was a mistake, Clavain – even though we did our best to reinforce your thinking with the shuttle launches. But now we're well outside your sensor footprint.'

Clavain nodded. 'But that won't help us once we're far from the surface. Then, we'll just look like another ship trying to reach deep space. The web may be late locking onto us, but it'll still get us in the end.'

'It would,' Galiana said. 'If deep space was where we were going.'

Felka stirred next to him. She had withdrawn into some kind of catatonia. Separation from the Wall had undermined her entire existence; now she was free-falling through an abyss of meaninglessness. Perhaps, Clavain, thought, she would fall forever. If that was the case, he had only brought forward her fate. Was that much of a cruelty? Perhaps he was deluding himself, but with time, was it out of the question that Galiana's machines could undo the harm they had inflicted ten years earlier? Surely they could try. It depended, of course, on where exactly they were headed. One of the system's other Conjoiner nests had been Clavain's initial guess – even though it seemed unlikely that they would ever survive the crossing. At ten klicks per second it would take years . . .

'Where are you taking us?' he asked.

Galiana issued some neural command which made the bullet seem to become transparent.

'There,' she said.

Something lay distantly ahead. Galiana made the forward view zoom in, until the object was much clearer.

Dark – misshapen. Like Deimos without fortifications.

'Phobos,' Clavain said, wonderingly. 'We're going to Phobos.'

'Yes,' Galiana said.

'But the worms—'

'Don't exist anymore.' She spoke with the same tutorly patience with which Remontoire had addressed him on the same subject not long before. 'Your attempt to oust the worms failed. You assumed our subsequent attempt failed . . . but that was only what we wanted you to think.'

For a moment he was lost for words. 'You've had people in Phobos all along?'

'Ever since the ceasefire, yes. They've been quite busy, too.'

Phobos altered. Layers of it were peeled away, revealing the glittering device which lay hidden in its heart, poised and ready for flight. Clavain had never seen anything like it, but the nature of the thing was instantly obvious. He was looking at something wonderful; something which had never existed before in the whole of human experience.

He was looking at a starship.

'We'll be leaving soon,' Galiana said. 'They'll try and stop us, of course. But now that their forces are concentrated near the surface, they won't succeed. We'll leave Phobos and Mars behind, and send messages to the other nests. If they can break out and meet us, we'll take them as well. We'll leave this whole system behind.'

'Where are you going?'

'Shouldn't that be where are we going? You're coming with us, after all.' She paused. 'There are a number of candidate systems. Our choice will depend on the trajectory the Coalition forces upon us.'

'What about the Demarchists?'

'They won't stop us.' It was said with total assurance – implying, what? That the Demarchy knew of this ship? Perhaps. It had long been rumoured that the Demarchists and the Conjoiners were closer than they admitted.

Clavain thought of something. 'What about the worms' altering the orbit?'

'That was our doing,' Galiana said. 'We couldn't help it. Every time we send up one of these canisters, we nudge Phobos into a different orbit. Even after we sent up a thousand canisters, the effect was tiny – we changed Phobos's velocity by less than one tenth of a millimetre per second – but there was no way to hide it.' Then she paused and looked at Clavain with something like apprehension. 'We'll be arriving in two hundred seconds. Do you want to live?'

'I'm sorry?'

'Think about it. The tube in Mars was a thousand kilometres long, which allowed us to spread the acceleration over ten minutes. Even then it was three gees. But there simply isn't room for anything like that in Phobos. We'll be slowing down much more abruptly.'

Clavain felt the hairs on the back of his neck prickle. 'How much more abruptly?'

'Complete deceleration in one fifth of a second.' She let that sink home. 'That's around five thousand gees.'

'I can't survive that.'

'No; you can't. Not now, anyway. But there are machines in your head now. If you allow it, there's time for them to establish a structural web across your brain. We'll flood the cabin with foam. We'll all die temporarily, but there won't be anything they can't fix in Phobos.'

'It won't just be a structural web, will it? I'll be like you, then. There won't be any difference between us.'

'You'll become Conjoined, yes.' Galiana offered the faintest of smiles. 'The procedure is reversible. It's just that no one's ever wanted to go back.'

'And you still tell me none of this was planned?'

'No; but I don't expect you to believe me. For what it's worth, though . . . you're a good man, Nevil. The Transenlightenment could use you. Maybe at the back of my mind . . . at the back of our mind . . .'

'You always hoped it might come to this?'

Galiana smiled.

He looked at Phobos. Even without Galiana's magnification, it was clearly bigger. They would be arriving very shortly. He would have liked longer to think about it, but the one thing not on his side now was time. Then he looked at Felka, and wondered which of them was about to embark on the stranger journey. Felka's search for meaning in a universe without her beloved Wall, or his passage into Transenlightenment? Neither would necessarily be easy. But together, perhaps, they might even find a way to help each other. That was all he could hope for now.

Clavain nodded assent, ready for the loom of machines to embrace his mind.

He was ready to defect.

GLACIAL

Nevil Clavain picked his way across a mosaic of shattered ice. The field stretched away in all directions, gouged by sleek-sided crevasses. They had mapped the largest cracks before landing, but he was still wary of surprises; his breath caught every time his booted foot cracked through a layer of ice. He was aware of how dangerous it would be to wander from the red path his implants were painting across the glacier field.

He only had to remind himself of what had happened to Martin Setterholm.

They had found his body a month ago, shortly after their arrival on the planet. It had been near the main American base; a stroll from the perimetre of the huge, deserted complex of stilted domes and ice-walled caverns. Clavain's friends had found dozens of dead within the buildings, and most of them had been easily identified against the lists of base personnel that the expedition had pieced together. But Clavain had been troubled by the gaps, and had wondered if any further dead might be found in the surrounding ice fields. He had explored the warrens of the base until he found an airlock that had never been closed, and though snowfalls had long since obliterated any footprints, there was little doubt in which direction a wanderer would have set off.

Long before the base had vanished over the horizon behind him, Clavain had run into the edge of a deep, wide crevasse. And there at the bottom – just visible if he leaned over the edge – was a man's outstretched arm and hand. Clavain had gone back to the others and had them return with a winch to lower him into the depths, descending thirty or forty metres into a cathedral of stained and sculpted ice. The body had come into view: a figure in an old-fashioned atmospheric survival suit. The man's legs were bent in a horrible way, like those of a strangely articulated alien. Clavain knew it was a man because the fall had jolted his helmet from its neck-ring; the corpse's well-preserved face was pressed halfway into a pillow of ice. The helmet had ended up a few metres away.

No one died instantly on Diadem. The air was breathable for short periods, and the man had clearly had time to ponder his predicament. Even in his confused state of mind he must have known that he was going to die.

'Martin Setterholm,' Clavain had said aloud, picking up the helmet and reading the nameplate on the crown. He felt sorry for him, but could not deny himself the small satisfaction of accounting for another of the dead. Setterholm had been amongst the missing, and though he had waited the better part of a century for it, he would at least receive a proper funeral now.

There was something else, but Clavain very nearly missed it. Setterholm had lived long enough to scratch out a message in the ice. Sheltered at the base of the glacier, the marks he had gouged were still legible. Three letters, it seemed to Clavain: an 'I', a 'V' and an 'F'.

IVF.

The message meant nothing to Clavain, and even a deep search of the Conjoiner collective memory threw up only a handful of vaguely plausible candidates. The least ridiculous was '*in vitro* fertilisation', but even that seemed to have no immediate connection with Setterholm. But then again, he had been a biologist, according to the base records. Did the message spell out the chilling truth about what had happened to the colony on Diadem: a biology lab experiment that had gone terribly wrong? Something to do with the worms, perhaps?

But after a while, overwhelmed by the sheer number of dead, Clavain had allowed the exact details of Setterholm's death to slip from his mind. He was hardly unique anyway, just one more example of the way most of them had died: not by suicide or violence but through carelessness, recklessness or just plain stupidity. Basic safety procedures – like not wandering into a crevasse zone without the right equipment – had been forgotten or ignored. Machines had been used improperly. Drugs had been administered incorrectly. Sometimes the victim had taken only themselves to the grave, but in other cases the death toll had been much higher. And it had all happened swiftly.

Galiana talked about it as if it was some kind of psychosis, while the other Conjoiners speculated about an emergent neural condition, buried in the gene pool of the entire colony, lurking for years until it was activated by an environmental trigger.

Clavain, while not discounting his friends' theories, could not help but think of the worms. They were everywhere, after all, and the Americans had certainly been interested in them – Setterholm especially. Clavain himself had pressed his faceplate against the ice and observed that the worms reached down to the depth where the man had died. Their fine burrowing trails scratched into the vertical ice walls like the branchings of a river delta, with dark nodes of breeding tangles at the intersections of the larger tunnels. The tiny black worms had infested the glacier completely, and this would only be one distinct colony out of the millions that existed throughout Diadem's frozen regions. The worm biomass in this single colony must have been several dozen tonnes at the very least. Had the Americans' studies of the worms unleashed something that shattered the mind, turning them all into stumbling fools?

He sensed Galiana's quiet presence at the back of his thoughts, where she had not been a moment earlier.

'Nevil,' she said. 'We're ready to leave again.'

'You're done with the ruin already?'

'It isn't very interesting – just a few equipment shacks. There are still some remains to the north we have to look over, and it'd be good to get there before nightfall.'

'But I've only been gone half an hour or—'

'Two hours, Nevil.'

He checked his wrist display disbelievingly, but Galiana was right: he had been out alone on the glacier for all that time. Time away from the others always seemed to fly by, like sleep to an exhausted man. Perhaps the analogy was accurate, at that: sleep was when the mammalian brain took a rest from the business of processing the external universe, allowing the accumulated experience of the day to filter down into long-term memory; collating useful memories and discarding what did not need to be remembered. And for Clavain – who still needed normal sleep – these periods away from the others were when his mind took a rest from the business of engaging in frantic neural communion with the other Conjoiners. He could almost feel his neurons breathing a vast collective groan of relief, now that all they had to do was process the thoughts of a single mind.

Two hours was nowhere near enough.

'I'll be back shortly,' Clavain said. 'I just want to pick up some more worm samples, then I'll be on my way.'

'You've picked up hundreds of the damned things already, Nevil, and they're all the same, give or take a few trivial differences.'

'I know. But it can't hurt to indulge an old man's irrational fancies, can it?'

As if to justify himself, he knelt down and began scooping surface ice into a small sample container. The leech-like worms riddled the ice so thoroughly that he was bound to have picked up a few individuals in this sample, even though he would not know for sure until he got back to the shuttle's lab. If he was lucky, the sample might even hold a breeding tangle: a knot of several dozen worms engaged in a slow, complicated orgy of cannibalism and sex. There, he would complete the same comprehensive scans he had run on all the other worms he had picked up, trying to guess just why the Americans had devoted so much effort to studying them. And doubtless he would get exactly the same results he had found previously. The worms never changed; there was no astonishing mutation buried in every hundredth or even thousandth specimen; no stunning biochemical trickery going on inside them. They secreted a few simple enzymes and they ate pollen grains and ice-bound algae and they wriggled their way through cracks in the ice, and when they met other worms they obeyed the brainless rules of life, death and procreation.

That was all they did.

Galiana, in other words, was right: the worms had simply become an excuse for him to spend time away from the rest of the Conjoiners.

At the beginning of the expedition, a month ago, it had been much easier to justify these excursions. Even some of the true Conjoined had been drawn by a primal human urge to walk out into the wilderness, surrounding themselves with kilometres of beautifully tinted, elegantly fractured, unthinking ice. It was good to be somewhere quiet and pristine after the war-torn solar system they had left behind.

Diadem was an Earth-like planet orbiting the star Ross 248. It had oceans, ice caps, plate tectonics and signs of reasonably advanced multi-cellular life. Plants had already invaded Diadem's land, and some animals – the equivalents of arthropods, molluscs and worms – had begun to follow in their wake. The largest land-based animals were still small by terrestrial standards, since nothing in the oceans had yet evolved an internal skeleton. There was nothing that showed any signs of intelligence, but that was only a minor disappointment. It would still take a lifetime's study just to explore the fantastic array of body-plans, metabolisms and survival strategies Diadem life had blindly evolved.

Yet even before Galiana had sent down the first survey shuttles, a shattering truth had become apparent.

Someone had reached Diadem before them.

The signs were unmistakable: glints of refined metal on the surface, picked out by radar. Upon inspection from orbit they turned out to be ruined structures and equipment, obviously of human origin.

'It's not possible,' Clavain had said. 'We're the first. We have to be the first. No one else has ever built anything like the *Sandra Voi*; nothing capable of travelling this far.'

'Somewhere in there,' Galiana had answered, 'I think there might be a mistaken assumption, don't you?'

Meekly, Clavain had nodded.

Now – later still than he had promised – Clavain made his way back to the waiting shuttle. The red carpet of safety led straight to the access ramp beneath the craft's belly. He climbed up and stepped through the transparent membrane that spanned the entrance door, most of his suit slithering away on contact with the membrane. By the time he was inside the ship he wore only a lightweight breather mask and a few communications devices. He could have survived outside naked for many minutes – Diadem's atmosphere now had enough oxygen to support humans – but Galiana refused to allow any intermingling of micro-organisms.

He returned the equipment to a storage locker, placed the worm sample in a refrigeration rack and clothed himself in a paper-thin black tunic and trousers, before moving into the aft compartment where Galiana was waiting.

She and Felka were sitting facing each other across the blank-walled, austerely furnished room. They were staring into the space between them without quite meeting each other's eyes. They looked like a mother and daughter locked in argumentative stalemate, but Clavain knew better.

He issued the mental command, well-rehearsed now, that opened his mind to communion with the others. It was like opening a tiny aperture in the side of a dam: he was never adequately prepared for the force with which the flow of data hit him. The room changed: colour bleeding out of the walls, lacing itself into abstract structures that permeated the room's volume. Galiana and Felka, dressed dourly a moment earlier, were now veiled in light, and appeared superhumanly beautiful. He could feel their thoughts, as if he were overhearing a heated conversation in the room next door. Most of it was non-verbal; Galiana and Felka were playing an intense, abstract game. The thing floating between them was a solid lattice of light, resembling the plumbing diagram of an insanely complex refinery. It was constantly adjusting itself, with coloured flows racing this way and that as the geometry changed. About half the volume was green, the remainder lilac, but suddenly the former encroached dramatically on the latter.

Felka laughed; she was winning.

Galiana conceded and crashed back into her seat with a sigh of exhaustion, but she was smiling as well.

'Sorry. I appear to have distracted you,' Clavain said.

'No; you just hastened the inevitable. I'm afraid Felka was always going to win.'

The girl smiled again, still saying nothing, though Clavain sensed her victory; a hard-edged thing, which for a moment outshone all other thoughts from her direction, eclipsing even Galiana's air of weary resignation.

Felka had been a failed Conjoiner experiment in the manipulation of foetal brain development; a child with a mind more machine than human. When he had first met her – in Galiana's nest on Mars – he had encountered a girl absorbed in a profound, endless game: directing the faltering self-repair processes of the terraforming structure known as the Great Wall of Mars, in which the nest sheltered. She had no interest in people – indeed, she could not even discriminate between faces. But when the nest was being evacuated, Clavain had risked his life to save hers, even though Galiana had told him that the kindest thing would be to let her die. As Clavain had struggled to adjust to life as part of Galiana's commune, he had set himself the task of helping Felka to develop her latent humanity. She had begun to show signs of recognition in his presence, perhaps sensing on some level that they had a kinship; that they were both strangers stumbling towards a mysterious new light.

Galiana rose from her chair, carpets of light wrapping around her. 'It was time to end the game, anyway. We've got work to do.' She looked down at the girl, who was still staring at the lattice. 'Sorry, Felka. Later, maybe.'

Clavain said, 'How's she doing?'

'She's laughing, Nevil. That has to be progress, doesn't it?'

'I'd say that depends what she's laughing about.'

'She beat me. She thought it was funny. I'd say that was a fairly human reaction, wouldn't you?'

'I'd still be happier if I could convince myself she recognised my face, and not my smell, or the sound my footfalls make.'

'You're the only one of us with a beard, Nevil. It doesn't take vast amounts of neural processing to spot *that*.'

Clavain scratched his chin self-consciously as they stepped through into the shuttle's flight deck. He liked his beard, even though it was trimmed to little more than grey stubble so that he could slip a breather mask on without difficulty. It was as much a link to his past as his memories, or the wrinkles Galiana had studiously built into his remodelled body.

'You're right, of course. Sometimes I just have to remind myself how far we've come.'

Galiana smiled – she was getting better at that, though there was still something a little forced about it – and pushed her long, grey-veined black hair behind her ears. 'I tell myself the same things when I think about you, Nevil.'

'Mm. But I have come some way, haven't I?'

'Yes, but that doesn't mean you haven't got a considerable distance ahead of you. I could have put that thought into your head in a microsecond, if you allowed me to do so – but you still insist that we communicate by making noises in our throats, the way monkeys do.'

'Well, it's good practice for you,' Clavain said, hoping that his irritation was not too obvious.

They settled into adjacent seats while avionics displays slithered into take-off configuration. Clavain's implants allowed him to fly the machine without any manual inputs at all, but – old soldier that he was – he generally preferred tactile controls. So his implants obliged, hallucinating a joystick inset with buttons and levers, and when he reached out to grasp it, his hands appeared to close around something solid. He shuddered to think how thoroughly his perceptions of the real world were being doctored to support this illusion; but once he had been flying for a few minutes he generally forgot about it, lost in the joy of piloting.

He got them airborne, then settled the shuttle into level flight towards the fifth ruin they would be visiting that day. Kilometres of ice slid beneath them, only occasionally broken by a protruding ridge or a patch of dry, boulder-strewn ground.

'Just a few shacks, you said?'

Galiana nodded. 'A waste of time, but we had to check it out.'

'Any closer to understanding what happened to them?'

'They died, more or less overnight. Mostly through incidents related to the breakdown of normal thought – although one or two may simply have died, as if they had some greater susceptibility to a toxin than the others.'

Clavain smiled, feeling that a small victory was his. 'Now you're looking at a toxin, rather than a psychosis?'

'A toxin's difficult to explain, Nevil.'

'From Martin Setterholm's worms, perhaps?'

'Not very likely. Their biohazard containment measures weren't as good as ours – but they were still adequate. We've analysed those worms and we know they don't carry anything obviously hostile to us. And even if there was a neurotoxin, how would it affect everyone so quickly? Even if the lab workers had caught something, they'd have fallen ill before anyone else did, sending a warning to the others – but nothing like that happened.' She paused, anticipating Clavain's next question. 'And no, I don't think that what happened to them is necessarily something we need worry about, though that doesn't mean I'm going to rule anything out. But even our oldest technology's a century ahead of the best they had – and we have the *Sandra Voi* to retreat to if we run into anything the medichines in our heads can't handle.'

Clavain always did his best not to think too much about the swarms of subcellular machines lacing his brain – supplanting much of it, in fact – but there were times when it was unavoidable. He still had a squeamish reaction to the idea, though it was becoming milder. Now, though, he could not help but view the machines as his allies; as intimately a part of him as his immune system. Galiana was right: they would resist anything that tried to interfere with what now passed as the 'normal' functioning of his mind.

'Still,' he said, not yet willing to drop his pet theory, 'you've got to admit something: the Americans – Setterholm especially – were interested in the worms. Too interested, if you ask me.'

'Look who's talking.'

'Ah, but my interest is strictly forensic. And I can't help but put the two things together. They were interested in the worms. And they went mad.'

This was an oversimplification, of course: it was clear enough that the worms had preoccupied only some of the Americans: those who were most interested in xenobiology. According to the evidence the Conjoiners had so far gathered, the effort had been largely spearheaded by Setterholm, the man Clavain had found dead at the bottom of the crevasse. Setterholm had travelled widely across Diadem's snowy wastes, gathering a handful of allies to assist in his work. He had found worms in dozens of ice fields, grouped into vast colonies. For the most part, the other members of the expedition had let him get on with his activities, even as they struggled with the day-to-day business of staying alive in what was still a hostile, alien environment.

Even before they had all died, things had been far from easy. The self-replicating robots that had brought them there in the first place had failed years before, leaving the delicate life-support systems of their shelters to slowly collapse; each malfunction a little more difficult to rectify than the last. Diadem was getting colder, too – sliding inexorably into a deep ice age. It had been the Americans' misfortune to arrive at the onset of a great, centuries-long winter. Now, Clavain thought, it was colder still; the polar ice caps rushing towards each other like long-separated lovers.

'It must have been fast, whatever it was,' Clavain mused. 'They'd already abandoned most of the outlying bases by then, huddling together back at the main settlement. By that point they only had enough spare parts and technical know-how to run a single fusion power plant.'

'Which failed.'

'Yes – but that doesn't mean much. It couldn't run itself, not by then – it needed constant tinkering. Eventually the people with the right know-how must have succumbed to the . . . whatever it was – and then the reactor stopped working and they all died of the cold. But they were in trouble long before the reactor failed.'

Galiana seemed on the point of saying something. Clavain could always tell when she was about to speak: it was as if some leakage from her thoughts reached his brain even as she composed what she would say.

'Well?' he said, when the silence had stretched long enough.

'I was just thinking,' she said. 'A reactor of that type – it doesn't need any exotic isotopes, does it? No tritium, or deuterium?'

'No. Just plain old hydrogen. You could get all you needed from sea water.'

'Or ice,' Galiana said.

They vectored in for the next landing site. Toadstools, Clavain thought: half a dozen black metal towers of varying height surmounted by domed black habitat modules, interlinked by a web of elevated, pressurised walkways. Each of the domes was thirty or forty metres wide, perched a hundred or more metres above the ice, festooned with narrow, armoured windows, sensors and communications antennas. A tongue-like extension from one of the tallest domes was clearly a landing pad. In fact, as he came closer, he saw that there was an aircraft parked on it: one of the blunt-winged machines that the Americans had used to get around in. It was dusted with ice, but it would probably still fly with a little persuasion.

He inched the shuttle down, one of its skids coming to rest only just inside the edge of the pad. Clearly the landing pad had only really been intended for one aircraft at a time.

'Nevil . . .' Galiana said. 'I'm not sure I like this.'

He felt tension leaking into his head, but could not be sure if it was his own or Galiana's.

'What don't you like?'

'There shouldn't be an aircraft here,' Galiana said.

'Why not?'

She spoke softly, reminding him that the evacuation of the outlying settlements had been orderly, compared to the subsequent crisis. 'This base should have been shut down and mothballed with all the others.'

'Then maybe someone stayed behind here,' Clavain suggested.

Galiana nodded. 'Or someone came back.'

There was a third presence with them now; another hue of thought bleeding into his mind. Felka had come into the cockpit. He could taste her apprehension.

'You sense it, too,' he said wonderingly, looking into the face of the terribly damaged girl. 'Our discomfort. And you don't like it any more than we do, do you?'

Galiana took the girl's hand. 'It's all right, Felka.'

She must have spoken aloud just for Clavain's benefit. Before her mouth had even opened Galiana would have planted reassuring thoughts in Felka's mind, attempting to still the disquiet with the subtlest of neural adjustments. Clavain thought of an expert ikebana artist minutely altering the placement of a single flower in the interests of harmony.

'Everything will be okay,' Clavain said. 'There's nothing here that can harm you.'

Galiana took a moment, blank-eyed, to commune with the other Conjoiners in and around Diadem. Most of them were still in orbit, observing things from the ship. She told them about the aircraft and notified them that she and Clavain were going to enter the structure.

He saw Felka's hand tighten around Galiana's wrist.

'She wants to come as well,' Galiana said.

'She'll be safer if she stays here.'

'She doesn't want to be alone.'

Clavain chose his words carefully. 'I thought Conjoiners – I mean we – could never be truly alone, Galiana.'

'There might be a communicational block inside the structure. It'll be better if she stays physically close to us.'

'Is that the only reason?'

'No, of course not.' For a moment he felt a sting of her anger, prickling his mind like sea-spray. 'She's still human, Nevil – no matter what we've done to her mind. We can't erase a million years of evolution. She may not be very good at recognising faces, but she recognises the need for companionship.'

He raised his hands. 'I never doubted it.'

'Then why are you arguing?'

Clavain smiled. He'd had this conversation so many times before, with so many women. He had been married to some of them. It was oddly comforting to be having it again, light-years from home, wearing a new body, his mind clotted with machines and confronting the matriarch of what should have been a feared and hated hive-mind. At the epicentre of so much strangeness, a tiff was almost to be welcomed.

'I just don't want anything to hurt her.'

'Oh. And I do?'

'Never mind,' he said, gritting his teeth. 'Let's just get in and out, shall we?'

The base, like all the American structures, had been built for posterity. Not by people, however, but by swarms of diligent self-replicating robots. That was how the Americans had reached Diadem: they had been brought there as frozen fertilised cells in the armoured, radiation-proofed bellies of star-crossing von Neumann robots. The robots had been launched towards several solar systems about a century before the *Sandra Voi* had left Mars. Upon arrival on Diadem they had set about breeding, making copies of themselves from local ores. When their numbers had reached some threshold, they had turned over their energies to the construction of bases: luxurious accommodation for the human children who would then be grown in their wombs.

'The entrance door's intact,' Galiana said when they had crossed from the shuttle to the smooth black side of the dome, stooping against the wind. 'And there's still some residual power in its circuits.'

That was a Conjoiner trick that always faintly unnerved Clavain. Like sharks, Conjoiners were sensitive to ambient electrical fields. Mapped into her vision, Galiana would see the energised circuits superimposed on the door like a ghostly neon maze. Now she extended her hand towards the lock, palm first.

'I'm accessing the opening mechanism. Interfacing with it now.' Behind her mask, he saw her face scrunch in concentration. Galiana only ever frowned when having to think hard. With her hand outstretched she looked like a wizard attempting some particularly demanding enchantment.

'Hmm,' she said. 'Nice old software protocols. Nothing too difficult.'

'Careful,' Clavain said. 'I wouldn't put it past them to have installed some kind of trap here—'

'There's no trap,' she said. 'But there is – ah, yes – a verbal entry code. Well, here goes.' She spoke louder, so that her voice would travel through the air to the door even above the howl of the wind. 'Open sesame.'

Lights flicked from red to green; dislodging a frosting of ice, the door slid ponderously aside to reveal a dimly lit interior chamber. The base must have been running on a trickle of emergency power for decades.

Felka and Clavain lingered while Galiana crossed the threshold.

'Well?' she challenged, turning around. 'Are you two sissies coming or not?'

Felka offered a hand. He took hers and the two of them – the old soldier and the girl who could barely grasp the difference between two human faces – took a series of tentative steps inside.

'What you just did, that business with your hand and the password . . .' Clavain paused. 'That *was* a joke, wasn't it?'

Galiana looked at him, blank-faced. 'How could it have been? Everyone knows Conjoiners haven't got anything remotely resembling a sense of humour.'

Clavain nodded gravely. 'That was my understanding, but I just wanted to be sure.'

There was no trace of the wind inside, but it would still have been too cold to remove their suits, even had they not been concerned about contamination. They worked their way along a series of winding corridors, some of which were dark, others bathed in feeble, pea-green lighting. Now and then they passed the entrance to a room full of equipment, but nothing that looked like a laboratory or living quarters. Then they descended a series of stairs and found themselves crossing one of the sealed walkways between the toadstools. Clavain had seen a few other American settlements built like this one; they were designed to remain useful even as they sank slowly into the ice.

The bridge led to what was obviously the main habitation section. Now there were lounges, bedrooms, laboratories and kitchens – enough for a crew of perhaps fifty or sixty. But there were no signs of any bodies, and the place did not look as if it had been abandoned in a hurry. The equipment was neatly packed away and there were no half-eaten meals on the tables. There was frost everywhere, but that was just the moisture that had frozen out of the air when the base cooled down.

'They were expecting to come back,' Galiana said.

Clavain nodded. 'They couldn't have had much of an idea of what lay ahead of them.'

They moved on, crossing another bridge, until they arrived in a toadstool almost entirely dedicated to bio-analysis laboratories. Galiana had to use her neural trick again to get them inside, the machines in her head sweet-talking the duller machines entombed in the doors. The low-ceilinged labs were bathed in green light, but Galiana found a wall panel that brought the lighting up a notch and even caused some bench equipment to wake up, pulsing with stand-by lights.

Clavain looked around, recognising centrifuges, gene-sequencers, gas chromatographs and scanning-tunnelling microscopes. There were at least a dozen other hunks of gleaming machinery whose function eluded him. A wall-sized cabinet held dozens of pull-out drawers, each of which contained hundreds of culture dishes, test tubes and gel slides. Clavain glanced at the samples, reading the tiny labels. There were bacteria and single-cell cultures with unpronounceable codenames, most of which were marked with Diadem map co-ordinates and a date. But there were also drawers full of samples with Latin names, comparison samples which must have come from Earth. The robots could easily have carried the tiny parent organisms from which these larger samples had been grown or cloned. Perhaps the Americans had been experimenting with the hardiness of Earth-born organisms, with a view to terraforming Diadem at some point in the future.

He closed the drawer silently and moved to a set of larger sample tubes racked on a desk. He picked one from the rack and raised it to the light, examining the smoky things inside. It was a sample of worms, indistinguishable from those he had collected on the glacier a few hours earlier. A breeding tangle, probably harvested from the intersection point of two worm tunnels. Some of the worms in the tangle would be exchanging genes; others would be fighting; others would be allowing themselves to be digested by adults or newly hatched young; all behaving according to rigidly deterministic laws of caste and sex. The tangle looked dead, but that meant nothing with the worms. Their metabolism was fantastically slow, each individual easily capable of living for thousands of years. It would take them months just to crawl along some of the longer cracks in the ice, let alone move between some of the larger tangles.

But the worms were not really all that alien. They had a close terrestrial analogue: the sun-avoiding ice-worms that had first been discovered in the Malaspina Glacier in Alaska towards the end of the nineteenth century. The Alaskan ice-worms were a lot smaller than their Diadem counterparts, but they also nourished themselves on the slim pickings that drifted onto the ice, or had been frozen into it years earlier. Like the Diadem worms, their most notable anatomical feature was a pore at the head end, just above the mouth. In the case of the terrestrial worms, the pore served a single function: secreting a salty solution that helped the worms melt their way into ice when there was no tunnel already present – an escape strategy that helped them get beneath the ice before the sun dried them up. The Diadem worms had a similar structure, but according to Setterholm's notes they had evolved a second use for it: secreting a chemically rich 'scent trail' which helped other worms navigate through the tunnel system. The chemistry of that scent trail turned out to be very complex, with each worm capable of secreting not merely a unique signature but a variety of flavours. Conceivably, more complex message schemes were embedded in some of the other flavours: not just 'follow me' but 'follow me only if you are female' – the Diadem worms had at least three sexes – 'and this is breeding season'. There were many other possibilities, which Setterholm seemed to have been attempting to decode and catalogue when the end had come.

It was interesting . . . up to a point. But even if the worms followed a complex set of rules dependent on the scent trails they were picking up, and perhaps other environmental cues, it would still only be rigidly mechanistic behaviour.

'Nevil, come here.'

It was Galiana's voice, but it had a tone he had barely heard before. It was one that made him run to where Felka and Galiana were waiting on the other side of the lab.

They were facing an array of lockers occupying an entire wall. A small status panel was set into each locker, but only one locker – placed at chest height – showed any activity. Clavain looked back towards the door through which they had entered, but from there it was hidden by intervening lab equipment. They would not have seen this locker even if it had been illuminated before Galiana brought the room's power back on.

'It might have been on all along,' he said.

'I know,' Galiana agreed.

She reached a hand up to the panel, tapping the control keys with unnerving fluency. Machines to Galiana were like musical instruments to a prodigy. She could pick one up cold and play it like an old friend.

The array of status lights changed configuration abruptly, then there was a bustle of activity somewhere behind the locker's metal face – latches and servomotors clicking after decades of stasis.

'Stand back,' Galiana said.

A rime of frost shattered into a billion sugary pieces. The locker began to slide out of the wall, the unhurried motion giving them adequate time to digest what lay inside. Clavain felt Felka grip his hand, and then noticed that her other hand was curled tightly around Galiana's wrist. For the first time, he began to wonder if it had really been such a good idea to allow the girl to join them.

The locker was two metres in length and half that in width and height; just sufficient to contain a human body. It had probably been designed to hold animal specimens culled from

Diadem's oceans, but it was equally capable of functioning as a mortuary tray. That the man inside the locker was dead was beyond question, but there was no sign of injury. His composure – flat on his back, his blue-grey face serenely blank, his eyes closed and his hands clasped neatly just below his ribcage – suggested to Clavain a saint lying in grace. His beard was neatly pointed and his hair long, frozen into a solid sculptural mass. He was still wearing several heavy layers of thermal clothing.

Clavain knelt closer and read the name-tag above the man's heart.

'Andrew Iverson. Ring a bell?'

A moment passed while Galiana established a link to the rest of the Conjoiners, ferreting the name out of some database. 'Yes. One of the missing. Seems he was a climatologist with an interest in terraforming techniques.'

Clavain nodded shrewdly. 'That figures, with all the micro-organisms I've seen in this place. Well: the trillion-dollar question – how do you think he got in there?'

'I think he climbed in,' Galiana said, and nodded at something Clavain had missed, almost tucked away beneath the man's shoulder. Clavain reached into the gap, his fingers brushing against the rock-hard fabric of Iverson's outfit. A cannula vanished into the man's forearm, where he had cut away a square of fabric. The cannula's black feed-line reached back into the cabinet, vanishing into a socket at the rear.

'You're saying he killed himself?' Clavain asked.

'He must have put something in that which would stop his heart. Then he probably flushed out his blood and replaced it with glycerol, or something similar, to prevent ice crystals forming in his cells. It would have taken some automation to make it work, but I'm sure everything he needed was here.'

Clavain thought back to what he knew about the cryonic immersion techniques that had been around a century or so earlier. They left something to be desired now, but back then they had not been much of an advance over mummification.

'When he sank that cannula into himself, he can't have been certain we'd ever find him,' Clavain remarked.

'Which would still have been preferable to suicide.'

'Yes, but . . . the thoughts that must have gone through his head. Knowing he had to kill himself first, to stand a chance of living again – and then hope someone else stumbled on Diadem.'

'You made a harder choice than that, once.'

'Yes. But at least I wasn't alone when I made it.'

Iverson's body was astonishingly well preserved, Clavain thought. The skin tissue looked almost intact, even if it had a deathly, granite-like colour. The bones of his face had not ruptured under the strain of the temperature drop. Bacterial processes had stopped dead. All in all, things could have been a lot worse.

'We shouldn't leave him like this,' Galiana said, pushing the locker so that it began to slide back into the wall.

'I don't think he cares much about that now,' Clavain said.

'No. You don't understand. He mustn't warm – not even to the ambient temperature of the room. Otherwise we won't be able to wake him up.'

It took five days to bring him back to consciousness.

The decision to reanimate had not been taken lightly; it had only been arrived at after intense discussion amongst the Conjoined, debates in which Clavain participated to the best of his ability. Iverson, they all agreed, could probably be resurrected with current Conjoiner methods. *In situ* scans of his mind had revealed preserved synaptic structures that a scaffold of machines could coax back towards consciousness. However, since they had not yet identified the cause of the madness that had killed Iverson's colleagues – and the evidence was pointing towards some kind of infectious agent – Iverson would be kept on the surface; reborn on the same world where he had died.

They had, however, moved him: shuttling him halfway across the world back to the main base. Clavain had travelled with the corpse, marvelling at the idea that this solid chunk of man-shaped ice – tainted, admittedly, with a few vital impurities – would soon be a breathing, thinking human being with memories and feelings. To him it was astonishing that this was possible; that so much latent structure had been preserved across the decades. Even more astonishing that the infusions of tiny machines the Conjoiners were brewing would be able to stitch together damaged cells and kick-start them back to life. And out of that inert loom of frozen brain structure – a thing that was at this moment nothing more than a fixed geometric entity, like a finely eroded piece of rock – something as malleable as consciousness would emerge.

But the Conjoiners were blasé at the prospect, viewing Iverson the way expert picture-restorers might view a damaged old master. Yes, there would be difficulties ahead – work that would require great skill – but nothing to lose sleep over.

Except, Clavain reminded himself, none of them slept anyway.

While the others were working to bring Iverson back to life, Clavain wandered the outskirts of the base, trying to get a better feel for what it must have been like during the last days. The debilitating mental illness must have been terrifying as it struck even those who might have stood a chance of developing some kind of counter-agent to it. Perhaps in the old days, when the base had been under the stewardship of the von Neumann machines, something might have been done . . . but in the end it must have been like trying to crack a particularly tricky algebra problem while growing steadily more drunk; losing first the ability to focus sharply, then to focus on the problem at all, and then to remember what was so important about it anyway. The labs in the main complex had an abandoned look to them: experiments half-finished; notes scrawled on the wall in ever more incoherent handwriting.

Down in the lower levels – the transport bays and storage areas – it was almost as if nothing had happened. Equipment was still neatly racked, surface vehicles neatly parked, and – with the base sub-systems back on – the place was bathed in light and not so cold as to require extra clothing. It was quite therapeutic, too: the Conjoiners had not extended their communicational fields into these regions, so Clavain's mind was mercifully isolated again; freed of the clamour of other voices. Despite that, he was still tempted by the idea of spending some time outdoors.

With that in mind he found an airlock, one that must have been added late in the base's history as it was absent from the blue-prints. There was no membrane stretched across this one; if he stepped through it he would be outside as soon as the doors cycled, with no more protection than the clothes he was wearing now. He considered going back into the base proper to find a membrane suit, but by the time he did that, the mood – the urge to go outside – would be gone.

Clavain noticed a locker. Inside, to his delight, was a rack of old-style suits such as Setterholm had been wearing. They looked brand new, alloy neck-rings gleaming. Racked above each one was a bulbous helmet. He experimented until he found a suit that fitted him, then struggled with the various latches and seals that coupled the suit parts together. Even when he thought he had donned the suit properly, the airlock detected that one of his gloves wasn't latched correctly. It refused to let him outside until he reversed the cycle and fixed the problem.

But then he was outside, and it was glorious.

He walked around the base until he found his bearings, and then – always ensuring that the base was in view and that his air supply was adequate – he set off across the ice. Above, Diadem's sky was a deep enamelled blue, and the ice – though fundamentally white – seemed to contain a billion nuances of pale turquoise, pale aquamarine; even hints of the palest of pinks. Beneath his feet he imagined the crack-like networks of the worms, threading down for hundreds of metres; and he imagined the worms, wriggling through that network, responding to and secreting chemical scent trails. The worms themselves were biologically simple – almost dismayingly so – but that network was a vast, intricate thing. It hardly mattered that the traffic along it – the to-and-fro motions of the worms as they went about their lives – was so agonisingly slow. The worms, after all, had endured longer than human comprehension. They had seen people come and go in an eyeblink.

He walked on until he arrived at the crevasse where he had found Setterholm. They had long since removed Setterholm's body, of course, but the experience had imprinted itself deeply on Clavain's mind. He found it easy to relive the moment at the lip of the crevasse when he had first seen the end of Setterholm's arm. At the time he had told himself that there must be worse places to die; surrounded by beauty that was so pristine, so utterly untouched by human influence. Now, the more he thought about it, the more that Setterholm's death played on his mind – he wondered if there could be any worse place. It was undeniably beautiful, but it was also crushingly dead; crushingly oblivious to life. Setterholm must have felt himself draining away, soon to become as inanimate as the palace of ice that was to become his tomb.

Clavain thought about it for many more minutes, enjoying the silence and the solitude and the odd awkwardness of the suit. He thought back to the way Setterholm had been found, and his mind niggled at something not quite right; a detail that had not seemed wrong at the time but which now troubled him.

It was Setterholm's helmet.

He remembered the way it had been lying away from the man's corpse, as if the impact had knocked it off. But now that Clavain had locked an identical helmet onto his own suit, that was more difficult to believe. The latches were sturdy, and he doubted that the drop into the crevasse would have been sufficient to break the mechanism. He considered the possibility that Setterholm had put his suit on hastily, but even that seemed unlikely now. The airlock had detected that Clavain's glove was badly attached; it – or any of the other locks – would surely have refused to allow Setterholm outside if his helmet had not been correctly latched.

Clavain wondered if Setterholm's death had been something other than an accident.

He thought about it, trying the idea on for size, then slowly shook his head. There were myriad possibilities he had yet to rule out. Setterholm could have left the base with his suit intact and then – confused and disoriented – he could have fiddled with the latch, depriving himself of oxygen until he stumbled into the crevasse. Or perhaps the airlocks were not as foolproof as they appeared; the safety mechanism capable of being disabled by people in a hurry to get outside.

No. A man had died, but there was no need to assume it had been anything other than an accident. Clavain turned, and began to walk back to the base.

*

'He's awake,' Galiana said, a day or so after the final wave of machines had swum into Iverson's mind. 'I think it might be better if he spoke to you first, Nevil, don't you? Rather than one of us?' She bit her tongue. 'I mean, rather than someone who's been Conjoined for as long as the rest of us?'

Clavain shrugged. 'Then again, an attractive face might be preferable to a grizzled old relic like myself. But I take your point. Is it safe to go in now?'

'Perfectly. If Iverson was carrying anything infectious, the machines would have flagged it.'

'I hope you're right.'

'Well, look at the evidence. He was acting rationally up to the end. He did everything to ensure we'd have an excellent chance of reviving him. His suicide was just a coldly calculated attempt to escape his situation.'

'Coldly calculated,' Clavain echoed. 'Yes, I suppose it would have been. Cold, I mean.'

Galiana said nothing, but gestured towards the door into Iverson's room.

Clavain stepped through the opening. And it was as he crossed the threshold that a thought occurred to him. He could once again see, in his mind's eye, Martin Setterholm's body lying at the bottom of the crevasse, his fingers pointing to the letters 'IVF'.

In vitro fertilisation.

But suppose Setterholm had been trying to write 'IVERSON', but had died before finishing the word? If Setterholm had been murdered – pushed into the crevasse – he might have been trying to pass on a message about his murderer. Clavain imagined his pain, legs smashed; knowing with absolute certainty he was going to die alone and cold, but willing himself to write Iverson's name . . .

But why would the climatologist have wanted to kill Setterholm? Setterholm's fascination with the worms was perplexing but harmless. The information Clavain had collected pointed to Setterholm being a single-minded loner; the kind of man who would inspire pity or indifference in his colleagues rather than hatred. And everyone was dying anyway – against such a background, a murder seemed almost irrelevant.

Maybe he was attributing too much to the six faint marks a dying man had scratched on the ice.

Forcing suspicion from his mind – for now – Clavain walked further into Iverson's room. The room was spartan but serene, with a small blue holographic window set high in one white wall. Clavain was responsible for that. Left to the Conjoiners – who had taken over an area of the main American base and filled it with their own pressurised spaces – Iverson's room would have been a grim, grey cube. That was fine for the Conjoiners – they moved through informational fields draped like an extra layer over reality. But though Iverson's head was now drenched with their machines, they were only there to assist his normal patterns of thought; reinforcing weak synaptic signals and compensating for a far-from-equilibrium mix of neurotransmitters.

So Clavain had insisted on cheering the place up a bit; Iverson's sheets and pillow were now the same pure white as the walls, so that his head bobbed in a sea of whiteness. His hair had been trimmed, but Clavain had made sure that no one had done more than neaten Iverson's beard.

'Andrew?' he said. 'I'm told you're awake now. I'm Nevil Clavain. How are you feeling?'

Iverson wet his lips before answering. 'Better, I suspect, than I have any reason to feel.'

'Ah.' Clavain beamed, feeling as if a large burden had just been lifted from his shoulders. 'Then you've some recollection of what happened to you.'

'I died, didn't I? Pumped myself full of antifreeze and hoped for the best. Did it work, or is this just some weird-ass dream as I'm sliding towards brain death?'

'No, it sure as hell worked. That was one weird-heck-ass of a risk . . .' Clavain halted, not entirely certain that he could emulate Iverson's century-old speech patterns. 'That was quite some risk you took. But it did work, you'll be glad to hear.'

Iverson lifted a hand from beneath the sheets, examining his palm and the pattern of veins and tendons on the back. 'This is the same body I went under with? You haven't stuck me in a robot, or cloned me, or hooked up my disembodied brain to a virtual-reality generator?'

'None of those things, no. Just mopped up some cell damage, fixed a few things here and there and – um – kick-started you back into the land of the living.'

Iverson nodded, but Clavain could tell he was far from convinced. Which was unsurprising: Clavain, after all, had already told a small lie.

'So how long was I under?'

'About a century, Andrew. We're an expedition from back home. We came by starship.'

Iverson nodded again, as if this was mere incidental detail. 'We're aboard it now, right?'

'No . . . no. We're still on the planet. The ship's parked in orbit.'

'And everyone else?'

No point sugaring the pill. 'Dead, as far as we can make out. But you must have known that would happen.'

'Yeah. But I didn't know for sure, even at the end.'

'So what happened? How did you escape the infection, or whatever it was?'

'Sheer luck.' Iverson asked for a drink. Clavain fetched him one, and at the same time had the room extrude a chair next to the bed.

'I didn't see much sign of luck,' Clavain said.

'No; it was terrible. But I was the lucky one – that's all I meant. I don't know how much you know. We had to evacuate the outlying bases towards the end, when we couldn't keep more than one fusion reactor running.' Iverson took a sip from the glass of water Clavain had brought him. 'If we'd still had the machines to look after us—'

'Yes. That's something we never really understood.' Clavain leant closer to the bed. 'Those von Neumann machines were built to self-repair themselves, weren't they? We still don't see how they broke down.'

Iverson eyed him. 'They didn't. Break down, I mean.'

'No? Then what happened?'

'We smashed them up. Like rebellious teenagers overthrowing parental control. The machines were nannying us, and we were sick of it. In hindsight, it wasn't such a good idea.'

'Didn't the machines put up a fight?'

'Not exactly. I don't think the people who designed them ever thought they'd get trashed by the kids they'd lovingly cared for.'

So, Clavain thought – whatever had happened here, whatever he went on to learn, it was clear that the Americans had been at least partially the authors of their own misfortunes. He still felt sympathy for them, but now it was cooler, tempered with something close to disgust. He wondered if that feeling of disappointed appraisal would have come so easily without Galiana's machines in his head. *It would be just a tiny step to go from feeling that way towards Iverson's people to feeling that way about the rest of humanity . . . and then I'd know that I'd truly attained Transenlightenment . . .*

Clavain snapped out of his morbid line of thinking. It was not Transenlightenment that engendered those feelings, just ancient, bone-deep cynicism.

'Well, there's no point dwelling on what was done years ago. But how did you survive?'

'After the evacuation, we realised that we'd left something behind – a spare component for the remaining fusion reactor. So I went back for it, taking one of the planes. I landed just as a bad weather front was coming in, which kept me grounded there for two days. That was when the others began to get sick. It happened pretty quickly, and all I knew about it was what I could figure out from the comm links back to the main base.'

'Tell me what you did figure out.'

'Not much,' Iverson said. 'It was fast, and it seemed to attack the central nervous system. No one survived it. Those that didn't die of it directly went on to get themselves killed through accidents or sloppy procedure.'

'We noticed. Eventually someone died who was responsible for keeping the fusion reactor running properly. It didn't blow up, did it?'

'No. Just spewed out a lot more neutrons than normal; too much for the shielding to contain. Then it went into emergency shutdown mode. Some people were killed by the radiation, but most died of the cold that came afterwards.'

'Hm. Except you.'

Iverson nodded. 'If I hadn't had to go back for that component, I'd have been one of them. Obviously, I couldn't risk returning. Even if I could have got the reactor working again, there was still the problem of the contaminant.' He breathed in deeply, as if steeling himself to recollect what had happened next. 'So I weighed my options and decided dying – freezing myself – was my only hope. No one was going to come from Earth to help me, even if I could have kept myself alive. Not for decades, anyway. So I took a chance.'

'One that paid off.'

'Like I said, I was the lucky one.' Iverson took another sip from the glass Clavain had brought him. 'Man, that tastes better than anything I've ever drunk in my life. What's in this, by the way?'

'Just water. Glacial water. Purified, of course.'

Iverson nodded, slowly, and put the glass down next to his bed.

'Not thirsty now?'

'Quenched my thirst nicely, thank you.'

'Good.' Clavain stood up. 'I'll let you get some rest, Andrew. If there's anything you need, anything we can do – just call out.'

'I'll be sure to.'

Clavain smiled and walked to the door, observing Iverson's obvious relief that the questioning session was over for now. But Iverson had said nothing incriminating, Clavain reminded himself, and his responses were entirely consistent with the fatigue and confusion anyone would feel after so long asleep – or dead, depending on how you defined Iverson's period on ice. It was unfair to associate him with Setterholm's death just because of a few indistinct marks gouged in ice, and the faint possibility that Setterholm had been murdered.

Still, Clavain paused before leaving the room. 'One other thing, Andrew – just something that's been bothering me, and I wondered if you could help.'

'Go ahead.'

'Do the initials "I", "V" and "F" mean anything to you?'

Iverson thought about it for a moment, then shook his head. 'Sorry, Nevil. You've got me there.'

'Well, it was just a shot in the dark,' Clavain said.

Iverson was strong enough to walk around the next day. He insisted on exploring the rest of the base, not simply the parts the Conjoiners had taken over. He wanted to see for himself the damage that he had heard about, and look over the lists of the dead – and the manner in which they had died – that Clavain and his friends had assiduously compiled. Clavain kept a watchful eye on the man, aware of how emotionally traumatic the whole experience must be. He was bearing it well, but that might easily have been a front. Galiana's machines could tell a lot about how his brain was functioning, but they were unable to probe Iverson's state of mind at the resolution needed to map emotional well-being.

Clavain, meanwhile, strove as best he could to keep Iverson in the dark about the Conjoiners. He did not want to overwhelm Iverson with strangeness at this delicate time; did not want to shatter the man's illusion that he had been rescued by a group of 'normal' human beings. But it turned out to be easier than he had expected, as Iverson showed surprisingly little interest in the history he had missed. Clavain had gone as far as telling him that the *Sandra Voi* was technically a ship full of refugees, fleeing the aftermath of a war between various factions of solar-system humanity – but Iverson had done little more than nod, never probing Clavain for more details about the war. Once or twice Clavain had even alluded accidentally to the Transenlightenment – that shared consciousness state the Conjoiners had reached – but Iverson had shown the same lack of interest. He was not even curious about the *Sandra Voi* herself, never once asking Clavain what the ship was like. It was not quite what Clavain had been expecting.

But there were rewards, too.

Iverson, it turned out, was fascinated by Felka, and Felka herself seemed pleasantly amused by the newcomer. It was, perhaps, not all that surprising: Galiana and the others had been busy helping Felka grow the neural circuitry necessary for normal human interactions, adding new layers to supplant the functional regions that had never worked properly – but in all that time, they had never introduced her to another human being she had not already met. And here was Iverson: not just a new voice but a new smell; a new face; a new way of walking – a deluge of new input for her starved mental routines. Clavain watched the way Felka latched on to Iverson when he entered a room, her attention snapping to him, her delight evident. And Iverson seemed perfectly happy to play the games that so wearied the others, the kinds of intricate challenge Felka adored. For hours on end Clavain watched the two of them lost in concentration; Iverson pulling mock faces of sorrow or – on the rare occasions when he beat her – extravagant joy. Felka responded in kind, her face more animated – more plausibly human – than Clavain had ever believed possible. She spoke more often in Iverson's presence than she had ever done in his, and the utterances she made more closely approximated well-formed, grammatically sound sentences than the disjointed shards of language Clavain had grown to recognise. It was like watching a difficult, backward child suddenly come alight in the presence of a skilled teacher. Clavain thought back to the time when he had rescued Felka from Mars, and how unlikely it had seemed then that she would ever grow into something resembling a normal adult human, as sensitised to others' feelings as she was to her own. Now, he could almost believe it would happen – yet half the distance she had come had been due to Iverson's influence, rather than his own.

Afterwards, when even Iverson had wearied of Felka's ceaseless demands for games, Clavain spoke to him quietly, away from the others.

'You're good with her, aren't you?'

Iverson shrugged, as if the matter was of no great consequence to him. 'Yeah. I like her. We both enjoy the same kinds of game. If there's a problem—'

He must have detected Clavain's irritation. 'No – no problem at all.' Clavain put a hand on his shoulder. 'There's more to it than just games, though, you have to admit—'

'She's a pretty fascinating case, Nevil.'

'I don't disagree. We value her highly.' He flinched, aware of how much the remark sounded like one of Galiana's typically flat statements. 'But I'm puzzled. You've been revived after nearly a century asleep. We've travelled here on a ship that couldn't even have been considered a distant possibility in your own era. We've undergone massive social and technical upheavals in the last hundred years. There are things about us – things about me – I haven't told you yet. Things about *you* I haven't even told you yet.'

'I'm just taking things one step at a time, that's all.' Iverson shrugged and looked distantly past Clavain, through the window behind him. His gaze must have been skating across kilometres of ice towards Diadem's white horizon, unable to find a purchase. 'I admit, I'm not really interested in technological innovations. I'm sure your ship's really nice, but . . . it's just applied physics. Just engineering. There may be some new quantum principles underlying your propulsion system, but if that's the case, it's probably just an elaborate curlicue on something that was already pretty baroque to begin with. You haven't smashed the light barrier, have you?' He read Clavain's expression accurately. 'No – didn't think so. Maybe if you had—'

'So what exactly does interest you?'

Iverson seemed to hesitate before answering, but when he did speak Clavain had no doubt that he was telling the truth. There was a sudden, missionary fervour in his voice. 'Emergence. Specifically, the emergence of complex, almost unpredictable patterns from systems governed by a few simple laws. Consciousness is an excellent example. A human mind's really just a web of simple neuronal cells wired together in a particular way. The laws governing the functioning of those individual cells aren't all that difficult to grasp – a cascade of well-studied electrical, chemical and enzymic processes. The tricky part is the wiring diagram. It certainly isn't encoded in DNA in any but the crudest sense. Otherwise why would a baby bother growing neural connections that are pruned down before birth? That'd be a real waste – if you had a perfect blueprint for the conscious mind, you'd only bother forming the connections you needed. No; the mind organises itself during growth, and that's why it needs so many more neurons than it'll eventually incorporate into functioning networks. It needs the raw material to work with as it gropes its way towards a functioning consciousness. The pattern emerges, bootstrapping itself into existence, and the pathways that aren't used – or aren't as efficient as others – are discarded.' Iverson paused. 'But how this organisation happens really isn't understood in any depth. Do you know how many neurons it takes to control the first part of a lobster's gut, Nevil? Have a guess, to the nearest hundred.'

Clavain shrugged. 'I don't know. Five hundred? A thousand?'

'No. Six. Not six hundred, just six. Six damned neurons. You can't get much simpler than that. But it took decades to understand how those six worked together, let alone how that particular network evolved. The problems aren't inseparable, either. You can't really hope to understand how ten billion neurons organise themselves into a functioning whole unless you understand how the whole actually functions. Oh, we've made some progress – we can tell you exactly which spinal neurons fire to make a lamprey swim, and how that firing pattern maps into muscle motion – but we're a long way from understanding how something as elusive as the concept of "I" emerges in the developing human mind. Well, at least we were before I went under. You may be about to reveal that you've achieved stunning progress in the last century, but something tells me you were too busy with social upheaval for that.'

Clavain felt an urge to argue – angered by the man's tone – but suppressed it, willing himself into a state of serene acceptance. 'You're probably right. We've made progress in the other direction – augmenting the mind as it is – but if we genuinely understood brain development, we wouldn't have ended up with a failure like Felka.'

'Oh, I wouldn't call her a failure, Nevil.'

'I didn't mean it like that.'

'Of course not.' Now it was Iverson's turn to place a hand on Clavain's shoulder. 'But you must see now why I find so Felka so fascinating. Her mind is damaged – you told me that yourself, and there's no need to go into the details – but despite that damage, despite the vast abysses in her head, she's beginning to self-assemble the kinds of higher-level neural routines we all take for granted. It's as if the patterns were always there as latent potentials, and it's only now that they're beginning to emerge. Isn't that fascinating? Isn't it something worthy of study?'

Delicately, Clavain removed the man's hand from his shoulder. 'I suppose so. I had hoped, however, that there might be something more to it than study.'

'I've offended you, and I apologise. My choice of phrase was poor. Of course I care for her.'

Clavain felt suddenly awkward, as if he had misjudged a fundamentally decent man. 'I understand. Look, ignore what I said.'

'Yeah, of course. It – um – will be all right for me to see her again, won't it?'

Clavain nodded. 'I'm sure she'd miss you if you weren't around.'

Over the next few days, Clavain left the two of them to their games, only rarely eavesdropping to see how things were going. Iverson had asked permission to show Felka around some of the other areas of the base, and after a few initial misgivings Clavain and Galiana had both agreed to his request. After that, long hours went by when the two of them were not to be found. Clavain had tracked them once, watching as Iverson led the girl into a disused lab and showed her intricate molecular models. They clearly delighted her; vast fuzzy holographic assemblages of atoms and chemical bonds that floated in the air like Chinese dragons. Wearing cumbersome gloves and goggles, Iverson and Felka were able to manipulate the mega-molecules, forcing them to fold into minimum-energy configurations that brute-force computation would have struggled to predict. As they gestured into the air and made the dragons contort and twist, Clavain watched for the inevitable moment when Felka would grow bored and demand something more challenging. But it never came. Afterwards – when she had returned to the fold, her face shining with wonder – it was as if Felka had undergone a spiritual experience. Iverson had shown her something her mind could not instantly encompass; a problem too large and subtle to be stormed in a flash of intuitive insight.

Seeing that, Clavain again felt guilty about the way he had spoken to Iverson, and knew that he had not completely put aside his doubts about the message Setterholm had left in the ice. But – the riddle of the helmet aside – there was no reason to think that Iverson might be a murderer beyond those haphazard marks. Clavain had looked into Iverson's personnel records from the time before he was frozen, and the man's history was flawless. He had been a solid, professional member of the expedition, well-liked and trusted by the others. Granted, the records were patchy, and since they were stored digitally they could have been doctored to almost any extent. But then much the same story was told by the handwritten diary and verbal log entries of some of the other victims. Andrew Iverson's name came up again and again as a man regarded with affection by his fellows; most certainly not someone capable of murder. Best, then, to discard the evidence of the marks and give him the benefit of the doubt.

Clavain spoke of his fears to Galiana, and while she listened to him, she only came back with exactly the same rational counter-arguments he had already provided for himself.

'The problem is,' Galiana said, 'that the man you found in the crevasse could have been severely confused, perhaps even hallucinatory. That message he left – if it was a message, and not just a set of random gouge marks he made while convulsing – could mean anything at all.'

'We don't know that Setterholm was confused,' Clavain protested.

'We don't? Then why didn't he make sure his helmet was on properly? It can't have been latched fully, or it wouldn't have rolled off him when he hit the bottom of the crevasse.'

'Yes,' Clavain said. 'But I'm reasonably sure he wouldn't have been able to leave the base if his helmet hadn't been latched.'

'In which case he must have undone it afterwards.'

'Yes, but there's no reason for him to have done that, unless . . .'

Galiana gave him a thin-lipped smile. 'Unless he was confused. Back to square one, Nevil.'

'No,' he said, conscious that he could almost see the shape of something; something that was close to the truth if not the truth itself. 'There's another possibility, one I hadn't thought of until now.'

Galiana squinted at him, that rare frown appearing. 'Which is?'

'That someone else removed his helmet for him.'

They went down into the bowels of the base. In the dead space of the equipment bays Galiana became ill at ease. She was not used to being out of communicational range of her colleagues. Normally, systems buried in the environment picked up neural signals from individuals, amplifying and rebroadcasting them to other people, but there were no such systems here. Clavain could hear Galiana's thoughts, but they came in weakly, like a voice from the sea almost drowned by the roar of surf.

'This had better be worth it,' Galiana said.

'I want to show you the airlock,' Clavain answered. 'I'm sure Setterholm must have left here with his helmet properly attached.'

'You still think he was murdered?'

'I think it's a remote possibility that we should be very careful not to discount.'

'But why would anyone kill a man whose only interest was a lot of harmless ice-worms?'

'That's been bothering me as well.'

'And?'

'I think I have an answer. Half of one, anyway. What if his interest in the worms brought him into conflict with the others? I'm thinking about the reactor.'

Galiana nodded. 'They'd have needed to harvest ice for it.'

'Which Setterholm might have seen as interfering with the worms' ecology. Maybe he made a nuisance of himself and someone decided to get rid of him.'

'That would be a pretty extreme way of dealing with him.'

'I know,' Clavain said, stepping through a connecting door into the transport bay. 'I said I had half an answer, not all of one.'

As soon as he was through he knew something was amiss. The bay was not as it had been before, when he had come down here scouting for clues. He dropped his train of thought immediately, focusing only on the now.

The room was much, much colder than it should have been. And brighter. There was an oblong of chill blue daylight spilling across the floor from the huge open door of one of the vehicle exit ramps. Clavain looked at it in mute disbelief, wanting it to be a temporary glitch in his vision. But Galiana was with him, and she had seen it, too.

'Someone's left the base,' she said.

Clavain looked out across the ice. He could see the wake the vehicle had left in the snow, arcing out towards the horizon. For a long moment they stood at the top of the ramp, frozen into inaction. Clavain's mind screamed with the implications. He had never really liked the idea of Iverson taking Felka away with him elsewhere in the base, but he had never considered the possibility that he might take her into one of the blind zones. From here, Iverson must have known enough little tricks to open a surface door, start a rover and leave, without any of the Conjoiners realising.

'Nevil, listen to me,' Galiana said. 'He doesn't necessarily mean her any harm. He might just want to show her something.'

He turned to her. 'There isn't time to arrange a shuttle. That party trick of yours – talking to the door? Do you think you can manage it again?'

'I don't need to. The door's already open.'

Clavain nodded at one of the other rovers, hulking behind them. 'It's not the door I'm thinking about.'

Galiana was disappointed: it took her three minutes to convince the machine to start, rather than the few dozen seconds she said it should have taken. She was, she told Clavain, in serious danger of getting rusty at that sort of thing. Clavain just thanked the gods that there had been no mechanical sabotage to the rover; no amount of neural intervention could have fixed that.

'That's another thing that makes it look as if this is just an innocent trip outside,' Galiana said. 'If he'd really wanted to abduct her, it wouldn't have taken much additional effort to stop us following him. If he'd closed the door, as well, we might not even have noticed he was gone.'

'Haven't you ever heard of reverse psychology?' Clavain said.

'I still can't see Iverson as a murderer, Nevil.' She checked his expression, her own face calm despite the effort of driving the machine. Her hands were folded in her lap. She was less isolated now, having used the rover's comm systems to establish a link back to the other Conjoiners. 'Setterholm, maybe. The obsessive loner and all that. Just a shame he's the dead one.'

'Yes,' Clavain said, uneasily.

The rover itself ran on six wheels, a squat, pressurised hull perched low between absurd-looking balloon tyres. Galiana gunned them hard down the ramp and across the ice, trusting the machine to glide harmlessly over the smaller crevasses. It seemed reckless, but if they followed the trail Iverson had left, they were almost guaranteed not to hit any fatal obstacles.

'Did you get anywhere with the source of the sickness?' Clavain asked.

'No breakthroughs yet—'

'Then here's a suggestion. Can you read my visual memory accurately?' Clavain did not need an answer. 'While you were finding Iverson's body, I was looking over the lab samples. There were a lot of terrestrial organisms there. Could one of those have been responsible?'

'You'd better replay the memory.'

Clavain did so: picturing himself looking over the rows of culture dishes, test tubes and gel slides; concentrating especially on those that had come from Earth rather than the locally obtained samples. In his mind's eye the sample names refused to snap into clarity, but the machines Galiana had seeded through his head would already be locating the eidetically stored short-term memories and retrieving them with a clarity beyond the capabilities of Clavain's own brain.

'Now see if there's anything there that might do the job.'

'A terrestrial organism?' Galiana sounded surprised. 'Well, there might be something there, but I can't see how it could have spread beyond the laboratory unless someone wanted it to.'

'I think that's exactly what happened.'

'Sabotage?'

'Yes.'

'Well, we'll know sooner or later. I've passed the information to the others. They'll get back to me if they find a candidate. But I still don't see why anyone would sabotage the entire base, even if it was possible. Overthrowing the von Neumann machines is one thing . . . mass suicide is another.'

'I don't think it was mass suicide. Mass murder, maybe.'

'And Iverson's your main suspect?'

'He survived, didn't he? And Setterholm scrawled a message in the ice just before he died. It must have been a warning about him.' But even as he spoke, he knew there was a second possibility; one that he could not quite focus on.

Galiana swerved the rover to avoid a particularly deep and yawning chasm, shaded with vivid veins of turquoise blue.

'There's a small matter of missing motive.'

Clavain looked ahead, wondering if the thing he saw glinting in the distance was a trick of the eye. 'I'm working on that,' he said.

Galiana halted them next to the other rover. The two machines were parked at the lip of a slope-sided depression in the ice. It was not really steep enough to call a crevasse, although it was at least thirty or forty metres deep. From the rover's cab it was not possible to see all the way into the powdery blue depths, although Clavain could certainly make out the fresh footprints descending into them. Up on the surface, marks like that would have been scoured away by the wind in days or hours, so these prints were very fresh. There were, he observed, two sets – someone heavy and confident and someone lighter, less sure of their footing.

Before they had taken the rover they had made sure there were two suits aboard it. They struggled into them, fiddling with the latches.

'If I'm right,' Clavain said, 'this kind of precaution isn't really necessary. Not for avoiding the sickness, anyway. But better safe than sorry.'

'Excellent timing,' Galiana said, snapping down her helmet and giving it a quarter twist to lock into place. 'They've just pulled something from your memory, Nevil. There's a family of single-celled organisms called dinoflagellates, one of which was present in the lab where we found Iverson. Something called *Pfiesteria piscicida*. Normally it's an ambush predator that attacks fish.'

'Could it have been responsible for the madness?'

'It's at least a strong contender. It has a taste for mammalian tissue as well. If it gets into the human nervous system it produces memory loss, disorientation – as well as a host of physical effects. It could have been dispersed as a toxic aerosol, released into the base's air system. Someone with access to the lab's facilities could have turned it from something merely nasty into something deadly, I think.'

'We should have pinpointed it, Galiana. Didn't we swab the air ducts?'

'Yes, but we weren't looking for something terrestrial. In fact we were excluding terrestrial organisms, only filtering for the basic biochemical building blocks of Diadem life. We just weren't thinking in criminal terms.'

'More fool us,' Clavain said.

Suited now, they stepped outside. Clavain began to regret his haste in leaving the base so quickly; at having to make do with these old suits and lacking any means of defence. Wanting something in his hand for moral support, he examined the equipment stowed around the outside of the rover until he found an ice pick. It would not be much of a weapon, but he felt better for it.

'You won't need that,' Galiana said.

'What if Iverson turns nasty?'

'You still won't need it.'

But he kept hold of it anyway – an ice pick was an ice pick, after all – and the two of them walked to the point where the icy ground began to curve over the lip of the depression. Clavain examined the wrist of his suit, studying the cryptic and old-fashioned matrix of keypads that controlled the suit's functions. On a whim he pressed something promising and was gratified when he felt crampons spike from the soles of his boots, anchoring him to the ice.

'Iverson!' he shouted. 'Felka!'

But sound carried poorly beyond his helmet, and the ceaseless, whipping wind would have snatched his words away from the crevasse. There was nothing for it but to make the difficult trek into the blue depths. He led the way, his heart pounding in his chest, the old suit awkward and top-heavy. He almost lost his footing once or twice, and had to stop to catch his breath when he reached the level bottom of the depression, sweat running into his eyes.

He looked around. The footprints led horizontally for ten or fifteen metres, weaving between fragile, curtain-like formations of opal ice. On some clinical level he acknowledged that the place had a sinister charm – he imagined the wind breathing through those curtains of ice, making ethereal music – but the need to find Felka eclipsed such considerations. He focused only on the low, dark-blue hole of a tunnel in the ice ahead of them. The footprints vanished into the tunnel.

'If the bastard's taken her . . .' Clavain said, tightening his grip on the pick. He switched on his helmet light and stooped into the tunnel, Galiana behind him. It was hard going; the tunnel wriggled, rose and descended for many tens of metres, and Clavain was unable to decide whether it was some weird natural feature – carved, perhaps, by a hot sub-glacial river – or whether it had been dug by hand, much more recently. The walls were veined with worm tracks: a marbling like an immense magnification of the human retina. Here and there Clavain saw the dark smudges of worms moving through cracks that were very close to the surface, though he knew it would be necessary to stare at them for long seconds before any movement was discernible. He groaned, the stooping becoming painful, and then the tunnel widened out dramatically. He realised that he had emerged into a much larger space.

It was still underground, although the ceiling glowed with the blue translucence of filtered daylight. The covering of ice could not have been more than a metre or two thick; a thin shell stretched like a dome over tens of metres of yawing nothing. Nearly sheer walls of delicately patterned ice rose up from a level, footprint-dappled floor.

'Ah,' said Iverson, who was standing near one wall of the chamber. 'You decided to join us.'

Clavain felt a stab of relief seeing that Felka was standing not far from him, next to a piece of equipment Clavain failed to recognise. Felka appeared unharmed. She turned towards him, the peculiar play of light and shade on her helmeted face making her look older than she was.

'Nevil,' he heard Felka say. 'Hello.'

He crossed the ice, fearful that the whole marvellous edifice was about to come crashing down on them all.

'Why did you bring her here, Iverson?'

'There's something I wanted to show her. Something I knew she'd like, even more than the other things.' He turned to the smaller figure near him. 'Isn't that right, Felka?'

'Yes.'

'And do you like it?'

Her answer was matter of fact, but it was closer to conversation than anything Clavain had ever heard from her lips.

'Yes. I do like it.'

Galiana stepped ahead of him and extended a hand to the girl. 'Felka? I'm glad you like this place. I like it, too. But now it's time to come back home.'

Clavain steeled himself for an argument, some kind of showdown between the two women, but to his immense relief Felka walked casually towards Galiana.

'I'll take her back to the rover,' Galiana said. 'I want to

make sure she hasn't had any problems breathing with that old suit on.'

A transparent lie, but it would suffice.

Then she spoke to Clavain. It was a tiny thing, almost inconsequential, but she placed it directly in his head.

And he understood what he would have to do.

When they were alone, Clavain said, 'You killed him.'

'Setterholm?'

'No. You couldn't have killed Setterholm because you *are* Setterholm.' Clavain looked up, the arc of his helmet light tracing the filamentary patterning until it became too tiny to resolve; blurring into an indistinct haze of detail that curved over into the ceiling itself. It was like admiring a staggeringly ornate fresco.

'Nevil – do me a favour? Check the settings on your suit, in case you're not getting enough oxygen.'

'There's nothing wrong with my suit.' Clavain smiled, the irony of it all delicious. 'In fact, it was the suit that tipped me off. When you pushed Iverson into the crevasse, his helmet came off. That couldn't have happened unless it wasn't fixed on properly in the first place – and *that* couldn't have happened unless someone had removed it after the two of you left the base.'

Setterholm – he was sure the man was Setterholm – snorted derisively, but Clavain continued speaking.

'Here's my stab at what happened, for what it's worth. You needed to swap identities with Iverson because Iverson had no obvious motive for murdering the others, whereas Setterholm certainly did.'

'And I don't suppose you have any idea what that motive might have been?'

'Give me time; I'll get there eventually. Let's just deal with the lone murder first. Changing the electronic records was easy enough – you could even swap Iverson's picture and medical data for your own – but that was only part of it. You also needed to get Iverson into your clothes and suit, so that we'd assume the body in the crevasse belonged to you, Setterholm. I don't know exactly how you did it.'

'Then perhaps – '

Clavain carried on. 'But my guess is you let him catch a dose of the bug you let loose in the main base – *Pfiesteria*, wasn't it? – then followed him when he went walking outside. You jumped him, knocked him down on the ice and got him out of his suit and into yours. He was probably unconscious by then, I suppose. But then he must have started coming round, or you panicked for another reason. You jammed the helmet on and pushed him into the crevasse. Maybe if all that had happened was his helmet coming off, I wouldn't have dwelled on it. But he wasn't dead, and he lived long enough to scratch a message in the ice. I thought it concerned his murderer, but I was wrong. He was trying to tell me who he was. Not Setterholm, but Iverson.'

'Nice theory.' Setterholm glanced down at a display screen in the back of the machine squatting next to him. Mounted on a tripod, it resembled a huge pair of binoculars, pointed with a slight elevation towards one wall of the chamber.

'Sometimes a theory's all you need. That's quite a toy you've got there, by the way. What is it, some kind of ground-penetrating radar?'

Setterholm brushed aside the question. 'If I was him – why would I have done it? Just because I was interested in the ice-worms?'

'It's simple,' Clavain said, hoping the uncertainty he felt was not apparent in his voice. 'The others weren't as convinced as you were of the worms' significance. Only you saw them for what they were.' He was treading carefully here; masking his ignorance of Setterholm's deeper motives by playing on the man's vanity.

'Clever of me if I did.'

'Oh, yes. I wouldn't doubt that at all. And it must have driven you to distraction, that you could see what the others couldn't. Naturally, you wanted to protect the worms, when you saw them under threat.'

'Sorry, Nevil, but you're going to have to try a lot harder than that.' He paused and patted the machine's matt-silver casing, clearly unable to pretend that he did not know what it was. 'It's radar, yes. It can probe the interior of the glacier with sub-centimetre resolution, to a depth of several tens of metres.'

'Which would be rather useful if you wanted to study the worms.'

Setterholm shrugged. 'I suppose so. A climatologist interested in glacial flow might also have use for the information.'

'Like Iverson?' Clavain took a step closer to Setterholm and the radar equipment. He could see the display more clearly now: a fibrous tangle of mainly green lines slowly spinning in space, with a denser structure traced out in red near its heart. 'Like the man you killed?'

'I told you: I'm Iverson.'

Clavain stepped towards him with the ice pick held double-handed, but when he was a few metres from the man he veered past and made his way to the wall. Setterholm had flinched, but he had not seemed unduly worried that Clavain was about to try to hurt him.

'I'll be frank with you,' Clavain said, raising the pick. 'I don't really understand what it is about the worms.'

'What are you going to do?'

'This.'

Clavain smashed the pick against the wall as hard as he was able. It was enough: a layer of ice fractured noisily away, sliding down like a miniature avalanche to land in pieces at his feet; each fist-sized shard was veined with worm trails.

'Stop,' Setterholm said.

'Why? What do you care, if you're not interested in the worms?'

Clavain smashed the ice again, dislodging another layer.

'You . . .' Setterholm paused. 'You could bring the whole place down on us if you're not careful.'

Clavain raised the pick again, letting out a groan of effort as he swung. This time he put all his weight behind the swing, all his fury, and a chunk the size of his upper body calved noisily from the wall.

'I'll take that risk,' Clavain said.

'No. You've got to stop.'

'Why? It's only ice.'

'No!'

Setterholm rushed him, knocking him off his feet. The ice pick spun from his hand and the two of them crashed into the ground, Setterholm landing on his chest. He pressed his faceplate close to Clavain's, every bead of sweat on his forehead gleaming like a precise little jewel.

'I told you to stop.'

Clavain found it difficult to speak with the pressure on his chest, but forced out the words with effort. 'I think we can dispense with the charade that you're Iverson now, can't we?'

'You shouldn't have harmed it.'

'No . . . and neither should the others, eh? But they needed that ice very badly.'

Now Setterholm's voice held a tone of dull resignation. 'For the reactor, you mean?'

'Yes. The fusion plant.' Clavain allowed himself to feel some small satisfaction before adding, 'Actually, it was Galiana who made the connection, not me. That the reactor ran on ice, I mean. And after all the outlying bases had been evacuated, they had to keep everyone alive back at the main one. And that meant more load on the reactor. Which meant it needed more ice, of which there was hardly a shortage in the immediate vicinity.'

'But they couldn't be allowed to harvest the ice. Not after what I'd discovered.'

Clavain nodded, observing that the reversion from Iverson to Setterholm was now complete.

'No. The ice is precious, isn't it? Infinitely more so than anyone else realised. Without that ice the worms would have died—'

'You don't understand either, do you?'

Clavain swallowed. 'I think I understand more than the others, Setterholm. You realised that the worms—'

'It wasn't the damned worms!' He had shouted – Setterholm had turned on a loudspeaker function in his suit that Clavain had not yet located – and for a moment the words crashed around the great ice chamber, threatening to start the tiny chain reaction of fractures that would collapse the whole structure. But when silence had returned – disturbed only by the rasp of Clavain's breathing – nothing had changed.

'It wasn't the worms?'

'No.' Setterholm was calmer now, as if the point had been made. 'No – not really. They were important, yes – but only as low-level elements in a much more complex system. Don't you understand?'

Clavain strove for honesty. 'I never really understood what it was that fascinated you about them. They seem quite simple to me.'

Setterholm removed his weight from Clavain and rose up onto his feet again. 'That's because they are. A child could grasp the biology of a single ice-worm in an afternoon. Felka did, in fact. Oh, she's wonderful, Nevil.' Setterholm's teeth flashed a smile that chilled Clavain. 'The things she could unravel . . . she isn't a failure; not at all. I think she's something miraculous we barely comprehend.'

'Unlike the worms.'

'Yes. They're like clockwork toys, programmed with a few simple rules.' Setterholm stooped down and grabbed the ice pick for himself. 'They always respond in exactly the same way to the same input stimulus. And the kinds of stimuli they respond to are simple in the extreme: a few gradations of temperature; a few biochemical cues picked up from the ice itself. But the emergent properties . . .'

Clavain forced himself to a sitting position. 'There's that word again.'

'It's the network, Nevil. The system of tunnels the worms dig through the ice. Don't you understand? That's where the real complexity lies. That's what I was always more interested in. Of course, it took me years to see it for what it is—'

'Which is?'

'A self-evolving network. One that has the capacity to adapt; to learn.'

'It's just a series of channels bored through ice, Setterholm.'

'No. It's infinitely more than that.' The man craned his neck as far as the architecture of his suit would allow, revelling in the palatial beauty of the chamber. 'There are two essential elements in any neural network, Nevil. Connections and nodes are necessary, but not enough. The connections must be capable of being weighted; adjusted in strength according to usefulness. And the nodes must be capable of processing the inputs from the connections in a deterministic manner, like logic gates.' He gestured around the chamber. 'Here, there is no absolutely sharp distinction between the connections and the nodes, but the essences remain. The worms lay down secretions when they travel, and those secretions determine how other worms make use of the same channels; whether they utilise one route or another. There are many determining factors – the sexes of the worms, the seasons, others I won't bore you with. But the point is simple. The secretions – and the effect they have on the worms – mean that the topology of the network is governed by subtle emergent principles. And the breeding tangles function as logic gates; processing the inputs from their connecting nodes according to the rules of worm sex, caste and hierarchy. It's messy, slow and biological – but the end result is that the worm colony as a whole functions as a neural network. It's a program that the worms themselves are running, even though any given worm hasn't a clue that it's a part of a larger whole.'

Clavain absorbed all that and thought carefully before asking the question that occurred to him. 'How does it change?'

'Slowly,' Setterholm said. 'Sometimes routes fall into disuse because the secretions inhibit other worms from using them. Gradually, the glacier seals them shut. At the same time other cracks open by chance – the glacier's own fracturing imposes a constant chaotic background on the network – or the worms bore new holes. Seen in slow motion – our time frame – almost nothing ever seems to happen, let alone change. But imagine speeding things up, Nevil. Imagine if we could see the way the network has changed over the last century, or the last thousand years . . . imagine what we might find. A constantly evolving loom of connections, shifting and changing eternally. Now – does that remind you of anything?'

Clavain answered in the only way that he knew would satisfy Setterholm. 'A mind, I suppose. A newborn one, still forging neural connections.'

'Yes. Oh, you'd doubtless like to point out that the network is isolated, so it can't be responding to stimuli beyond itself – but we can't know that for certain. A season is like a heartbeat here, Nevil! What we think of as geologically slow processes – a glacier cracking, two glaciers colliding – those events could be as forceful as caresses and sounds to a blind child.' He paused and glanced at the screen in the back of the imaging radar. 'That's what I wanted to find out. A century ago, I was able to study the network for a handful of decades, and I found something that astonished me. The colony moves, reshapes itself constantly, as the glacier shifts and breaks up. But no matter how radically the network changes its periphery, no matter how thoroughly the loom evolves, there are deep structures inside the network that are always preserved.' Setterholm's finger traced the red mass at the heart of the green tunnel map. 'In the language of network topology, the tunnel system is scale-free rather than exponential. It's the hallmark of a highly organised network with a few rather specialised processing centres – hubs, if you like. This is one. I believe its function is to cause the whole network to move away from a widening fracture in the glacier. It would take me much more than a century to find out for sure, although everything I've seen here confirms what I originally thought. I mapped other structures in other colonies, too. They can be huge, spread across cubic kilometres of ice. But they always persist. Don't you see what that means? The network has begun to develop specialised areas of function. It's begun to process information, Nevil. It's begun to creep its way towards thought.'

Clavain looked around him once more, trying to see the chamber in the new light that Setterholm had revealed. Think not of the worms as entities in their own right, he thought, but as electrical signals, ghosting along synaptic pathways in a neural network made of solid ice . . .

He shivered. It was the only appropriate response.

'Even if the network processes information . . . there's no reason to think it could ever become conscious.'

'Why not, Nevil? What's the fundamental difference between perceiving the universe via electrical signals transmitted along nerve tissue, and via fracture patterns moving through a vast block of ice?'

'I suppose you have a point.'

'I had to save them, Nevil. Not just the worms, but the network they were a part of. We couldn't come all this way and just wipe out the first thinking thing we'd ever encountered in the universe, simply because it didn't fit into our neat little preconceived notions of what alien thought would actually be like.'

'But saving the worms meant killing everyone else.'

'You think I didn't realise that? You think it didn't agonise me to do what I had to do? I'm a human being, Nevil – not a monster. I knew exactly what I was doing and I knew exactly what it would make me look like to anyone who came here afterwards.'

'But you still did it.'

'Put yourself in my shoes. How would you have acted?'

Clavain opened his mouth, expecting an easy answer to spring to mind. But nothing came; not for several seconds. He was thinking about Setterholm's question, more thoroughly than he had done so far. Until then he had satisfied himself with the quiet, unquestioned assumption that he would not have acted the way Setterholm had done. But could he really be so sure? Setterholm, after all, had truly believed that the network formed a sentient whole; a thinking being. Possessing that knowledge must have made him feel divinely chosen; sanctioned to commit any act to preserve the fabulously rare thing he had found. And he had, after all, been right.

'You haven't answered me.'

'That's because I thought the question warranted something more than a flippant answer, Setterholm. I like to think I wouldn't have acted the way you did, but I don't suppose I can ever be sure of that.'

Clavain stood up, inspecting his suit for damage; relieved that the scuffle had not injured him.

'You'll never know.'

'No. I never will. But one thing's clear enough. I've heard you talk; heard the fire in your words. You believe in your network, and yet you still couldn't make the others see it. I doubt I'd have been able to do much better, and I doubt that I'd have thought of a better way to preserve what you'd found.'

'Then you'd have killed everyone, just like I did?'

The realisation of it was like a heavy burden someone had just placed on his shoulders. It was so much easier to feel incapable of such acts. But Clavain had been a soldier. He had killed more people than he could remember, even though those days had been a long time ago. It was really a lot less difficult to do when you had a cause to believe in.

And Setterholm had definitely had a cause.

'Perhaps,' Clavain said. 'Perhaps I might have, yes.'

He heard Setterholm sigh. 'I'm glad. For a moment there—'

'For a moment what?'

'When you showed up with that pick, I thought you were planning to kill me.' Setterholm hefted the pick, much as Clavain had done earlier. 'You wouldn't have done that, would you? I don't deny that what I did was regrettable, but I had to do it.'

'I understand.'

'But what happens to me now? I can stay with you all, can't I?'

'We probably won't be staying on Diadem, I'm afraid. And I don't think you'd really want to come with us; not if you knew what we're really like.'

'You can't leave me alone here, not again.'

'Why not? You'll have your worms. And you can always kill yourself again and see who shows up next.' Clavain turned to leave.

'No. You can't go now.'

'I'll leave your rover on the surface. Maybe there are some supplies in it. Just don't come anywhere near the base again. You won't find a welcome there.'

'I'll die out here,' Setterholm said.

'Start getting used to it.'

He heard Setterholm's feet scuffing across the ice; a walk breaking into a run. Clavain turned around calmly, unsurprised to see Setterholm coming towards him with the pick raised high, as a weapon.

Clavain sighed.

He reached into Setterholm's skull, addressing the webs of machines that still floated in the man's head, and instructed them to execute their host in a sudden, painless orgy of neural deconstruction. It was not a trick he could have done an hour ago, but after Galiana had planted the method in his mind, it was easy as sneezing. For a moment he understood what it must feel like to be a god.

And in that same moment Setterholm dropped the ice pick and stumbled, falling forward onto one end of the pick's blade. It pierced his faceplate, but by then he was dead anyway.

'What I said was the truth,' Clavain said. 'I might have killed them as well, just like I said. I don't want to think so, but I can't say it isn't in me. No; I don't blame you for that; not at all.'

With his boot he began to kick a dusting of frost over the dead man's body. It would be too much bother to remove Setterholm from this place, and the machines inside him would sterilise his body, ensuring that none of his cells ever contaminated the glacier. And, as Clavain had told himself only a few days earlier, there were worse places to die than here. Or worse places to be left for dead, anyway.

When he was done, when what remained of Setterholm was just an ice-covered mound in the middle of a cavern, Clavain addressed him one final time.

'But that doesn't make it right, either. It was still murder, Setterholm.' He kicked a final divot of ice over the corpse. 'Someone had to pay for it.'

DIAMOND DOGS

ONE

I met Childe in the Monument to the Eighty.

It was one of those days when I had the place largely to myself, able to walk from aisle to aisle without seeing another visitor; only my footsteps disturbed the air of funereal silence and stillness.

I was visiting my parents' shrine. It was a modest affair: a smooth wedge of obsidian shaped like a metronome, undecorated save for two cameo portraits set in elliptical borders. The sole moving part was a black blade which was attached near the base of the shrine, ticking back and forth with magisterial slowness. Mechanisms buried inside the shrine ensured that it was winding down, destined to count out days and then years with each tick. Eventually it would require careful measurement to detect its movement.

I was watching the blade when a voice disturbed me.

'Visiting the dead again, Richard?'

'Who's there?' I said, looking around, faintly recognising the speaker but not immediately able to place him.

'Just another ghost.'

Various possibilities flashed through my mind as I listened to the man's deep and taunting voice – a kidnapping, an assassination – before I stopped flattering myself that I was worthy of such attention.

Then the man emerged from between two shrines a little way down from the metronome.

'My God,' I said.

'Now do you recognise me?'

He smiled and stepped closer: as tall and imposing as I remembered. He had lost the devil's horns since our last meeting – they had only ever been a bio-engineered affectation – but there was still something satanic about his appearance, an effect not lessened by the small and slightly pointed goatee he had cultivated in the meantime.

Dust swirled around him as he walked towards me, suggesting that he was not a projection.

'I thought you were dead, Roland.'

'No, Richard,' he said, stepping close enough to shake my hand. 'But that was most certainly the effect I desired to achieve.'

'Why?' I said.

'Long story.'

'Start at the beginning, then.'

Roland Childe placed a hand on the smooth side of my parents' shrine. 'Not quite your style, I'd have thought?'

'It was all I could do to argue against something even more ostentatious and morbid. But don't change the subject. What happened to you?'

He removed his hand, leaving a faint damp imprint. 'I faked my own death. The Eighty was the perfect cover. The fact that it all went so horrendously wrong was even better. I couldn't have planned it like that if I'd tried.'

No arguing with that, I thought. It *had* gone horrendously wrong.

More than a century and a half ago, a clique of researchers led by Calvin Sylveste had resurrected the old idea of copying the essence of a living human being into a computer-generated simulation. The procedure – then in its infancy – had the slight drawback that it killed the subject. But there had still been volunteers, and my parents had been amongst the first to sign up and support Calvin's work. They had offered him political protection when the powerful Mixmaster lobby opposed the project, and they had been amongst the first to be scanned.

Less than fourteen months later, their simulations had also been amongst the first to crash.

None could ever be restarted. Most of the remaining Eighty had succumbed, and now only a handful remained unaffected.

'You must hate Calvin for what he did,' Childe said, still with that taunting quality in his voice.

'Would it surprise you if I said I didn't?'

'Then why did you set yourself so vocally against his family after the tragedy?'

'Because I felt justice still needed to be served.' I turned from the shrine and started walking away, curious as to whether Childe would follow me.

'Fair enough,' he said. 'But that opposition cost you dearly, didn't it?'

I bridled, halting next to what appeared a highly realistic sculpture but was almost certainly an embalmed corpse.

'Meaning what?'

'The Resurgam expedition, of course, which just happened to be bankrolled by House Sylveste. By rights, you should have been on it. You were Richard Swift, for heaven's sake. You'd spent the better part of your life thinking about possible modes of alien sentience. There should have been a place for you on that ship, and you damned well knew it.'

'It wasn't that simple,' I said, resuming my walk. 'There were a limited number of slots available and they needed practical types first – biologists, geologists, that kind of thing. By the time they'd filled the most essential slots, there simply wasn't any room for abstract dreamers like myself.'

'And the fact that you'd pissed off House Sylveste had nothing whatsoever to do with it? Come off it, Richard.'

We descended a series of steps down into the lower level of the Monument. The atrium's ceiling was a cloudy mass of jagged sculptures: interlocked metal birds. A party of visitors was arriving, attended by servitors and a swarm of bright, marble-sized float-cams. Childe breezed through the group, drawing annoyed frowns but no actual recognition, although one or two of the people in the party were vague acquaintances of mine.

'What is this about?' I asked, once we were outside.

'Concern for an old friend. I've had my tabs on you, and it was pretty obvious that not being selected for that expedition was a crushing disappointment. You'd thrown your life into contemplation of the alien. One marriage down the drain because of your self-absorption. What was her name again?'

I'd had her memory buried so deeply that it took a real effort of will to recall any exact details about my marriage.

'Celestine. I think.'

'Since then you've had a few relationships, but nothing lasting more than a decade. A decade's a mere fling in this town, Richard.'

'My private life's my own business,' I responded sullenly. 'Hey. Where's my volantor? I parked it here.'

'I sent it away. We'll take mine instead.'

Where my volantor had been was a larger, blood-red model. It was as baroquely ornamented as a funeral barge. At a gesture from Childe it clammed open, revealing a plush gold interior with four seats, one of which was occupied by a dark, slouched figure.

'What's going on, Roland?'

'I've found something. Something astonishing that I want you to be a part of; a challenge that makes every game you and I ever played in our youth pale in comparison.'

'A challenge?'

'The ultimate one, I think.'

He had pricked my curiosity, but I hoped it was not too obvious. 'The city's vigilant. It'll be a matter of public record that I came to the Monument, and we'll have been recorded together by those float-cams.'

'Exactly,' Childe said, nodding enthusiastically. 'So you risk nothing by getting in the volantor.'

'And should I at any point weary of your company?'

'You have my word that I'll let you leave.'

I decided to play along with him for the time being. Childe and I took the volantor's front pair of seats. Once ensconced, I turned around to acquaint myself with the other passenger, and then flinched as I saw him properly.

He wore a high-necked leather coat which concealed much of the lower half of his face. The upper part was shadowed under the generous rim of a Homburg, tipped down to shade his brow. Yet what remained visible was sufficient to shock me. There was only a blandly handsome silver mask; sculpted into an expression of quiet serenity. The eyes were blank silver surfaces, what I could see of his mouth a thin, slightly smiling slot.

'Doctor Trintignant,' I said.

He reached forward with a gloved hand, allowing me to shake it as one would the hand of a woman. Beneath the black velvet of the glove I felt armatures of hard metal. Metal that could crush diamond. 'The pleasure is entirely mine,' he said.

*

Airborne, the volantor's baroque ornamentation melted away to mirror-smoothness. Childe pushed ivory-handled control sticks forward, gaining altitude and speed. We seemed to be moving faster than the city ordinances allowed, avoiding the usual traffic corridors. I thought of the way he had followed me, researched my past and had my own volantor desert me. It would also have taken considerable resourcefulness to locate the reclusive Trintignant and persuade him to emerge from hiding.

Clearly Childe's influence in the city exceeded my own, even though he had been absent for so long.

'The old place hasn't changed much,' Childe said, swooping us through a dense conglomeration of golden buildings, as extravagantly tiered as the dream pagodas of a fever-racked Emperor.

'Then you've really been away? When you told me you'd faked your death, I wondered if you'd just gone into hiding.'

He answered with a trace of hesitation, 'I've been away, but not as far as you'd think. A family matter came up that was best dealt with confidentially, and I really couldn't be bothered explaining to everyone why I needed some peace and quiet on my own.'

'And faking your death was the best way to go about it?'

'Like I said, I couldn't have planned the Eighty if I'd tried. I had to bribe a lot of minor players in the project, of course, and I'll spare you the details of how we provided a corpse . . . but it all worked swimmingly, didn't it?'

'I never had any doubts that you'd died along with the rest of them.'

'I didn't like deceiving my friends. But I couldn't go to all that trouble and then ruin my plan with a few indiscretions.'

'You were friends, then?' solicited Trintignant.

'Yes, Doctor,' Childe said, glancing back at him. 'Way back when. Richard and I were rich kids – relatively rich, anyway

– with not enough to do. Neither of us were interested in the stock market or the social whirl. We were only interested in games.'

'Oh. How charming. What kinds of games, might I ask?'

'We'd build simulations to test each other – extraordinarily elaborate worlds filled with subtle dangers and temptations. Mazes and labyrinths; secret passages; trapdoors; dungeons and dragons. We'd spend months inside them, driving each other crazy. Then we'd go away and make them even harder.'

'But in due course you grew apart,' the doctor said. His synthesised voice had a curious piping quality.

'Yeah,' Childe said. 'But we never stopped being friends. It was just that Richard had spent so much time devising increasingly alien scenarios that he'd become more interested in the implied psychologies behind the tests. And I'd become interested only in the playing of the games; not their construction. Unfortunately Richard was no longer there to provide challenges for me.'

'You were always much better than me at playing them,' I said. 'In the end it got too hard to come up with something you'd find difficult. You knew the way my mind worked too well.'

'He's convinced that he's a failure,' Childe said, turning round to smile at the doctor.

'As are we all,' Trintignant answered. 'And with some justification, it must be said. I have never been allowed to pursue my admittedly controversial interests to their logical ends. You, Mister Swift, were shunned by those who you felt should have recognised your worth in the field of speculative alien psychology. And you, Mister Childe, have never discovered a challenge worthy of your undoubted talents.'

'I didn't think you'd paid me any attention, Doctor.'

'Nor had I. I have surmised this much since our meeting.'

The volantor dropped below ground level, descending into a brightly lit commercial plaza lined with shops and boutiques. With insouciant ease, Childe skimmed us between aerial walkways and then nosed the car into a dark side-tunnel. He gunned the machine faster, our speed indicated only by the passing of red set into the tunnel sides. Now and then another vehicle passed us, but once the tunnel had branched and rebranched half a dozen times, no further traffic appeared. The tunnel lights were gone now and when the volantor's headlights grazed the walls they revealed ugly cracks and huge, scarred absences of cladding. These old sub-surface ducts dated back to the city's earliest days, before the domes were thrown across the crater.

Even if I had recognised the part of the city where we had entered the tunnel system, I would have been hopelessly lost by now.

'Do you think Childe has brought us together to taunt us about our respective failures, Doctor?' I asked, beginning to feel uneasy again despite my earlier attempts at reassurance.

'I would consider that a distinct possibility, were Childe himself not conspicuously tainted by the same lack of success.'

'Then there must be another reason.'

'Which I'll reveal in due course,' Childe said. 'Just bear with me, will you? You two aren't the only ones I've gathered together.'

Presently we arrived somewhere.

It was a cave in the form of a near-perfect hemisphere, the great domed roof arching a clear three hundred metres from the floor. We were obviously well below Yellowstone's surface now. It was even possible that we had passed beyond the city's crater wall, so that above us lay only poisonous skies.

But the domed chamber was inhabited.

The roof was studded with an enormous number of lamps, flooding the interior with synthetic daylight. An island stood in the middle of the chamber, moated by a ring of uninviting water. A single bone-white bridge connected the mainland to the island, shaped like a great curved femur. The island was dominated by a thicket of slender, dark poplars partly concealing a pale structure situated near its middle.

Childe brought the volantor to a rest near the edge of the water and invited us to disembark.

'Where are we?' I asked, once I had stepped down.

'Query the city and find out for yourself,' Trintignant said.

The result was not what I was expecting. For a moment there was a shocking absence inside my head, the neural equivalent of a sudden, unexpected amputation.

The doctor's chuckle was an arpeggio played on a pipe organ. 'We have been out of range of city services from the moment we entered his conveyance.'

'You needn't worry,' Childe said. 'You are beyond city services, but only because I value the secrecy of this place. If I imagined it'd have come as a shock to you, I'd have told you already.'

'I'd have at least appreciated a warning, Roland,' I said.

'Would it have changed your mind about coming here?'

'Conceivably.'

The echo of his laughter betrayed the chamber's peculiar acoustics. 'Then are you at all surprised that I didn't tell you?'

I turned to Trintignant. 'What about you?'

'I confess my use of city services has been as limited as your own, but for rather different reasons.'

'The good Doctor needed to lie low,' Childe said. 'That meant he couldn't participate very actively in city affairs. Not if he didn't want to be tracked down and assassinated.'

I stamped my feet, beginning to feel cold. 'Good. What now?'

'It's only a short ride to the house,' Childe said, glancing towards the island.

Now a noise came steadily nearer. It was an antiquated, rumbling sound, accompanied by an odd, rhythmic sort of drumming, quite unlike any machine I had experienced. I looked towards the femoral bridge, suspecting as I did that it was exactly what it looked like: a giant, bio-engineered bone, carved with a flat roadbed. And something was approaching us over the span: a dark, complicated and unfamiliar contraption, which at first glance resembled an iron tarantula.

I felt the back of my neck prickle.

The thing reached the end of the bridge and swerved towards us. Two mechanical black horses provided the motive power. They were emaciated black machines with sinewy, piston-driven limbs, venting steam and snorting from intakes. Malignant red laser-eyes swept over us. The horses were harnessed to a four-wheeled carriage slightly larger than the volantor, above which was perched a headless humanoid robot. Skeletal hands gripped iron control cables which plunged into the backs of the horses' steel necks.

'Meant to inspire confidence, is it?' I asked.

'It's an old family heirloom,' Childe said, swinging open a black door in the side of the carriage. 'My uncle Giles made automata. Unfortunately – for reasons we'll come to – he was a bit of a miserable bastard. But don't let it put you off.'

He helped us aboard, then climbed inside himself, sealed the door and knocked on the roof. I heard the mechanical horses snort; alloy hooves hammered the ground impatiently. Then we were moving, curving around and ascending the gentle arc of the bridge of bone.

'Have you been here during the entire period of your absence, Mister Childe?' Trintignant asked.

He nodded. 'Ever since that family business came up. I've allowed myself the occasional visit back to the city – just like I did today – but I've tried to keep such excursions to a minimum.'

'Didn't you have horns the last time we met?' I said.

He rubbed the smooth skin of his scalp where the horns had been. 'Had to have them removed. I couldn't very well disguise myself otherwise.'

We crossed the bridge and navigated a path between the tall trees which sheltered the island's structure. Childe's carriage pulled up to a smart stop in front of the building and I was afforded my first unobstructed view of our destination. It was not one to induce great cheer. The house's architecture was haphazard: whatever basic symmetry it might once have had was lost under a profusion of additions and modifications. The roof was a jumbled collision of angles and spires, jutting turrets and sinister oubliettes. Not all of the embellishments had been arranged at strict right angles to their neighbours, and the style and apparent age of the house varied jarringly from place to place. Since our arrival in the cave the overhead lights had dimmed, simulating the onset of dusk, but only a few windows were illuminated, clustered together in the left-hand wing. The rest of the house had a forbidding aspect, the paleness of its stone, the irregularity of its construction and the darkness of its many windows suggesting a pile of skulls.

Almost before we had disembarked from the carriage, a reception party emerged from the house. It was a troupe of servitors – humanoid household robots, of the kind anyone would have felt comfortable with in the city proper – but they had been reworked to resemble skeletal ghouls or headless knights. Their mechanisms had been sabotaged so that they limped and creaked, and they had all had their voiceboxes disabled.

'Had a lot of time on his hands, your uncle,' I said.

'You'd have loved Giles, Richard. He was a scream.'

'I'll take your word for it, I think.'

The servitors escorted us into the central part of house, then took us through a maze of chill, dark corridors.

Finally we reached a large room walled in plush red velvet. A holoclavier sat in one corner, with a book of sheet music spread open above the projected keyboard. There was a malachite escritoire, a number of well-stocked bookcases, a single chandelier, three smaller candelabra and two fireplaces of distinctly gothic appearance, in one of which roared an actual fire. But the room's central feature was a mahogany table, around which three additional guests were gathered.

'Sorry to keep everyone waiting,' Childe said, closing a pair of sturdy wooden doors behind us. 'Now. Introductions.'

The others looked at us with no more than mild interest.

The only man amongst them wore an elaborately ornamented exoskeleton: a baroque support structure of struts, hinged plates, cables and servo-mechanisms. His face was a skull papered with deathly white skin, shading to black under his bladelike cheekbones. His eyes were concealed behind goggles, his hair a spray of stiff black dreadlocks.

Periodically he inhaled from a glass pipe, connected to a miniature refinery of bubbling apparatus placed before him on the table.

'Allow me to introduce Captain Forqueray,' Childe said. 'Captain – this is Richard Swift and . . . um, Doctor Trintignant.'

'Pleased to meet you,' I said, leaning across the table to shake Forqueray's hand. His grip felt like the cold clasp of a squid.

'The Captain is an Ultra; the master of the lighthugger *Apollyon*, currently in orbit around Yellowstone,' Childe added.

Trintignant refrained from approaching him.

'Shy, Doctor?' Forqueray said, his voice simultaneously deep and flawed, like a cracked bell.

'No, merely cautious. It is a matter of common knowledge that I have enemies amongst the Ultras.'

Trintignant removed his Homburg and patted his crown delicately, as if smoothing down errant hairs. Silver waves had been sculpted into his head-mask, so that he resembled a bewigged Regency fop dipped in mercury.

'You've enemies everywhere,' said Forqueray between gurgling inhalations. 'But I bear you no personal animosity for your atrocities, and I guarantee that my crew will extend you the same courtesy.'

'Very gracious of you,' Trintignant said, before shaking the Ultra's hand for the minimum time compatible with politeness. 'But why should your crew concern me?'

'Never mind that.' It was one of the two women speaking now. 'Who is this guy, and why does everyone hate him?'

'Allow me to introduce Hirz,' Childe said, indicating the woman who had spoken. She was small enough to have been a child, except that her face was clearly that of an adult woman. She was dressed in austere, tight-fitting black clothes which only emphasised her diminutive build. 'Hirz is – for want of a better word – a mercenary.'

'Except I prefer to think of myself as an information retrieval specialist. I specialise in clandestine infiltration for high-level corporate clients in the Glitter Band – physical espionage, some of the time. Mostly, though, I'm what used to be called a hacker. I'm also pretty damned good at my job.'

Hirz paused to swig down some wine. 'But enough about me. Who's the silver dude, and what did Forqueray mean about atrocities?'

'You're seriously telling me you're unaware of Trintignant's reputation?' I said.

'Hey, listen. I get myself frozen between assignments. That means I miss a lot of shit that goes down in Chasm City. Get over it.'

I shrugged and – with one eye on the doctor himself – told Hirz what I knew about Trintignant. I sketched in his early career as an experimental cyberneticist, how his reputation for fearless innovation had eventually brought him to Calvin Sylveste's attention.

Calvin had recruited Trintignant to his own research team, but the collaboration had not been a happy one. Trintignant's desire to find the ultimate fusion of flesh and machine had become obsessive; even – some said – perverse. After a scandal involving experimentation on unconsenting subjects, Trintignant had been forced to pursue his work alone, his methods too extreme even for Calvin.

So Trintignant had gone to ground, and continued his gruesome experiments with his only remaining subject.

Himself.

'So let's see,' said the final guest. 'Who have we got? An obsessive and thwarted cyberneticist with a taste for extreme modification. An intrusion specialist with a talent for breaking into highly protected – and dangerous – environments. A man with a starship at his disposal and the crew to operate it.'

Then she looked at Childe, and while her gaze was averted I admired the fine, faintly familiar profile of her face. Her long hair was the sheer black of interstellar space, pinned back from her face by a jewelled clasp which flickered with a constellation of embedded pastel lights. Who was she? I felt sure we had met once or maybe twice before. Perhaps we had passed each other amongst the shrines in the Monument to the Eighty, visiting the dead.

'And Childe,' she continued. 'A man once known for his love of intricate challenges, but long assumed dead.' Then she turned her piercing eyes upon me. 'And, finally, you.'

'I know you, I think—' I said, her name on the tip of my tongue.

'Of course you do.' Her look, suddenly, was contemptuous. 'I'm Celestine. You used to be married to me.'

All along, Childe had known she was here.

'Do you mind if I ask what this is about?' I said, doing my best to sound as reasonable as possible, rather than someone on the verge of losing their temper in polite company.

Celestine withdrew her hand once I had shaken it. 'Roland invited me here, Richard. Just the same way he did you, with the same veiled hints about having found something.'

'But you're . . .'

'Your ex-wife?' She nodded. 'Exactly how much do you remember, Richard? I heard the strangest rumours, you know. That you'd had me deleted from your long-term memory.'

'I had you suppressed, not deleted. There's a subtle distinction.'

She nodded knowingly. 'So I gather.'

I looked at the other guests, who were observing us. Even Forqueray was waiting, the pipe of his apparatus poised an inch from his mouth in expectation. They were waiting for me to say something; anything.

'Why exactly are you here, Celestine?'

'You don't remember, do you?'

'Remember what?'

'What it was I used to do, Richard, when we were married.'

'I confess I don't, no.'

Childe coughed. 'Your wife, Richard, was as fascinated by the alien as you were. She was one of the city's foremost specialists on the Pattern Jugglers, although she'd be entirely too modest to admit it herself.' He paused, apparently seeking Celestine's permission to continue. 'She visited them, long before you met, spending several years of her life at the study station on Spindrift. You swam with the Jugglers, didn't you, Celestine?'

'Once or twice.'

'And allowed them to reshape your mind, transforming its neural pathways into something deeply – albeit usually temporarily – alien.'

'It wasn't that big a deal,' Celestine said.

'Not if you'd been fortunate enough to have it happen to you, no. But for someone like Richard – who craved knowledge of the alien with every fibre of his existence – it would have been anything but mundane.' He turned to me. 'Isn't that true?'

'I admit I'd have done a great deal to experience communion with the Jugglers,' I said, knowing that it was pointless to deny it. 'But it just wasn't possible. My family lacked the resources to send me to one of the Juggler worlds, and the bodies that might ordinarily have funded that kind of trip – the Sylveste Institute, for instance – had turned their attentions elsewhere.'

'In which case Celestine was deeply fortunate, wouldn't you say?'

'I don't think anyone would deny that,' I said. 'To speculate about the shape of alien consciousness is one thing; but to drink it; to bathe in the full flood of it – to know it intimately, like a lover . . .' I trailed off for a moment. 'Wait a minute. Shouldn't you be on Resurgam, Celestine? There isn't time for the expedition to have gone there and come back.'

She eyed me with raptorial intent before answering, 'I never went.'

Childe leant over and refreshed my glass. 'She was turned down at the last minute, Richard. Sylveste had a grudge against anyone who'd visited the Jugglers; he suddenly decided they were all unstable and couldn't be trusted.'

I looked at Celestine wonderingly. 'Then all this time . . .?'

'I've been here, in Chasm City. Oh, don't look so crushed, Richard. By the time I learned I'd been turned down, you'd already decided to flush me out of your past. It was better for both of us this way.'

'But the deception . . .'

Childe put one hand on my shoulder, calmingly. 'There wasn't any. She just didn't make contact again. No lies; no deception; nothing to hold a grudge about.'

I looked at him, angrily. 'Then why the hell is she here?'

'Because I happen to have use for someone with the skills that the Jugglers gave to Celestine.'

'Which included?' I said.

'Extreme mathematical prowess.'

'And why would that have been useful?'

Childe turned to the Ultra, indicating that the man should remove his bubbling apparatus.

'I'm about to show you.'

The table housed an antique holo-projection system. Childe handed out viewers which resembled lorgnette binoculars, and, like so many myopic opera buffs, we studied the apparitions which floated into existence above the polished mahogany surface.

Stars: incalculable numbers of them – hard white and blood-red gems, strewn in lacy patterns against deep velvet blue.

Childe narrated: 'The better part of two and a half centuries ago, my uncle Giles – whose somewhat pessimistic handiwork you have already seen – made a momentous decision. He embarked on what we in the family referred to as the Programme, and then only in terms of extreme secrecy.'

Childe told us that the Programme was an attempt at covert deep space exploration.

Giles had conceived the work, funding it directly from the family's finances. He had done this with such ingenuity that the apparent wealth of House Childe had never faltered, even as the Programme entered its most expensive phase. Only a few select members of the Childe dynasty had even known of the Programme's existence, and that number had dwindled as time passed.

The bulk of the money had been paid to the Ultras, who had already emerged as a powerful faction by that time.

They had built the autonomous robot space probes according to this uncle's desires, and then launched them towards a variety of target systems. The Ultras could have delivered his probes to any system within range of their lighthugger ships, but the whole point of the exercise was to restrict the knowledge of any possible discoveries to the family alone. So the envoys crossed space by themselves, at only a fraction of the speed of light, and the targets they were sent to were all poorly explored systems on the ragged edge of human space.

The probes decelerated by use of solar sails, picked the most interesting worlds to explore, and then fell into orbit around them.

Robots were sent down, equipped to survive on the surface for many decades.

Childe waved his hand across the table. Lines radiated out from one of the redder suns in the display, which I assumed was Yellowstone's star. The lines reached out towards other stars, forming a three-dimensional scarlet dandelion several dozen light-years wide.

'These machines must have been reasonably intelligent,' Celestine said. 'Especially by the standards of the time.'

Childe nodded keenly. 'Oh, they were. Cunning little blighters. Subtle and stealthy and diligent. They had to be, to operate so far from human supervision.'

'And I presume they found something?' I said.

'Yes,' Childe said testily, like a conjurer whose carefully scripted patter was being ruined by a persistent heckler. 'But not immediately. Giles didn't expect it to be immediate, of course – the envoys would take decades to reach the closest systems they'd been assigned to, and there'd still be the communicational time lag to take into consideration. So my uncle resigned himself to forty or fifty years of waiting, and that was erring on the optimistic side.' He paused and sipped from his wine. 'Too bloody optimistic, as it happened. Fifty years passed . . . then sixty . . . but nothing of any consequence was ever reported back to Yellowstone, at least not in his lifetime. The envoys did, on occasion, find something interesting – but by then other human explorers had usually stumbled on the same find. And as the decades wore on, and the envoys failed to justify their invention, my uncle grew steadily more maudlin and bitter.'

'I'd never have guessed,' Celestine said.

'He died, eventually – bitter and resentful; feeling that the universe had played some sick cosmic trick on him. He could have lived for another fifty or sixty years with the right treatments, but I think by then he knew it would be a waste of time.'

'You faked your death a century and a half ago,' I said. 'Didn't you tell me it had something to do with the family business?'

He nodded in my direction. 'That was when my uncle told me about the Programme. I didn't know anything about it until then – hadn't heard even the tiniest hint of a rumour. No one in the family had. By then, of course, the project was costing us almost nothing, so there wasn't even a financial drain to be concealed.'

'And since then?'

'I vowed not to make my uncle's mistake. I resolved to sleep until the machines sent back a report, and then sleep again if the report turned out to be a false alarm.'

'Sleep?' I said.

He clicked his fingers and one entire wall of the room whisked back to reveal a sterile, machine-filled chamber.

I studied its contents.

There was a reefersleep casket of the kind Forqueray and his ilk used aboard their ships, attended by numerous complicated hunks of gleaming green support machinery. By use of such a casket, one might prolong the four-hundred-odd years of a normal human lifespan by many centuries, though reefersleep was not without its risks.

'I spent a century and a half in that contraption,' he said, 'waking every fifteen or twenty years whenever a report trickled in from one of the envoys. Waking is the worst part. It feels like you're made of glass; as if the next movement you make – the next breath you take – will cause you to shatter into a billion pieces. It always passes, and you always forget it an hour later, but it's never easier the next time.' He shuddered visibly. 'In fact, sometimes I think it gets harder each time.'

'Then your equipment needs servicing,' Forqueray said dismissively. I suspected it was bluff. Ultras often wore a lock of braided hair for every crossing they had made across interstellar space and survived all the myriad misfortunes which might befall a ship. But that braid also symbolised every occasion on which they had been woken from the dead, at the end of the journey.

They felt the pain as fully as Childe did, even if they were not willing to admit it.

'How long did you spend awake each time?' I asked.

'No more than thirteen hours. That was usually sufficient to tell if the message was interesting or not. I'd allow myself one or two hours to catch up on the news; what was going on in the wider universe. But I had to be disciplined. If I'd stayed awake longer, the attraction of returning to city life would have become overwhelming. That room began to feel like a prison.'

'Why?' I asked. 'Surely the subjective time must have passed very quickly?'

'You've obviously never spent any time in reefersleep, Richard. There's no consciousness when you're frozen, granted – but the transitions to and from the cold state are like an eternity, crammed with strange dreams.'

'But you hoped the rewards would be worth it?'

Childe nodded. 'And, indeed, they may well have been. I was last woken six months ago, and I've not returned to the chamber since. Instead, I've spent time gathering together the resources and the people for a highly unusual expedition.'

Now he made the table change its projection, zooming in on one particular star.

'I won't bore you with catalogue numbers, suffice to say that this is a system which no one around this table – with the possible exception of Forqueray – is likely to have heard of. There've never been any human colonies there, and no crewed vessel has ever passed within three light-years of it. At least, not until recently.'

The view zoomed in again, enlarging with dizzying speed.

A planet swelled up to the size of a skull, suspended above the table.

It was hued entirely in shades of grey and pale rust, cratered and gouged here and there by impacts and what must have been very ancient weathering processes. Though there was a suggestion of a wisp of atmosphere – a smoky blue halo encircling the planet – and though there were ice caps at either pole, the world looked neither habitable nor inviting.

'Cheerful-looking place, isn't it?' Childe said. 'I call it Golgotha.'

'Nice name,' Celestine said.

'But not, unfortunately, a very nice planet.' Childe made the view enlarge again, so that we were skimming the world's bleak, apparently lifeless surface. 'Pretty dismal, to be honest. It's about the same size as Yellowstone, receiving about the same amount of sunlight from its star. Doesn't have a moon. Surface gravity's close enough to one gee that you won't know the difference once you're suited up. A thin carbon dioxide atmosphere, and no sign that anything's ever evolved there. Plenty of radiation hitting the surface, but that's about your only hazard, and one we can easily deal with. Golgotha's tectonically dead, and there haven't been any large impacts on her surface for a few million years.'

'Sounds boring,' Hirz said.

'And it very probably is, but that isn't the point. You see, there's something on Golgotha.'

'What kind of something?' Celestine asked.

'That kind,' Childe said.

It came over the horizon.

It was tall and dark, its details indistinct. That first view of it was like the first glimpse of a cathedral's spire through morning fog. It tapered as it rose, constricting to a thin neck before flaring out again into a bulb-shaped finial, which in turn tapered to a needle-sharp point.

Though it was impossible to say how large the thing was, or what it was made of, it was very obviously a structure, as opposed to a peculiar biological or mineral formation. On Grand Teton, vast numbers of tiny single-celled organisms conspired to produce the slime towers which were that world's most famous natural feature, and while those towers reached impressive heights and were often strangely shaped, they were unmistakably the products of unthinking biological processes rather than conscious design. The structure on Golgotha was too symmetric for that, and entirely too solitary. If it had been a living thing, I would have expected to see others like it, with evidence of a supporting ecology of different organisms.

Even if it were a fossil, millions of years dead, I could not believe that there would be just one on the whole planet.

No. The thing had most definitely been put there.

'A structure?' I asked Childe.

'Yes. Or a machine. It isn't easy to decide.' He smiled. 'I call it Blood Spire. Almost looks innocent, doesn't it? Until you look closer.'

We spun round the Spire, or whatever it was, viewing it from all directions. Now that we were closer, it was clear that the thing's surface was densely detailed; patterned and textured with geometrically complex forms, around which snaked intestinal tubes and branching, veinlike bulges. The effect was to undermine my earlier certainty that the thing was non-biological.

Now it looked like some sinewy fusion of animal and machine: something that might have appealed in its grotesquerie to Childe's demented uncle.

'How tall is it?' I asked.

'Two hundred and fifty metres,' Childe said.

I saw that now there were tiny glints on Golgotha's surface, almost like metallic flakes which had fallen from the side of the structure.

'What are those?' I asked.

'Why don't I show you?' Childe said.

He enlarged the view still further, until the glints resolved into distinct shapes.

They were people.

Or – more accurately – the remains of what had once been people. It was impossible to say how many there had been. All had been mutilated in some fashion: crushed or pruned or bisected; the tattered ruins of their spacesuits were still visible in one or two places. Severed parts accompanied the bodies, often several tens of metres from the rightful owner.

It was as if they had been flung away in a fit a temper.

'Who were they?' Forqueray asked.

'A crew who happened to slow down in this system to make shield repairs,' Childe said. 'Their captain was called Argyle. They chanced upon the Spire and started exploring it, believing it to contain something of immense technological value.'

'And what happened to them?'

'They went inside in small teams, sometimes alone. Inside the Spire they passed through a series of challenges, each of which was harder than the last. If they made a mistake, the Spire punished them. The punishments were initially mild, but they became steadily more brutal. The trick was to know when to admit defeat.'

I leaned forward. 'How do you know all this?'

'Because Argyle survived. Not long, admittedly, but long enough for my machine to get some sense out of him. It had been on Golgotha the whole time, you see – watching Argyle's arrival, hiding and recording them as they confronted the Spire. And it watched him crawl out of the Spire, shortly before the last of his colleagues was ejected.'

'I'm not sure I'm prepared to trust either the testimony of a machine or a dying man,' I said.

'You don't have to,' Childe answered. 'You need only consider the evidence of your eyes. Do you see those tracks in the dust? They all lead into the Spire, and there are almost none leading to the bodies.'

'Meaning what?' I said.

'Meaning that they got inside, the way Argyle claimed. Observe also the way the remains are distributed. They're not all at the same distance from the Spire. They must have been ejected from different heights, suggesting that some got closer to the summit than others. Again, it accords with Argyle's story.'

With a sinking feeling of inevitability I saw where this was heading. 'And you want us to go there and find out what it was they were so interested in. Is that it?'

He smiled. 'You know me entirely too well, Richard.'

'I thought I did. But you'd have to be quite mad to go anywhere near that thing.'

'Mad? Possibly. Or simply very, very curious. The question is—' He paused and leaned across the table to refill my glass, all the while maintaining eye contact. 'Which are you?'

'Neither,' I said.

But Childe could be persuasive. A month later I was frozen aboard Forqueray's ship.

TWO

We reached orbit around Golgotha.

Thawed from reefersleep we convened for breakfast, riding a travel pod upship to the lighthugger's meeting room.

Everyone was there, including Trintignant and Forqueray, the latter inhaling from the same impressive array of flasks, retorts and spiralling tubes he had brought with him to Yellowstone. Trintignant had not slept with the rest of us, but looked none the worse for wear. He had, Childe said, his own rather specialised plumbing requirements, incompatible with standard reefersleep systems.

'Well, how was it?' Childe asked, throwing a comradely arm around my shoulders.

'Every bit as . . . dreadful as I'd been led to expect.' My voice was slurred, sentences taking an age to form in whatever part of my brain it was that handled language. 'Still a bit fuzzy.'

'Well, we'll soon fix that. Trintignant can synthesise a medichine infusion to pep up those neural functions, can't you, Doctor?'

Trintignant looked at me with his handsome, immobile mask of a face. 'It would be no trouble at all, my dear fellow . . .'

'Thanks.' I steadied myself; my mind crawled with half-remembered images of the botched cybernetic experiments which had earned Trintignant his notoriety. The thought of him pumping tiny machines into my skull made my skin crawl. 'But I'll pass on that for now. No offence intended.'

'And absolutely none taken.' Trintignant gestured towards a vacant chair. 'Come. Sit with us and join in the discussion. The topic, rather interestingly, is the dreams some of us experienced on the way here.'

'Dreams . . .?' I said. 'I thought it was just me. I wasn't the only one?'

'No,' Hirz said, 'you weren't the only one. I was on a moon in one of them. Earth's, I think. And I kept on trying to get inside this alien structure. Fucking thing kept killing me, but I'd always keep going back inside, like I was being brought back to life each time just for that.'

'I had the same dream,' I said, wonderingly. 'And there was another dream in which I was inside some kind of—' I halted, waiting for the words to assemble in my head. 'Some kind of underground tomb. I remember being chased down a corridor by an enormous stone ball which was going to roll over me.'

Hirz nodded. 'The dream with the hat, right?'

'My God, yes.' I grinned like a madman. 'I lost my hat, and I felt this ridiculous urge to rescue it!'

Celestine looked at me with something between icy detachment and outright hostility. 'I had that one too.'

'Me too,' Hirz said, chuckling. 'But I said fuck the hat. Sorry, but with the kind of money Childe's paying us, buying a new one ain't gonna be my biggest problem.'

An awkward moment followed, for only Hirz seemed at all comfortable about discussing the generous fees Childe had arranged as payment for the expedition. The initial sums had been large enough, but upon our return to Yellowstone we would all receive nine times as much; adjusted to match any inflation which might occur during the time – between sixty and eighty years – which Childe said the journey would span.

Generous, yes.

But I think Childe knew that some of us would have joined him even without that admittedly sweet bonus.

Celestine broke the silence, turning to Hirz. 'Did you have the one about the cubes, too?'

'Christ, yes,' the infiltration specialist said, as if suddenly remembering. 'The cubes. What about you, Richard?'

'Indeed,' I answered, flinching at the memory of that one. I had been one of a party of people trapped inside an endless series of cubic rooms, many of which contained lethal surprises. 'I was cut into pieces by a trap, actually. Diced, if I remember accurately.'

'Yeah. Not exactly on my top ten list of ways to die, either.'

Childe coughed. 'I feel I should apologise for the dreams. They were narratives I fed into your minds – Doctor Trintignant excepted – during the transition to and from reefersleep.'

'Narratives?' I said.

'I adapted them from a variety of sources, thinking they'd put us all in the right frame of mind for what lies ahead.'

'Dying nastily, you mean?' Hirz asked.

'Problem-solving, actually.' Childe served pitch-black coffee as he spoke, as if all that was ahead of us was a moderately bracing stroll. 'Of course, nothing that the dreams contained is likely to reflect anything that we'll find inside the Spire . . . but don't you feel better for having had them?'

I gave the matter some thought before responding.

'Not exactly, no,' I said.

Thirteen hours later we were on the surface, inspecting the suits Forqueray had provided for the expedition.

They were sleek white contraptions, armoured, powered and equipped with enough intelligence to fool a roomful of cyberneticians. They enveloped themselves around you, forming a seamless white surface which lent the wearer the appearance of a figurine moulded from soap. The suits quickly learned how you moved, adjusting and anticipating all the time like perfect dance partners.

Forqueray told us that each suit was capable of keeping its occupant alive almost indefinitely; that the suit would recycle bodily wastes in a near-perfect closed cycle, and could even freeze its occupant if circumstances merited such action. They could fly and would protect their user against just about any external environment, ranging from a vacuum to the crush of the deepest ocean.

'What about weapons?' Celestine asked, once we had been shown how to command the suits to do our bidding.

'Weapons?' Forqueray asked blankly.

'I've heard about these suits, Captain. They're supposed to contain enough firepower to take apart a small mountain.'

Childe coughed. 'There won't be any weapons, I'm afraid. I asked Forqueray to have them removed from the suits. No cutting tools, either. And you won't be able to achieve as much with brute force as you would with an unmodified suit. The servos won't allow it.'

'I'm not sure I understand. You're handicapping us before we go in?'

'No – far from it. I'm just abiding by the rules that the Spire sets. It doesn't allow weapons inside itself, you see – or anything else that might be used against it, like fusion torches. It senses such things and acts accordingly. It's very clever.'

I looked at him. 'Is this guesswork?'

'Of course not. Argyle already learned this much. No point making exactly the same mistakes again, is there?'

'I still don't get it,' Celestine said when we had assembled outside the shuttle, standing like so many white soap statuettes. 'Why fight the thing on its own terms at all? There are bound to be weapons on Forqueray's ship we could use from orbit; we could open it like a carcase.'

'Yes,' Childe said, 'and in the process destroy everything we came this far to learn?'

'I'm not talking about blowing it off the face of Golgotha. I'm just talking about clean, surgical dissection.'

'It won't work. The Spire is a living thing, Celestine. Or at least a machine intelligence many orders of magnitude cleverer than anything we've encountered to date. It won't tolerate violence being used against it. Argyle learned that much.

'Even if it can't defend itself against such attacks – and we don't know that – it will certainly destroy what it contains. We'll still have lost everything.'

'But still . . . no weapons?'

'Not quite,' Childe said, tapping the forehead region of his suit. 'We still have our minds, after all. That's why I assembled this team. If brute force would have been sufficient, I'd have had no need to scour Yellowstone for such fierce intellects.'

Hirz spoke from inside her own, smaller version of the armoured suit. 'You'd better not be taking the piss.'

'Forqueray?' Childe said. 'We're nearly there now. Put us down on the surface two klicks from the base of the Spire. We'll cross the remaining distance on foot.'

Forqueray obliged, bringing the triangular formation down. Our suits had been slaved to his, but now we regained independent control.

Through the suit's numerous layers of armour and padding I felt the rough texture of the ground beneath my feet. I held up a thickly gauntleted hand and felt the breeze of Golgotha's thin atmosphere caress my palm. The tactile transmission was flawless, and when I moved, the suit flowed with me so effortlessly that I had no sense of being encumbered by it. The view was equally impressive, with the suit projecting an image directly into my visual field rather than forcing me to peer through a visor.

A strip along the top of my visual field showed a three-hundred-and-sixty-degree view all around me, and I could zoom in on any part of it almost without thinking. Various overlays – sonar, radar, thermal, gravimetric – could be dropped over the existing visual field with the same ease. If I looked down I could even ask the suit to edit me out of the image, so that I could view the scene from a disembodied perspective. As we walked along the suit threw traceries of light across the scenery: an etchwork of neon which would now and then coalesce around an odd-shaped rock or peculiar pattern of ground markings. After several minutes of this I had adjusted the suit's alertness threshold to what I felt was a useful level of protectivity, neither too watchful nor too complacent.

Childe and Forqueray had taken the lead on the ground. They would have been difficult to distinguish, but my suit had partially erased their suits, so that they seemed to walk unprotected save for a ghostly second skin. When they looked at me they would perceive the same consensual illusion.

Trintignant followed a little way behind, moving with the automaton-like stiffness I had now grown almost accustomed to.

Celestine followed, with me a little to her stern.

Hirz brought up the rear, small and lethal and – now that I knew her a little better – quite unlike any of the few children I had ever met.

And ahead – rising, ever rising – was the thing we had come all this way to best.

It had been visible, of course, long before we set down. The Spire was a quarter of a kilometre high, after all. But I think we had all chosen to ignore it; to map it out of our perceptions, until we were much closer. It was only now that we were allowing those mental shields to collapse, forcing our imaginations to confront the fact of the tower's existence.

Huge and silent, it daggered into the sky.

It was much as Childe had shown us, except that it seemed infinitely more massive; infinitely more present. We were still a quarter of a kilometre from the thing's base, and yet the flared top – the bulb-shaped finial – seemed to be leaning back over us, constantly on the point of falling and crushing us. The effect was exacerbated by the occasional high-altitude cloud that passed overhead, writhing in Golgotha's fast, thin jet-streams. The whole tower looked as if it were toppling. For a long moment, taking in the immensity of what stood before us – its vast age; its vast, brooding capacity for harm – the idea of trying to reach the summit felt uncomfortably close to insanity.

Then a small, rational voice reminded me that this was exactly the effect the Spire's builders would have sought.

Knowing that, it was fractionally easier to take the next step closer to the base.

'Well,' Celestine said. 'It looks like we've found Argyle.'

Childe nodded. 'Yes. Or what's left of the poor bastard.'

We had found several body parts by then, but his was the only one that was anywhere near being complete. He had lost a leg inside the Spire, but had been able to crawl to the exit before the combination of bleeding and asphyxiation killed him. It was here – dying – that he had been interviewed by Childe's envoy, which had only then emerged from its hiding place.

Perhaps he had imagined himself in the presence of a benevolent steel angel.

He was not well preserved. There was no bacterial life on Golgotha, and nothing that could be charitably termed weather, but there were savage dust-storms, and these must have intermittently covered and revealed the body, scouring it in the process. Parts of his suit were missing, and his helmet had cracked open, exposing his skull. Papery sheets of skin adhered to the bone here and there, but not enough to suggest a face.

Childe and Forqueray regarded the corpse uneasily, while Trintignant knelt down and examined it in more detail. A float-cam belonging to the Ultra floated around, observing the scene with goggling arrays of tightly packed lenses.

'Whatever took his leg off did it cleanly,' the doctor reported, pulling back the tattered layers of the man's suit fabric to expose the stump. 'Witness how the bone and muscle have been neatly severed along the same plane, like a geometric slice through a platonic solid? I would speculate that a laser was responsible for this, except that I see no sign of cauterisation. A high-pressure water jet might have achieved the same precision of cut, or even an extremely sharp blade.'

'Fascinating, Doc,' Hirz said, kneeling down next to him. 'I'll bet it hurt like fuck, too, wouldn't you?'

'Not necessarily. The degree of pain would depend acutely on the manner in which the nerve ends were truncated. Shock does not appear to have been the primary agent in this man's demise.' Doctor Trintignant fingered the remains of a red fabric band a little distance above the end of the leg. 'Nor was the blood loss as rapid as might have been expected given the absence of cauterisation. This band was most likely a tourniquet, probably applied from his suit's medical kit. The same kit almost certainly included analgesics.'

'It wasn't enough to save him, though,' Childe said.

'No.' Trintignant stood up, the movement reminding me of an escalator. 'But you must concede that he did rather well, considering the impediments.'

For most of its height Blood Spire was no thicker than a few dozen metres, and considerably narrower just below the bulb-like upper part. But, like a slender chess piece, its lower parts swelled out considerably to form a wide base. That podium-like mass was perhaps fifty metres in diametre: a fifth of the structure's height. From a distance it appeared to rest solidly on the base: a mighty obelisk requiring the deepest of foundations to anchor it to the ground.

But it didn't.

The Spire's base failed to touch the surface of Golgotha at all, but floated above it, spaced by five or six clear metres of air. It was as if someone had constructed a building slightly above the ground, kicked away the stilts, and it had simply stayed there.

We all walked confidently towards the rim and then stopped; none of us were immediately willing to step under that overhang.

'Forqueray?' Childe said.

'Yes?'

'Let's see what that drone of yours has to say.'

Forqueray had his float-cam fly under the rim, orbiting the underside of the Spire in a lazily widening spiral. Now and then it fingered the base with a spray of laser-light, and once or twice even made contact, skittering against the flat surface. Forqueray remained impassive, glancing slightly down as he absorbed the data being sent back to his suit.

'Well?' Celestine said. 'What the hell's keeping it up?'

Forqueray took a step under the rim. 'No fields; not even a minor perturbation of Golgotha's own magnetosphere. No significant alteration in the local gravitational vector, either. And – before we assume more sophistication than is strictly necessary – there are no concealed supports.'

Celestine was silent for a few moments before answering, 'All right. What if the Spire doesn't weigh anything? There's air here; not much of it I'll grant you – but what if the Spire's mostly hollow? There might be enough buoyancy to make the thing float, like a balloon.'

'There isn't,' Forqueray said, opening a fist to catch the cam, which flew into his grasp like a trained kestrel. 'Whatever's above us is solid matter. I can't read its mass, but it's blocking an appreciable cosmic-ray flux, and none of our scanning methods can see through it.'

'Forqueray's right,' Childe said. 'But I understand your reluctance to accept this, Celestine. It's perfectly normal to feel a sense of denial.'

'Denial?'

'That what we are confronting is truly alien. But I'm afraid you'll get over it, just the way I did.'

'I'll get over it when I feel like getting over it,' Celestine said, joining Forqueray under the dark ceiling.

She looked up and around, less in the manner of someone admiring a fresco than in the manner of a mouse cowering beneath a boot.

But I knew exactly what she was thinking.

In four centuries of deep space travel there had been no more than glimpses of alien sentience. We had long expected they were out there somewhere. But that suspicion had grown less fervent as the years passed; world after world had revealed only faint, time-eroded traces of cultures that might once have been glorious but which were now utterly destroyed. The Pattern Jugglers were clearly the products of intelligence, but not necessarily intelligent themselves. And – though they had been spread from star to star in the distant past – they did not now depend on any form of technology that we recognised. The Shrouders were little better: secretive minds cocooned inside shells of restructured spacetime.

They had never been glimpsed, and their nature and intentions remained worryingly unclear.

Yet Blood Spire was different.

For all its strangeness, for all that it mocked our petty assumptions about the way matter and gravity should conduct themselves, it was recognisably a manufactured thing. And, I told myself, if it had managed to hang above Golgotha's surface until now, it was extremely unlikely to choose this moment to come crashing down.

I stepped across the threshold, followed by the others.

'Makes you wonder what kind of beings built it,' I said. 'Whether they had the same hopes and fears as us, or whether they were so far beyond us as to seem like gods.'

'I don't give a shit who built it,' Hirz said. 'I just want to know how to get into the fucking thing. Any bright ideas, Childe?'

'There's a way,' he said.

We followed him until we stood in a small, nervous huddle under the centre of the ceiling. It had not been visible before, but directly above us was a circle of utter blackness against the mere gloom of the Spire's underside.

'That?' Hirz said.

'That's the only way in,' Childe said. 'And the only way you get out alive.'

I said, 'Roland – how exactly did Argyle and his team get inside?'

'They must have brought something to stand on. A ladder or something.'

I looked around. 'There's no sign of it now, is there?'

'No, and it doesn't matter. We don't need anything like that – not with these suits. Forqueray?'

The Ultra nodded and tossed the float-cam upwards.

It caught flight and vanished into the aperture. Nothing happened for several seconds, other than the occasional stutter of red light from the hole. Then the cam emerged, descending again into Forqueray's hand.

'There's a chamber up there,' Forqueray said. 'Flat-floored, surrounding the hole. It's twenty metres across, with a ceiling just high enough to let us stand upright. It's empty. There's what looks like a sealed door leading out of the chamber into the rest of the Spire.'

'Can we be sure there's nothing harmful in it?' I asked.

'No,' Childe said. 'But Argyle said the first room was safe. We'll just have to take his word on that one.'

'And there's room for all of us up there?'

Forqueray nodded. 'Easily.'

I suppose there should have been more ceremony to the act, but there was no sense of significance, or even foreboding, as we rose into the ceiling. It was like the first casual step onto the tame footslopes of a mountain, unweighted by any sense of the dangers that undoubtedly lay ahead.

Inside it was exactly as Forqueray had described.

The chamber was dark, but the float-cam provided some illumination and our suits' sensors were able to map out the chamber's shape and overlay this information on our visual fields.

The floor had a metalled quality to it, dented here and there, and the edge where it met the hole was rounded and worn.

I reached down to touch it, feeling a hard, dull alloy which nonetheless seemed as if it would yield given sufficient pressure. Data scrolled onto my visual read-out, informing me that the floor had a temperature only one hundred and fifteen degrees above absolute zero. My palm chemosensor reported that the floor was mainly iron, laced with carbon woven into allotropic forms it could not match against any in its experience. There were microscopic traces of almost every other stable isotope in the periodic table, with the odd exception of silver. All of this was inferred, for when the chemosensor attempted to shave off a microscopic layer of the flooring for more detailed analysis, it gave a series of increasingly heated error messages before falling silent.

I tried the chemosensor against part of my own suit.

It had stopped working.

'Fix that,' I instructed my suit, authorising it to divert whatever resources it required to the task.

'Problem, Richard?' asked Childe.

'My suit's damaged. Minor, but annoying. I don't think the Spire was too thrilled about my taking a sample of it.'

'Shit. I probably should have warned you of that. Argyle's lot had the same problem. It doesn't like being cut into, either. I suspect you got off with a polite warning.'

'Generous of it,' I said.

'Be careful, all right?' Childe then told everyone else to disable their chemosensors until told otherwise. Hirz grumbled, but everyone else quietly accepted what had to be done.

In the meantime I continued my own survey of the room, counting myself lucky that my suit had not provoked a stronger reaction. The chamber's circular wall was fashioned from what looked like the same hard, dull alloy, devoid of detail except for the point where it framed what was obviously a door, raised a metre above the floor. Three blocky steps led up to it.

The door itself was one metre wide and perhaps twice that in height.

'Hey,' Hirz said. 'Feel this.'

She was kneeling down, pressing a palm against the floor.

'Careful,' I said. 'I just did that and—'

'I've turned off my chemo-whatsit, don't worry.'

'Then what are you—'

'Why don't you reach down and see for yourself?'

Slowly, we all knelt down and touched the floor. When I had felt it before it had been as cold and dead as the floor of a crypt, yet that was no longer the case. Now it was vibrating; as if somewhere not too far from here a mighty engine was shaking itself to pieces: a turbine on the point of breaking loose from its shackles. The vibration rose and fell in throbbing waves. Once every thirty seconds or so it reached a kind of crescendo, like a great slow inhalation.

'It's alive,' Hirz said.

'It wasn't like that just now.'

'I know.' Hirz turned and looked at me. 'The fucking thing just woke up, that's why. It knows we're here.'

THREE

I moved to the door and studied it properly for the first time.

Its proportions were reassuringly normal, requiring only that we stoop down slightly to step through. But for now the door was sealed by a smooth sheet of metal, which would presumably slide across once we had determined how to open it. The only guidance came from the door's thick metal frame, which was inscribed with faint geometric markings.

I had not noticed them before.

The markings were on either side of the door, on the uprights of the frame. Beginning from the bottom on the left-hand side, there was a dot – it was too neatly circular to be accidental – a flat-topped equilateral triangle, a pentagon and then a heptagonal figure. On the right-hand side there were three more figures with eleven, thirteen and twenty sides respectively.

'Well?' Hirz was looking over my shoulder. 'Any bright ideas?'

'Prime numbers,' I said. 'At least, that's the simplest explanation I can think of. The number of vertices of the shapes on the left-hand frame are the first four primes: one, three, five and seven.'

'And on the other frame?'

Childe answered for me. 'The eleven-sided figure is the next one in the sequence. Thirteen's one prime too high, and twenty isn't a prime at all.'

'So you're saying if we choose eleven, we win?' Hirz reached out her hand, ready to push her hand against the lowest figure on the right, which she could reach without ascending the three steps. 'I hope the rest of the tests are this simp—'

'Steady, old girl.' Childe had caught her wrist. 'Mustn't be too hasty. We shouldn't do anything until we've arrived at a consensus. Agreed?'

Hirz pulled back her hand. 'Agreed . . .'

It took only a few minutes for everyone to agree that the eleven-sided figure was the obvious choice. Celestine did not immediately accede; she looked long and hard at the right-hand frame before concurring with the original choice.

'I just want to be careful, that's all,' she said. 'We can't assume anything. They might think from right to left, so that the figures on the right form the sequence which those on the left are supposed to complete. Or they might think diagonally, or something even less obvious.'

Childe nodded. 'And the obvious choice might not always be the right one. There might be a deeper sequence – something more elegant – which we're just not seeing. That's why I wanted Celestine along. If anyone'll pick out those subtleties, it's her.'

She turned to him. 'Just don't put too much faith in whatever gifts the Jugglers might have given me, Childe.'

'I won't. Unless I have to.' Then he turned to the infiltration specialist, still standing by the frame. 'Hirz – you may go ahead.'

She reached out and touched the frame, covering the eleven-sided figure with her palm.

After a heart-stopping pause there was a clunk, and I felt the floor vibrate even more strongly than it had before. Ponderously, the door slid aside, revealing another dark chamber.

We all looked around, assessing each other.

Nothing had changed; none of us had suffered any sudden, violent injuries.

'Forqueray?' Childe said.

The Ultra knew what he meant. He tossed the float-cam through the open doorway and waited several seconds until it flew back into his grasp.

'Another metallic chamber, considerably smaller than this one. The floor is level with the door, so we'll have gained a metre or so in height. There's another door on the opposite side, again with markings. Other than that, I don't see anything except bare metal.'

'What about the other side of *this* door?' Childe said. 'Are there markings on it as well?'

'Nothing that the drone could make out.'

'Then let me be the guinea pig. I'll step through and we'll see what happens. I'm assuming that even if the door seals behind me, I'll still be able to open it. Argyle said the Spire didn't prevent anyone from leaving provided they hadn't attempted to access a new room.'

'Try it and see,' Hirz said. 'We'll wait on this side. If the door shuts on you, we'll give you a minute and then we'll open it ourselves.'

Childe walked up the three steps and across the threshold. He paused, looked around and then turned back to face us, looking down on us now.

Nothing had happened.

'Looks like the door stays open for now. Who wants to join me?'

'Wait,' I said. 'Before we all cross over, shouldn't we take a look at the problem? We don't want to be trapped in there if it's something we can't solve.'

Childe walked over to the far door. 'Good thinking. Forqueray, pipe my visual field through to the rest of the team, will you?'

'Done.'

We saw what Childe was seeing, his gaze tracking along the doorframe. The markings looked much like those we had just solved, except that the symbols were different. Four unfamiliar shapes were inscribed on the left side of the door, spaced vertically. Each of the shapes was composed of four rectangular elements of differing sizes, butted together in varying configurations. Childe then looked at the other side of the door. There were four more shapes on the right, superficially similar to those we had already seen.

'Definitely not a geometric progression,' Childe said.

'No. Looks more like a test of conservation of symmetry through different translations,' Celestine said, her voice barely a murmur. 'The lowest three shapes on the left have just been rotated through an integer number of right angles, giving their corresponding forms on the right. But the top two shapes aren't rotationally symmetric. They're mirror images, plus a rotation.'

'So we press the top right shape, right?'

'Could be. But the left one's just as valid.'

Hirz said, 'Yeah. But only if we ignore what the last test taught us. Whoever the suckers were that made thing, they think from left to right.'

Childe raised his hand above the right-side shape. 'I'm prepared to press it.'

'Wait.' I climbed the steps and walked over the threshold, joining Childe. 'I don't think you should be in here alone.'

He looked at me with something resembling gratitude. None of the others had stepped over yet, and I wondered if I would have done so had Childe and I not been friends.

'Go ahead and press it,' I said. 'Even if we get it wrong, the punishment's not likely to be too severe at this stage.'

He nodded and palmed the right-side symbol.

Nothing happened.

'Maybe the left side . . .?'

'Try it. It can't hurt. We've obviously done *something* wrong already.'

Childe moved over and palmed the other symbol on the top row.

Nothing.

I gritted my teeth. 'All right. Might as well try one of the ones we definitely know is wrong. Are you ready for that?'

He glanced at me and nodded. 'I didn't go to the hassle of bringing in Forqueray just for the free ride, you know. These suits are built to take a lot of crap.'

'Even alien crap?'

'About to find out, aren't we?'

He moved to palm one of the lower symmetry pairs.

I braced myself, unsure what to expect when we made a deliberate error, wondering if the Spire's punishment code would even apply in such a case. After all, what was clearly the correct choice had elicited no response, so what was the sense in being penalised for making the wrong one?

He palmed the shape; still nothing happened.

'Wait,' Celestine said, joining us. 'I've had an idea. Maybe it won't respond – positively or negatively – until we're all in the same room.'

'Only one way to find out,' Hirz said, joining her.

Forqueray and Trintignant followed.

When the last of them had crossed the threshold, the rear door – the one we had all come through – slid shut. There were no markings on it, but nothing that Forqueray did made it open again.

Which, I supposed, made a kind of sense. We had committed to accepting the next challenge now; the time for dignified retreats had passed. The thought was not a pleasant one. This room was smaller than the last one, and the environment was suddenly a lot more claustrophobic.

We were standing almost shoulder to shoulder.

'You know, I think the first chamber was just a warm-up,' Celestine said. 'This is where it starts getting more serious.'

'Just press the fucking thing,' Hirz said.

Childe did as he was told. As before, there was an uncomfortable pause which probably lasted only half a second, but which felt abyssally longer, as if our fates were being weighed by distant judicial machinery. Then thumps and vibrations signalled the opening of the door.

Simultaneously, the door behind us had opened again. The route out of the Spire was now clear again.

'Forqueray . . .' Childe said.

The Ultra tossed the float-cam into the darkness.

'Well?'

'This is getting a tiny bit monotonous. Another chamber, another door, another set of markings.'

'No booby traps?'

'Nothing the drone can resolve, which I'm afraid isn't saying much.'

'I'll go in this time,' Celestine said. 'No one follow me until I've checked out the problem, understood?'

'Fine by me,' Hirz said, peering back at the escape route.

Celestine stepped into the darkness.

I decided that I was no longer enjoying the illusion of seeing everyone as if we were not wearing suits – we all looked far too vulnerable, suddenly – and ordered my own to stop editing my visual field to that extent. The transition was smooth; suits formed around us like thickening auras. Only the helmet parts remained semi-transparent, so that I could still identify who was who without cumbersome visual tags.

'It's another mathematical puzzle,' Celestine said. 'Still fairly simple. We're not really being stretched yet.'

'Yeah, well, I'll settle for not being really stretched,' Hirz said.

Childe looked unimpressed. 'Are you certain of the answer?'

'Trust me,' Celestine said. 'It's perfectly safe to enter.'

This time the markings looked more complicated; at first I feared that Celestine had been over-confident.

On the left-hand side of the door – extending the height of the frame – was a vertical strip marked by many equally spaced horizontal grooves, in the manner of a ruler. But some of the cleanly cut grooves were deeper than the others. On the other side of the door was a similar ruler, but with a different arrangement of deeper grooves, not lining up with any of those on the right.

I stared at the frame for several seconds, thinking the solution would click into my mind; willing myself back into the problem-solving mode that had once seemed so natural. But the pattern of grooves refused to snap into any neat mathematical order.

I looked at Childe, seeing no greater comprehension in his face.

'Don't you see it?' Celestine said.

'Not quite,' I said.

'There are ninety-one grooves, Richard.' She spoke with the tone of a teacher who had begun to lose patience with a tardy pupil. 'Now counting from the bottom, the following grooves are deeper than the rest: the third, the sixth, the tenth, the fifteenth . . . shall I continue?'

'I think you'd better,' Childe said.

'There are seven other deep grooves, concluding with the ninety-first. You must see it now, surely. Think geometrically.'

'I am,' I said testily.

'Tell us, Celestine,' Childe said, between what was obviously gritted teeth.

She sighed. 'They're triangular numbers.'

'Fine,' Childe said. 'But I'm not sure I know what a triangular number is.'

Celestine glanced at the ceiling for a moment, as if seeking inspiration. 'Look. Think of a dot, will you?'

'I'm thinking,' Childe said.

'Now surround that dot by six neighbours, all the same distance from each other. Got that?'

'Yes.'

'Now keep on adding dots, extending out in all directions, as far as you can imagine – each dot having six neighbours.'

'With you so far.'

'You should have something resembling a Chinese chequer-board. Now concentrate on a single dot again, near the middle. Draw a line from it to one of its six neighbours, and then another line to one of the two dots either side of the neighbour you just chose. Then join the two neighbouring dots. What have you got?'

'An equilateral triangle.'

'Good. That's three taken care of. Now imagine that the triangle's sides are twice as long. How many dots are connected together now?'

Childe answered after only a slight hesitation, 'Six. I think.'

'Yes.' Celestine turned to me. 'Are you following, Richard?'

'More or less . . .' I said, trying to hold the shapes in my head.

'Then we'll continue. If we triple the size of the triangle, we link together nine dots along the sides, with an additional dot in the middle. That's ten. Continue – with a quadruple-sized triangle – and we hit fifteen.'

She paused, giving us time to catch up. 'There are eight more; up to ninety-one, which has thirteen dots along each side.'

'The final groove,' I said, accepting for myself that whatever this problem was, Celestine had definitely understood it.

'But there are only seven deep grooves in that interval,' she continued. 'That means all we have to do is identify the groove on the right which corresponds to the missing triangular number.'

'All?' Hirz said.

'Look, it's simple. I *know* the answer, but you don't have to take my word for it. The triangles follow a simple sequence. If there are N dots in the lower row of the last triangle, the next one will have N plus one more. Add one to two and you've got three. Add one to two to three, and you've got six. One to two to three to four, and you've got ten. Then fifteen, then twenty-one . . .' Celestine paused. 'Look, it's senseless taking my word for it. Graph up a chequerboard display on your suits – Forqueray, can you oblige? – and start arranging dots in triangular patterns.'

We did. It took quarter of an hour, but after that time we had all – Hirz included – convinced ourselves by brute force that Celestine was right. The only missing pattern was for the fifty-five-dot case, which happened to coincide with one of the deep grooves on the right side of the door.

It was obvious, then. That *was* the one to press.

'I don't like it,' Hirz said. 'I see it now . . . but I didn't see it until it was pointed out to me. What if there's another pattern none of us are seeing?'

Celestine looked at her coldly. 'There isn't.'

'Look, there's no point arguing,' Childe said. 'Celestine saw it first, but we always knew she would. Don't feel bad about it, Hirz. You're not here for your mathematical prowess. Nor's Trintignant, nor's Forqueray.'

'Yeah, well, remind me when I can do something useful,' Hirz said.

Then she pushed forward and pressed the groove on the right side of the door.

Progress was smooth and steady for the next five chambers. The problems to be solved grew harder, but after consultation the solution was never so esoteric that we could not all agree on it. As the complexity of the task increased, so did the area taken up by the frames, but other than that there was no change in the basic nature of the challenges. We were never forced to proceed more quickly than we chose, and the Spire always provided a clear route back to the exit every time a doorway had been traversed. The door immediately behind us would seal only once we had all entered the room where the current problem lay, which meant that we were able to assess any given problem before committing ourselves to its solution. To convince ourselves that were indeed able to leave, we had Hirz go back the way we had come in. She was able to return to the first room unimpeded – the rear-facing doors opened and closed in sequence to allow her to pass – and then make her way back to the rest of us by using the entry codes we had already discovered.

But something she said upon her return disturbed us.

'I'm not sure if it's my imagination or not . . .'

'What?' Childe snapped.

'I think the doorways are getting narrower. And lower. There was definitely more headroom at the start than there is now. I guess we didn't notice when we took so long to move from room to room.'

'That doesn't make much sense,' Celestine said.

'As I said, maybe I imagined it.'

But we all knew she had done no such thing. The last two times I had stepped across a door's threshold my suit had bumped against the frame. I had thought nothing of it at the time – putting it down to carelessness – but that had evidently been wishful thinking.

'I wondered about the doors already,' I said. 'Doesn't it seem a little convenient that the first one we met was just the right size for us? It could have come from a human building.'

'Then why are they getting smaller?' Childe asked.

'I don't know. But I think Hirz is right. And it does worry me.'

'Me too. But it'll be a long time before it becomes a problem.' Childe turned to the Ultra. 'Forqueray – do the honours, will you?'

I turned and looked at the chamber ahead of us. The door was open now, but none of us had yet stepped across the threshold. As always, we waited for Forqueray to send his float-cam snooping ahead of us, establishing that the room contained no glaring pitfalls.

Forqueray tossed the float-cam through the open door.

We saw the usual red stutters as it swept the room in visible light. 'No surprises,' Forqueray said, in the usual slightly absent tone he adopted when reporting the cam's findings. 'Empty metallic chamber . . . only slightly smaller than the one we're standing in now. A door at the far end with a frame that extends half a metre out on either side. Complex inscriptions this time, Celestine.'

'I'll cope, don't you worry.'

Forqueray stepped a little closer to the door, one arm raised with his palm open. His expression remained calm as he waited for the drone to return to its master. We all watched, and then – as the moment elongated into seconds – began to suspect that something was wrong.

The room beyond was utterly dark; no stammering flashes now.

'The cam—' Forqueray said.

Childe's gaze snapped to the Ultra's face. 'Yes?'

'It isn't transmitting anymore. I can't detect it.'

'That isn't possible.'

'I'm telling you.' The Ultra looked at us, his fear not well concealed. 'It's gone.'

Childe moved into the darkness, through the frame.

Just as I was admiring his bravery I felt the floor shudder. Out of the corner of my eye I saw a flicker of rapid motion, like an eyelid closing.

The rear door – the one that led out of the chamber in which we were standing – had just slammed shut.

Celestine fell forward. She had been standing in the gap.

'No . . .' she said, hitting the ground with a detectable thump.

'Childe!' I shouted, unnecessarily. 'Stay where you are – something just happened.'

'What?'

'The door behind us closed on Celestine. She's been injured . . .'

I was fearing the worst – that the door might have snipped off an arm or a leg as it closed – but it was, mercifully, not that serious. The door had damaged the thigh of her suit, grazing an inch of its armour away as it closed, but Celestine herself had not been injured. The damaged part was still airtight, and the suit's mobility and critical systems remained unimpaired.

Already, in fact, the self-healing mechanisms were coming into play repairing the wound.

She sat up on the ground. 'I'm OK. The impact was hard, but I don't think I've done any permanent damage.

'You sure?' I said, offering her a hand.

'Perfectly sure,' she said, standing up without my assistance.

'You were lucky,' Trintignant said. 'You were only partly blocking the door. Had that not been the case, I suspect your injuries would have been more interesting.'

'What happened?' Hirz asked.

'Childe must have triggered it,' Forqueray said. 'As soon as he stepped into the other room, it closed the rear door.' The Ultra stepped closer to the aperture. 'What happened to my float-cam, Childe?'

'I don't know. It just isn't here. There isn't even a trace of debris, and there's no sign of anything that could have destroyed it.'

The silence that followed was broken by Trintignant's piping tones. 'I believe this makes a queer kind of sense.'

'You do, do you?' I said.

'Yes, my dear fellow. It is my suspicion that the Spire has been tolerating the drone until now – lulling us, if you will, into a false sense of security. Yet now the Spire has decreed that we must discard that particular mental crutch. It will no longer permit us to gain any knowledge of the contents of a room until one of us steps into it. And at that moment it will prevent any of us *leaving* until we have solved that problem.'

'You mean it's changing the rules as it goes along?' Hirz asked.

The doctor turned his exquisite silver mask towards her. 'Which rules did you have in mind, Hirz?'

'Don't fuck with me, Doc. You know what I mean.'

Trintignant touched a finger to the chin of his helmet. 'I confess I do not. Unless it is your contention that the Spire has at some point agreed to bind by a set of strictures, which I would ardently suggest is far from the case.'

'No,' I said. 'Hirz is right, in one way. There *have* been rules. It's clear that it won't tolerate us inflicting physical harm against it. And it won't allow us to enter a room until we've all stepped into the preceding one. I think those are pretty fundamental rules.'

'Then what about the drone, and the door?' asked Childe.

'It's like Trintignant said. It tolerated us playing outside the rules until now, but we shouldn't have assumed that was always going to be the case.'

Hirz nodded. 'Great. What else is it tolerating now?'

'I don't know.' I managed a thin smile. 'I suppose the only way to find out is to keep going.'

We passed through another eight rooms, taking between one and two hours to solve each.

There had been a couple of occasions when we had debated whether to continue, with Hirz usually the least keen of us, but so far the problems had not been insurmountably difficult. And we were making a kind of progress. Mostly the rooms were blank, but every now and then there was a narrow, trellised window, panelled in stained sheets of what was obviously a substance very much more resilient than glass or even diamond. Sometimes these windows opened only into gloomy interior spaces, but on one occasion we were able to look outside, able to sense some of the height we had attained. Forqueray, who had been monitoring our journey with an inertial compass and gravitometre, confirmed that we had ascended at least fifteen vertical metres since the first chamber. That almost sounded impressive, until one considered the several hundred metres of Spire that undoubtedly lay above us. Another few hundred rooms, each posing a challenge more testing than the last?

And the doors were definitely getting smaller.

It was an effort to squeeze through now, and while the suits were able to reshape themselves to some extent, there was a limit to how compact they could become.

It had taken us sixteen hours to reach this point. At this rate it would take many days to get anywhere near the summit.

But none of us had imagined that this would be over quickly.

'Tricky,' Celestine said, after studying the latest puzzle for many minutes. 'I think I see what's going on here, but . . .'

Childe looked at her. 'You think, or you know?'

'I mean what I said. It's not easy, you know. Would you rather I let someone else take first crack at it?'

I put a hand on Celestine's arm and spoke to her privately. 'Easy. He's just anxious, that's all.'

She brushed my hand away. 'I didn't ask you to defend me, Richard.'

'I'm sorry. I didn't mean—'

'Never mind.' Celestine switched off private and addressed the group. 'I think these markings are shadows. Look.'

By now we had all become reasonably adept at drawing figures using our suits' visualisation systems. These sketchy hallucinations could be painted on any surface, apparently visible to all.

Celestine, who was the best at this, drew a short red hyphen on the wall.

'See this? A one-dimensional line. Now watch.' She made the line become a square; splitting into two parallel lines joined at their ends. Then she made the square rotate until it was edge-on again, and all we could see was the line.

'We see it . . .' Childe said.

'You can think of a line as the one-dimensional shadow of a two-dimensional object, in this case a square. Understand?'

'I think we get the gist,' Trintignant said.

Celestine made the square freeze, and then slide diagonally, leaving a copy of itself to which it was joined at the corners.

'Now. We're looking at a two-dimensional figure this time; the shadow of a three-dimensional cube. See how it changes if I rotate the cube, how it elongates and contracts?'

'Yes. Got that,' Childe said, watching the two joined squares slide across each other with a hypnotically smooth motion, only one square visible, as the imagined cube presented itself face-on to the wall.

'Well, I think what these figures . . .' Celestine sketched a hand an inch over the intricate designs worked into the frame, 'I think what these figures represent are two-dimensional shadows of four-dimensional objects.'

'Fuck off,' Hirz said.

'Look, just concentrate, will you? This one's easy. It's a hypercube. That's the four-dimensional analogue of a cube. You just take a cube and extend it *outwards*; just the same way that you make a cube from a square.' Celestine paused, and for a moment I thought she was going to throw up her hands in despair. 'Look. Look at this.' And then she sketched something on the wall: a cube set inside a slightly larger one, to which it was joined by diagonal lines. 'That's what the three-dimensional shadow of a hypercube would look like. Now all you have to do is collapse that shadow by one more dimension, down to two, to get *this*—' She jabbed at the beguiling design marked on the door.

'I think I see it,' Childe said, without anything resembling confidence.

Maybe I did, too – though I felt the same lack of certainty. Childe and I had certainly taunted each other with higher-dimensional puzzles in our youth, but never had so much depended on an intuitive grasp of those mind-shattering mathematical realms. 'All right,' I said. 'Supposing that *is* the shadow of a tesseract . . . what's the puzzle?'

'This,' Celestine said, pointing to the other side of the door, to what seemed like an utterly different – though no less complex – design. 'It's the same object, after a rotation.'

'The shadow changes that drastically?'

'Start getting used to it, Richard.'

'All right.' I realised she was still annoyed with me for touching her. 'What about the others?'

'They're all four-dimensional objects; relatively simple geometric forms. This one's a four-simplex; a hypertetrahedon. It's a hyper pyramid with five tetrahedral faces . . .' Celestine trailed off, looking at us with an odd expression on her face. 'Never mind. The point is, all the corresponding forms on the right should be the shadows of the same polytopes after a simple rotation through higher-dimensional space. But one isn't.'

'Which is?'

She pointed to one of the forms. 'This one.'

'And you're certain of that?' Hirz said. 'Because I'm sure as fuck not.'

Celestine nodded. 'Yes. I'm completely sure of it now.'

'But you can't make any of us see that this is the case?'

She shrugged. 'I guess you either see it or you don't.'

'Yeah? Well maybe we should have all taken a trip to the Pattern Jugglers. Then maybe I wouldn't be about to shit myself.'

Celestine said nothing, but merely reached out and touched the errant figure.

'There's good news and there's bad news,' Forqueray said after we had traversed another dozen or so rooms without injury.

'Give us the bad news first,' Celestine said.

Forqueray obliged, with what sounded like the tiniest degree of pleasure. 'We won't be able to get through more than two or three more doors. Not with these suits on.'

There had been no real need to tell us that. It had become crushingly obvious during the last three or four rooms that we were near the limit; that the Spire's subtly shifting internal architecture would not permit further movement within the bulky suits. It had been an effort to squeeze through the last door; only Hirz was oblivious to these difficulties.

'Then we might as well give up,' I said.

'Not exactly.' Forqueray smiled his vampiric smile. 'I said there was good news as well, didn't I?'

'Which is?' Childe said.

'You remember when we sent Hirz back to the beginning, to see if the Spire was going to allow us to leave at any point?'

'Yes,' Childe said. Hirz had not repeated the complete exercise since, but she had gone back a dozen rooms, and found that the Spire was just as operative as it had been before. There was no reason to think she would not have been able to make her way to the exit, had she wished.

'Something bothered me,' Forqueray said. 'When she went back, the Spire opened and closed doors in sequence to allow her to pass. I couldn't see the sense in that. Why not just open all the doors all the doors along her route?'

'I confess it troubled me as well,' Trintignant said.

'So I thought about it, and decided there must be a reason not to have all the doors open at once.'

Childe sighed. 'Which was?'

'Air,' Forqueray said.

'You're kidding, aren't you?'

The Ultra shook his head. 'When we began, we were moving in vacuum – or at least through air that was as thin as that on Golgotha's surface. That continued to be the case for the next few rooms. Then it began to change. Very slowly, I'll grant you – but my suit sensors picked up on it immediately.'

Childe pulled a face. 'And it didn't cross your mind to tell any of us about this?'

'I thought it best to wait until a pattern became apparent.' Forqueray glanced at Celestine, whose face was impassive.

'He's right,' Trintignant said. 'I too have become aware of the changing atmospheric conditions. Forqueray has also doubtless noticed that the temperature in each room has been a little warmer than the last. I have extrapolated these trends and arrived at a tentative conclusion. Within two – possibly three – rooms, we will be able to discard our suits and breathe normally.'

'Discard our suits?' Hirz looked at him as if he were insane. 'You have got to be fucking kidding.'

Childe raised a hand. 'Wait a minute. When you said air, Doctor Trintignant, you didn't say it was anything we could breathe.'

The doctor's answer was a melodious piped refrain. 'Except it is. The ratios of the various gases are remarkably close to those we employ in our suits.'

'Which isn't possible. I don't remember providing a sample.'

Trintignant dipped his head in a nod. 'Nonetheless, it appears that one has been taken. The mix, incidentally, corresponds to precisely the atmospheric preferences of Ultras. Argyle's expedition would surely have employed a slightly different mix, so it is not simply the case that the Spire has a long memory.'

I shivered.

The thought that the Spire – this vast breathing thing through which we were scurrying like rats – had somehow reached inside the hard armour of our suits to snatch a sample of air, without our knowing, made my guts turn cold. It not only knew of our presence, but it knew – intimately – what we were.

It understood our fragility.

As if wishing to reward Forqueray for his observation, the next room contained a substantially thicker atmosphere than any of its predecessors, and was also much warmer. It was not yet capable of supporting life, but one would not have died instantly without the protection of a suit.

The challenge that the room held was by far the hardest, even by Celestine's reckoning. Once again the essence of the task lay in the figures marked on either side of the door, but now these figures were linked by various symbols and connecting loops, like the subway map of a foreign city. We had encountered some of these hieroglyphics before – they were akin to mathematical operators, like the addition and subtraction symbol – but we had never seen so many. And the problem itself was not simply a numerical exercise, but – as far as Celestine could say with any certainty – a problem about topological transformations in four dimensions.

'Please tell me you see the answer immediately,' Childe said.

'I . . .' Celestine trailed off. 'I think I do. I'm just not absolutely certain. I need to think about this for a minute.'

'Fine. Take all the time you want.'

Celestine fell into a reverie which lasted minutes, and then tens of minutes. Once or twice she would open her mouth and take a breath of air as if in readiness to speak, and on one or two other occasions she took a promising step closer to the door, but none of these things heralded the sudden, intuitive breakthrough we were all hoping for. She always returned to same silent, standing posture. The time dragged on; first an hour and then the better part of two hours.

All this, I thought, before even Celestine had seen the answer. It might take days if we were all expected to follow her reasoning.

Finally, however, she spoke. 'Yes, I see it.'

Childe was the first to answer. 'Is it the one you thought it was originally?'

'No.'

'Great,' Hirz said.

'Celestine . . .' I said, trying to defuse the situation. 'Do you understand why you made the wrong choice originally?'

'Yes. I think so. It was a trick answer; an apparently correct solution which contained a subtle flaw. And what looked like the clearly wrong answer turned out to be the right one.'

'Right. And you're certain of that?'

'I'm not certain of anything, Richard. I'm just saying this is what I believe the answer to be.'

I nodded. 'I think that's all any of us can honestly expect. Do you think there's any chance of the rest of us following your line of argument?'

'I don't know. How much do you understand about Kaluza-Klein spaces?'

'Not a vast amount, I have to admit.'

'That's what I feared. I could probably explain my reasoning to some of you, but there'd always be someone who didn't get it—' Celestine looked pointedly at Hirz. 'We could be in this bloody room for weeks before any of us grasp the solution. And the Spire may not tolerate that kind of delay.'

'We don't know that,' I cautioned.

'No,' Childe said. 'On the other hand, we can't afford to spend weeks solving every room. There's going to have to come a point where we put our faith in Celestine's judgement. I think that time may have come.'

I looked at him, remembering that his mathematical fluency had always been superior to mine. The puzzles I had set him had seldom defeated him, even if it had taken weeks for his intensely methodical mind to arrive at the solution. Conversely, he had often managed to beat me by setting a mathematical challenge of similar intricacy to the one now facing Celestine. They were not quite equals, I knew, but neither were their abilities radically different. It was just that, thanks to her experiences with the Pattern Jugglers, Celestine would always arrive at the answer with the superhuman speed of a savant.

'Are you saying I should just press it, with no consultation?' Celestine said.

Childe nodded. 'Provided everyone else agrees with me . . .'

It was not an easy decision to make, especially after having navigated so many rooms via such a ruthlessly democratic process. But we all saw the sense, even Hirz coming around to our line of thinking in the end.

'I'm telling you,' she said. 'We get through this door, I'm out of here, money or not.'

'You're giving up?' Childe asked.

'You saw what happened to those poor bastards outside. They must have thought they could keep on solving next test.'

Childe looked sad, but said, 'I understand perfectly. But I trust you'll reassess your decision as soon as we're through?'

'Sorry, but my mind's made up. I've had enough of this shit.' Hirz turned to Celestine. 'Put us all out of our misery, will you? Make the choice.'

Celestine looked at each of us in turn. 'Are you ready for this?'

'We are,' Childe said, answering for the group. 'Go ahead.'

Celestine pressed the symbol. There was the usual yawning moment of expectation; a moment that stretched agonisingly. We all stared at the door, willing it to begin sliding open.

This time nothing happened.

'Oh God . . .' Hirz began.

Something happened then, almost before she had finished speaking, but it was over almost before we had sensed any change in the room. It was only afterwards – playing back the visual record captured by our suits – that we were able to make any sense of events.

The walls of the chamber – like every room we had passed through, in fact – had looked totally seamless. But in a flash something emerged from the wall: a rigid, sharp-ended metal rod spearing out at waist-height. It flashed through the air from wall to wall, vanishing like a javelin thrown into water. None of us had time to notice it, let alone react bodily. Even the suits – programmed to move out of the way of obvious moving hazards – were too slow. By the time they began moving, the javelin had been and gone. And if there had been only that one javelin, we might have missed it happening at all.

But a second emerged, a fraction of a second after the first, spearing across the room at a slightly different angle.

Forqueray happened to be standing in the way.

The javelin passed through him as if he were made of smoke; its progress was unimpeded by his presence. But it dragged behind it a comet-tail of gore, exploding out of his suit where he had been speared, just below the elbow. The pressure in the room was still considerably less than atmospheric.

Forqueray's suit reacted with impressive speed, but it was still sluggish compared to the javelin.

It assessed the damage that had been inflicted on the arm, aware of how quickly its self-repair systems could work to seal that inch-wide hole, and came to a rapid conclusion. The integrity could be restored, but not before unacceptable blood and pressure loss. Since its duty was always to keep its wearer alive, no matter what the costs, it opted to sever the arm above the wound; hyper-sharp irised blades snicked through flesh and bone in an instant.

All that took place long before any pain signals had a chance to reach his brain. The first thing Forqueray knew of his misfortune was when his arm clanged to his feet.

'I think—' he started saying. Hirz dashed over to the Ultra and did her best to support him.

Forqueray's truncated arm ended in a smooth silver iris.

'Don't talk,' Childe said.

Forqueray, who was still standing, looked at his injury with something close to fascination. 'I—'

'I said don't talk.' Childe knelt down and picked up the amputated arm, showing the evidence to Forqueray. The hole went right through it, as cleanly bored as a rifle barrel.

'I'll live,' Forqueray managed.

'Yes, you will,' Trintignant said. 'And you may also count yourself fortunate. Had the projectile pierced your body, rather than one of its extremities, I do not believe we would be having this conversation.'

'You call this fortunate?'

'A wound such as yours can be made good with only trivial intervention. We have all the equipment we need aboard the shuttle.'

Hirz looked around uneasily. 'You think the punishment's over?'

'I think we'd know if it wasn't,' I said. 'That was our first mistake, after all. We can expect things to be a little worse in future, of course.'

'Then we'd better not make any more screw-ups, had we?' Hirz was directing her words at Celestine.

I had expected an angry rebuttal. Celestine would have been perfectly correct to remind Hirz that – had the rest of us been forced to make that choice – our chances of hitting the correct answer would have been a miserable one in six.

But instead Celestine just spoke with the flat, soporific tones of one who could not quite believe she had made such an error.

'I'm sorry . . . I must have . . .'

'Made the wrong decision. Yes.' I nodded. 'And there'll undoubtedly be others. You did your best, Celestine – better than any of us could have managed.'

'It wasn't good enough.'

'No, but you narrowed the field down to two possibilities. That's a lot better than six.'

'He's right,' Childe said. 'Celestine, don't cut yourself up about this. Without you we wouldn't have got as far as we did. Now go ahead and press the other answer – the one you settled on originally – and we'll get Forqueray back to base camp.'

The Ultra glared at him. 'I'm fine, Childe. I can continue.'

'Maybe you can, but it's still time for a temporary retreat. We'll get that arm looked at properly, and then we'll come back with lightweight suits. We can't carry on much further with these, anyway – and I don't particularly fancy continuing with no armour at all.'

Celestine turned back to the frame. 'I can't promise that this is the right one, either.'

'We'll take that chance. Just hit them in sequence – best choice first – until the Spire opens a route back to the start.'

She pressed the symbol that had been her first choice, before she had analysed the problem more deeply and seen a phantom trap.

As always, Blood Spire did not oblige us with an instant judgement on the choice we had made. There was a moment when all of us tensed, expecting the javelins to come again . . . but this time we were spared further punishment.

The door opened, exposing the next chamber.

We did not step through, of course. Instead, we turned around and made our way back through the succession of rooms we had already traversed, descending all the while, almost laughing at the childish simplicity of the very earliest puzzles compared to those we had faced before the attack.

As the doors opened and closed in sequence, the air thinned out and the skin of Blood Spire became colder, less like a living thing, more like an ancient, brooding machine. But still that distant, throbbing respiratory vibration rattled the floors, lower now, and slower: the Spire letting us know it was aware of our presence and, perhaps, the tiniest bit disappointed at this turning back.

'All right, you bastard,' Childe said. 'We're retreating, but only for now. We're coming back, understand?'

'You don't have to take it personally,' I said.

'Oh, but I do,' Childe said. 'I take it very personally indeed.'

We reached the first chamber, and then dropped down through what had been the entrance hole. After that, it was just a short flight back to the waiting shuttle.

It was dark outside.

We had been in the Spire for more than nineteen hours.

FOUR

'It'll do,' Forqueray said, tilting his new arm this way and that.

'Do?' Trintignant sounded mortally wounded. 'My dear fellow, it is a work of exquisite craftsmanship; a thing of beauty. It is unlikely that you will see its like again, unless of course I am called upon to perform a similar procedure.'

We were sitting inside the shuttle, still parked on Golgotha's surface. The ship was a squat, aerodynamically blunt cylinder which had landed tail-down and then expanded a cluster of eight bubbletents around itself: six for our personal quarters during the expedition, one commons area, and a general medical bay equipped with all the equipment Trintignant needed to do his work. Surprisingly – to me, at least, who admitted to some unfamiliarity with these things – the shuttle's fabricators had been more than able to come up with the various cybernetic components that the doctor required, and the surgical tools at his disposal – glistening, semi-sentient things which moved to his will almost before they were summoned – were clearly state of the art by any reasonable measure.

'Yes, well, I'd have rather you'd reattached my old arm,' Forqueray said, opening and closing the sleek metal gauntlet of his replacement.

'It would have been almost insultingly trivial to do that,' Trintignant said. 'A new hand could have been cultured and regrafted in a few hours. If that did not appeal to you, I could have programmed your stump to regenerate a hand of its own accord; a perfectly simple matter of stem-cell manipulation. But what would have been the point? You would be very likely to lose it as soon as we suffer our next punishment. Now you will only be losing machinery – a far less traumatic prospect.'

'You're enjoying this,' Hirz said, 'aren't you?'

'It would be churlish to deny it,' Trintignant said. 'When you have been deprived of willing subjects as long as I have, it's only natural to take pleasure in those little opportunities for practice that fate seems fit to present.'

Hirz nodded knowingly. She had not heard of Trintignant upon our first meeting, I recalled, but she had lost no time in forming her subsequent opinion of the man. 'Except you won't just stop with a hand, will you? I checked up on you, Doc – after that meeting in Childe's house. I hacked into some of the medical records that the Stoner authorities still haven't declassified, because they're just too damned disturbing. You really went the whole hog, didn't you? Some of the things I saw in those files – your victims – they stopped me from sleeping.'

And yet still she had chosen to come with us, I thought. Evidently the allure of Childe's promised reward outweighed any reservations she might have had about sharing a room with Trintignant. But I wondered about those medical records. Certainly, the publicly released data had contained more than enough atrocities for the average nightmare. It chilled the blood to think that Trintignant's most heinous crimes had never been fully revealed.

'Is it true?' I said. 'Were there really worse things?'

'That depends,' Trintignant said. 'There were subjects upon whom I pushed my experimental techniques further than is generally realised, if that is what you mean. But did I ever approach what I considered were the true limits? No. I was always hindered.'

'Until, perhaps, now,' I said.

The rigid silver mask swivelled to face us all in turn. 'That is as may be. But please give the following matter some consideration. I can surgically remove all your limbs now, cleanly, with the minimum of complications. The detached members could be put into cryogenic storage, replaced by prosthetic systems until we have completed the task that lies ahead of us.'

'Thanks . . .' I said, looking around at the others. 'But I think we'll pass on that one, Doctor.'

Trintignant offered his palms magnanimously. 'I am at your disposal, should you wish to reconsider.'

We spent a full day in the shuttle before returning to the Spire. I had been mortally tired, but when I finally slept, it was only to submerge myself in yet more labyrinthine dreams, much like those Childe had pumped into our heads during the reefersleep transition. I woke feeling angry and cheated, and resolved to confront him about it.

But something else snagged my attention. There was something wrong with my wrist. Buried just beneath the skin was a hard rectangle, showing darkly through my flesh. Turning my wrist this way and that, I admired the object, acutely – and strangely conscious of its rectilinearity. I looked around me, and felt the same visceral awareness of the other shapes which formed my surroundings. I did not know whether I was more disturbed at the presence of the alien object under my flesh, or my unnatural reaction to it.

I stumbled groggily into the common quarters of the shuttle, presenting my wrist to Childe, who was sitting there with Celestine.

She looked at me before Childe had a chance to answer. 'So you've got one too,' she said, showing me the similar shape lurking just below her own skin. The shape rhymed – there was no other word for it – with the surrounding panels and extrusions of the commons. 'Um, Richard?' she added.

'I'm feeling a little strange.'

'Blame Childe. He put them there. Didn't you, you lying rat?'

'It's easily removed,' he said, all innocence. 'It just seemed more prudent to implant the devices while you were all asleep anyway, so as not to waste any more time than necessary.'

'It's not just the thing in my wrist,' I said, 'whatever it is.'

'It's something to keep us awake,' Celestine said, her anger just barely under control. Feeling less myself than ever, I watched the way her face changed shape as she spoke, conscious of the armature of muscle and bone lying just beneath the skin.

'Awake?' I managed.

'A . . . shunt, of some kind,' she said. 'Ultras use them, I gather. It sucks fatigue poisons out of the blood, and puts other chemicals back into the blood to upset the brain's normal sleeping cycle. With one of these you can stay conscious for weeks, with almost no psychological problems.'

I forced a smile, ignoring the sense of wrongness I felt. 'It's the almost part that worries me.'

'Me too.' She glared at Childe. 'But much as I hate the little rat for doing this without my permission, I admit to seeing the sense in it.'

I felt the bump in my wrist again. 'Trintignant's work, I presume?'

'Count yourself lucky he didn't hack your arms and legs off while he was at it.'

Childe interrupted her. 'I told him to install the shunts. We can still catnap, if we have the chance. But these devices will let us stay alert when we need alertness. They're really no more sinister than that.'

'There's something else . . .' I said tentatively. I glanced at Celestine, trying to judge if she felt as oddly as I did. 'Since I've been awake, I've . . . experienced things differently. I keep seeing shapes in a new light. What exactly have you done to me, Childe?'

'Again, nothing irreversible. Just a small medichine infusion—'

I tried to keep my temper. 'What sort of medichines?'

'Neural modifiers.' He raised a hand defensively, and I saw the same rectangular bulge under his skin. 'Your brain is already swarming with Demarchist implants and cellular machines, Richard, so why pretend that what I've done is anything more than a continuation of what was already there?'

'What the fuck is he talking about?' said Hirz, who had been standing at the door to the commons for the last few seconds. 'Is it to do with the weird shit I've been dealing with since waking up?'

'Very probably,' I said, relieved that at least I was not going insane. 'Let me guess – heightened mathematical and spatial awareness?'

'If that's what you call it, yeah. Seeing shapes everywhere, and thinking of them fitting together . . .'

Hirz turned to look at Childe. Small as she was, she looked easily capable of inflicting injury. 'Start talking, dickhead.'

Childe spoke with quiet calm. 'I put modifiers in your brain, via the wrist shunt. The modifiers haven't performed any radical neural restructuring, but they are suppressing and enhancing certain regions of brain function. The effect – crudely speaking

– is to enhance your spatial abilities, at the expense of some less essential functions. What you are getting is a glimpse into the cognitive realms that Celestine inhabits as a matter of routine.' Celestine opened her mouth to speak, but he cut her off with a raised palm. 'No more than a glimpse, no, but I think you'll agree that – given the kinds of challenges the Spire likes to throw at us – the modifiers will give us an edge that we lacked previously.'

'You mean you've turned us all into maths geniuses, overnight?'

'Broadly speaking, yes.'

'Well, that'll come in handy,' Hirz said.

'It will?'

'Yeah, when you try and fit the pieces of your dick back together.'

She lunged for him.

'Hirz, I . . .'

'Stop,' I said, interceding. 'Childe was wrong to do this without our consent, but – given the situation we find ourselves in – the idea makes sense.'

'Whose side are you on?' Hirz said, backing away with a look of righteous fury in her eyes.

'Nobody's,' I said. 'I just want to do whatever it takes to beat the Spire.'

Hirz glared at Childe. 'All right. This time. But you try another stunt like that, and . . .'

But even then it was obvious that Hirz had come to the conclusion that I had already arrived at myself that, given what the Spire was likely to test us with, it was better to accept these machines than ask for them to be flushed out of our systems.

There was just one troubling thought which I could not quite dismiss.

Would I have welcomed the machines so willingly before they had invaded my head, or were they influencing my decision?

I had no idea.

But I decided to worry about that later.

FIVE

'Three hours,' Childe said triumphantly. 'Took us nineteen to reach this point on our last trip through. That has to mean something, doesn't it?'

'Yeah,' Hirz said snidely. 'It means it's a piece of piss when you know the answers.'

We were standing by the door where Celestine had made her mistake the last time. She had just pressed the correct topological symbol and the door had opened to admit us to the chamber beyond, one we had not so far stepped into. From now on we would be facing fresh challenges again, rather than passing through those we had already faced. The Spire, it appeared, was more interested in probing the limits of our understanding than getting us simply to solve permutations of the same basic challenge.

It wanted to break us, not stress us.

More and more I was thinking of it as a sentient thing: inquisitive and patient and – when the mood took it – immensely capable of cruelty.

'What's in there?' Forqueray said.

Hirz had gone ahead into the unexplored room.

'Well, fuck me if it isn't another puzzle.'

'Describe it, would you?'

'Weird shape shit, I think.' She was quiet for a few seconds. 'Yeah. Shapes in four dimensions again. Celestine – you wanna take a look at this? I think it's right up your street.'

'Any idea what the nature of the task is?' Celestine asked.

'Fuck, I don't know. Something to do with stretching, I think . . .'

'Topological deformations,' Celestine murmured before joining Hirz in the chamber.

For a minute or so the two of them conferred, studying the marked doorframe like a pair of discerning art critics.

On the last run through, Hirz and Celestine had shared almost no common ground: it was unnerving to see how much Hirz now grasped. The machines Childe had pumped into our skulls had improved the mathematical skills of all of us – with the possible exception of Trintignant, who I suspected had not received the therapy – but the effects had differed in nuance, degree and stability. My mathematical brilliance came in feverish, unpredictable waves, like inspiration to a laudanum-addicted poet. Forqueray had gained astonishing fluency in arithmetic, able to count huge numbers of things simply by looking at them for a moment.

But Hirz's change had been the most dramatic of all, something even Childe was taken aback by. On the second pass through the Spire she had been intuiting the answers to many of the problems at a glance, and I was certain that she was not always remembering what the correct answer had been. Now, as we encountered the tasks that had challenged even Celestine, Hirz was still able to perceive the essence of a problem, even if it was beyond her to articulate the details in the formal language of mathematics.

And if she could not yet see her way to selecting the correct answer, she could at least see the one or two answers that were clearly wrong.

'Hirz is right,' Celestine said eventually. 'It's about topological deformations, stretching operations on solid shapes.'

Once again we were seeing the projected shadows of four-dimensional lattices. On the right side of the door, however, the shadows were of the same objects after they had been stretched and squeezed and generally distorted. The problem was to identify the shadow that could only be formed with a shearing, in addition to the other operations.

It took an hour, but eventually Celestine felt certain that she had selected the right answer. Hirz and I attempted to follow her arguments, but the best we could do was agree that two of the other answers would have been wrong. That, at least, was an improvement on anything we would have been capable of before the medichine infusions, but it was only moderately comforting.

Nonetheless, Celestine had selected the right answer. We moved into the next chamber.

'This is as far as we can go with these suits,' Childe said, indicating the door that lay ahead of us. 'It'll be a squeeze, even with the lighter suits – except for Hirz, of course.'

'What's the air like in here?' I asked.

'We could breathe it,' Forqueray said. 'And we'll have to, briefly. But I don't recommend that we do that for any length of time – at least not until we're forced into it.'

'Forced?' Celestine said. 'You think the doors are going to keep getting smaller?'

'I don't know. But doesn't it feel as if this place is forcing us to expose ourselves to it, to make ourselves maximally vulnerable? I don't think it's done with us just yet.' He paused, his suit beginning to remove itself. 'But that doesn't mean we have to humour it.'

I understood his reluctance. The Spire had hurt him, not us.

Beneath the Ultra suits which had brought us this far we had donned as much of the lightweight versions as was possible. They were skintight suits of reasonably modern design, but they were museum pieces compared to the Ultra equipment. The helmets and much of the breathing gear had been impossible to put on, so we had carried the extra parts strapped to our backs. Despite my fears, the Spire had not objected to this, but I remained acutely aware that we did not yet know all the rules under which we played.

It only took three or four minutes to get out of the bulky suits and into the new ones; most of this time was taken up running status checks. For a minute or so, with the exception of Hirz, we had all breathed Spire air.

It was astringent, blood-hot, humid, and smelt faintly of machine oil.

It was a relief when the helmets flooded with the cold, tasteless air of the suits' backpack recyclers.

'Hey.' Hirz, the only one still wearing her original suit, knelt down and touched the floor. 'Check this out.'

I followed her, pressing the flimsy fabric of my glove against the surface.

The structure's vibrations rose and fell with increased strength, as if we had excited it by removing our hard protective shells.

'It's like the fucking thing's getting a hard-on,' Hirz said.

'Let's push on,' Childe said. 'We're still armoured – just not as effectively as before – but if we keep being smart, it won't matter.'

'Yeah. But it's the being smart part that worries me. No one smart would come within pissing distance of this fucking place.'

'What does that make you, Hirz?' Celestine asked.

'Greedier than you'll ever know,' she said.

Nonetheless we made good progress for another eleven rooms. Now and then a stained-glass window allowed a view out of Golgotha's surface, which looked very far below us. By Forqueray's estimate we had gained forty-five vertical metres since entering the Spire. Although two hundred further metres lay ahead – the bulk of the climb, in fact – for the first time it began to appear possible that we might succeed. That, of course, was contingent on several assumptions. One was that the problems, while growing steadily more difficult, would not become insoluble. The other was that the doorways would not continue to narrow now that we had discarded the bulky suits.

But they did.

As always, the narrowing was imperceptible from room to room, but after five or six it could not be ignored. After ten or fifteen more rooms we would again have to scrape our way between them.

And what if the narrowing continued beyond that point?

'We won't be able to go on,' I said. 'We won't fit – even if we're naked.'

'You are entirely too defeatist,' Trintignant said.

Childe sounded reasonable. 'What would you propose, Doctor?'

'Nothing more than a few minor adjustments of the basic human body-plan. Just enough to enable us to squeeze through apertures which would be impassable with our current . . . encumbrances.'

Trintignant looked avariciously at my arms and legs.

'It wouldn't be worth it,' I said. 'I'll accept your help after I've been injured, but if you're thinking that I'd submit to anything more drastic . . . well, I'm afraid you're severely mistaken, Doctor.'

'Amen to that,' Hirz said. 'For a while back there, Swift, I really thought this place was getting to you.'

'It isn't,' I said. 'Not remotely. And in any case, we're thinking many rooms ahead here, when we might not even be able to get through the next.'

'I agree,' Childe said. 'We'll take it one at a time. Doctor Trintignant, put your wilder fantasies aside, at least for now.'

'Consider them relegated to mere daydreams,' Trintignant said.

So we pushed on.

Now that we had passed through so many doors, it was possible to see that the Spire's tasks came in waves; that there might, for instance, be a series of problems which depended on prime number theory, followed by another series which hinged on the properties of higher-dimensional solids. For several rooms in sequence we were confronted by questions related to tiling patterns – tessellations – while another sequence tested our understanding of cellular automata: odd chequerboard armies of shapes which obeyed simple rules and yet interacted in stunningly complex ways. The final challenge in each set would always be the hardest; the one where we were most likely to make a mistake. We were quite prepared to take three or four hours to pass each door, if that was the time it took to be certain – in Celestine's mind at least – that the answer was clear.

And though the shunts were leaching fatigue poisons from our blood, and though the modifiers were enabling us to think with a clarity we had never known before, a kind of exhaustion always crept over us after solving one of the harder challenges. It normally passed in a few tens of minutes, but until then we generally waited before venturing through the now open door, gathering our strength again.

In those quiet minutes we spoke amongst ourselves, discussing what had happened and what we could expect.

'It's happened again,' I said, addressing Celestine on the private channel.

Her answer came back, no more terse than I had expected. 'What?'

'For a while the rest of us could keep up with you. Even Hirz. Or, if not keep up, then at least not lose sight of you completely. But you're pulling ahead again, aren't you? Those Juggler routines are kicking in again.'

She took her time replying. 'You have Childe's medichines.'

'Yes. But all they can do is work with the basic neural topology, suppressing and enhancing activity without altering the layout of the connections in any significant way. And the 'chines are broad-spectrum; not tuned specifically to any one of us.'

Celestine looked at the only one of us still wearing one of the original suits. 'They worked on Hirz.'

'Must have been luck. But yes, you're right. She couldn't see as far as you, though, even with the modifiers.'

Celestine tapped the shunt in her wrist, still faintly visible beneath the tight-fitting fabric of her suit. 'I took a spike of the modifiers as well.'

'I doubt that it gave you much of an edge over what you already had.'

'Maybe not.' She paused. 'Is there a point to this conversation, Richard?'

'Not really,' I said, stung by her response. 'I just . . .'

'Wanted to talk, yes.'

'And you don't?'

'You can hardly blame me if I don't, can you? This isn't exactly the place for small talk, let alone with someone who chose to have me erased from his memory.'

'Would it make any difference if I said I was sorry about that?'

I could tell from the tone of her response that my answer had not been quite the one she was expecting. 'It's easy to say you're sorry, now . . . now that it suits you to say as much. That's not how you felt at the time.'

I fumbled for an answer which was not too distant from the truth. 'Would you believe me if I said I'd had you suppressed because I still loved you, and not for any other reason?'

'That's just a little too convenient, isn't it?'

'But not necessarily a lie. And can you blame me for it? We were in love, Celestine. You can't deny that. Just because things happened between us . . .' A question I had been meaning to ask her forced itself to the front of my mind. 'Why didn't you contact me again, after you were told you couldn't go to Resurgam?'

'Our relationship was over, Richard.'

'But we'd parted on reasonably amicable terms. If the Resurgam expedition hadn't come up, we might not have parted at all.'

Celestine sighed; one of exasperation. 'Well, since you asked, I *did* try and contact you.'

'You did?'

'But by the time I'd made my mind up, I learned about the way you'd had me suppressed. How do you imagine that made me feel, Richard? Like a small, disposable part of your past – something to be wadded up and flicked away when it offended you?'

'It wasn't like that at all. I never thought I'd see you again.'

She snorted. 'And maybe you wouldn't have, if it wasn't for dear old Roland Childe.'

I kept my voice level. 'He asked me along because we both used to test each other with challenges like this. I presume he needed someone with your kind of Juggler transform. Childe wouldn't have cared about our past.'

Her eyes flashed behind the visor of her helmet. 'And you don't care either, do you?'

'About Childe's motives? No. They're neither my concern nor my interest. All that bothers me now is this.'

I patted the Spire's thrumming floor.

'There's more here than meets the eye, Richard.'

'What do you mean by that?'

'Haven't you noticed how—' She looked at me for several seconds, as if on the verge of revealing something, then shook her head. 'Never mind.'

'What, for pity's sake?'

'Doesn't it strike you that Childe has been just a little too well prepared?'

'I wouldn't say there's any such thing as being too well prepared for a thing like the Blood Spire, Celestine.'

'That's not what I mean.' She fingered the fabric of her skin-tight. 'These suits, for instance. How did he know we wouldn't be able to go all the way with the larger ones?'

I shrugged, a gesture that was now perfectly visible. 'I don't know. Maybe he learned a few things from Argyle, before he died.'

'Then what about Doctor Trintignant? That ghoul isn't remotely interested in solving the Spire. He hasn't contributed to a single problem yet. And yet he's already proved his value, hasn't he?'

'I don't follow.'

Celestine rubbed her shunt. 'These things. And the neural modifiers – Trintignant supervised their installation. And I haven't even mentioned Forqueray's arm, or the medical equipment aboard the shuttle.'

'I still don't see what you're getting at.'

'I don't know what leverage Childe's used to get his co-operation – it's got to be more than bribery or avarice – but I have a very, very nasty idea. And all of it points to something even more disturbing.'

I was wearying of this. With the challenge of the next door ahead of us, the last thing I needed was paranoiac theory-mongering.

'Which is?'

'Childe knows too much about this place.'

Another room, another wrong answer, another punishment.

It made the last look like a minor reprimand. I remembered a swift metallic flicker of machines emerging from hatches which opened in the seamless walls: not javelins now, but jointed, articulated pincers and viciously curved scissors. I remembered high-pressure jets of vivid arterial blood spraying the room like pink banners, the shards of shattered bone hammered against the walls like shrapnel. I remembered an unwanted and brutal lesson in the anatomy of the human body; the elegance with which muscle, bone and sinew were anchored to each other and the horrid ease with which they could be flensed apart – filleted – by surgically sharp metallic instruments.

I remembered screams.

I remembered indescribable pain, before the analgesics kicked in.

Afterwards, when we had time to think about what had happened, I do not think any of us thought of blaming Celestine for making another mistake. Childe's modifiers had given us a healthy respect for the difficulty of what she was doing, and – as before – her second choice had been the correct one; the one that opened a route back to the Spire's exit.

And besides . . .

Celestine had suffered as well.

It was Forqueray who had caught the worst of it, though. Perhaps the Spire, having tasted his blood once, had decided it wanted much more of it – more than could be provided by the sacrifice of a mere limb. It had quartered him: two quick opposed snips with the nightmarish scissors; a bisection followed an instant later by a hideous transection.

Four pieces of Forqueray had thudded to the Spire's floor; his interior organs were laid open like a wax model in a medical school. Various machines nestled neatly amongst his innards, sliced along the same planes. What remained of him spasmed once or twice, then – with the exception of his replacement arm, which continued to twitch – he was mercifully still. A moment or two passed, and then – with whiplash speed – jointed arms seized his pieces and pulled him into the wall, leaving slick red skid marks.

Forqueray's death would have been bad enough, but by then the Spire was already inflicting further punishment.

I saw Celestine drop to the ground, one arm pressed around the stump of another, blood spraying from the wound despite the pressure she was applying. Through her visor her face turned ghostly.

Childe's right hand was missing all the fingers. He pressed the ruined hand against his chest, grimacing but managing to stay on his feet.

Trintignant had lost a leg. But there was no blood gushing from the wound; no evidence of severed muscle and bone. I saw only damaged mechanisms; twisted and snapped steel and plastic armatures, buzzing cables and stuttering optic fibres; interrupted feedlines oozing sickly green fluids.

Trintignant, nonetheless, fell to the floor.

I also felt myself falling, looking down to see that my right leg ended just below the knee; realising that my own blood was hosing out in a hard scarlet stream. I hit the floor – the pain of the injury having yet to reach my brain – and reached out in reflex for the stump. But only one hand presented itself, my left arm had been curtailed neatly above the wrist. In my peripheral vision I saw my detached hand, still gloved, perched on the floor like an absurd white crab.

Pain flowered in my skull.

I screamed.

SIX

'I've had enough of this shit,' Hirz said.

Childe looked up at her from his recovery couch. 'You're leaving us?'

'Damn right I am.'

'You disappoint me.'

'Fine, but I'm still shipping out.'

Childe stroked his forehead, tracing its shape with the new steel gauntlet Trintignant had attached to his arm. 'If anyone should be quitting, it isn't you, Hirz. You walked out of the Spire without a scratch. Look at the rest of us.'

'Thanks, but I've just had dinner.'

Trintignant lifted his silver mask towards her. 'Now, there is no call for that. I admit the replacements I have fashioned here possess a certain brutal *esthétique*, but in functional terms they are without equal.' As if to demonstrate his point, he flexed his own replacement leg.

It was a replacement, rather than simply the old one salvaged, repaired and reattached. Hirz – who had picked up as many pieces of us as she could manage – had never found the other part of Trintignant. Nor had an examination of the area around the Spire – where we had found the pieces of Forqueray – revealed any significant part of the doctor. The Spire had allowed us to take back Forqueray's arm after it had been severed, but it appeared to have decided to keep all metallic things for itself.

I stood up from my own couch, testing the way my new leg supported my weight. There was no denying the excellence of Trintignant's work. The prosthesis had interfaced with my existing nervous system so perfectly that I had already accepted the leg into my body image. When I walked on it I did so with only the tiniest trace of a limp, and that would surely vanish once I had grown accustomed to the replacement.

'I could take the other one off as well,' Trintignant piped up, rubbing his hands together. 'Then you would have perfect neural equilibrium . . . shall I do it?'

'You want to, don't you?'

'I admit I have always been offended by asymmetry.'

I felt my other leg; the flesh and blood one felt so vulnerable, so unlikely to last the course.

'You'll just have to be patient,' I said.

'Well, all things come to he who waits. And how is the arm doing?'

Like Childe, I now boasted one steel gauntlet instead of a hand. I flexed it, hearing the tiny, shrill whine of actuators. When I touched something I felt prickles of sensation; the hand was capable of registering subtle gradations of warmth or coldness. Celestine's replacement was very similar, although sleeker and somehow more feminine. At least our injuries had demanded as much, I thought; unlike Childe, who had lost only his fingers, but who had appeared to welcome more of the doctor's gleaming handiwork than was strictly necessary.

'It'll do,' I said, remembering how much Forqueray had irritated the doctor with the same remark.

'Don't you get it?' Hirz said. 'If Trintignant had his way, you'd be like him by now. Christ only knows where he'll stop.'

Trintignant shrugged. 'I merely repair what the Spire damages.'

'Yeah. The two of you make a great team, Doc.' She looked at him with an expression of pure loathing. 'Well, sorry, but you're not getting your hands on me.'

Trintignant appraised her. 'No great loss, when there is so little raw material with which to work.'

'Screw you, creep.'

Hirz left the room.

'Looks like she means it when she says she's quitting,' I said, breaking the silence that ensued.

Celestine nodded. 'I can't say I entirely blame her either.'

'You don't?' Childe asked.

'No. She's right. This whole thing is in serious danger of turning into some kind of sick exercise in self-mutilation.' Celestine looked at her own steel hand, not quite masking her own revulsion. 'What will it take, Childe? What will we turn into by the time we beat this thing?'

He shrugged. 'Nothing that can't be reversed.'

'But maybe by then we won't want it reversed, will we?'

'Listen, Celestine.' Childe propped himself against a bulkhead. 'What we're doing here is trying to beat an elemental thing. Reach its summit, if you will. In that respect the Blood Spire isn't very different to a mountain. It punishes us when we make mistakes, but then so do mountains. Occasionally, it kills. More often than not it leaves us only with a reminder of what it can do. Blood Spire snips off a finger or two. A mountain achieves the same effect with frostbite. Where's the difference?'

'A mountain doesn't enjoy doing it, for a start. But the Spire *does*. It's alive, Childe, living and breathing.'

'It's a machine, that's all.'

'But maybe a cleverer one than anything we've ever known before. A machine with a taste for blood, too. That's not a great combination, Childe.'

He sighed. 'Then you're giving up as well?'

'I didn't say that.'

'Fine.'

He stepped through the door which Hirz had just used.

'Where are you going?' I said.

'To try and talk some sense into her, that's all.'

SEVEN

Ten hours later – buzzing with unnatural alertness; the need for sleep a distant, fading memory – we returned to Blood Spire.

'What did he say to make you come back?' I said to Hirz, between one of the challenges.

'What do you think?'

'Just a wild stab in the dark, but did he by any chance up your cut?'

'Let's just say the terms were renegotiated. Call it a performance -related bonus.'

I smiled. 'Then calling you a mercenary wasn't so far off the mark, was it?'

'Sticks and stones may break my bones . . . sorry. Given the circumstances, that's not in the best possible taste, is it?'

'Never mind.'

We were struggling out of our suits now. Several rooms earlier we had reached a point where it was impossible to squeeze through the door without first disconnecting our air lines and removing our backpacks. We could have done without the packs, of course, but none of us wanted to breathe Spire air until it was absolutely necessary. And we would still need the packs to make our retreat, back through the unpressurised rooms. So we kept hold of them as we wriggled between rooms, fearful of letting go. We had seen the way the Spire harvested first Forqueray's drone and then Trintignant's leg, and it was likely it would do the same with our equipment if we left it unattended.

'Why are you doing it, then?' asked Hirz.

'It certainly isn't the money,' I said.

'No. I figured that part out. What, then?'

'*Because it's there.* Because Childe and I go back a long way, and I can't stand to give up on a challenge once I've accepted it.'

'Old-fashioned bullheadedness, in other words,' Celestine said.

Hirz was putting on a helmet and backpack assembly for the first time. She had just been forced to get out of her original suit and put on one of the skintights; even her small frame was now too large to pass through the constricted doors. Childe had attached some additional armour to her skintight – scablike patches of woven diamond – but she must have felt more vulnerable.

I answered Celestine. 'What about you, if it isn't the same thing that keeps me coming back?'

'I want to solve the problems, that's all. For you they're just a means to an end, but for me they're the only thing of interest.'

I felt slighted, but she was right. The nature of the challenges was less important to me than discovering what was at the summit; the secret the Spire so jealously guarded.

'And you're hoping that through the problems they set us you'll eventually understand the Spire's makers?'

'Not just that. I mean, that's a significant part of it, but I also want to know what my own limitations are.'

'You mean you want to explore the gift that the Jugglers have given you?' Before she had time to answer I continued, 'I understand. And it's never been possible before, has it? You've only ever been able to test yourself against problems set by other humans. You could never map the limits of your ability, any more than a lion could test its strength against paper.'

She looked around her. 'But now I've met something that tests me.'

'And?'

Celestine smiled thinly. 'I'm not sure I like it.'

We did not speak again until we had traversed half a dozen new rooms, and then rested while the shunts mopped up the excess of tiredness which came after such efforts.

The mathematical problems had now grown so arcane that I could barely describe them, let alone grope my way towards a solution. Celestine had to do most of the thinking, therefore, but the emotional strain which we all felt was just as wearying. For an hour during the rest period I teetered on the edge of sleep, but then alertness returned like a pale, cold dawn. There was something harsh and clinical about that state of mind – it did not feel completely normal – but it enabled us to get the job done, and that was all that mattered.

We continued, passing the seventieth room – fifteen further than we had reached before. We were now at least sixty metres higher than when we had entered, and for a while it looked like we had found a tempo that suited us. It was a long time since Celestine had shown any hesitation in her answers, even if it took a couple of hours for her to reach the solution. It was as if she had found the right way of thinking, and now none of the challenges felt truly alien to her. For a while, as we passed room after room, a dangerous optimism began to creep over us.

It was a mistake.

In the seventy-first room, the Spire began to enforce a new rule. Celestine, as usual, spent at least twenty minutes studying the problem, skating her fingers over the shallowly etched markings on the frame, her lips moving silently as she mouthed possibilities.

Childe studied her with a peculiar watchfulness I had not observed before.

'Any ideas?' he said, looking over her shoulder.

'Don't crowd me, Childe. I'm thinking.'

'I know, I know. Just try and do it a little faster, that's all.'

Celestine turned away from the frame. 'Why? Are we on a schedule suddenly?'

'I'm just a little concerned about the amount of time it's taking us, that's all.' He stroked the bulge on his forearm. 'These shunts aren't perfect, and—'

'There's something else, isn't there?'

'Don't worry. Just concentrate on the problem.'

But this time the punishment began before we had begun our solution.

It was lenient, I suppose, compared to the savage dismembering that had concluded our last attempt to reach the summit. It was more of a stern admonishment to make our selection; the crack of a whip rather than the swish of a guillotine.

Something popped out of the wall and dropped to the floor.

It looked like a metal ball, about the size of a marble. For several seconds it did nothing at all. We all stared at it, knowing that something unpleasant was going to happen, but unsure what.

Then the ball trembled, and – without deforming in any way – bounced itself off the ground to knee-height.

It hit the ground and bounced again, a little higher this time.

'Celestine,' Childe said, 'I strongly suggest you come to a decision—'

Horrified, Celestine forced her attention back to the puzzle marked on the frame. The ball continued bouncing; reaching higher each time.

'I don't like this,' Hirz said.

'I'm not exactly thrilled by it myself,' Childe told her, watching as the ball hit the ceiling and slammed back to the floor, landing to one side of the place where it had begun its bouncing. This time its rebound was enough to make it hit the ceiling again, and on the recoil it streaked diagonally across the room, hitting one of the side walls before glancing off at a different angle. The ball slammed into Trintignant, ricocheting off his metal leg, and then connected with the walls twice – gaining speed with each collision – before hitting me in the chest. The force of it was like a hard punch, driving the air from my lungs.

I fell to the ground, emitting a groan of discomfort.

The little ball continued arcing around the room, its momentum not sapped in any appreciable way. It kept getting faster, in fact, so that its trajectory came to resemble a constantly shifting silver loom which occasionally intersected with one of us. I heard groans, and then felt a sudden pain in my leg, and the ball kept on getting faster. The sound it made was like a fusillade of gunshots, the space between detonation growing smaller.

Childe, who had been hit himself, shouted: 'Celestine! Make your choice!'

The ball chose that moment to slam into her, making her gasp in pain. She buckled down on one knee, but in the process reached out and palmed one of the markings on the right side of the frame.

The gunshot sounds – the silver loom – even the ball itself – vanished.

Nothing happened for several more seconds, and then the door ahead of us began to open.

We inspected our injuries. There was nothing life-threatening, but we had all been bruised badly, and it was likely that a bone or two had been fractured. I was sure I had broken a rib, and Childe grimaced when he tried to put weight on his right ankle. My leg felt tender where the ball had struck me, but I could still walk, and after a few minutes the pain abated, soothed by a combination of my own medichines and the shunt's analgesics.

'Thank God we'd put the helmets back on,' I said, fingering a deep bump in the crown. 'We'd have been pulped otherwise.'

'Would someone please tell me what just happened?' Celestine asked, inspecting her own wounds.

'I guess the Spire thought we were taking too long,' Childe said. 'It's given us as long as we like to solve the problems until now, but from now on it looks we'll be up against the clock.'

Hirz said: 'And how long did we have?'

'After the last door opened? Forty minutes or so.'

'Forty-three, to be precise,' Trintignant said.

'I strongly suggest we start work on the next door,' Childe said. 'How long do you think we have, Doctor?'

'As an upper limit? In the region of twenty-eight minutes.'

'That's nowhere near enough time,' I said. 'We'd better retreat and come back.'

'No,' Childe said. 'Not until we're injured.'

'You're insane,' Celestine said.

But Childe ignored her. He just stepped through the door, into the next room. Behind us the exit door slammed shut.

'Not insane,' he said, turning back to us. 'Just very eager to continue.'

It was never the same thing twice.

Celestine made her selection as quickly as she could, every muscle tense with concentration, and that gave us – by Trintignant's estimation – five or six clear minutes before the Spire would demand an answer.

'We'll wait it out,' Childe said, eyeing us all to see if anyone disagreed. 'Celestine can keep checking her results. There's no sense in giving the fucking thing an answer before we have to; not when so much is at stake.'

'I'm sure of the answer,' Celestine said, pointing to the part of the frame she would eventually palm.

'Then take five minutes to clear your head. Whatever. Just don't make the choice until we're forced into it.'

'If we get through this room, Childe . . .'

'Yes?'

'I'm going back. You can't stop me.'

'You won't do it, Celestine, and you know it.'

She glared at him, but said nothing. I think what followed was the longest five minutes in my life. None of us dared speak again, unwilling to begin anything – even a word – for fear that something like the ball would return. All I heard for five minutes was our own breathing; backgrounded by the awful slow thrumming of the Spire itself.

Then something slithered out of one wall.

It hit the floor, writhing. It was an inch-thick, three-metre-long length of flexible metal.

'Back off . . .' Childe told us.

Celestine looked over her shoulder. 'You want me to press this, or not?'

'On my word. Not a moment before.'

The cable continued writhing: flexing, coiling and uncoiling like a demented eel. Childe stared at it, fascinated. The writhing grew in strength, accompanied by the slithering, hissing sounds of metal on metal.

'Childe?' Celestine asked.

'I just want to see what this thing actually—'

The cable flexed and writhed, and then propelled itself rapidly across the floor in Childe's direction. He hopped nimbly out of the way, the cable passing under his feet. The writhing had become a continuous whip-cracking now, and we all pressed ourselves against the walls. The cable – having missed Childe – retreated to the middle of the room and hissed furiously. It looked much longer and thinner than it had a moment ago, as if it had elongated itself.

'Childe,' Celestine said, 'I'm making the choice in five seconds, whether you like it or not.'

'Wait, will you?'

The cable moved with blinding speed now, rearing up so that its motion was no longer confined to a few inches above the floor. Its writhing was so fast that it took on a quasi-solidity: an irregularly shaped pillar of flickering, whistling metal. I looked at Celestine, willing her to palm the frame, no matter what Childe said. I appreciated his fascination – the thing was entrancing to look at – but I suspected he was pushing curiosity slightly too far.

'Celestine . . .' I started saying.

But what happened next happened with lightning speed: a silver-grey tentacle of the blur – a thin loop of the cable – whipped out to form a double coil around Celestine's arm. It was the one Trintignant had already worked on. She looked at it in horror; the cable tightened itself and snipped the arm off. Celestine slumped to the floor, screaming.

The tentacle tugged her arm to the centre of the room, retreating back into the hissing, flickering pillar of whirling metal.

I dashed for the door, remembering the symbol she pressed. The whirl reached a loop out to me, but I threw myself against the wall and the loop merely brushed the chest of my suit before flicking back into the mass. From the whirl, tiny pieces of flesh and bone dribbled to the ground. Then another loop flicked out and snared Hirz, wrapping around her midsection and pulling her towards the centre.

She struggled – cartwheeling her arms, her feet skidding against the floor – but it was no good. She started shouting, and then screaming.

I reached the door.

My hand hesitated over the markings. Was I remembering accurately, or had Celestine intended to press a different solution? They all looked so similar now.

Then Celestine, who was still clutching her ruined arm, nodded emphatically.

I palmed the door.

I stared at it, willing it to move. After all this, what if her choice had been wrong? The Spire seemed to draw out the moment sadistically while behind me I continued to hear the frantic hissing of the whirling cable. And something else, which I preferred not to think about.

Suddenly the noise stopped.

In my peripheral vision I saw the cable retreating back into the wall, like a snake's tongue laden with scent.

Before me, the door began to open.

Celestine's choice had been correct. I examined my state of mind and decided that I ought to be feeling relief. And perhaps, distantly, I did. At least now we would have a clear route back out of the Spire. But we would not be going forward, and I knew not all us would be leaving.

I turned around, steeling myself against what I was about to see.

Childe and Trintignant were undamaged.

Celestine was already attending to her injury, fixing a tourniquet from her medical kit above the point where her arm ended. She had lost very little blood, and did not appear to be in very much discomfort.

'Are you all right?' I said.

'I'll make it out, Richard.' She grimaced, tugging the tourniquet tighter. 'Which is more than can be said for Hirz.'

'Where is she?'

'It got her.'

With her good hand, Celestine pointed to the place where the whirl had been only moments before. On the floor – just below the volume of air where the cable had hovered and thrashed – lay a small, neat pile of flailed human tissue.

'There's no sign of Celestine's hand,' I said. 'Or Hirz's suit.'

'It pulled her apart,' Childe said, his face drained of blood.

'Where is she?'

'It was very fast. There was just a . . . blur. It pulled her apart and then the parts disappeared into the walls. I don't think she could have felt much.'

'I hope to God she didn't.'

Doctor Trintignant stooped down and examined the pieces.

EIGHT

Outside, in the long, steely-shadowed light of what was either dusk or dawn, we found the pieces of Hirz for which the Spire had had no use.

They were half-buried in dust, like the bluffs and arches of some ancient landscape rendered in miniature. My mind played gruesome tricks with the shapes, turning them from brutally detached pieces of human anatomy into abstract sculptures: jointed formations that caught the light in a certain way and cast their own pleasing shadows. Though some pieces of fabric remained, the Spire had retained all the metallic parts of her suit for itself. Even her skull had been cracked open and sucked dry, so that the Spire could winnow the few small precious pieces of metal she carried in her head.

And what it could not use, it had thrown away.

'We can't just leave her here,' I said. 'We've got to do something, bury her . . . at least put up some kind of marker.'

'She's already got one,' Childe said.

'What?'

'The Spire. And the sooner we get back to the shuttle, the sooner we can fix Celestine and get back to it.'

'A moment please,' Trintignant said, fingering through another pile of human remains.

'Those aren't anything to do with Hirz,' Childe said.

Trintignant rose to his feet slipping something into his suit's utility belt pocket in the process.

Whatever it had been was small; no larger than a marble or small stone.

'I'm going home,' Celestine said, when we were back in the safety of the shuttle. 'And before you try and talk me out of it, that's final.'

We were alone in her quarters. Childe had just given up trying to convince her to stay, but he had sent me in to see if I could be more persuasive. My heart, however, was not in it. I had seen what the Spire could do, and I was damned if I was going to be responsible for any blood other than my own.

'At least let Trintignant take care of your hand,' I said.

'I don't need steel now,' she said, stroking the glistening blue surgical sleeve which terminated her arm. 'I can manage without a hand until we're back in Chasm City. They can grow me a new one while I'm sleeping.'

The doctor's musical voice interrupted us, Trintignant's impassive silver mask poking through into Celestine's bubble-tent partition. 'If I may be so bold . . . it may be that my services are the best you can now reasonably hope to attain.'

Celestine looked at Childe, and then at the doctor, and then at the glistening surgical sleeve.

'What are you talking about?'

'Nothing. Only some news from home which Childe has allowed me to see.' Uninvited, Trintignant stepped fully into the room and sealed the partition behind him.

'What, Doctor?'

'Rather disturbing news, as it happens. Not long after our departure, something upsetting happened to Chasm City. A blight which afflicted everything contingent upon any microscopic, self-replicating system. Nanotechnology, in other words. I gather the fatalities were numbered in the millions . . .'

'You don't have to sound so bloody cheerful about it.'

Trintignant navigated to the side of the couch where Celestine was resting. 'I merely stress the point that what we consider state of the art medicine may be somewhat beyond the city's present capabilities. Of course, much may change before our return . . .'

'Then I'll just have to take that risk, won't I?' Celestine said.

'On your own head be it.' Trintignant paused and placed something small and hard on Celestine's table. Then he turned as if to leave, but stopped and spoke again. 'I am accustomed to it, you know.'

'Used to what?' I said.

'Fear and revulsion. Because of what I have become, and what I have done. But I am not an evil man. Perverse, yes. Given to peculiar desires, most certainly. But emphatically not a monster.'

'What about your victims, Doctor?'

'I have always maintained that they gave consent for the procedures I inflicted' – he corrected himself – 'performed upon them.'

'That's not what the records say.'

'And who are we to argue with records?' The light played on his mask in such a fashion as to enhance the half-smile that was always there. 'Who are we, indeed.'

When Trintignant was gone, I turned to Celestine and said, 'I'm going back into the Spire. You realise that, don't you?'

'I'd guessed, but I still hope I can talk you out of it.' With her good hand, she fingered the small, hard thing Trintignant had placed on the table. It looked like a misshapen dark stone – whatever the doctor had found amongst the dead – and for a moment I wondered why he had left it behind.

Then I said, 'I really don't think there's much point. It's between me and Childe now. He must have known there'd come a point when I wouldn't be able to turn away.'

'No matter what the costs?' Celestine asked.

'Nothing's without a little risk.'

She shook her head, slowly and wonderingly. 'He really got to you, didn't he.'

'No,' I said, feeling a perverse need to defend my old friend, even when I knew that what Celestine said was perfectly true. 'It wasn't Childe, in the end. It was the Spire.'

'Please, Richard. Think carefully, won't you?'

I said I would. But we both knew it was a lie.

NINE

Childe and I went back.

I gazed up at it, towering over us like some brutal cenotaph. I saw it with astonishing, diamond-hard clarity. It was as if a smoky veil had been lifted from my vision, permitting thousands of new details and nuances of hue and shade to blast through. Only the tiniest, faintest hint of pixelation – seen whenever I changed my angle of view too sharply – betrayed the fact that this was not quite normal vision, but a cybernetic augmentation.

Our eyes had been removed, the sockets scrubbed and packed with far more efficient sensory devices, wired back into our visual cortices. Our eyeballs waited back at the shuttle, floating in jars like grotesque delicacies. They would be popped back in when we had conquered the Spire.

'Why not goggles?' I said when Trintignant had first explained his plans.

'Too bulky, and too liable to be snatched away. The Spire has a definite taste for metal. From now on, anything vital had better be carried as part of us – not just worn, but internalised.' The doctor steepled his silver fingers. 'If that repulses you, I suggest you concede defeat now.'

'I'll decide what repulses me,' I said.

'What else?' Childe said. 'Without Celestine we'll need to crack those problems ourselves.'

'I will increase the density of medichines in your brains,' Trintignant said. 'They will weave a web of fullerene tubes, artificial neuronal connections supplanting your existing synaptic topology.'

'What good will that do?'

'The fullerene tubes will conduct nerve signals hundreds of times more rapidly than your existing synaptic pathways. Your neural computation rate will increase. Your subjective sense of elapsed time will slow.'

I stared at the doctor, horrified and fascinated at the same time. 'You can do that?'

'It's actually rather trivial. The Conjoiners have been doing it since the Transenlightenment, and their methods are well documented. With them I can make time slow to a subjective crawl. The Spire may give you only twenty minutes to solve a room, but I can make it feel like several hours; even one or two days.'

I turned to Childe. 'You think that'll be enough?'

'I think it'll be a lot better than nothing, but we'll see.'

But it was better than that.

Trintignant's machines did more than just supplant our existing and clumsily slow neural pathways. They reshaped them, configuring the topology to enhance mathematical prowess, which took us onto a plateau beyond what the neural modifiers had been capable of doing. We lacked Celestine's intuitive brilliance, but we had the advantage of being able to spend longer – subjectively, at least – on a given problem.

And, for a while at least, it worked.

TEN

'You're turning into a monster,' she said.

I answered, 'I'm turning into whatever it takes to beat the Spire.'

I stalked away from the shuttle, moving on slender, articulated legs like piston-driven stilts. I no longer needed armour now: Trintignant had grafted it to my skin. Tough black plaques slid over each other like the carapacial segments of a lobster.

'You even sound like Trintignant now,' Celestine said, following me. I watched her asymmetric shape loom next to mine: she lopsided; me a thin, elongated wraith.

'I can't help that,' I said, my voice piping from the speech synthesiser that replaced my sealed-up mouth.

'You can stop. It isn't too late.'

'Not until Childe stops.'

'And then? Will even that be enough to make you give up, Richard?'

I turned to face her. Behind her faceplate I watched her try to conceal the revulsion she obviously felt.

'He won't give up,' I said.

Celestine held out her hand. At first I thought she was beckoning me, but then I saw there was something in her palm. Small, dark and hard.

'Trintignant found this outside, by the Spire. It's what he left in my room. I think he was trying to tell us something. Trying to redeem himself. Do you recognise it, Richard?'

I zoomed in on the object. Numbers flickered around it. Enhancement phased in. Surface irregularity. Topological contours. Albedo. Likely composition. I drank in the data like a drunkard.

Data was what I lived for now.

'No.'

ELEVEN

'I can hear something.'

'Of course you can. It's the Spire, the same as it's always been.'

'No.' I was silent for several moments, wondering whether my augmented auditory system was sending false signals into my brain.

But there it was again: an occasional rumble of distant machinery, but one that was coming closer.

'I hear it now,' Childe said. 'It's coming from behind us. Along the way we've come.'

'It sounds like the doors opening and closing in sequence.'

'Yes.'

'Why would they do that?'

'Something must be coming through the rooms towards us.'

Childe thought about that for what felt like minutes, but was probably only a matter of actual seconds. Then be shook his head, dismissively. 'We have eleven minutes to get through this door, or we'll be punished. We don't have time to worry about anything extraneous.'

Reluctantly, I agreed.

I forced my attention back to the puzzle, feeling the machinery in my head pluck at the mathematical barbs of the problem. The ferocious clockwork that Trintignant had installed in my skull spun giddily. I had never understood mathematics with any great agility, but now I sensed it as a hard grid of truth underlying everything: bones shining through the thin flesh of the world.

It was almost the only thing I was now capable of thinking of at all. Everything else felt painfully abstract, whereas before the opposite had been the case. This, I knew, must be what it felt like to an idiot savant, gifted with astonishing skill in one highly specialised field of human expertise.

I had become a tool shaped so efficiently for one purpose that it could serve no other.

I had become a machine for solving the Spire.

Now that we were alone – and no longer reliant on Celestine – Childe had revealed himself as a more than adequately capable problem-solver. Several times I had found myself staring at a problem, with even my new mathematical skills momentarily unable to crack the solution, when Childe had seen the answer. Generally he was able to articulate the reasoning behind his choice, but sometimes there was nothing for it but for me to either accept his judgement or wait for my own sluggard thought processes to arrive at the same conclusion.

And I began to wonder.

Childe was brilliant now, but I sensed there was more to it than the extra layers of cognitive machinery Trintignant had installed. He was so confident now that I began to wonder if he had merely been holding back before, preferring to let the rest of us make the decisions. If that was the case, he was in some way responsible for the deaths that had already happened.

But, I reminded myself, we had all volunteered.

With three minutes to spare, the door eased open, revealing the room beyond. At the same moment the door we had come through opened as well, as it always did at this point. We could leave now, if we wished. At this time, as had been the case with every room we had passed through, Childe and I made a decision on whether to proceed further or not. There was always the danger that the next room would be the one that killed us – and every second that we spent before stepping through the doorway meant one second less available for cracking the next problem.

'Well?' I said.

His answer came back, clipped and automatic. 'Onwards.'

'We only had three minutes to spare on this one, Childe. They're getting harder now. A hell of a lot harder.'

'I'm fully aware of that.'

'Then maybe we should retreat. Gather our strength and return. We'll lose nothing by doing so.'

'You can't be sure of that. You don't know that the Spire will keep letting us make these attempts. Perhaps it's already tiring of us.'

'I still—'

But I stopped, my new, wasp-waisted body flexing easily at the approach of a footfall.

My visual system scanned the approaching object, resolving it into a figure, stepping over the threshold from the previous room. It was a human figure, but one that had, admittedly, undergone some alterations – although none that were as drastic as those that Trintignant had wrought on me. I studied the slow, painful way she made her progress. Our own movements seemed slow, but were lightning-fast by comparison.

I groped for a memory; a name; a face.

My mind, clotted with routines designed to smash mathematics, could not at first retrieve such mundane data.

Finally, however, it obliged.

'Celestine,' I said.

I did not actually speak. Instead, laser light stuttered the mass of sensors and scanners jammed into my eye sockets. Our minds now ran too rapidly to communicate verbally, but, though she moved slowly herself, she deigned to reply.

'Yes. It's me. Are you really Richard?'

'Why do you ask?'

'Because I can hardly tell the difference between you and Childe.'

I looked at Childe, paying proper attention to his shape for what seemed the first time.

At last, after so many frustrations, Trintignant had been given free rein to do with us as he wished. He had pumped our heads full of more processing machinery, until our skulls had to be reshaped to accommodate it, becoming sleekly elongated. He cracked our ribcages open and carefully removed our lungs and hearts, putting these organs into storage. The space vacated by one lung was replaced by a closed-cycle blood oxygenating system of the kind carried in spacesuit backpacks, so that we could endure vacuum and had no need to breathe ambient air. The other lung's volume was filled by a device which circulated refrigerated fluid along a loop of tube, draining the excess heat generated by the stew of neural machines filling our heads. Nutrient systems crammed the remaining thoracic spaces; our hearts were tiny fusion-powered pumps. All other organs – stomach, intestines, genitalia – were removed, along with many bones and muscles. Our remaining limbs were detached and put into storage, replaced by skeletal prosthetics of immense strength, but which could fold and deform to enable us to squeeze through the tightest door. Our bodies were encased in exoskeletal frames to which these limbs were anchored. Finally, Trintignant gave us whiplike counterbalancing tails, and then caused our skins to envelop our metal parts, hardening here and there in lustrous grey patches of organic armour, woven from the same diamond mesh that had been used to reinforce Hirz's suit.

When he was done, we looked like diamond-hided greyhounds.

Diamond dogs.

I bowed my head. 'I am Richard.'

'Then for God's sake please come back.'

'Why have you followed us?'

'To ask you. One final time.'

'You changed yourself just to come after me?'

Slowly, with the stone grace of a statue, she extended a beckoning hand. Her limbs, like ours, were mechanical, but her basic form was far less canine.

'Please.'

'You know I can't go back now. Not when I've come so far.'

Her answer was an eternity arriving. 'You don't understand, Richard. This is not what it seems.'

Childe turned his sleek, snouted face to mine.

'Ignore her,' he said.

'No,' Celestine said, who must have also been attuned to Childe's laser signals. 'Don't listen to him, Richard. He's tricked and lied to you all along. To all of us. Even to Trintignant. That's why I came back.'

'She's lying,' Childe said.

'No. I'm not. Haven't you got it yet, Richard? Childe's been here before. This isn't his first visit to the Spire.'

I convulsed my canine body in a shrug. 'Nor mine.'

'I don't mean since we arrived on Golgotha. I mean before that. Childe's been to this planet already.'

'She's lying,' Childe repeated.

'Then how did you know what to expect, in so much detail?'

'I didn't. I was just prudent.' He turned to me, so that only I could read the stammer of his lasers. 'We are wasting valuable time here, Richard.'

'Prudent?' Celestine said. 'Oh yes; you were damned prudent. Bringing along those other suits, so that when the first ones became too bulky we could still go on. And Trintignant – how did you know he'd come in so handy?'

'I saw the bodies lying around the base of the Spire,' Childe answered. 'They'd been butchered by it.'

'And?'

'I decided it would be good to have someone along who had the medical aptitude to put right such injuries.'

'Yes.' Celestine nodded. 'I don't disagree with that. But that's no more than part of the truth, is it?'

I looked at Childe and Celestine in turn. 'Then what is the whole truth?'

'Those bodies aren't anything to do with Captain Argyle.'

'They're not?' I said.

'No.' Celestine's words arrived agonisingly slowly, and I began to wish that Trintignant had turned her into a diamond-skinned dog as well. 'No. Because Argyle never existed. He was a necessary fiction – a reason for Childe knowing at least something about what the Spire entailed. But the truth . . . well, why don't you tell us, Childe?'

'I don't know what you want me to say.'

Celestine smiled. 'Only that the bodies are yours.'

His tail flexed impatiently, brushing the floor. 'I won't listen to this.'

'Then don't. But Trintignant will tell you the same thing. He guessed first, not me.'

She threw something towards me.

I willed time to move more slowly. What she had thrown curved lazily through the air, following a parabola. My mind processed its course and extrapolated its trajectory with deadening precision.

I moved and opened my foreclaw to catch the falling thing.

'I don't recognise it,' I said.

'Trintignant must have thought you would.'

I looked down at the thing, trying to see it anew. I remembered the doctor fishing amongst the bones around the Spire's base; placing something in one of his pockets. This hard, black, irregular, dully pointed thing.

What was it?

I half remembered.

'There has to be more than this,' I said.

'Of course there is,' Celestine said. 'The human remains – with the exception of what's been added since we arrived – are all from the same genetic individual. I know. Trintignant told me.'

'That isn't possible.'

'Oh, it is. With cloning, it's almost child's play.'

'This is nonsense,' Childe said.

I turned to him now, feeling the faint ghost of an emotion Trintignant had not completely excised. 'Is it really?'

'Why would I clone myself?'

'I'll answer for him,' Celestine said. 'He found this thing, but long, long before he said he did. And he visited it, and set about exploring it, using clones of himself.'

I looked at Childe, expecting him to at least proffer some shred of explanation. Instead, padding on all fours, he crossed into the next room.

The door behind Celestine slammed shut like a steel eyelid.

Childe spoke to us from the next room. 'My estimate is that we have nine or ten minutes in which to solve the next problem. I am studying it now and it strikes me as . . . challenging, to say the least. Shall we adjourn any further discussion of trivialities until we're through?'

'Childe,' I said. 'You shouldn't have done that. Celestine wasn't consulted . . .'

'I assumed she was on the team.'

Celestine stepped into the new room. 'I wasn't. At least I didn't think I was. But it looks like I am now.'

'That's the spirit,' Childe said. And I realised then where I had seen the small, dark thing that Trintignant had retrieved from the surface of Golgotha.

I might have been mistaken.

But it looked a lot like a devil's horn.

TWELVE

The problem was as elegant Byzantine, multi-layered and potentially treacherous as any we had encountered.

Simply looking at it sent my mind careering down avenues of mathematical possibility, glimpsing deep connections between what I had always assumed were theoretically distant realms of logical space. I could have stared at it for hours, in a state of ecstatic transfixion. Unfortunately, we had to solve it, not admire it. And we now had less than nine minutes.

We crowded around the door and for two or three minutes – what felt like two or three hours – nothing was said.

I broke the silence, when I sensed that I needed to think about something else for a moment.

'Was Celestine right? Did you clone yourself?'

'Of course he did,' she said. 'He was exploring hazardous territory, so he'd have been certain to bring the kind of equipment necessary to regenerate organs.'

Childe turned away from the problem. 'That isn't the same as cloning equipment.'

'Only because of artificially imposed safeguards,' Celestine answered. 'Strip those away and you can clone to your heart's content. Why regenerate a single hand or arm when you can culture a whole body?'

'What good would that do me? All I'd have done was make a mindless copy of myself.'

I said, 'Not necessarily. With memory trawls and medichines, you could go some way towards imprinting your personality and memory on any clone you chose.'

'He's right,' Celestine said. 'It's easy enough to rescript memories. Richard should know.'

Childe looked back at the problem, which was still as fiercely intractable as when we had entered.

'Six minutes left,' he said.

'Don't change the fucking subject,' Celestine said. 'I want Richard to know exactly what happened here.

'Why?' Childe said. 'Do you honestly care what happens to him? I saw that look of revulsion when you saw what we'd done to ourselves.'

'Maybe you do revolt me,' she said, nodding. 'But I also care about someone being manipulated.'

'I haven't manipulated anyone.'

'Then tell him the truth about the clones. And the Spire, for that matter.'

Childe returned his attention to the door, evidently torn between solving the problem and silencing Celestine. Less than six minutes now remained, and though I had distracted myself, I had not come closer to grasping the solution, or even seeing a hint of how to begin.

I snapped my attention back to Childe. 'What happened with the clones? Did you send them in, one by one, hoping to find a way into the Spire for you?'

'No.' He almost laughed at my failure to grasp the truth. 'I didn't send them in ahead of me, Richard. Not at all. I sent them in *after* me.'

'Sorry, but I don't understand.'

'I went in first, and the Spire killed me. But before I did that, I trawled myself and installed those memories in a recently grown clone. The clone wasn't a perfect copy of me, by any means – it had some memories, and some of my grosser personality traits, but it was under no illusions that it was anything but a recently made construct.' Childe looked back towards the problem. 'Look, this is all very interesting, but I really think—'

'The problem can wait,' Celestine said. 'I think I see a solution, in any case.'

Childe's slender body stiffened in anticipation. 'You do?'

'Just a hint of one, Childe. Keep your hackles down.'

'We don't have much time, Celestine. I'd very much like to hear your solution.'

She looked at the pattern, smiling faintly. 'I'm sure you would. I'd also like to hear what happened to the clone.'

I sensed him seethe with anger, then bring it under control. 'It – the new me – went back into the Spire and attempted to make further progress than its predecessor. Which it did, advancing several rooms beyond the point where the old me died.'

'What made it go in?' Celestine said. 'It must have known it would die in there as well.'

'It thought it had a significantly better chance of survival than the last one. It studied what had happened to the first victim and took precautions – better armour; drugs to enhance mathematical skills; some crude stabs at the medichine therapies we have been using.'

'And?' I said. 'What happened after that one died?'

'It didn't die on its first attempt. Like us, it retreated once it sensed it had gone as far as it reasonably could. Each time, it trawled itself – making a copy of its memories. These were inherited by the next clone.'

'I still don't get it,' I said. 'Why would the clone care what happened to the one after it?'

'Because . . . it never expected to die. None of us did. Call that a character trait, if you will.'

'Overweening arrogance?' Celestine offered.

'I'd prefer to think of it as a profound lack of self-doubt. Each clone imagined itself better than its predecessor; incapable of making the same errors. But they still wanted to be trawled, so that – in the unlikely event that they were killed – something would go on. So that, even if that particular clone did not solve the Spire, it would still be something with my genetic heritage that did. Part of the same lineage. Family, if you will.' His tail flicked impatiently. 'Four minutes. Celestine . . . are you ready now?'

'Almost, but not quite. How many clones were there, Childe? Before you, I mean?'

'That's a pretty personal question.'

She shrugged. 'Fine. I'll just withhold my solution.'

'Seventeen,' Childe said. 'Plus my original; the first one to go in.'

I absorbed this number, stunned at what it implied. 'Then you're . . . the nineteenth to try and solve the Spire?'

I think he would have smiled at that point, had it been anatomically possible. 'Like I said, I try and keep it in the family.'

'You've become a monster,' Celestine said, almost beneath her breath.

It was hard not to see it that way as well. He had inherited the memories from eighteen predecessors, all of whom had died within the Spire's pain-wracked chambers. It hardly mattered that he had probably never inherited the precise moment of death; the lineage was no less monstrous for that small mercy. And who was to say that some of his ancestor clones had not crawled out of the Spire, horribly mutilated, dying, but still sufficiently alive to succumb to one last trawl?

They said a trawl was all the sharper if it was performed at the moment of death, when damage to the scanned mind mattered less.

'Celestine's right,' I said. 'You've become something worse than the thing you set out to beat.'

Childe appraised me, those dense clusters of optics sweeping over me like gun barrels. 'Have you looked in a mirror lately, Richard? You're not exactly the way nature intended, you know.'

'This is just cosmetic,' I said. 'I still have my memories. I haven't allowed myself to become a' – I faltered, my brain struggling with vocabulary now that so much of it had been reassigned to the task of cracking the Spire – 'a perversion,' I finished.

'Fine.' Childe lowered his head; a posture of sadness and resignation. 'Then go back, if that's what you want. Let me stay to finish the challenge.'

'Yes,' I said. 'I think I will. Celestine? Get us through this door and I'll come back with you. We'll leave Childe to his bloody Spire.'

Celestine's sigh was one of heartfelt relief. 'Thank God, Richard. I didn't think I'd be able to convince you quite that easily.'

I nodded towards the door, suggesting that she sketch out what she thought was the likely solution. It still looked devilishly hard to me, but now that I refocused my mind on it, I thought I began to see the faintest hint of an approach, if not a full-blooded solution.

But Childe was speaking again. 'Oh, you shouldn't sound so surprised,' he said. 'I always knew he'd turn back as soon as the going got tough. That's always been his way. I shouldn't have deceived myself that he'd have changed.'

I bristled. 'That isn't true.'

'Then why turn back when we've come so far?'

'Because it isn't worth it.'

'Or is it simply that the problem's become too difficult; the challenge too great?'

'Ignore him,' Celestine said. 'He's just trying to goad you into following him. That's what this has always been about, hasn't it, Childe? You think you can solve the Spire, where eighteen previous versions of you have failed. Where eighteen previous versions of you were butchered and flayed by the thing.' She looked around, almost as if she expected the Spire to punish her for speaking so profanely. 'And perhaps you're right, too. Perhaps you really have come closer than any of the others.'

Childe said nothing, perhaps unwilling to contradict her.

'But simply beating the Spire wouldn't be good enough,' Celestine said. 'For you'd have no witnesses. No one to see how clever you'd been.'

'That isn't true at all.'

'Then why did we all have to come here? You found Trintignant useful, I'll grant you that. And I helped you as well. But you could have done without us, ultimately. It would have been bloodier, and you might have needed to run off a few more clones . . . but I don't doubt that you could have done it.'

'The solution, Celestine.'

By my estimate we had not much more than two minutes left in which to make our selection. And yet I sensed that it was time enough. Magically, the problem had opened up before me where a moment ago it had been insoluble; like one of those optical illusions which suddenly flip from one state to another. The moment was as close to a religious experience as I cared to come.

'It's all right,' I said. 'I see it now. Have you got it?'

'Not quite. Give me a moment . . .' Childe stared at it, and I watched as the lasers from his eyes washed over the labyrinthine engravings. The red glare skittered over the wrong solution and lingered there. It flickered away and alighted on the correct answer, but only momentarily.

Childe flicked his tail. 'I think I've got it.'

'Good,' Celestine replied. 'I agree with you. Richard? Are you ready to make this unanimous?'

I thought I had misheard her, but I had not. She was saying that Childe's answer was the right one; that the one I had been sure of was the wrong one . . .

'I thought . . .' I began. Then, desperately, I stared at the problem again. Had I missed something? Childe had looked to have his doubts, but Celestine was so certain of herself. And yet what I had glimpsed had appeared beyond question. 'I don't know,' I said weakly. 'I don't know.'

'We haven't time to debate it. We've got less than a minute.'

The feeling in my belly was one of ice. Somehow, despite the layers of humanity that had been stripped from me, I could still taste terror. It was reaching me anyway, refusing to be daunted. I felt so certain of my choice. And yet I was outnumbered.

'Richard?' Childe said again, more insistent this time.

I looked at the two of them, helplessly. 'Press it,' I said.

Childe placed his forepaw over the solution that he and Celestine had agreed on, and pressed.

I think I knew, even before the Spire responded, that the choice had not been the correct one. And yet when I looked at Celestine I saw nothing resembling shock or surprise in her expression. Instead, she looked completely calm and resigned.

And then the punishment commenced.

It was brutal, and once it would have killed us. Even with the augmentations Trintignant had given us, the damage inflicted was considerable as a scythe-tipped, triple-jointed pendulum descended from the ceiling and began swinging in viciously widening arcs. Our minds might have been able to compute the future position of a simpler pendulum, steering our bodies out of its harmful path. But the trajectory of a jointed pendulum was ferociously difficult to predict: a nightmarish demonstration of the mathematics of chaos.

But we survived, as we had survived the previous attacks. Even Celestine made it through, the flashing arc snipping off only one of her arms. I lost an arm and leg on one side, and watched – half in horror, half in fascination – as the room claimed these parts for itself; tendrils whipped out from the wall to salvage those useful conglomerations of metal and plastic. There was pain, of a sort, for Trintignant had wired those limbs into our nervous systems, so that we could feel heat and cold. But the pain abated quickly, replaced by digital numbness.

Childe got the worst of it, though. The blade had sliced him through the middle, just below what had once been his ribcage, spilling steel and plastic guts, bone, viscera, blood and noxious lubricants onto the floor. The tendrils squirmed out and captured the twitching prize of his detached rear end, flicking tail and all.

With the hand that she still had, Celestine pressed the correct symbol. The punishment ceased and the door opened.

In the comparative calm that followed, Childe looked down at his severed trunk.

'I seem to be quite badly damaged,' he said.

But already various valves and gaskets were stemming the fluid loss; clicking shut with neat precision. Trintignant, I saw, had done very well. He had equipped Childe to survive the most extreme injuries.

'You'll live,' Celestine said, with what struck me as less than total sympathy.

'What happened?' I asked. 'Why didn't you press that one first?'

She looked at me. 'Because I knew what had to be done.'

Despite her injuries she helped us on the retreat.

I was able to stumble from room to room, balancing myself against the wall and hopping on my good leg. I had lost no great quantity of blood, for while I had suffered one or two gashes from close approaches of the pendulum, my limbs had been detached below the points where they were anchored to flesh and bone. But I still felt the shivering onset of shock, and all I wanted to do was make it out of the Spire, back to the sanctuary of the shuttle. There, I knew, Trintignant could make me whole again. Human again, for that matter. He had always promised it would be possible, and while there was much about him that I did not like, I did not think he would lie about that. It would be a matter of professional pride that his work was technically reversible.

Celestine carried Childe, tucked under her arm. What remained of him was very light, she said, and he was able to cling to her with his undamaged forepaws. I felt a spasm of horror every time I saw how little of him there was, while shuddering to think how much more intense that spasm would have been were I not numbed by the medichines.

We had made it back through perhaps one third of the rooms when he slithered from her grip, thudding to the floor.

'What are you doing?' Celestine asked.

'What do you think?' He supported himself by his forelimbs, his severed trunk resting against the ground. The wound had begun to close, I saw, his diamond skin puckering tight to seal the damage.

Before very long he would look as if he had been made this way.

Celestine took her time before answering, 'Quite honestly, I don't know what to think.'

'I'm going back. I'm carrying on.'

Still propping myself against a wall, I said, 'You can't. You need treatment. For God's sake; you've been cut in half.'

'It doesn't matter,' Childe said. 'All I've done is lose a part of me I would have been forced to discard before very long. Eventually the doors would have been a tight squeeze even for something shaped like a dog.'

'It'll kill you,' I said.

'Or I'll beat it. It's still possible, you know.' He turned around, his rear part scraping against the floor, and then looked back over his shoulder. 'I'm going to retrace my steps back to the room where this happened. I don't think the Spire will obstruct your retreat until I step – or crawl, as it may be – into the last room we opened. But if I were you, I wouldn't take too long on the way back.' Then he looked at me, and again switched on the private frequency. 'It's not too late, Richard. You can still come back with me.'

'No,' I said. 'You're wrong. It's much too late.'

Celestine reached out to help me make my awkward way to the next door. 'Leave him, Richard. Leave him to the Spire. It's what he's always wanted, and he's had his witnesses now.'

Childe eased himself onto the lip of the door leading into the room we had just come through.

'Well?' he said.

'She's right. Whatever happens now, it's between you and the Spire. I suppose I should wish you the best of luck, except it would sound irredeemably trite.'

He shrugged; one of the few human gestures now available to him. 'I'll take whatever I can get. And I assure you that we *will* meet again, whether you like it or not.'

'I hope so,' I said, while knowing it would never be the case. 'In the meantime, I'll give your regards to Chasm City.'

'Do that, please. Just don't be too specific about where I went.'

'I promise you that. Roland?'

'Yes?'

'I think I should say goodbye now.'

Childe turned around and slithered into the darkness, propelling himself with quick, piston-like movement of his forearms.

Then Celestine took my arm and helped me towards the exit.

THIRTEEN

'You were right,' I told her as we made our way back to the shuttle. 'I think I would have followed him.'

Celestine smiled. 'But I'm glad you didn't.'

'Do you mind if I ask you something?'

'As long as it isn't to do with mathematics.'

'Why did you care about what happened to me, and not Childe?'

'I did care about Childe,' she said firmly. 'But I didn't think any of us were going to be able to persuade him to turn back.'

'And that was the only reason?'

'No. I also thought you deserved something better than to be killed by the Spire.'

'You risked your life to get me out,' I said. 'I'm not ungrateful.'

'Not ungrateful? Is that your idea of an expression of gratitude?' But she was smiling, and I felt a faint impulse to smile as well. 'Well, at least that sounds like the old Richard.'

'There's hope for me yet, then. Trintignant can put me back the way I should be, after he's done with you.'

But when we got back to the shuttle there was no sign of Doctor Trintignant. We searched for him, but found nothing; not even a set of tracks leading away. None of the remaining suits were missing, and when we contacted the orbiting ship they had no knowledge of the doctor's whereabouts.

Then we found him.

He had placed himself on his operating couch, beneath the loom of swift, beautiful surgical machinery. And the machines had dismantled him, separating him into his constituent components, placing some pieces of him in neatly labelled fluid-filled flasks and others in vials. Chunks of eviscerated biomachinery floated like stinger-laden jellyfish. Implants and mechanisms glittered like small, precisely jewelled ornaments. There was surprisingly little in the way of organic matter.

'He killed himself,' Celestine said. Then she found his hat – the Homburg – which he had placed at the head of the operating couch. Inside, tightly folded and marked in precise handwriting, was what amounted to Trintignant's suicide note.

My dear friends, he had written.

After giving the matter no little consideration, I have decided to dispose of myself. I find the prospect of my own dismantling a more palatable one than continuing to endure revulsion for a crime I do not believe I committed. Please do not attempt to put me back together; the endeavour would, I assure you, be quite futile. I trust however that the manner of my demise – and the annotated state to which I have reduced myself – will provide some small amusement to future scholars of cybernetics.

I must confess that there is another reason why I have chosen to bring about this somewhat terminal state of affairs. Why, after all, did I not end myself on Yellowstone?

The answer, I am afraid, lies as much in vanity as anything else.

Thanks to the Spire – and to the good offices of Mister Childe – I have been given the opportunity to continue the work that was so abruptly terminated by the unpleasantness in Chasm City. And thanks to yourselves – who were so keen to learn the Spire's secrets – I have been gifted with subjects willing to submit to some of my less orthodox procedures.

You in particular, Mister Swift, have been a Godsend. I consider the series of transformations I have wrought upon you to be my finest achievement to date. You have become my magnum opus. I fully accept that you saw the surgery merely as a means to an end and that you would not otherwise have consented to my ministrations, but that in no way lessens the magnificence of what you have become.

And therein, I am afraid lies the problem.

Whether you conquer the Spire or retreat from it – assuming, of course, that it does not kill you – there will surely come a time when you will desire to return to your prior form. And that would mean that I would be compelled to undo my single greatest work.

Something I would rather die than do.

I offer my apologies, such as they are, while remaining –

Your obedient servant,

T

Childe never returned. After ten days we searched the area about the Spire's base, but there were no remains that had not been there before. I supposed that there was nothing for it but to assume that he was still inside; still working his way to whatever lay at the summit.

And I wondered.

What ultimate function did the Spire serve? Was it possible that it served none but its own self-preservation? Perhaps it simply lured the curious into it, and forced them to adapt – becoming more like machines themselves – until they reached the point when they were of use to it.

At which point it harvested them.

Was it possible that the Spire was no more purposeful than a flytrap?

I had no answers. And I did not want to remain on Golgotha pondering such things. I did not trust myself not to return to the Spire. I still felt its feral pull.

So we left.

'Promise me,' Celestine said.

'What?'

'That whatever happens when we get home – whatever's become of the city – you won't go back to the Spire.'

'I won't go back,' I said. 'And I promise you that. I can even have the memory of it suppressed, so it doesn't haunt my dreams.'

'Why not,' she said. 'You've done it before, after all.'

But when we returned to Chasm City we found that Childe had not been lying. Things had changed, but not for the better. The thing that they called the Melding Plague had plunged our city back into a festering, technologically-decadent dark age. The wealth we had accrued on Childe's expedition meant nothing now, and what small influence my family had possessed before the crisis had diminished even further.

In better days, Trintignant's work could probably have been undone. It would not have been simple, but there were those who relished such a challenge, and I would probably have had to fight off several competing offers: rival cyberneticists vying for the prestige of tackling such a difficult project. Things were different. Even the crudest kinds of surgery were now difficult or impossibly expensive. Only a handful of specialists retained the means to even attempt such work, and they were free to charge whatever they liked.

Even Celestine, who had been wealthier than me, could only afford to have me repaired, not rectified. That – and the other matter – almost bankrupted us.

And yet she cared for me.

There were those who saw us and imagined that the creature with her – the thing that trotted by her like a stiff, diamond-skinned, grotesque mechanical dog – was merely a strange choice of pet. Sometimes they sensed something unusual in our relationship – the way she might whisper an aside to me, or the way I might appear to be leading her – and they would look at me, intently, before I stared into their eyes with the blinding red scrutiny of my vision.

Then they would always look away.

And for a long time – until the dreams became too much – that was how it was.

Yet now I pad into the night, Celestine unaware that I have left our apartment. Outside, dangerous gangs infiltrate the shadowed, half-flooded streets. They call this part of Chasm City the Mulch and it is the only place where we can afford to live now. Certainly we could have afforded something better – something much better – if I had not been forced to put aside money in readiness for this day. But Celestine knows nothing of that.

The Mulch is not as bad as it used to be, but it would still have struck the earlier me as a vile place in which to exist. Even now I am instinctively wary, my enhanced eyes dwelling on the various crudely fashioned blades and crossbows that the gangs flaunt. Not all of the creatures who haunt the night are technically human. There are things with gills that can barely breathe in open air. There are other things that resemble pigs, and they are the worst of all.

But I do not fear them.

I slink between shadows, my thin, doglike form confusing them. I squeeze through the gaps in collapsed buildings, effortlessly escaping the few who are foolish enough to chase me.

Now and then I even stop and confront them, standing with my back arched.

My red gaze stabs through them.

I continue on my way.

Presently I reach the appointed area. At first it looks deserted – there are no gangs here – but then a figure emerges from the gloom, trudging through ankle-deep caramel-brown flood water. The figure is thin and dark, and with each step it makes there is a small, precise whine. It comes into view and I observe that the woman – for it is a woman, I think – is wearing an exoskeleton. Her skin is the black of interstellar space, and her small, exquisitely featured head is perched above a neck which has been extended by several vertebrae. She wears copper rings around her neck, and her fingernails – which I see clicking against the thighs of her exoskeleton – are as long as stilettos.

I think she is strange, but she sees me and flinches.

'Are you . . .?' she starts to say.

'I am Richard Swift,' I answer.

She nods almost imperceptibly – it cannot be easy, bending that neck – and introduces herself. 'I am Triumvir Verika Abebi, of the lighthugger *Poseidon*. I sincerely hope you are not wasting my time.'

'I can pay you, don't you worry.'

She looks at me with something between pity and awe. 'You haven't even told me what it is you want.'

'That's easy,' I say. 'I want you to take me somewhere.'